A Family Christmas

Katie
Flynn

A Family Christmas

CENTURY

Published by Century Books in 2014

2 4 6 8 10 9 7 5 3 1

First published in Great Britain in 2014 by Century
The Random House Group Limited
20 Vauxhall Bridge Road, London, SW1V 2SA

www.randomhouse.co.uk

Addresses for companies within The Random House Group Limited can be found at: www.randomhouse.co.uk/offices.htm

The Random House Group Limited Reg. No. 954009

A CIP catalogue record for this book
is available from the British Library

ISBN 9781780892290

The Random House Group Limited supports the Forest Stewardship Council® (FSC®), the leading international forest-certification organisation. Our books carrying the FSC label are printed on FSC®-certified paper. FSC is the only forest-certification scheme supported by the leading environmental organisations, including Greenpeace. Our paper procurement policy can be found at: www.randomhouse.co.uk/environment

Typeset i   Paladino 11/13.5 pt by Palimpsest Book Production   imited,

Print   (UK) Ltd, Croydon, CR   1YY

For Jean Hughes: If there are any mistakes in the book they are mine; the bits I got right are thanks to Jean.

Acknowledgements

I am extremely grateful to Lyn Davies who heard I was hoping to meet someone who would be willing to talk to me about their life in WWII in the ATS. She put me in touch with Jean Hughes who at the age of 92 still has fantastic memories of being on the AckAck sites and kept a marvellous diary of her experiences, a copy of which she gave me.

Dear Jean, I am so grateful to you for your help: you should write a book yourself.

Dear Reader,

Ever since returning from seeing my son and grand-daughters in Australia, I feel as though I've been running which, in a way, I have been because I've been trying to catch up. I had written a third of *A Family Christmas* before I left, but on arriving back at my desk I realised with some horror that the plot, which had seemed simple enough when I left, had changed into a story so complex that I could see no way of resolving it!

I had been away for just over two months and having to virtually scrap a third of a book and start at the beginning again . . . well, I'm sure you can imagine how I felt, and how my poor editor felt too. So instead of getting quietly on with the new story, I began to fiddle with what I had already written . . . and the awful thing was that though I had completely changed the plot, the names remained the same! And for some unknown reason I had named a goody Sam, in this book, whereas a couple of books ago (I think it was in *A Sixpenny Christmas*), the baddy had been called Sam. I cannot tell you how muddled this made us all, though we managed to sort it in the end!

But enough of muddles! Flash is now getting on for sixteen years old and was not at all delighted to come out of the marvellous cattery, where he is an elder statesman, after being incarcerated for over two months. At first he retreated into his bedroom and refused totally to come out, then he tried his 'litter room', and when we finally got him out of his cosy retreat he refused to look at us, turning his back and laying his ears flat whenever he thought himself observed.

ix

He now takes in his stride the presence of my daughter-next-door's two lurchers and two black cats, and they very wisely take no notice of him. But age has made him cautious and he no longer stalks the birds when they come to feed from the seed, peanut and fat hangers. They know in some mysterious way that he is no longer a threat and when we have a sunny day (rare!) he lies in a warm patch and observes in an avuncular manner – you would think him a model bird watcher with no more interest in our feathered friends than was proper.

And I am comfortably into my next book, the early part of which is set in the Yorkshire Dales, though that may change . . . plots have a habit of twisting round and biting you on the nose if you take them for granted. I search for a title, groan groan, always the most difficult part of starting a new book. How about *The Seventh Wave*? Only so far the sea hasn't come into it. Or *The Straight and Narrow*? I don't think so! Or *Searching for Tom*? That might do, because the story starts with Madeleine, who is around ten, trying to follow in the footsteps of Charles Kingsley, who wrote *The Water Babies*, when she discovers that Mr Kingsley actually wrote the book in the Dales near where she lives, and she begins to hope that he really did find the little creatures . . . well, you never know . . . if anyone out there gets a better idea . . . I leave it in your capable hands!

All best wishes,
Sincerely,

Katie Flynn.

Prologue

It was a hot day, but then most days are hot in Malvonia, a small South American republic, and the tall, dark-haired man appeared to be sunk in thought and not taking much interest in his surroundings. Below him the water of the dock had small fish investigating the mud, but the man hardly seemed to notice. There were few people about, for it was siesta, when all the shops and offices closed and respectable people took to their beds and slept away the hottest part of the day.

The man was scarcely aware of the heat, for he was thinking of his home and his children. His mind played wistfully with a mental picture of snow on holly branches, children skating on the nearest pond and gifts beneath the Christmas tree.

He had already bought presents for his son and daughter and wrapped them with great care in several layers of tissue. Then he had placed the gifts in a stout box, sealing it with what seemed to be yards and yards of sticky tape, and enclosing the whole thing in brown paper, adding string and even some sealing wax. Then, with the parcel well secured, he had walked up from the docks into the seedy little town, found a post office, bought the necessary stamps and left the parcel with the clerk, who would dispatch it by the first ship heading for England.

He had left the post office feeling relieved that the job was done, and headed for the dock where his ship, the *Mary Anne*, lay at anchor. The heat was beginning to get to him, and he ran a hand through his tightly curling dark hair, then produced a large handkerchief and wiped his glistening forehead. He was thinking again of snow and red berries, so he did not even glance at the group of men coming towards him. They were talking and laughing, and just as he reached the *Mary Anne*'s anchorage one of them addressed him. The man began to say he did not speak Portuguese, but even as his mouth formed the words he felt a sickening blow on the back of his head and found himself face down in the water of the dock. Desperately he struggled and managed to rise to the surface, but then something struck him another stunning blow, this time on the forehead, and he lost consciousness.

Chapter 1

It had been raining when Jimmy emerged from No. 4 Solomon Court, but by the time he had run his little sister to earth, playing shop in the Latimers' woodshed, the rain had turned to sleet and a sharp wind was blowing what felt like icy needles into his unprotected face. He had looked at Mo, happily selling a piece of broken china to Nelly Latimer, and grinned ruefully. It would have been nice to have her company, but he acknowledged that to request it would not have been fair. Mo was six, too young to be able to help with the laundry. It was far better to leave her playing happily whilst he undertook the errand which might or might not result in the sixpence that Aunt Huxtable had promised, so he had leaned down, patted Mo's curly head and told her he was going to the wash house for Aunt Huxtable and might not be back before dusk, for the December days were short and in a few days it would be Christmas.

Mo had been sitting cross-legged behind the makeshift counter – she was clearly the shopkeeper on this occasion and Nelly Latimer the customer – and had risen reluctantly to her feet, but Jimmy had waved her to sit down again. 'No point both of us getting soaked,' he had said kindly, 'so go on wi' your game.'

And he had set off, slinging the canvas bag across one shoulder as he tried to avoid the worst of the puddles, for the cardboard soles he'd inserted into his ancient boots did not do much to keep his feet dry. He was bound for the tearooms to deliver the clean laundry in his bag and collect the dirty stuff, which he would then take to the wash house. Normally Aunt Huxtable would do the delivery herself, but today she had handed the carefully ironed linen to Jimmy with instructions to take it to the little café and collect the appropriate payment. He had planned to spend the day cutting holly in Princes Park and selling it on Homer Street market to make a bit of money for the holiday, and had just been telling himself that he could still do this when Aunt Huxtable had added a rider to her instructions. 'And when you've delivered the clean linen, just you take all the dirty stuff what she'll give you straight round to the wash house,' she had ordered him. 'Find yourself a sink and put the cloths in it; there's a bar of yellow soap in the bottom of the bag that you can use to get 'em clean. Then, when there ain't a stain on 'em, you must rinse 'em well and put 'em through the mangle. When that's done grab yourself a bit of line and hang 'em out. And don't you go leaving 'em there else you can be sure someone'll prig 'em. Gather 'em up whilst they's still damp but not really wet, and bring 'em home so's I can iron 'em. Then tomorrer you 'n' your sister can take 'em back to Mrs Simpson.' She had looked at him craftily, her mean little eyes sliding from the top of his head to his leaky boots. 'If you does as I say I'll give you a tanner; always provided the stuff's as clean as a new pin acourse.'

Jimmy had stared at her, aghast. 'But I've never done more'n carry the dirty linen up to the wash house for you,' he had said. 'Lads don't go in the wash house, lerralone do the washin'. Why can't you do it, Aunt Huxtable? I'm bound to make a mess of it, and then where will we be?'

Mrs Huxtable had laughed harshly and given Jimmy a shove so hard that he staggered. 'None of that snivellin'!' she had said sharply. 'I've gorra job in the pub scrubbin' down, which will take most of the day. There's nowt to stop a lad usin' the wash house, 'specially so near Christmas. If your sister were a bit older . . . but she can give you a hand. I reckon she knows how to wash a dozen or so tablecloths even if you don't. Where is she, anyroad? It ain't often the pair of youse is parted.'

'Mo? I dunno,' Jimmy had said vaguely. 'Well, if I'm to do your washing as well as deliver the linen I'd best be off. And if you don't come up with that tanner, Aunt Huxtable, it's the last time I'll run any errand for you, and that's a promise.'

'Don't you threaten me . . .' the woman had said menacingly, but perhaps there was something in the look Jimmy had given her which warned her that even worms will turn, so she gave a high, artificial laugh and actually smiled at him, though

5

there had been little humour in the set of her thin-lipped mouth. 'Awright, awright, you'll get your perishin' money, provided you do a good job, as I said. If you don't, if there's so much as one tea stain on one piece o' linen, then you'll not gerra penny. And bear in mind that me son's ship docks at noon today; he won't let me be cheated by a snivellin' kid.'

At her words Jimmy's heart had given a couple of extra beats. He and Mo hated and feared Cyril Huxtable, for the man was a bully and enjoyed giving pain. Jimmy had known Cyril's ship was about to dock and wished he had remembered to warn his sister to steer clear of the man, until he recollected that Cyril was always first in at the pub door as soon as he was paid off. He would be in no condition to bully anyone for a couple of days at least.

Jimmy sloshed on, wondering whether he could get someone to give an eye to the washing once it was on the line. Maybe then he would still have time to cut some holly and make some real money, not just the measly sixpence which Aunt Huxtable had promised. But the sleet was turning to snow and Jimmy quickened his pace, seeing his destination ahead. He was looking forward to getting out of the wet, but when he reached the wash house he discovered that the steam from a dozen sinks and four enormous coppers made the atmosphere almost as damp as that of the street outside. Peering around him, he could not see one empty sink; every one seemed to be occupied. He looked for someone who might be ready to exchange their washing sink for a rinsing one, then turned as his name was called.

'Hello, Jimmy. Wharrever are you doin' in here? If you're wantin' for an empty sink you can take mine on once I've got these perishin' sheets an' that over to the rinser. Come to that you could earn me grateful t'anks by helpin' me to move 'em. Normally I wouldn't ask, only I'm that wore out wi' a-scrubbin' at the stains . . . here, put your lot on me drainin' board, then no one else will try to take over the sink.'

Jimmy beamed at the speaker, a big Irish woman who lived in Solomon Court a couple of doors down from No. 4. Her name was Mrs McTavish and Jimmy knew she took in a great deal of laundry, doing not only the washing but also the ironing, and turning out piles of crisp, dazzlingly white sheets, tablecloths and the like every day. She was a hard worker and popular with the other women who used the wash house, but for a moment he hesitated, for Aunt Huxtable was also in the business of laundering for others, though in a very small way as yet. Suppose Mrs McTavish resented the competition and meant to splash him with scalding hot water, or wait until his attention was elsewhere so that she might pull Aunt Huxtable's laundry out of the sink and on to the dirty, puddled floor? It was the sort of thing Aunt Huxtable would have done herself if she could get away with it, but Mrs McTavish was a very different kettle of fish. He caught the fat woman's eye and saw only appeal, and a sort of rueful friendliness, and so he took the copper stick from her huge, water-softened fingers and began to fish sheets, pillowslips and a couple of big white handkerchiefs out of the hot water.

'Where d'you want 'em?' he said gruffly. 'Which sink is you rinsin' in?'

The small, skinny woman on the far side of Mrs McTavish gestured to the sink next to her own. 'Drop 'em in there, lad,' she said. 'We's all up to our 'oxters in washin', what wi' Christmas so close.' She grinned at the big Irishwoman. 'I'd gi' you a hand meself, Feena, only I's gorra sink full, a-waitin' for a mangle to come free; the minute that happens I'll get this lot across.' She turned back to Jimmy. 'This near the 'oliday we's all at full stretch and workin' our fingers into holes so's we get paid in time to buy a bit of pork, or even a last-minute bird on Great Homey market.'

'Aye, that's why every sink's in use,' another woman remarked, twisting round to smile at Jimmy. She was younger than most of the others and was pegging out a line of nappies. 'When I saw you in here, lad, I thought t'ings is desperate so dey are, else you wouldn't find a lad in the wash house, not if it were ever so.' She chuckled and wiped the sweat off her forehead with the back of her hand. 'Your mam gorra big order?' she enquired.

Jimmy shook his head, feeling a blush burn up his neck and invade his face. 'Nah,' he said quickly.

'And she ain't my mam, neither. She said she'd gimme a tanner if I brought her tablecloths an' that up to the wash house and stayed until the stuff was dry enough to iron.'

Mrs McTavish snorted and patted Jimmy's skinny shoulder. 'Tell you what, lad – you put your things in to soak and help me wit' me rinsin', then I'll help you wit' yours an we'll be done in no time.' She turned to the younger woman. 'You wasn't to know, Annie. I doubt you ever met Grace Trewin, this young feller's mam. She died a while back in a sannytorium of what we used to call consumption, though there's a big long name for it these days, and a nicer woman – Welsh, mind you – you'd have to go far to find. Her man went back to sea immediately after the funeral.' She lowered her voice. 'And if you ask me, he were took advantage of. They lived at four Solomon Court and Mrs Huxtable told him she'd move in and look after his children as if they were her own, only he'd have to keep paying the rent and hand over summat for their keep as well.' She turned back to Jimmy. 'I'll warrant you've guessed that your pa agreed in a hurry and don't know the half of what goes on,' she said. 'He barely knew the woman by all accounts – he were away at sea most of the time, and then when your mam were so ill at the end he never left her side, ain't that so, young feller? And now you and your sister gets more kicks than ha'p'orths from the Widow Huxtable, what you calls your aunt.' She looked around, and

Jimmy saw for the first time that most of the women were listening and grinning. 'She ain't your aunt, is she? Though even if she were she don't do right by you. Your pa's payin' through the nose and would be fit to kill if he could see how you're treated. You ought to tell 'im, lad, next time his ship's in port. Will you do that?'

Jimmy, dropping the Irishwoman's first two sheets into the sink and beginning to pump cold water over them, nodded uneasily. If Aunt Huxtable heard he had been discussing her with these friendly but forthright women he would get the thrashing of his life; if she could catch him, that was. Despite himself, Jimmy gave a tight little grin. If living with the Widow Huxtable – lor', she'd belt him if she heard him call her *that*! – had taught him anything it had been how to run like the wind, to hide, to stay clear until her fury had worn off, and never to utter a word in her hearing which she could construe as criticism. So he simply nodded at Mrs McTavish's words and continued to pump until the rinsing sink was full. Then he began to heave the rinsed sheets out of the water and on to the wide wooden draining board, looking round to see if there was a mangle free.

Around him, the women chattered, scrubbed, and helped each other to wring out sheets and straighten the big towels which rich folk sent down for washing. Jimmy let his mind wander to past Christmases, when his mother had been alive – and to her last moments, when he and Mo had gone to the sanatorium and seen her, so white and thin and only able to smile at them, to hold out a slender, blue-veined hand, before her head had fallen sideways on the pillow and blood had gushed . . . but it was no use wishing. He knew she had loved them, had not wanted to leave them. Now there was just Aunt Huxtable, who crowed over having someone else to pay her rent and a nice little sum towards any expenses she might have. He knew she would lie inventively when his father wanted to know where the money was going . . . but that day had not yet come and in the meantime all he could do was make sure he and Mo spent as little time as possible in No. 4 Solomon Court . . . and learned to dodge and run when Aunt Huxtable's spiteful temper was at its worst.

Mrs McTavish started to wring the worst of the water out of the sheets, and then he helped her to fold the linen and feed it into the maw of the mangle. He quite enjoyed the work, only half listening to the chaff and laughter and letting his thoughts go back to Christmas, only a few days away. Not that it would make much difference to his and Mo's lives; Aunt Huxtable would see to that. Even if his father sent extra money for the holiday, Jimmy knew he and Mo would never see it.

The Irishwoman's voice brought Jimmy back to the present. 'True, ain't it?' she said. 'That woman's awful quick wit' a slap or a crack across the legs wit' a stick.' Mrs McTavish's voice was sympathetic, and Jimmy warmed to her. It would be a relief to tell someone of all the mean tricks Aunt Huxtable played on him and his small sister. Promises of food or money if they did her messages or cleaned the house, promises which were never kept; days when he was not allowed out of the house, not even to attend school, because she wanted him to fetch and carry, or to clean the pub on the corner when the landlord was out and would not realise that the two children had done the work for which their 'aunt' had been paid. Then there was her scarcely veiled amusement when Jimmy was caned for non-attendance, though it was scarcely his fault since she herself had forbidden him to leave the Court. And he would never forget her spiteful gloating when Mo's letter to her father, begging him to come home, was destroyed before her six-year-old eyes.

Feena McTavish was looking at him, eyebrows raised, and Jimmy glanced cautiously around him before replying. 'Yes, she's hard on me little sister,' he said, keeping his voice low. 'I can take it if I have to – though I can run like the wind when she's close on me heels – but it's different for Mo. I tell her over and over not to stand her ground – there's no point in askin' for trouble – but the kid won't listen. And that Cyril near on broke her arm last time he were in port. If our da knew . . .'

He stopped speaking. Another woman had entered the wash house. Jimmy sighed. This was their neighbour, Mrs Grimshaw, and Mrs Huxtable's crony. She was in her forties, with thin greying hair pulled back from a sharp, spiteful face, and the minute she saw Jimmy she burst into speech. 'Here, jest you let Mrs Mac mangle her own perishin' sheets! Your aunt said you'd gi' me a hand if I fed you a morsel, 'cos she were too busy to go cookin' treats for two kids what give her nothin' but cheek! So what did you do after eatin' more'n your fair share of that there meat and tater pie? Lit out, that's what, so your aunt said to tell you there'd be no Christmas cheer for you unless me laundry was delivered, dry and ironed, afore the holiday. Now what does I find you doin'? Makin' yourself a nice little sum by givin' this good lady a hand wi' her manglin' while my tablecloths an' serviettes wait to be scrubbed. I'm tellin' you . . .'

Jimmy immediately released his hold on the sheets, but the Irishwoman winked at him and jerked a thumb. 'Leave off, Mrs Grimshaw,' she said, her voice calm but authoritative. 'The lad's not workin' for money, though I don't deny I'll gladly hand out a copper or two for the help he's give willingly. You find yourself another to do the work . . . which won't over-burden you, by the looks.'

Jimmy waited for an explosion of wrath from Mrs Grimshaw, but though she mumbled a complaint beneath her breath she said nothing more, merely crossing the puddled floor and dumping her washing – there was, indeed, not much of it – into the nearest unoccupied sink. Jimmy hastily picked up the next sheet and soon he and the Irishwoman were working once more. Jimmy decided that mangling was quite fun, or it was with Mrs McTavish cracking jokes to make him laugh and discussing the forthcoming holiday as though he, too, might get some enjoyment from it. She did not say a lot whilst Mrs Grimshaw was within hearing, but as soon as the sharp-faced woman had gone she began to talk freely once more.

'You and your little sister will have some Christmas cheer, don't you worry, for your pa's bound to send a bit extry, a few little t'ings for his kids,' she observed. 'Tell you what, young feller; I'll nip round to number four and put a word in. I reckon you'd rather I did that than paid you a few coppers for your help.'

Jimmy smiled politely, but wished he dared remind Mrs McTavish of the existence of Aunt Huxtable's grown-up son. He, Jimmy, could outrun Mrs Huxtable, but he had suffered many times at Cyril's hands. Last time he had come back he had accused Jimmy of some small sin, and when Jimmy had shot out of the house had grabbed Mo, dragged her to the door and bellowed out that if Jimmy didn't return at once he'd break her perishing arm for her. Jimmy knew that if challenged Cyril would say he had been joking, just teasing the kid to keep him in line, but Jimmy had seen his sister's face drain of colour as her small arm was forced up her back and he had returned at once, saying nothing when Cyril had hauled him into the kitchen and Aunt Huxtable had slashed his legs with the stick she kept handy by the kitchen fire.

But it was pointless worrying about Cyril, so Jimmy thanked Mrs McTavish but said that he hoped his pa might actually come home this year. The Irishwoman looked a little doubtful, but she said nothing more on the subject and the two continued to work in harmony.

An hour later, when Mrs Huxtable's linen was dry enough to iron, Jimmy tucked the money she had given him into the pocket of his patched trousers. Then he ventured out of the wash house and looked doubtfully up at the darkened sky. The sleet had eased and lazy flakes of snow fell from the lowering clouds, but Jimmy hated the thought of returning to No. 4 without so much as glancing at the stalls on Great Homer Street. He had done the washing in record time, thanks to the kindly Irishwoman, so there could be no harm in a quick look at the second-hand stalls, where he might find some small gift for Mo which he could now afford to buy with the money Mrs McTavish had given him.

He glanced left and right, hesitated, and turned towards Great Homer Street. As soon as he reached the brightly lit stalls he headed for one where he knew from past experience that amongst the second-hand clothing small toys could sometimes be found. He was just examining a little dog with a torn ear when the stallholder addressed him. 'Hello there, young Jimmy! Lookin' for a gift for that pretty little sister of yourn?' Harry Theaker, who Jimmy's mother had always maintained paid a fair price for anything she brought in, and had frequently employed Jimmy to help on the stall, shivered expressively. 'Why the devil they calls this a green Christmas I'll never bleedin' well know. Grey, yes, I'd go along wi' that. Ah well, since you're here you can gi' me a hand to get me goods stowed away. Are you on? Trade's terrible, 'cos no one wants to be out in weather like this, so I'm for home.' He smacked his lips. 'My old woman come past ten or twenty minutes ago and said she'd have the kettle a-boilin' and the muffins on the toastin' fork, so I don't mean to linger.'

Jimmy beamed at his old friend. 'Of course I'll help you. I meant to cut some holly, but I've been to the wash house for Aunt Huxtable and it's too late now. Mebbe I'll do it tomorrer instead. How much is this little dog? It's only got half an ear, but you know our Mo, she'll just love it.'

He held out the little dog as he spoke and Harry Theaker took it from him, cast a look round the stall and sighed deeply. 'A threepenny joe,' he said decisively. 'And if you help me to get packed up before it's full dark you can have a bag of broken biscuits too; I were goin' to have 'em for my tea but now it'll be toasted muffins instead so you might as well eat them up for me. Is that fair?'

'It's real good of you, Mr Theaker,' Jimmy said gratefully, handing over the coins Mrs McTavish had given him and tucking the little dog and the biscuits into the bosom of his ragged shirt. He began to pack the items nearest him into a large tea chest. 'And don't you worry. I reckon tomorrow is bound to be better and you'll sell the rest of your stock.'

Harry Theaker laughed. 'You're a cheery little beggar,' he said jovially. 'And ain't you lucky young Mo weren't with you to see you buy that dog? Come to think of it, where is she?'

Jimmy thought that Mo was unlikely to have gone back into No. 4, because she was still in Aunt Huxtable's bad books. Some days before, Mrs Huxtable had been chatting to one of the neighbours as Mo descended the front steps and the woman had smiled at the small girl and said, 'Ain't you the lucky one? Your aunt's put money down to buy a nice fat chicken for your Christmas dinner. Ain't she a queen, Mo?'

'Yes, she is. I heared Mrs Carruthers what lives up the other end of the Court say she's the queen of liars,' Mo had said innocently. 'She said she has a new lie for every day of the week.'

It might not have been so bad if the other woman had not laughed, but laugh she did, for Aunt Huxtable's reputation had gone ahead of her. Normally Mo would have got a whipping, but because they were in the open with neighbours coming and going it had been passed off as a joke, albeit in rather bad taste. Mo had been shaken, slapped and sent supperless to bed, and she was still wary in Aunt Huxtable's presence.

So now Jimmy grinned at the older man. 'Playin' shop in the Latimers' woodshed,' he said, continuing to pack Harry's stock neatly away. 'Are you going to collapse the stall? Only it looks as though it might rain again later.'

His companion shook his head. 'No point, me laddo,' he said. 'I'll be back here bright an' early settin' up shop, so I just cover the top with this here tarpaulin and I'm ready to start tradin' as soon as customers appear.'

'Right,' Jimmy said briskly, and very soon he was bidding Mr Theaker goodbye and setting off for the Court.

As he walked he began to wonder whether there really was any chance of his father's returning for the holiday. It had been more than a year since his mother's death, and though most folk were too tactful to remark on Mr Trewin's absence Jimmy knew that there were mutterings from kindly folk in the Court, who saw how Mrs Huxtable treated them and knew that their father would be horrified if he knew one half of what went on. Naturally enough Jimmy and Mo agreed with their well-wishers, for they yearned for their father's return and could not understand why he had left them for so long. Jimmy told Mo constantly that Dad loved them both and would come home one day and take them away from Mrs Huxtable, but recently he had overheard something which at least partially explained why he had not yet done so.

Jimmy had been queuing at the big brass water tap at the end of the Court with two empty buckets to fill, trying to think how he could get a letter to his father when he had no idea which ship he was

18

on, when he suddenly heard a neighbour ahead of him in the queue mention his name.

'You know young Jimmy Trewin's pa haven't been home not once since his wife died? Did you know her?'

Her companion had shrugged, looking puzzled. 'I dunno. What did she look like?'

The neighbour sighed. 'She had wonderful ash blonde hair soft as a dandelion clock, big blue eyes and a rare lovely complexion, though as she got worse the colour faded from her cheeks and left her very pale.'

The other woman pulled a doubtful face. 'There's a kid round here what's got ash blonde curls,' she said, and Jimmy saw her friend nod.

'That's why we reckon he won't come back no matter what, 'cos he worshipped that Grace and just the sight of the little 'un brings his loss back.'

Jimmy had broken away from the queue with a mumbled excuse. He needed to think. It had never occurred to him that Mo was like anyone but herself, but now he realised the truth of the woman's statement. Mo was the image of their dead mother, in colouring at least. He thought the resemblance ended there, but could not help despising his father for staying away when he must know how their mother would have reproached him for his behaviour.

But right now, with the toy dog and the biscuits tucked away safely in his shirt, Jimmy decided there was nothing he could do about it, so there was no point in worrying. He was just thinking that if the

19

weather was better the following day he would get Mo to help him cut holly when he saw her small figure tearing along the wet pavement as though the devil himself was on her heels. He guessed she was heading for the wash house to help him carry the laundry home, and stepped out in the middle of the pavement to bar her way.

Far from turning to accompany him back to Solomon Court and asking how his day had gone, however, she tore herself free from his arms, grabbed his hand and began to hustle him back the way he had come. Jimmy protested, reminding Mo that he had to deliver the old girl's washing so that she could iron the tablecloths and napkins damp and finish off the drying process by spreading them on the old wooden clothes horse before the fire. But Mo interrupted him, tugging as hard as she could on his arm, and Jimmy saw that her eyes were dilated with fear and she was trembling.

'What's up?' Jimmy said, turning at his sister's imperious pulling. 'You in Aunt Huxtable's bad books again? We've no need to go back to the wash house; Mrs McTavish has given me a hand and the stuff's just the way it should be, so you can stop worryin'. It's all done, right and tight, so let's go home and see what the old devil's got us for tea.'

Glancing down at his sister, he realised that Mo was not wet through; even her pale curls were dry and fluffy, so whatever the reason for her flight along the road it was something which had only just happened. 'Don't say Mrs Latimer were cross because you and Nelly were playin' in the woodshed? If so, I'll have a word . . .' He glanced up at the sky. 'Only I reckon there's more rain and sleet up there, just waitin' to come tumblin' down and drench us to the skin. We ought to get back to Solomon Court just as soon as we can.'

Mo pulled him to a halt as a few feathery flakes floated down to land on her crisp curls. 'I can't go back to Solomon Court ever,' she said mournfully. 'Oh, Jimmy, I never meant to do it, but I've been and gone and killed Cyril, and everyone's after me!'

Chapter 2

Jimmy stared at his small sister, his mouth dropping open. 'You couldn't kill a great hefty bloke like Cyril Huxtable; I expect you just frightened him,' he said at last, though he continued to let Mo pull him back along Scotland Road. 'Tell me what happened and I'll see what we must do, only first we'd best get into some shelter because it's going to snow again any minute.' He made for Harry Theaker's stall, and he and Mo crawled under the canvas covering and made themselves quite a little nest by half emptying a tea chest of clothing, squeezing into it and pulling the displaced clothing in after them.

'Go on, fire ahead,' Jimmy said as they settled themselves, and Mo, nothing loth, began to speak. Cyril's ship had docked and as was his habit he had gone straight to the nearest pub and drunk nearly all his wages away. Then he had returned to No. 4, so sozzled that he had not even seen Mo curled up in her favourite spot on the hearth rug within the enclosing arms of the clothes horse upon which Mrs Huxtable had spread various articles of clothing. Mo had taken into her little refuge a sack of sprouts which Mrs Huxtable had given her to clean before she sold them to the neighbours for their Christmas dinners. Warmed by the fire, knowing she was well hidden, Mo did not worry when she heard Cyril Huxtable come stumbling across the kitchen. She saw that he had a bottle of rum in one hand and what looked like a parcel in the other. He dragged a chair up to the fire, muttering imprecations as to what he would do to anyone who interfered with him, and proceeded to tear the parcel open. It was well protected by several layers of brown paper, and as one of them fluttered to the floor Mo saw her own name and thought it might be a Christmas present from her father. Not that it really mattered, Mo reminded herself ruefully, because Cyril would simply take the contents of the parcel down the road, either to the nearest pawn shop or to one of the stalls on Paddy's Market, and sell the contents for whatever he could get.

The brown paper concealed a large white box reinforced with sticky tape, and though from where she was hidden it did not look particularly strong appearances were obviously deceptive, because in the end Cyril, with a curse, had to take his knife to it, wrenching it open with little regard for the contents. Mo, craning her neck, saw that her guess had been right. The parcel contained presents: a soft toy, a teddy so fluffy and sweet that Mo's susceptible heart went out to it, and a harmonica.

She gasped; Jimmy was musical, had longed for a real mouth organ, and here it was, his heart's desire! More important, these gifts could only have come from their father, for only he would remember Jimmy's passionate desire for a proper instrument rather than the tinny little pipe her brother played in the school orchestra.

Mo gave a small moan. She remembered her mother apologising to Jimmy a couple of years earlier for her inability to buy the present he most wanted, saying that a really good harmonica was way beyond their means. Even if Cyril did not recognise its value, Aunt Huxtable would take it away and sell it for sure. She had to rescue the parcel before that happened; taking a deep, silent breath, Mo waited to see what Cyril would do.

At last, frowning heavily and taking swigs from his bottle every now and then, he seemed to make up his mind. 'Load of rubbish, that lot. Won't get nothin' for them down the market.' He chuckled to himself. 'It's lucky I've got other plans for making gelt.' And he took what looked to Mo like a sparkling string out of his pocket. She had never seen anything so lovely as it glittered in the firelight. As she watched, entranced, Cyril pulled a face and hollered, 'Ma! Where's my dinner?'

There was no reply; Mrs Huxtable, Mo knew, was not in the house, having gone over to Mrs Grimshaw's for a chat. Grumbling, Cyril shambled across the kitchen, still clutching the children's presents as well as the pretty string, which Mo could now see was a jewelled necklace. He must have stolen it, she thought. 'Well, I'm for a spot of shut-eye until the pubs open,' he mumbled. He gave a last bellow of 'Ma, where the devil's you at?' and lurched towards the stairs.

As soon as he had gone, Mo gave a little moan of despair and crawled out from her clothes-horse shelter. She could hear Cyril still muttering as he crashed on to his bed. 'I'll get them bloody Trewins if it's the last thing I do, and if they give me any trouble I'll top the pair of 'em,' he slurred. 'Mam hates 'em, I hates 'em, anyone with a grain o' sense hates 'em. I'll catch 'em and shove 'em into the dock as soon as I'm sober.' He chuckled hoarsely. 'They're a burden on us Huxtables, that's what they are.'

Mo sat quite still for a few minutes, wondering whether Cyril's threat was real. Then common sense came to her aid. If he attacked her or Jimmy he would be in real trouble when their father came home, and besides, if he suspected she was listening it was just the sort of threat he'd use to frighten her. Oh, how she hated him! But she must go and warn Jimmy that he was home, and maybe they would be able to keep out of his way. First, though, she must rescue their presents, and perhaps take another look at the sparkly necklace. He would be deep in a drunken sleep by now, but might wake at any moment. However, she knew a way to slow him down if he tried to follow her, if she dared to do it. Softly, she stole up the stairs and crept silently into Cyril's room. He was snoring.

* * *

'I did right, didn't I, our Jimmy?' Mo asked anxiously. 'You always say come to you if I'm in trouble, and oh, Jimmy, I'm in trouble now!'

'I don't see why, kiddo,' Jimmy said after a thoughtful pause. 'You had every right to take our presents, and I'm sure you can't have killed Cyril. What makes you think you did? You've played the same trick before just to slow him down, and it worked.'

Mo gave a doleful sniff. 'Ye-es, but this time I stayed too long looking for the sparkly necklace – I really wanted to see it again, 'cos it were real pretty, but I never did find it – and I'd barely got back into the kitchen when Cyril started hollerin'. He come shufflin' to the top of the stairs, never noticin' I'd tied his bootlaces together, and saw me in the kitchen and his eyes sort of slithered sideways to the sack of sprouts and the clothes horse and he guessed I'd been spying on him. He roared like a bull, Jimmy, and screamed that he'd kill us both when he got his hands on us and then he took a big step forward, so of course he came down the stairs head first. I were hopin' he'd bruise himself like he's bruised us so many times, but then Mrs Grimshaw and Aunt Huxtable came running to see what had caused the commotion, an' Cyril were still lying at the foot of our stairs. Aunt Huxtable began to scream that he were dead and whiles everyone were clusterin' round – I saw Johnny Latimer give him a real good kick – I sneaked in and tried to undo the laces. Only the old girl must have seen, 'cos she began to screech that it were bound to be the work of the Trewin kids, you an' me, Jimmy. I tried to say that you were at the wash house and I were too little to hurt anybody but Aunt Huxtable just kept screechin' we'd killed her son and tellin' someone to fetch the scuffers. "They'll hang you from the yard arm," she said, and tried to grab me, so I lit out and come to you.' She looked at him anxiously. 'That were the right thing to do, weren't it, Jimmy?'

'Yes of course,' Jimmy said positively. Now that he thought about it he realised that his little sister had taken a step which he, as the older, should have taken long since; she had run from the Court and the Huxtables. Jimmy supposed that he had stayed with the old woman because when his father came for them he would naturally expect them to be at the Court. And then there was the problem of where Jimmy would run. Sam Trewin had married Grace against his parents' wishes and had cut himself off completely from his family; Jimmy did not even know where they lived. He gnawed his lip thoughtfully. His mother was Welsh, and had grown up on a farm, but that was all he knew. He could only assume that, like his father's family, the Griffiths had not approved of their offspring's marriage and wanted to cut the connection.

'Jimmy?' Mo's small piping voice sounded as though she was on the verge of tears. 'Oh, Jimmy, what'll we do when morning comes? Did I really kill Cyril? I didn't tie the knots real hard; I just meant to give me time to get to you at the wash house. I's

28

frightened when Cyril's drunk, 'cos he don't know his own strength, do he, Jimmy? But will the scuffers believe me, or will they take Aunt Huxtable's side and hang me from the yard arm?'

Jimmy gave Mo a reassuring squeeze. 'Don't you mention tying the laces together, not to anyone but me,' he ordered. 'As for what we ought to do, I think we'll lie low for a bit. No point in going back to number four. Oh, I know there are some people who'll take our side, but there's bound to be trouble, and you know what a liar old Huxtable is. If only we had relatives who would take us in . . .'

Mo gave a squeak. 'If only we could go to our mam's mam. Do you remember, Jimmy? Mam said they lived in a house with roses round the door.'

Jimmy stared. 'But that were years ago; you can't possibly remember Mam sayin' that,' he objected. 'Why, I couldn't have been more than three or four – you weren't even born then!'

A cold little hand reached out of the darkness and patted his cheek. 'No, of course I don't remember; but you've told me over and over that we had relations what lived in the country. Why, only last week you were tellin' me about how one day you hoped to be a farmer too, and you said I could help with the work, feed the animals and that, when I's growed.'

'Well I'm damned. Wharra memory you've got, little 'un,' Jimmy said admiringly. 'I think you've had a really good idea. We could catch a train and go into Wales. We could tell folk we're lookin' for our Griffiths relatives; someone would be bound to know 'em. Wales isn't very big, is it?'

'I dunno,' Mo said sleepily. Then her voice sharpened. 'But we've got no money, Jimmy; they wouldn't let us on the train with no money, and we'd need to buy food and things until we find our fambly.'

Jimmy sighed. Shifting a little to find a comfortable position, he was about to suggest that they should follow his original plan, to cut holly and sell it at the market, when something jabbed into his side, and he remembered not only the biscuits, to which he had not given a thought, but also the money that the tearoom lady had paid for the linen delivery. He plunged his hand into his shirt front and produced the biscuits, handing a couple to Mo and taking one for himself. 'Broken biscuits from Mr Theaker, and we *have* got money,' he said triumphantly. 'It's what the tearoom paid for their laundry. I ought to give it to the old girl, but she's cheated us often enough, so she can whistle for it.'

Mo gave a sleepy chuckle. 'Serve her right,' she said dreamily. 'Then I'm a murderer and youse a thief . . . Cor, won't old Huxtable like that!'

Jimmy chuckled. 'Tomorrer mornin', right early, before anyone is up, I'll go back to the Court and find out whether Cyril's dead or alive,' he said. 'I'd take a bet that someone as horrible as him is all right, but I dare say you'll feel better if you know you've not killed him. I'll leave the washing outside the door. Do you want to come with me, or would you rather stay here? You can duck down under the stall if anyone from the Court comes by.' He waited for a reply, and presently smiled to himself. Mo, bless her, was fast asleep, and he decided that if the weather was bad next day she would be best tucked away under Mr Theaker's careful eye. The friendly stallholder would not let her down.

Outside on Great Homer Street the rain began to fall once more, and Jimmy, like a little mouse in its nest, heard the rain pattering on Mr Theaker's stout canvas and felt happy. He had money in his pocket, the sweet taste of broken biscuits in his mouth and the prospect of cutting enough holly next day to make a nice little sum. Life, it seemed, had taken a turn for the better, for though the idea of setting off to find their Welsh relations might seem unrealistic in the cold light of day, he had made up his mind on another score. It was bad enough being bullied, taunted and half starved by Mrs Huxtable; why should his little sister feel physically threatened as well? No, he would sneak back to No. 4 whilst it was still dark, check on Cyril and dump the washing, and then he and Mo would stay clear of Solomon Court until Cyril was on the high seas once more.

Miss Glenys Trent, until recently deputy headmistress at the Peabody Academy for girls, came out on to the pavement without looking in either direction, and almost bowled over a passing boy. For a moment she just stood there in the rain feeling as though her legs were made of jelly, but then she remembered her umbrella, unfurled it and turned rather blindly away from the school. She must take hold of herself and face the awful truth that she was now one of the great army of unemployed. There were a number of things she would have to do: pay her landlady, settle any bills – for at least the board of governors had had the decency to pay an extra month's salary for breaking their contract – and go to the labour exchange to see what the prospects of work for an experienced teacher might be. Fortunately she had always lived well within her means, so she still had most of her salary for that term's teaching, tucked away in her post office savings book. Slogging along without the faintest idea of where she was going, the erstwhile deputy headmistress of the Peabody Academy could have wept with rage and frustration. She had held the post for one term and had received many congratulations on her work, yet the board had merely stared stonily at her as they gave her the bad news.

She had protested, of course; her initial contract with the school had been for a year's employment, provided she was satisfactory. And she had been, as at least two members of the committee had told her after the meeting. They had been sympathetic but powerless, and when they tried awkwardly to express their sympathy pride had come to Miss Trent's aid. She had said loftily that she expected to be given an excellent reference and would doubtless soon find employment more to her taste than that offered by the Peabody Academy.

They had been brave words but she had not believed them herself; a teacher who had been contractually bound for a year would have to grow accustomed to raised eyebrows when prospective employers saw that she had only worked for one term. Indeed, she was bitterly regretting now that she had ever seen the deputy headship advertised. She had been happy enough in the small rural school where she had taught the seven- to eleven-year-olds. The children had liked her and enjoyed her approach to lessons, which she had managed to make fun rather than chores to be got over as quickly as possible.

One member of the board, a woman who had taught at the university in her time and whom Glenys Trent had never much liked, had stopped her in the corridor as she was leaving the building. 'Nepotism,' she had hissed. 'If you need a personal reference, my dear, just send me a letter.' She had thrust a sheet of paper on which she had printed her name and address at the younger woman. 'Mr Jenkins and myself voted against the decision to ask you to leave, but the others were like a flock of sheep, so eager to please the chairman that they would have agreed with anything he suggested. But they'll regret it; it's not easy to keep lively young ladies happily occupied once they're old enough to leave school and take their place in the world of work, but you managed it. So if you need that reference . . .'

Miss Trent had thanked her and taken the sheet

of paper, noting with a small inward smile that it was a page torn from a school exercise book. Then she had gone to her room and been doubly disgusted by the hypocrisy of those who had only days earlier been congratulating her on her success with the senior girls. There on her desk in a sizeable cardboard box were all her possessions: the fountain pen – a Parker – which had been a leaving present from her former employers, a neat pencil box containing a big squashy rubber and a variety of different lead pencils; even the box in which she brought her cold lunch to school and the teacup with her name painted on it, presented to her by her former pupils, had been put in the box. It seemed suddenly like the cruellest insult of all, that she was being dispossessed in such a public and unpleasant manner. She realised that the chairman had followed her into the room, almost as though he expected her to steal something, and turned to face him. 'I shall call for my things tomorrow . . .' she began, only to be swiftly interrupted.

'The school will be closed tomorrow,' Mr Coleman had said coldly. 'Please take your things away at once, otherwise I shall be forced to leave them on the front steps to await collection.'

It would have been lovely to gather up the box and crown him with it before hailing a taxi and leaving with her pride more or less intact, but it was also out of the question. Money was going to be extremely scarce in the weeks to come; she must save such luxuries as humiliating Mr Coleman until she had a job once more. If she could get one, that was. In two more days it would be Christmas Eve, and unless she could get temporary work in one of the big stores in the city centre she would be having a poor holiday indeed.

So she had picked up her cardboard box and without a word to anyone else had left, telling herself that she had had a lucky escape. At least no one had even suggested that she was not suitable for the post. They had merely said that the school was overstaffed, that salaries were too high, so management had decided to retrench. I'm better off without them, Miss Trent told herself, sloshing along the pavement. Oh, and I'll have to tell Myrtle that I can't share that lovely little flat over the green-grocer's shop after all. Oh, dear, and Myrtle's been begging furniture and bits and pieces from her family . . . gracious, and I put down the deposit on a bed and a square of carpet for my bedroom floor from that nice Mr Isaacs on Brownlow Hill. I wonder if I can explain to him, get him to give my money back, since I won't be needing carpets or beds. She felt a sob rising in her throat and stopped short for a moment, determined to regain control. She dreaded having to tell her friend what had happened, but after all it was not her fault and she was sure Myrtle would understand. There must be another staff member who would jump at the chance of sharing with Miss Taylor, who was very popular, but it was out of the question for Miss Trent herself. She simply could not move in with

Myrtle on the first of January knowing that she would be moving out, possibly within days. The trouble is, Liverpool is a busy port, and that means accommodation is expensive, she told herself. When I was working in the Yorkshire Dales my room cost me five shillings a week, but even a half share in the flat was going to be twice that. If I were to move out of the city it would save me quite a lot.

At least her new spectacles had not cost very much. When she had first taken up the position of deputy head at the Peabody Academy she had heard one of the staff commenting on her looks. 'All that fluffy blonde hair! She looks more like a chorus girl than a deputy head,' the woman had complained. 'I don't deny she's got all the right qualifications, but really! I can't see the girls doing what she tells them to do, even when she scrapes her hair back and knots it into that sort of bun arrangement – is it called a French pleat? She just doesn't look the part.'

Glenys had seen her point and had promptly gone out in her lunch hour and bought a pair of tortoiseshell spectacles with lenses of blank glass. She was glad she had, because not only did they make her look older and more – oh, more responsible – but when she wanted time to think she took off the spectacles and thoughtfully polished them, keeping a little cloth especially for the purpose. Yes, she would continue wearing the spectacles; she thought it quite possible that she might need to look older and more responsible when she tackled the labour exchange the next day.

Walking fast now, Miss Trent continued to try to count her blessings. There are other savings to be taken into account; I shan't need to buy the text books which the school seemed to think I had to have in order to teach my 'young ladies', nor the exercise books, which I always thought a school provided anyway.

She stopped walking for a moment and looked around her. Where on earth was she? On either side of the road were dozens and dozens of stalls. Miss Trent gave herself a mental shake. She really must pull herself together. Why, she had walked right into the middle of the Great Homer Street market; now she would have to retrace her steps to her lodgings in Orange Street. She had warned Mrs Stockyard that she was intending to move out on the first of January, but now she would have to admit that she had been dismissed and would need to keep her room on for a bit longer if possible. She would be searching for work and ought to be in the centre of Liverpool where most jobs were to be found. So her best move now would be to go back to her lodgings, get a good night's sleep if she could, and visit the nearest labour exchange in the morning. In her heart she knew that there was no hope of a teaching job at this time of year, but there must be something else she could do, something which would bring in, if not a living wage, at least enough money to keep her until she did find a post. Resolutely, Miss Trent made for Orange Street.

*   *   *

Cyril awoke. He lay in his untidy and rather smelly bed and for a moment could not remember where he was. Slowly, the events of the afternoon came back to him. He was in his ma's house in Solomon Court and the reason that he ached all over was because he'd had a bad fall. Nothing to do with being drunk, he told himself hazily. No, it was them bloody kids; one of them must have given him a shove and he'd gone arse over tit down the perishing stairs. It were lucky for them he'd not broke a bone, but even so, when he caught up with them . . .

For a moment he simply lay there planning his revenge on the Trewin brats, but then another memory rose sluggishly to the surface. He had been in the pub with his mates, celebrating the start of their shore leave, when another seaman, even drunker than they were, had begun to boast about stealing jewellery from one of the big houses on Princes Avenue. The man had even taken a necklace out of his pocket and shown it off, holding it up to the light so that the sparkling stones flashed fire, and basking in the slurred admiration of his friends. There and then Cyril had known what he was going to do, and two hours later he had been waiting outside when the other man left the pub, had bashed him on the head, and had stolen the necklace . . . the necklace!

Hastily, Cyril sat up, aware that his heart was thumping, and sweat was breaking out both on his low brow and on the palms of his ham-like hands.

The memories were clearer now; he remembered jerking awake on this very bed, minutes ago – or was it hours? – fully clothed and booted, as though he had simply come upstairs for a rest, and feeling for the necklace he was sure he had been holding when he lay down. He had not found it. Panicking, he had stumbled from the room, roaring for his mother, and that was when those scum had tripped him and pushed him down the stairs. What a fool he had been! Of course no one could have taken the necklace. It must be here somewhere. He threw off the blankets and began to root around in the rumpled bedding, but when no jewellery met his frantic fingers he gave a bellow of rage which brought his mother stomping heavily up the stairs.

'Wharron earth's wrong, Cyril me lad?' she asked crossly. 'I were dozin' in front of the fire, wonderin' when you'd wake, when you shruck out.' She gave a rather unpleasant grin. 'You sounded like a bleedin' bull a-bawlin'. Lost a quid and found a penny?'

'When you hears what I've got to say you won't be laughin',' Cyril said grimly. 'Someone's been in here and taken a grand gold necklace all set about with sparkly stones, what I found lyin' on a street corner on the Scottie Road.'

His mother snorted. 'Oh aye? Expect me to believe that?' she asked derisively. 'You've lost it, that's what. If you strip the bed it'll probably be amongst the covers, see if I ain't right.'

Cyril gave a howl of rage. 'I done all that, you stupid old biddy. I were goin' to sell it to a feller

39

I know what would have paid good money. Well, you were the only other person in the house when it disappeared; what do you say to that, eh?'

Mrs Huxtable's thin mouth set in a hard line. 'As if I'd steal from me own flesh and blood,' she said bitterly. 'Besides, I weren't the only person in the house. The Trewin brat were here, cleanin' the veggies so's we could sell 'em for Christmas dinners, so don't you go blamin' your poor old ma for what that devil's daughter's done. Who do you think tipped you downstairs? Would I do a thing like that?'

Cyril was so distraught that he nearly answered 'yes', but just in time he remembered two things. The first was his mother's strong right hand and ebony cane, and the second was that the teddy and the harmonica which had been on the foot of his bed were there no longer. He leapt to his feet. 'Sorry, Ma. You're in the right of it, as always. I shouldn't ha' said what I did. O' course that bloody kid were here – I remember now. It'll be her what took my property, and I mean to get it back right fast, before she's had a chance to show her pals, or the scuffers for that matter. Wait till I get my hands on her – she'll be sorry she were ever born.'

Chapter 3

Jimmy woke to find that the sky was growing light.
All around him was silence; it seemed that it was
still too early for the market traders to have arrived,
which must mean that a stealthy trip to the Court
was perfectly possible.

Jimmy wriggled out of their warm little nest with
great caution, managing not to wake his little sister.
He smoothed his hair back from his face with both
hands and picked up the canvas bag with its burden
of clean but unironed linen, trying to make as little
noise as possible. Mo looked comfortable and he
had no wish to wake her, so he gently replaced the
clothing he had disturbed the previous night and
watched with satisfaction as she gave a little mew
of pleasure and snuggled down.

He padded along the crisp pavement, wishing
he had had the forethought to borrow an article of
warm clothing from Mr Theaker's stock, but as the
sky gradually lightened he broke into a run; exercise was warming, he decided, and by the time he
reached the Court he had forgotten the icy temperature. Now that he was back, hovering outside No.
4, he realised that he had no idea how to find out
what had happened to Cyril. He had no intention

of banging on the door and demanding to know whether his little sister had killed Mrs Huxtable's precious son, and thought that if he hung around someone who was working an early shift might appear and tell him how things stood.

He had decided last night not to give Aunt Huxtable the money from the tearoom, but now that he was actually on the spot he realised that this might not be a good idea. Aunt Huxtable was a vicious and vengeful woman and would be only too happy to tell anyone who would listen that he had stolen it. He would keep the sixpence which she had promised him, but he tucked the rest of the cash well down amongst the linen, and propped the bag and its contents against the door. On the top step, he bent his head to listen. Cyril had a resounding snore which had often kept Jimmy awake for hours, but now there was no sound from the silent house. Jimmy frowned, then looked quickly at the parlour window which overlooked the Court, relieved to see no drawn blinds, which was the usual way of indicating a death. Perhaps Cyril had simply closed the bedroom door.

Tentatively, Jimmy tried the front door handle and was pleasantly surprised to find that the door swung inward at his touch. For a moment he stood there, still listening, then slid quietly into the cold kitchen. Had he and Mo been there the night before they would have made up the fire and then damped it down with ash, but it appeared that either Mrs Huxtable had not bothered with the mundane task, or Cyril really had been more badly hurt than Jimmy had imagined. Perhaps even now he was in hospital, and if so, Jimmy thought apprehensively, he would have to steer clear of the scuffers and anyone else who might be interested to know how Cyril came by his injuries. But he was quickly reassured by a peculiar gobbling noise and a couple of groans, which proved that Cyril's fall had not been fatal, for Jimmy knew those sounds all too well. Cyril Huxtable had indeed shut himself into his bedroom, or perhaps his mother had shut the door in order to get some sleep herself. In any case, Jimmy would be able to re-assure his sister that, far from being dead, Cyril was merely, as usual, the worse for drink.

Having satisfied himself that poor little Mo was not a murderer Jimmy stole down the hall and let himself out into the ice-cold morning. He was just about to turn back to Scotland Road when he saw a movement and presently recognised Edmund Nuttall, commonly known as Nutty. Like Jimmy, Nutty often helped out at one of the markets, and now a big smile crossed his face and he opened his mouth, clearly about to shout a greeting.

Jimmy had never known he could move so fast, but he had reached Nutty and clapped a hand over his mouth before the other boy had drawn breath. 'Shurrup, old feller,' he hissed. 'I come back here early, on the sly like, 'cos I wanted to know what's been happenin'. There was a rare ol' fuss yesterday and I heard that Cyril Huxtable had had a bit of a fall. Good job if you ask me, only it won't sweeten

43

the old gal's temper. Were you around when it happened?' He drew Nutty out of the Court as he spoke, and the two settled themselves on a pile of orange boxes outside a greengrocer's shop whose owner was clearly still abed.

'Well, you're right about one thing,' Nutty agreed. 'There were a hellish fuss. That drunken sot come roarin' out of his pit all set to beat up anyone in his way and fell from top to bottom of the stairs. His ma would have it he were dead and tried to blame Mo, but they say drunks can fall a good deal further than just down one flight of stairs without doing themselves any harm.' He chuckled. 'I didn't see it myself, but my mam told me that he were on his feet again and vowing revenge only a couple of hours after he hit the bottom.'

Cautiously, Jimmy tried to extract a little more information from his friend. 'How did he come to fall?' he asked with well-simulated curiosity. 'After all, he knows where the stairs are; he's stumbled up and down 'em often enough.'

Nutty shrugged. 'His old ma said somethin' about bootlaces, I'm not sure what. I reckon he could have tripped over them, wouldn't you say? But bein' a Huxtable, of course he had to try and find someone to blame; stands to reason. And now he's sayin' he'll get whoever tripped him if it takes him the rest of his life, but I reckon that's just talk. After all, it'll soon be Christmas Day, and knowin' him he'll be on the booze from the moment the pubs open. By Boxing Day it'll all be forgotten.' He jerked a thumb at the Court behind them. 'You goin' back there? I've gorra job in Paddy's Market makin' up bags of fruit and nuts so's Mrs Apply don't have to waste time weighin' 'em. You gorra job an' all?'

Jimmy opened his mouth to tell Nutty that he would be working for Mr Theaker, then changed his mind. Nutty was not a gabster, never had been, but what he did not know he could not tell, and the fewer people who knew where he and Mo were, the better. So he shrugged his shoulders, replying evasively that he had only come back to the Court to discover for himself just what had happened the previous evening.

Nutty grinned. 'Well now you know you might as well come along o' me and see if anyone on Paddy's Market needs a young fellow what's quick and honest and hard-workin'. Or you could try the Great Homer Street lot.' He looked up at the sky. 'Looks like it's goin' to be a fine day, even though it's cold,' he said encouragingly. 'Aw, c'mon, Jimmy. I bet Mrs Apply would be happy for you to help with deliveries.' He paused, looking with renewed curiosity at his friend. 'Where's that kid sister of yourn? It ain't often you see one without t'other; young Mo ain't never far from your side. But acourse, knowin' old Ma Huxtable, you'll have taken care neither of you gets within swipin' distance for a while yet. I reckon you've already got yourself a job an' Mo's holdin' it for you while you find out about yesterday. That's why you didn't jump at the chance of a delivery job.' He winked and patted the side of his nose with his forefinger as the two of them slid off the pile of orange boxes and set out along the Scotland Road. 'Am I right?'

Jimmy sighed. So much for hoping to keep Nutty in the dark. He might have known his friend would guess what was up; best tell him what had happened, swear him to secrecy and pray to God that he kept it to himself.

Nutty was staring at him, his sandy eyebrows gradually climbing. 'You can trust me, old feller,' he said rather reproachfully as the two lads fell into step and headed for the markets. 'Have I ever let you down? Have you ever known me blab? But we'd best gerra move on or we'll neither of us have a job, 'cos Mrs Apply expects me to turn up just as soon as there's light enough to tell a Brazil from a walnut.'

They had reached Great Homer Street and Jimmy was opening his mouth to admit that he and Mo would be working at one of the second-hand clothing stalls when Nutty gave a crow of triumph. 'It's awright, me old pal, you don't have to say a word. I see Mo behind Harry Theaker's stall, so I reckon you'll be workin' there once the customers start to come.' He looked curiously at his friend. 'What'll you do for Christmas Day, old feller? You won't want to go back to number four and the market will pack up, so no hope of a Christmas dinner there. But I'm sure me mam would let you come to our place. She's bought a leg of pork, a big bag of sprouts and the nicest taters we've seen for a long while. There's seven of us, but I reckon it'll feed nine. What say, Jim old mate?'

Jimmy smothered a sigh. 'Thanks very much; that's real kind of you, and I'd love to accept but I dursen't,' he said regretfully. 'We'll not be coming near nor by Solomon Court until Cyril's ship sails, and him with it. You don't know what he's like, honest to God you don't. He near on broke young Mo's arm last time he were home because he reckoned I'd took his share of a pie the old girl had bought cheap from Sample's. If he thinks either one of us had anything to do with his fall, he'll take it out on our hides.'

Nutty stared, eyes rounding. 'Surely he wouldn't hit a kid like Mo?' he asked incredulously. 'She's only a baby, when all's said and done, and me mam says she's that underfed that Mrs Huxtable ought to be prosecuted.' He cocked an eyebrow. 'Is your dad comin' home for the holiday? If so, you've got to tell 'im how you're treated, so—'

Jimmy snorted; he couldn't help it. 'Dad thinks sending money is all he has to do,' he said bitterly. 'Our mam died more'n a year ago and he's not been home once since then; he only stayed for a couple of days after the funeral, just long enough to agree to the Huxtables moving in to our house.' He lowered his voice. 'That's why me an' Mo's goin' to make ourselves scarce until after Cyril's ship sails. I dunno quite what we're goin' to do yet, but I'll think of summat.'

'And I won't breathe a word to a soul,' Nutty

promised. 'Wish I could do more to help, old feller, but me and my brother Sammy is goin' to put our money together to buy our mam one of them lovely cookin' aprons what I see'd on a stall next but one to Mrs Apply's. Tell you what, though, why don't the pair of us nip out when the market's quietened down an' cut some holly in Princes Park? Mam says that's stealing, but me da says it's no more stealing than a blackbird pickin' off hawthorn berries. Trees belong to everyone, he says.'

Jimmy grinned. 'Mo an' me always get our holly from them thick hedges what keeps us out of the rich people's gardens. Thanks, Nutty; that's a good idea of yours. I were goin' to go anyway, but between the pair of us we'll be able to cut a really good bunch and sell it door to door. It's funny really; most of the customers are buying their own holly back, when you come to think. Anyway, why don't you an' me meet in Princes Park when the markets shut, and if Mo an' myself can make enough gelt sellin' my half tomorrow then maybe our Christmas won't be too bad after all.'

Miss Trent tried every labour exchange in the city, but though some of the staff were sympathetic she was not offered work. She had explained that she had been deputy head at the Peabody Academy, that she had been 'last in, first out', having only joined the school in September, that she had references from both her previous employer and a governor of the Academy, but it had been useless.

48

'Put yourself on the supply list,' a friendly clerk advised her. 'After Christmas there's always flu or tummy bugs and schools need replacement teachers for weeks, sometimes. Only you'll need to go to the education department; we don't deal with short-term temporary jobs here. And if I were you I'd leave it until the new term starts.' The clerk, a middle-aged woman with a round face and twinkling dark eyes, smiled conspiratorially. 'Wait until they're desperate. Good luck, Miss . . .' she glanced down at the papers before her, 'Miss Trent.'

'And you've nothing I might take in the meantime?' Glenys asked hopefully. 'Most of the shops have sales after Christmas; I thought I might get a temporary post in one of the big stores . . .' She would have continued, but the clerk was shaking her head.

'With a hundred people jostling for every job and no previous retail experience you wouldn't stand a chance,' she said. 'Tell me, Miss Trent, have you considered returning to your home and trying there for work?'

Miss Trent opened her mouth to explain and closed it again. It was pointless after all and would only embarrass the woman if she replied, truthfully, that there was nowhere she could honestly call home. So she smiled and shook her head but did not go into detail. 'I'm living in lodgings at present,' she said evasively. 'But there's good sense in what you say, and I'll take your advice. I'll speak to the Education Department around the tenth of January, when in my experience temporary staff are beginning to be needed.'

The clerk stood up and held out her hand. 'Goodbye, Miss Trent, and good luck. If you don't find work before you are eligible to start drawing the dole, come back to me and I'll help you to fill in the forms.'

'Thank you,' Miss Trent said, trying to infuse gratitude into her tone, for the woman was only trying to help her. But I don't intend to draw the dole, she told herself as she left the office. After all, I've a term's salary, which should keep me going for some time if I can find cheaper lodgings, and so far as I remember the rules I can't draw on government support until my money runs out.

She let herself out of the office and tried not to notice the long queue of men who looked up hopefully as she closed the door behind her, then sank into apathy once more. And now, she told herself, turning towards Miss Taylor's lodgings, for the worst part. I must tell Myrtle that I've been dismissed and can't join her in the flat over the greengrocer's shop until I get another job, by which time she will have found someone else to share with, I'm sure.

An hour later Miss Trent left the house on Daisy Street feeling a little better, for Miss Taylor had been extremely understanding and had been loud in her condemnation of the way the board of governors had behaved. 'I'm afraid I shall have to get someone else, though, Glenys,' she had said regretfully. 'The rent's pretty reasonable really with two sharing but far too much for me on my own, even though I get a decent salary by most people's standards. Mind you, if you're desperate, you'd be very welcome to sleep on the floor – or even the sofa if my aunt lets me have her old one.'

'Thanks, Myrtle,' Glenys said. 'It's awfully nice of you, but I'm going to stay on at Mrs Stockyard's for the time being.' She saw the worry lines smoothe from her friend's face and knew that kindly though the offer was meant, Myrtle would have to spend a considerable time trying to find another person to share the flat as it was, and Miss Trent had no wish to further complicate her friend's life.

Having tackled the problem she had dreaded the most, she returned to Orange Street almost gaily. Once inside the house, she plucked up her courage and went to the kitchen to tell her landlady that she was no longer employed by the Peabody Academy.

Mrs Stockyard was a small fat woman with sharp dark eyes and a thin-lipped mouth, who provided her lodgers with breakfast and nothing more. The first time she had carried the tray of porridge and tea into Miss Trent's room she had explained brusquely that she had what she described as 'a little baking job', so preferred that her lodgers – Miss Trent herself, a shy young man called Frank Bloggs who worked for the railways, and a retired seaman – should remain in their own rooms and not invade her kitchen, even at breakfast time.

So now, as she hovered in the doorway, Miss

51

Trent glanced curiously around the room for from the way her landlady guarded it one would have thought it must contain rare or beautiful things. However, this was plainly not the case. The floor was quarry-tiled, a large wooden table in the middle was flanked by four bentwood chairs, and the large dresser contained a motley assortment of cheap china. The fire in the closed range did little to raise the temperature, and Miss Trent reflected that she must get this interview over quickly and return to her own room so that she might light her paraffin stove and get the chill of the December afternoon out of her bones.

She waited for her landlady to offer her a chair, but the invitation did not come, so she moved hesitantly forward and smiled at the older woman. Mrs Stockyard did not return the smile, and raised her grizzled eyebrows. 'Yes?' she said. 'I've been meanin' to have a word with you. As I understand it you're movin' into a flat share commencin' first January. Well—'

Miss Trent cut across her. 'That's right; I said I'd be going on the first of January, but I'm afraid that's changed. I am no longer working at the Peabody Academy, so—'

The landlady interrupted in her turn. 'Oh ho, so you've changed your mind, have you?' she said nastily. 'Well, you're too late, Miss Glenys Trent; I were going to say that young Mr Bloggs has a pal wantin' good cheap accommodation, so knowin' as you was leavin' I let him put down a week's rent and he moves in the day you move out. Which is the first of January as agreed, and I want that room spick and span when you go.' She looked Miss Trent up and down. 'I ought to take a week's rent from you for changin' your mind and askin' to stay on, but since you can't I'll waive me usual practice and let you go as arranged.'

She stared triumphantly at Miss Trent and her lodger reflected that it was the first time she had seen her landlady actually smiling. But what a nasty smile, she told herself, turning to leave the room. The woman was actively delighted to think she could thwart someone so easily. Miss Trent's hand was actually on the kitchen doorknob before she thought of a retort. 'Well, that's fine, Mrs Stockyard,' she said breezily. 'I'm afraid, however, that you jumped to the wrong conclusion. I wasn't going to ask you if I might extend my stay; in fact I was going to tell you that I would be leaving a day earlier than planned. Good afternoon.'

As she left the room she heard her landlady saying angrily that if so she would want extra rent, but Miss Trent heard the tremble of doubt in the older woman's voice and knew she had nothing to fear. Leaving a day early could not possibly affect Mrs Stockyard one way or the other and well she knew it. She was just being spiteful, and Miss Trent found that she was glad she would no longer be living under the same roof as such an unpleasant person.

She hurried back to her own room, lit the paraffin stove and sank into the only armchair her landlady provided, pulling it close to the window so that she could watch the passers-by whilst the warmth gradually increased. Pushing aside the net curtains and watching the people going past, she felt a glow of elation. She had worsted Mrs Stockyard, leaving the landlady gobbling with annoyance, and now felt in a mood to think about the holiday. In two days it would be Christmas and she must plan how to deal with it, for all the shops and markets would be shut and she was sure that her landlady would not allow her to cook even a potato in her precious kitchen.

She leaned back in her chair and considered what she knew of other people's Christmases. Myrtle had told her that the bakeries would be open to cook any meat, pies or poultry that their customers took in. I'll buy a tiny chicken, and if Sample's cook it for me, then that will leave my Primus stove for potatoes and vegetables, she thought busily. I shan't want a Christmas pudding because they're far too rich and probably cost too much as well, but I'll have a couple of those delicious-looking mince pies I've seen on the cake stalls. Myrtle said the stallholders start to reduce their prices on Christmas Eve, so I'll go out late tomorrow and buy all my Christmas treats then. And I won't jolly well worry about where I'll be sleeping on the thirty-first; I'll surely find somewhere, even if it's only an old car blanket on Myrtle's floor.

Chapter 4

When Harry heard that Jimmy and Mo did not intend to go back to Solomon Court for Christmas he was horrified. 'Once the market closes at four o'clock tomorrow it won't open again until after the holiday,' he reminded them. 'I dunno why you won't go home, but I've knowed the pair of you long enough to realise you fell into the wrong hands when your dad agreed to let them Huxtables move in with you. But you weren't ever scared to go home of a night time, nor you didn't keep duckin' out of sight whenever a man came too close to the stall. Oh aye, you're scared of someone, or summat, I knows that much.'

The three of them were sitting at the back of the stall eating apple turnovers, which Harry had provided in return, he said, for the help the children so willingly gave. Jimmy had looked shyly at him from under his lashes. 'But you lets us sleep under your stall,' he had pointed out. 'I reckon that's payment enough for any help what we give, so the grub is extry.'

Harry had laughed, but now he was looking worried. 'Well, you can't stay here after tonight,' he went on. 'So what plans do you have for the holiday, eh? Because if you've none, I've got a suggestion to make. I've a friend what's a major in the Sally Army. If I have a word with him, he'll see you right for a couple of nights and you'll get a grand Christmas dinner, 'cos they do that for everyone. What do you say I give him a shout?'

Mo gave a happy little squeak, and looked hopefully to her brother for his approval. 'Can we, Jimmy?' she asked wistfully. 'I feel safe as houses when I's cuddled up in our box under Mr Theaker's stall, but I won't go back to number four, 'cos that Cyril means to kill us, and Aunt Huxtable wants to hang me from the yard arm.'

Jimmy turned to Mr Theaker. 'It's hard to explain, Mr Theaker, 'cos we don't really know ourselves why Cyril keeps threatenin' to strangle the pair of us. But he's awful big and awful cruel, so we're keepin' clear until his ship sails.'

Harry nodded his understanding, but then had to get up from his perch on the row of orange boxes which marked the back of his stall to serve a customer. Before he returned Jimmy took Mo's small hand in his and squeezed it encouragingly. 'I know Mr Theaker's our pal and wouldn't do nothin' to hurt us,' he whispered. 'But we don't know this 'ere major, and he might not understand that there's evil men – and women too – who hurt kids. He might want to take us back to number four and tell Cyril and Aunt Huxtable off for the way they behave. Even if he keeps us by him until after the holiday, we have to face the fact that no

56

one ain't goin' to stick with us for ever. So just you keep your gob shut, young Mo, and mebbe we'll stay safe until Cyril's ship sails.'

He had barely finished his warning when Harry wrapped the garment the customer had chosen, took the money and returned to their side. 'Well?' he said. 'Have you made up your mind to trust Major Williams? I swear you'll never regret it. He's a good man – your mam thought he was one of the best, and you know me; I wouldn't let harm come to Grace's kids, not if it were ever so. So when trading's over for the day you can come with me and take a look at him. The army band and choir will be holding a service in the Salvation Hall. No charge, just donations in the box. Will you give it a go?'

Jimmy grinned. 'Tell you what, Mr Theaker, that major of yours ain't the only good man around here,' he said. 'And if we goes to this concert and feels we'll be safe with the major, then we'll pay our way; or we will if you'll keep an eye on Mo for me while I go cuttin' holly to sell round the streets.'

Mr Theaker chuckled. 'I dare say there's them as will part with a few coppers to have a bit of holly to stick behind a picture or put into a flower vase. The major won't ask for no payment, but you're just like your mam, Jimmy boy. She always insisted on paying her way, and you are just such another.'

Mo was tugging Jimmy's sleeve. 'Why can't I come to cut holly too?' she asked plaintively. 'You ain't goin' to leave me here all by my lonesome, are you? Why, Cyril could come in and nab me and you wouldn't even know. Oh, *please* let me come holly-cutting with you!'

Jimmy sighed. If he had been going on his own she would have been welcome to join him, but he knew from experience that Nutty would gather all his pals together to help, and they would not look with favour on Molly's joining the party. But as he gazed down at his sister's little face he knew he could not possibly leave her. Had things been normal he would have left her playing happily with one of her little pals in the Court, but now of course that was impossible. They had not seen Cyril amongst the crowds at the market and had only glimpsed Mrs Huxtable once as she waddled past the stall with her arms full of shopping and an expression of fury on her fat face, but there was no saying when one or both of them might suddenly appear. Jimmy and Mo had crouched below the level of the stall until Mrs Huxtable had passed by, and then Mo had whispered: 'Ain't she just mad though, our Jimmy! It's us as would be carryin' that heavy shoppin' if she had her way. D'you think she were lookin' for us? But we've kept a good look-out, haven't we, and of course Mr Theaker lendin' us different clo'es musta helped.'

Jimmy had nodded. He had been lent a corduroy jacket and cap and Mo was resplendent in a coloured headscarf tied under her chin and a long buttoned cardigan, and now, with her bright hair out of sight and her small body bulked out by the thick cardigan, she looked nothing like his skinny little sister. Nevertheless . . . He shrugged helplessly. 'You'll have to come, I suppose,' he said grudgingly. 'Nutty and the other fellers won't be too pleased, but if you just keep quiet and out of the way . . .'

But in the event this did not prove necessary. Harry's energetic wife appeared just then to help on the stall, and Harry took the opportunity to put his check cap on at a rakish angle, thrust his arms into his heavy greatcoat, and beckon to the two Trewins to follow him. 'I'm just a-goin' to introduce these nippers to Major Williams,' he explained to his wife. 'It won't take me more'n five minutes, an' then I'll come back an' start packin' up. All right wi' you, Mary me love?'

'Oh, aye,' Mrs Theaker said equably. 'Are you sure you want to take the little gairl along? If not she can stay wi' me.'

Harry tutted. 'Of course I want to take her along. I's goin' to introduce her to the major, ain't I, so that she can spend Christmas in the Salvation Hall.' He patted his wife's thin cheek affectionately. 'See you soon, chuck.'

'I wouldn't mind stayin' wi' Mrs Theaker. I like Mrs Theaker,' Mo said definitely as they moved away from the stall. 'She wouldn't let 'orrible Aunt Huxtable or even 'orribler Cyril carry me off. Only I s'pose she'll be goin' home wi' you when the stall's closed down. Oh, dear, I hope this 'ere major is as nice as you, Mr Theaker.'

59

'No one's as nice as Mr Theaker,' Jimmy said reproachfully, but he was presently forced to acknowledge he was wrong. Major Williams proved to be every bit as nice and understanding as Harry had promised, and when Jimmy had explained their predicament he had said at once that he understood. 'My wife and I will be spending a good deal of the Christmas holiday helping to feed and entertain those who have no one else to turn to,' he explained. 'But instead of sleeping in the Hall with the others you are welcome to use our spare bedroom; our eldest daughter, Roseanne, will be making a grand Christmas dinner in our house which we shall be delighted to share.' He held out a hand to Mo. 'Your brother tells me he is going to the park with his friends, so why don't you come and meet Roseanne and my other children?'

Jimmy expected Mo to cling to his hand and insist that she would not leave him, but instead she looked up into Major Williams's handsome, kindly face. 'I know a Roseanne,' she said eagerly. 'She teaches the infant class at my school . . . well, she isn't a teacher yet 'cos she's not old enough, but when she is she's goin' to go to college so she can come back and teach the little 'uns. Is that your Roseanne? We calls her by her first name 'cos there's three Miss Williamses already in our school.'

The conversation had taken place outside the Salvation Hall, and now Major Williams laughed and clapped a hand on Harry's shoulder. 'Yes, that's my daughter,' he said. 'Mr Theaker here will confirm it. And now if you've decided to accept our hospitality you and I will go straight to my house, and you shall meet the rest of the family and sit down to a nice tea whilst your brother goes off with his pals.'

Mo smiled happily, and Jimmy, much relieved, gave her a brief hug. 'Yes, you go with the major,' he said. 'I'm going to meet Nutty now, but I'll be back by ten o'clock, I promise. I'll see you then – if you're not asleep, that is.' He turned to Harry. 'Thank you very much. I don't know what we'd have done without you.'

Harry grinned. 'Couldn't let your mam down, God rest her soul. Good luck, the pair of you – and happy Christmas!'

And so it was that as dusk faded into dark Jimmy made his cautious way to Princes Park, where he and Nutty were to meet to carry out their task. His friend greeted him with a grin and Jimmy recognised several of the other lads from the surrounding Courts. They were all pals and knew him well enough not to give him away to the Huxtables. Jimmy began to feel positively irresponsible. Mo had been clinging closer to him than a limpet to a rock, but now he was with lads of his own age, he joined in with the laughter and the gossip with a clear conscience. He did not use swear words whilst he was with his sister, but now if he felt annoyed he could give vent to his feelings in the shared language which all the boys used.

Whistling softly beneath his breath, he decided

that Nutty's dad had been right when he likened taking holly to a bird plucking off a hawthorn berry, whereas scrumping fruit – a favourite summer pastime – really was stealing. He was expanding on this theory whilst Nutty nodded sagely when the moon, whose full silver face had shown the park up as bright as day, went behind a cloud. For a moment the boys paused in their stealthy onward progress, but then they moved forward once more until they reached a hedge which positively bristled with holly. Jimmy produced his clasp knife and began to look for well-berried pieces, but either the aforementioned bird or other lads had already been busy here; they would have to go deeper into the park if they wanted holly whose berries still remained on the branch.

As he and his pals crossed a piece of open ground, Jimmy remembered something he had always known really, which was that they were not alone in wanting to earn a bit extra for the holiday. Because of the Depression there were a great many men who had to take what they could get in order to make the dole go round, and some of these men, Jimmy had heard, were dangerous. They would attack an old woman for what was in her purse, even if it was only a few shillings, and if they decided that it was worth while to accost and steal from a group of boys then they would undoubtedly do it.

He was whispering this information into Nutty's ear, suggesting that they move away from ground which had already been virtually stripped, when they reached a tall holly tree whose upper branches were still heavy with berries. The reason for this peculiarity was soon clear, however: the briefest of examinations showed that the huge tree was quite unclimbable even for Jimmy, who was the best climber of all the lads. Fortunately, a large lime tree whose upper branches were within a few feet of the holly's presented few problems for an agile twelve-year-old, and within minutes Jimmy had ascended, reached across, grabbed the biggest – and best – branch of well-berried holly and cut it off from the main trunk, and was descending the lime tree once more. Glancing down, he saw in the tricky moonlight that whilst he had been climbing Nutty and the other lads had moved on. He looked about him, hoping Nutty had left the canvas bag in which Jimmy had meant to carry his trophy, but as his feet touched the ground he realised that Nutty must have taken it with him.

As Jimmy stood wondering which way his pals had gone, the moon went behind a cloud just as a hand descended on the back of his neck. He chuckled. It was one of the others, of course, jealous of his success, and thinking to show him he wasn't the only one who could get good-sized branches. 'Stow it, Freddy,' he began, then stopped as a voice he knew all too well spoke in his ear.

'Got you, you bloody little bag o' filth!' the voice grated. 'By Gor, I'll learn you an' your sister to keep your thievin' paws off other people's property.

You took my stash while I were asleep, and I'll be bound it were one o' you what made me fall down the stairs as well, though I still doesn't know how you did it!' Here Cyril shook Jimmy as vehemently as a dog shakes a rabbit. 'Where'd you put it? Don't you think you can keep shtum, because if you won't tell I'll beat the truth out of you. I'll thrash you till there's not a strip of skin left unmarked on your measly little pelt.'

Jimmy muttered that he did not know what his captor was talking about, whereupon Cyril jerked cruelly at the handful of hair on the nape of his neck.

'Ho, you thought you could keep out of my way if you stayed away from Solly Court, but that's where you was bleedin' well wrong. I remembered you was pally with that bleedin' Nuttall boy, and when I saw him headin' towards the park I remembered as how you kids used to cut holly and sell it on Christmas Eve. Well, you've cut all the holly you're going to get—' At this point Jimmy tore himself free from the older man's grasp and swung the big holly branch right across Cyril's face. Cyril give a shriek and let go of his captive for a moment to try to detach the prickly leaves from his skin.

'You little swine, you've bleedin' well blinded me,' he howled, causing himself more pain as he tore the holly free. 'Oh, I'll kill you, I'll kill the pair of you for this!' He let go of the branch and made an ineffectual grab for the boy just as the moon re-emerged from the cloud, and Jimmy saw that his face looked as though a cat had scratched it. He backed off, and then, as Cyril lurched towards him, set off across the park at a fast run. Looking over his shoulder as he burst into the road, he saw that though Cyril was some way behind he was still in hot pursuit. It would not do, therefore, to go to the house where Mo waited, and for obvious reasons he could not go to Solomon Court. There were a hundred little streets and jiggers where he might hide for a while, but he would have to think carefully before he decided which one to honour with his presence. Cyril might have friends who would be happy to join the chase, but on the good side he had to keep stopping to mop at the blood running down his face, so Jimmy did not think he was in immediate danger of being recaptured.

When Cyril got out into the main street, however, he began to shout 'Stop, thief', and though most people laughed and assumed that the man was referring to the holly the younger boy carried, one or two might have got in his way just for the hell of it, and this, Jimmy realised, could prove fatal for his chance of escape. As soon as he could he shot into a narrow side street, made sure he was out of Cyril's sight, and dived down the 'tunnel' between a row of terraced houses. He ran along the jigger for a short way, vaulted a low and crumbling wall, ran across the yard behind it and knocked urgently on the nearest back door.

For several moments there was no reply, no sign that there was anyone in the house, but even as he heard sounds of pursuit coming along the side street the back door shot open and a woman's voice said loudly: 'If I've told you once that I don't want any holly, or mistletoe, or a great swag of ivy, let alone your version of "Good King Wenceslas looked out", I've told you a hundred times. So go away, please, and let me watch my soup, because if it boils over on to the Primus stove I'll have a fine mess to clear up.'

Jimmy took a deep breath and tried to still the hammering of his heart long enough to plead that the woman would let him hide, but even as he did so she opened the door rather wider and pulled him inside just as Cyril, augmented by another couple of men, probably seamen off his ship, swerved round the corner and stopped short by the back gate which led from the jigger to the woman's house.

There was a muttered conversation between the men and then they moved on. Jimmy could hear their booted footsteps getting fainter and fainter as they traversed the narrow little jigger. When silence had returned once more, the woman spoke.

'I expect you could do with a cup of hot soup, though why I should give you anything when it's pretty clear you've stolen someone's holly I really can't understand – though why in God's name they should pursue you just for that I don't understand either. I've not been here for very long but wherever I've lived kids have cut holly and sold it on Christmas Eve.' She chuckled. 'From the sound of it, you must have chosen quite the wrong place to cut yours.' She

66

eyed the enormous branch which Jimmy was still holding, and tutted. 'You foolish boy, why on earth didn't you drop it? I suppose you could have thrown it in front of them if they got too close. Though it is a very fine specimen, I admit. If you cut all the twigs off and tie them into bundles you'd probably make more money than trying to sell the whole branch.' She looked keenly into Jimmy's face. 'Or wasn't that the reason for the kerfuffle? I must say . . .' and here she looked Jimmy over with a very shrewd eye, 'it doesn't seem likely. I suppose I ought to turn you out and let justice take its course, but I'd rather hear your story first.'

They had been standing in the narrow corridor which went from back to front of the terraced house, but now the woman gave a squeak and broke into a trot. 'Follow me,' she called over her shoulder. 'My soup! Oh, lor', if it boils over I'll be in the soup.' She gave what seemed to Jimmy a most uncharacteristic giggle. 'My story isn't as exciting as yours – if your story is exciting, that is – but I'm sure it's every bit as peculiar. My landlady, having been invited this morning to go away for Christmas, locked the kitchen door to prevent my using her precious "amenities", as she calls them, and left me two buckets of water which she said should last me until she returns. I suppose I could go next door if I need more than she's left me, but it has rather complicated my life . . .'

As she uttered the last words she pushed open her door and with a cry snatched a small saucepan

67

off the Primus stove which was standing in the hearth, then fanned her face in mock relief, for despite her fears the soup had only just begun to come to the boil. 'Pass me a couple of mugs, and then sit down,' she ordered him. You're a wretched nuisance, but since I saved you from those men I suppose we might as well share the soup while you tell me what it's all about.'

Jimmy opened his mouth to begin, realising suddenly how very hungry he was and how very good the soup smelled, but even as she handed him a mug an awful thought struck him. 'Oh, miss, you saved me bacon right enough, but I'm in awful trouble and I don't know as anyone can help me. You're right about one thing: I were out scrumpin' holly. I left me little sister with – with a sort of military person from the Salvation Army, someone she didn't mind staying with whilst I cut the holly. She's in their spare room, but oh, miss, I never saw the house or heard what number it was. In fact I can't even remember the name of the road. And if I don't join her by ten o'clock she'll be that worried she might do somethin' silly. She's only six, and the man that were chasin' me is after her as well.' He jumped to his feet and the soup swirled dangerously in the mug. 'I've gorra go, gorra find her. Where is we now?'

The woman shook her finger reprovingly and pinched the bridge of her nose. 'Calm down and drink your soup,' she said. 'It's already half past ten, so she's probably asleep, and I'm sure your pursuer will soon get tired of whatever game he's playing. If I'm to help you, you must tell me your story right from the beginning. I was going to offer you a bed for the night; in fact I can offer both you and your sister a bed until after the holiday, because the house is empty apart from myself. Mrs Stockyard – she's my landlady – only has three lodgers, and she didn't want any of us to stay over Christmas, only I had nowhere else to go, which is why she locked the kitchen door.' She pulled a face. 'It's made my life more difficult, which I imagine was her intention, but I'll manage.' She raised her eyebrows at her unexpected guest. 'And now tell me why that uncouth creature was chasing you. I'm sure if you stop worrying you'll remember the address of the people who have taken your sister in.'

'How did you know he were uncouth?' Jimmy said suspiciously. 'You can't have heard more than muttering.'

His new friend smiled. 'Didn't you wonder why I opened the back door so suddenly? My front window is a poor fit and I heard them outside, arguing about whether you'd gone down the side passage into the jigger. The language they used was pretty choice, I can tell you.'

'Oh, I see,' Jimmy said. He took a sip of his soup, then a large swallow. 'I say, this is delicious. It's days – no, more like weeks – since I had a proper hot meal; Mrs Huxtable is no cook. But she occasionally buys a shop pie and we might just get a smidgen of that.' He looked at the woman now

69

sitting opposite him. 'What I'm goin' to tell you will sound pretty far-fetched, and the worst of it is we don't know ourselves what's at the bottom of it. So I'd better start right at the beginning when old Ma Huxtable sent me to the wash house with a pile of tablecloths and that, and give our Mo a big sack of sprouts to clean so she could sell 'em to the neighbours for their Christmas dinner . . .'

When he had finished he looked hopefully at his companion. It was such an unlikely story; could she possibly make sense of it? But it seemed that she could, for she was nodding slowly. Jimmy saw no need to explain about Mo's activity with the boot-laces. After all, Cyril had fallen down the stairs many times before, and never suffered any lasting ill effects. 'What I can't make out, though, is what Cyril thinks we've stolen. Mo says he had a glittery necklace; I can't think where he would have got such a thing, but maybe that's what he thinks we took. Or maybe it was the Christmas presents – we just don't know.'

'Yes, I do see,' the woman said thoughtfully. 'But you haven't got to find whatever it is he thinks you stole, just prove you weren't the ones who took it.'

Jimmy shook his head. 'All Mo took were the things in the parcel, but they was meant for her and me anyhow – a teddy bear for Mo and a harmonica for me. But Cyril's the sort of feller what only has one idea in his mind at a time. Also, he's what you might call a man of violence. He'd enjoy beating me and Mo to a pulp whether or not he

70

believed we'd took his property. He's a wicked man, Miss – Miss . . .'

'Yes, it's about time we learned each other's names,' the woman said. She was tall and straight with pale blonde hair, rather like his mother's, done up in a fancy braid at the back of her head. She was neatly but not gaudily dressed, in a grey pleated skirt, a white blouse and a navy blue cardigan, with sensible lace-up shoes on her feet and the sort of stockings which Jimmy knew from his times on Harry's stall to be called lisle. The woman smiled as his eyes took in every detail of her appearance. 'My name's Miss Trent; Glenys Trent, to be exact. And you are . . .?'

Jimmy glanced at the mirror above the kitchen table and saw a skinny urchin in ragged trousers and shirt beneath a brown corduroy jacket much too big for him. He noticed that he must have lost his cap at some stage and felt guilty because Mr Theaker had loaned it to him. But perhaps next day he might scout around, see if he could find it. His straight dark hair was in need of a cut, his pale face was smeared with dirt from his tree-climbing activities, and there was a worry line between his dark brows, which was a result of his having virtually lost his little sister. If she stayed where she was and simply waited he was sure she would be safe, for the major and his family would see she came to no harm, but he knew Mo. The moment ten o'clock struck, she would have started to worry, and he, her protector, could do nothing to reassure her of his safety until he could remember the address of the house to which she had gone so happily. He realised with a stab of horror that he could not remember the major's name either; what on earth was he to do? But Miss Trent was looking at him enquiringly and Jimmy's mind, which had been wandering the moonlit streets, came back to the house in which he was now sitting. 'Sorry, Miss Trent. I'm Jimmy Trewin, and my sister's Maureen, only everyone calls her Mo. She's a darling. When you meet her you'll scarce believe we're brother and sister 'cos she's that pretty.' He hesitated. 'You're a teacher, aren't you?'

Miss Trent had been sipping her soup whilst frowning over the problem of what Jimmy should do, but at his words her eyebrows shot up. 'What? As it happens you are correct; was it just a lucky guess or do I have "teacher" tattooed on my forehead?'

Jimmy laughed with her, then shook his head and pointed to her small bookshelves. 'It's your spectacles and the way you do your hair, all pulled back off your face,' he explained. 'And the books. You've got *Pride and Prejudice*, *Sense and Sensibility*, *Bleak House*, *David Copperfield* and lots more whose titles I don't recognise, but a friend of our mam was a teacher and her bookshelves were full of stuff like that.'

Miss Trent stood up, patting Jimmy's shoulder and offering more soup. 'You're a clever lad,' she said approvingly. 'When we've finished the soup we'll go and search for your sister. Where did you part from her, can you remember?'

Jimmy brightened. 'Quite near where Mr Theaker sets up his stall on Great Homer Street,' he said. He glanced shyly at Miss Trent. 'Mr Theaker's a grand feller. He's been letting us sleep under his stall, like in a canvas tent, ever so warm and comfy, but of course I couldn't leave Mo there while I went cutting holly. So Mr Theaker took us to meet this major chap, who said that he'd look after her while I were busy making some money, and that we can both stay with them, just over Christmas like. Cyril's ship sails before the end of the year, so we'll have no worries after that. His mam is a beast but we can cope with her.'

'I see,' Miss Trent said thoughtfully. 'Well, I'm sure you're right. But in the meantime I suppose we might wake Mr Theaker and ask him for this major's address. After all . . .'

She stopped speaking. Jimmy's hearing had always been acute and now it was heightened by his fear for his sister. He put a finger to his lips, and even as he did so Miss Trent too heard what had caught Jimmy's attention. Footsteps! Someone was walking along the pavement, and even as she glanced towards the curtained window there was the squeak of the gate being pushed open and shut and then, before they could do more than exchange terrified glances, the sound of someone's key in the lock, and a muttered curse when it did not immediately turn. The front door creaked slowly open.

73

'Hide!' Miss Trent hissed to Jimmy, who immediately dived under the bed, whilst she herself walked boldly into the corridor, saying clearly, 'Who's that? How dare you come into a private house without even knocking, using what is no doubt a stolen key?' And without more ado she blocked the man's way. Then turned her head to speak over her shoulder: 'Will someone fetch the police? This man is trespassing.'

Chapter 5

Miss Trent's heart was beating so hard that she thought the intruder must surely hear it, but he made no move to come further into the house; indeed he backed off. It was dark in the passage and the moonlight behind him made it impossible for Miss Trent to see him as anything but a dark shadow – a fairly tall, broad man in a dark coat and cap. But as she moved forward to shut the door in his face he spoke.

'Don't call the scuffers, miss,' he said quietly. 'It's me, Frank Bloggs. Oh, Gawd, miss, wharra start you gave me! Mrs Stockyard told me the house would be empty and I'd have to go to relatives till New Year's Day – she never said no word about you being here. But I've no family left in these parts, so now she's gone I thought mebbe I could manage here on me own.'

Miss Trent pulled the door wide and ushered the young man inside. 'You can come out, Jimmy,' she called. 'This isn't an intruder, it's another of Mrs Stockyard's lodgers.' She turned back to Mr Bloggs. 'I'd better introduce you to my young friend, who's spending the holiday with me.' She paused a moment before opening the door of her room wide, giving

Jimmy a chance to wriggle out from under the bed, which he did with promptitude. 'Jimmy, this is Mr Bloggs, who works for the railways; he has one of the upstairs rooms. Mr Bloggs, this is Jimmy Trewin.'

'Nice to meet you Mr Bloggs,' Jimmy said. The two shook hands, eyeing one another covertly, in the warm light of the paraffin lamp.

Miss Trent smiled to herself. 'Come in and sit down, Mr Bloggs, and let me put you in the picture,' she said. 'It seems that Mrs Stockyard lied in order to keep us out of her house, but here we are and here we'll stay.'

Jimmy cleared his throat. 'Don't forget, miss, that we were just going off to search for my sister,' he said. He turned to the older man. 'She's only six and I just know that because I wasn't there at ten o'clock she'll have come out looking for me . . . Oh, I can't explain . . .'

'Well I can,' Miss Trent said quickly, and outlined the story which Jimmy had told her. 'So you see, we're going to try to find this major's house, even if it means rousing Mr Theaker. It's none of your concern, of course, but if you'd like to stay in my warm room until we return you're very welcome to do so. I'm sure your room will be icy cold, even though it's a mild night.'

'Hang on a minute, Miss Trent,' the young man said eagerly. 'When you say the major, are you referrin' to Major Williams, what runs the Salvation Army in these parts? If you are, I can lead you straight to his house. I'm a Salvationist, you see, so I know him well.' He grinned at Jimmy. 'Is your sister a little bit of a thing with very fair hair, all curls? If so, she's the reason I decided to come back to Orange Street. I were goin' to stay with Williams and his family, but when they took the little gal in as well as all the others I said I'd come back here.'

He stopped speaking as Jimmy began to struggle into his borrowed coat. 'She'll be safe with the major, lad . . .' he was beginning when Miss Trent interrupted.

'I think we'd better all go,' she said decisively, 'because from what I've heard she may have already fled from the major's protection.' She smiled at Jimmy. 'I gather your sister is a very spirited young lady, and if she has gone off to try to find you, Jimmy, we'll need as many searchers as we can get. Big cities are dangerous places at night, and we know there is a man out there who would do her a mischief if he could.' As she spoke she was taking her coat down from its hook, kicking off her slippers and sliding her feet into boots. Then it was the work of a moment to turn off the Primus stove, douse the lamp and go out into the brilliant moonlight.

Mr Bloggs pointed to a narrow street almost opposite where they stood. 'It might be safer to stay on the main roads, but I imagine the little gal would avoid bright lights,' he said in a low tone. He turned to Miss Trent. 'From what you told me, this here Huxtable feller isn't likely to creep around quietly, so we must make as little noise as possible and listen out for sounds of cursing and brawling.'

Jimmy began to remind the man that Cyril had been very quiet indeed when he had nabbed him in Princes Park, but though he nodded Mr Bloggs was quick to point out that some time had passed since that encounter.

'If I know his type he'll have had a few pints by this time, and he'll soon begin to shout and boast and make himself unpleasant,' he said. 'So take my advice, Jimmy, and we'll none of us talk unless we have something important to say. Right then, let's go.'

'And I always thought you were too timid to say boo to a goose,' Miss Trent marvelled. 'You are obviously going to be the leader in this expedition, so lay on, Macduff!'

Mo had thoroughly enjoyed her evening, greeting Roseanne as an old friend and taking part in a game of blind man's buff which the older girl had organised. At nine o'clock, however, the visiting children – and Mo – were invited into the kitchen for cocoa and biscuits, after which the visitors departed and Mo was put into a little truckle bed which pulled out from beneath Roseanne's.

She lay in bed reliving her evening with great enjoyment; what a lot she would have to tell Jimmy when he joined her, no doubt with his canvas bag bristling with holly. She did not often have money of her own but she had been saving the ha'pennies the old ladies of the Court handed out to anyone who would carry bags or fill buckets for them and had amassed what was to her a small fortune. She had counted it the day before Cyril's return and intended to spend it all on a stick of nougat, a quarter of a pound of striped humbugs and a bag of shelled peanuts, because these were all Jimmy's favourites. But now she thought she really ought to get a small gift for Roseanne, because the other girl had been so kind. She knew it was possible to buy two mince pies in a little fancy box, though she had no idea what these delicious creations cost.

She snuggled her head into her pillow, deciding to go out with Roseanne or Jimmy next morning to do her Christmas shopping, and even as the thought entered her head she heard the clock strike ten. Immediately she sat bolt upright; Jimmy would be back, telling the major and his family all about his expedition. She listened hard but could not pick out Jimmy's tones amongst the voices below. Oh, well, she knew he would come up just as soon as he was free to do so, although it had been a long and exciting day and perhaps, when he did appear, he would have so much to tell her that he might prefer to save his news until morning.

She snuggled down again, knowing she would not sleep until she was certain he was safely back, and when the door creaked open she shot up in her little bed, sure that this was Jimmy at last. But the voice which spoke was not Jimmy's.

'Hello, are you still awake?' Roseanne said. 'It's after ten o'clock; you should have been asleep ages ago. Are you finding it difficult to drop off because you're sleeping in a strange bed? Is there anything you want? A glass of water, or maybe a visit to the privy? It's a mild night, but even so you must put on that dressing gown we lent you before you venture out. And my old slippers – they'll be far too big for you, but you can shuffle along, can't you?'

'I could,' Mo said briefly, before broaching the subject uppermost in her mind. 'Has Jimmy come back yet? There are lots of people talking downstairs, but I don't think I can hear his voice, and he promised to be back by ten o'clock.'

Roseanne had come upstairs holding a candle, and by its flickering light Mo thought that her friend looked a trifle uncertain. 'Well, there are a lot of people downstairs and one of them might be Jimmy,' she admitted. 'But I've never seen your brother. What does he look like?'

Mo gave this serious consideration, sitting up in bed and twisting one of her yellow curls around her finger. 'Well, he's not a bit like me, because he's dark with straight hair and very straight eyebrows which make him look cross, although he isn't, of course. Jimmy says I take after our mam and he takes after our dad, that's why we're so different. He wasn't wearing his own coat because we were in disguise like, so's Cyril wouldn't reckernise us. He'll still be wearing the brown corduroy coat and cap Mr Theaker lent him, I guess.'

Roseanne looked doubtful. 'He's only eleven or twelve, isn't he? Well, there are one or two boys downstairs, but none of them are wearing corduroy, as far as I can recall. Do you want me to go down again and ask? Only I'm sure he must have come in by now; why, it's nearly half past ten. Has he gone cutting holly? Most of the lads do that so they can sell it round the markets on Christmas Eve. It's stealing really, of course, only nobody minds. I've heard my dad saying it's like country kids scrumping apples; so long as they don't take too many, not even the farmers object.'

'No, it's all right, you needn't go down again. I'm sure he's here,' Mo said slowly. A plan was forming in her mind, but she did not mean Roseanne to put two and two together. Instead, she snuggled down the bed again, and watched as Roseanne jumped between her own sheets and turned to her.

'Your brother has probably gone straight to bed with the other boys, so just you stop fretting and go to sleep. And no sneaking around the house trying to find him, because tonight the place is as full as it can hold, and we can't have young ladies tripping over boys in sleeping bags and maybe rousing the whole house. Promise?'

'Course I do, Roseanne,' Mo said, fingers crossed firmly behind her back. She gave an enormous yawn and patted her mouth. 'Gosh, I'm *sooo* tired. Goodnight.'

Very soon after this conversation the house went quiet. Roseanne's breathing slowed and steadied. Mo waited until she heard the major and his wife coming upstairs and shutting the door into their bedroom, then climbed out of bed and dressed hastily in the clothes Mr Theaker had lent her. She tied the headscarf under her chin, buttoned the long cardigan and put on the borrowed boots. They were too big but they were a great deal more comfortable than her battered and holey plimsolls; a good deal warmer, too. She kept a careful eye on Roseanne, but the older girl did not stir, and presently Mo let herself out of the bedroom and crept down the stairs. She had decided that if anyone queried her presence she would say she had to visit the privy, or perhaps that she was thirsty and needed a glass of water. However, though she had to be very careful in the kitchen because there were humped figures of boys and girls, blanket-wrapped, all over the quarry tiles, it was the work of a moment to slip into the back yard and close the kitchen door behind her. She glanced at the privy as she passed it, a lie already on her tongue should anyone emerge, but no one did. The jigger was in deep shadow on one side and bright moonlight on the other, but Mo did not care. She had known as soon as she entered the kitchen that Jimmy was not there, and now she was determined to find him. When she emerged on to the main road she stopped for a moment, trying to make up her mind which way to go. She knew of course that Jimmy had gone to Princes Park, but she also knew that he was a boy who always kept his promises, and he had promised to be at the major's house by ten o'clock. Now it was nearer eleven than ten, and Mo knew that only two things could have stopped him. Either the scuffers had decided to wage war on the little sinners who stripped the holly from the hedges and bushes in Princes Park, or Cyril Huxtable had realised where he would probably find one or both of the Trewins and had pounced on Jimmy just when her brother thought himself safe. Then she remembered that there might be a third reason for Jimmy's non-appearance: he might not have fully understood that he too was to come to the major's house to sleep in safety for a few nights. If so, she supposed he might easily have crawled into the canvas shelter under Mr Theaker's stall, knowing her to be safe and not realising that he, too, could have had a proper bed. This made up her mind in which direction to turn; she would go to Great Homer Street first. Silent as a little shadow, she began to steal quietly along the pavement towards her destination.

Fifteen minutes later she left Harry Theaker's stall, disappointment causing the tears to well up in her eyes. In her heart she had almost convinced herself that Jimmy would be here, and now there were but the two alternatives. She hated to think of Jimmy in a police cell, but after a little thought realised that this was unlikely. The scuffers were there to bring law and order to the streets. They would scarcely throw anyone into prison for snapping off a few twigs of holly, let alone a boy of twelve. And that left what she most dreaded: that Cyril Huxtable had caught Jimmy and dragged him off to No. 4 Solomon Court, where he would

83

try to beat the truth out of his victim, though of course since Jimmy did not know what they were supposed to have done it stood to reason that he couldn't admit or deny anything either.

Mo took a deep breath and knuckled her eyes, then blew her nose on her sleeve and turned in the direction of Solomon Court. She knew she might be heading for the lion's den, but she did not intend to abandon her brother. She would go to the Court, and if he was not there she would try the docks, the pubs, anywhere at all where Cyril Huxtable might be found, and when she found him she would go to the scuffers and do her very best to convince them of his wickedness – unless of course she could find some means to rescue Jimmy herself.

Resolutely, Mo set off.

Mo walked fast, but as she got nearer to Solomon Court her pace slowed. How could she find out whether Jimmy was incarcerated without searching No. 4 room by room? And that would simply be asking for trouble. She stopped just short of the entrance to the Court, where there was a bollard on the pavement to prevent heavy lorries from entering. She had perched upon it often, for it was 'home' when the kids were playing relievio, and now she automatically mounted it and sat there wishing fervently that Jimmy would suddenly appear and make her worries unnecessary. But this was wishful thinking; what she needed to do at this stage was try to put herself into Cyril's shoes.

Presuming he had caught Jimmy, she was pretty sure he would bring his captive back here and threaten him with the beating of his life if he didn't immediately admit to whatever it was he thought they had done. He must have put some sort of gag into poor Jimmy's mouth to stop him yelling, Mo told herself. There was nothing else for it: her first move would simply have to be as much of an exploration of No. 4 as she could manage.

She was halfway across the Court when she remembered something else. She was as much at risk from Cyril and his mother as Jimmy was. If Cyril hadn't managed to capture Jimmy he would be very pleased to capture her. So going close to the house, showing herself in the patchy moonlight, was just what the Huxtables wanted. If only there was some way of finding out whether they were at home. Mo chewed her lip. She could shout 'Fire! Fire!' but of course she would have to get close enough to set something alight or they would simply assume the cry concerned some other house and, being as selfish as they were horrible, simply go back to bed.

And suppose Cyril had realised the perils of bringing Jimmy back to No. 4? There were other places – Princes Park itself – where Cyril could work his wicked will on her brother. Perhaps I ought to have started in Princes Park, Mo thought despairingly. But I'm here now, so I'll go round by the jigger and see what I can see.

Keeping to the shadows, Mo approached the house from the back. She was silent as a little mouse, but as soon as she looked over the gate she saw that the privy was occupied. Mrs Huxtable, wrapped in a blanket and with a cushion behind her head, was sitting there with the door wide open, clearly on watch, except that both her eyes were closed and a rich and grumbling snore was issuing from her mean little mouth.

An enormous weight was lifted from Mo's mind and her lips curved into a delighted smile. If Mrs Huxtable was keeping watch over the back door, then it was almost certain that Cyril would be sitting in the bow window watching the front of the house. Well, that must mean that whatever the cause for Jimmy's non-appearance at the major's house it was not because he had been captured. She retraced her steps and crept, bent double, along the front of the house, keeping well below the level of the sill, and listening hard. At first she could hear nothing, but then a deep irritated sigh came to her ears. A match flared and the red tip of a cigarette glowed, and she heard the creak of Mrs Huxtable's rocking chair as Cyril shifted and sighed with frustration.

Now, elation made her careless. Jimmy was not here, and since Cyril was, it seemed most of her dread had been unnecessary. All that remained now was to go back to the major's house in the quiet little street off Everton Road and await her brother's arrival; why, he might already be there, and if he had gone up to the room she shared with Roseanne and found her missing . . . goodness, far from rescuing him she might have plunged him into real danger! Forgetting caution, Mo straightened up and fairly tore across the cobbles, hearing behind her a roar which warned her that Cyril had seen her and was already limbering up for pursuit.

Mo chuckled to herself. She had always been a very fast runner, and provided nobody got in her way she thought herself a match for Cyril. He was big and strong, but he was also overweight and consequently clumsy. She was sure she could lose him as soon as she left the main road for the tortuous and twisty little streets which were such a feature of the city.

She whipped on to the main road and heard a crash behind her. Risking a quick glance over her shoulder she saw Cyril sprawling on the pavement, and chuckled to herself as she heard him curse. Determined to take advantage of his fall she turned into the first little street she came to, certain that she could outrun him, but even as she swerved to avoid a cat which darted out of somebody's porch she was seized and held in an iron grip whilst a voice in her ear said: 'Got you! And don't you call out.'

The voice was one she had never heard before and she realised with dismay that Cyril must have whistled up some of his fellow seamen to help in his pursuit of Jimmy and herself. As for calling out, what chance did she have? Her captor had clapped a large hand over her mouth and held her against his body, making escape or shouting impossible. But just as she was contemplating sinking her teeth into the muffling hand, the voice whispered: 'Hush! I'm Jimmy's pal . . . I'll explain presently,' and she saw Cyril lumbering into view, his big head swinging from side to side as he sought a glimpse of her. She heard a low chuckle in her ear and then an authoritative voice on the main road said briskly: 'What's your hurry, sir? No, don't try to get away. When any member of the force asks a question, it's because they want an answer.'

Cyril muttered something, and her captor slackened his grip on Mo so that she could see the little scene being enacted at the top of the street. A large policeman had hold of Cyril by one brawny wrist, and when he began to shout, to say that he was in pursuit of a thief and must be allowed to continue on his way, the policeman gave a disbelieving laugh. 'Oh yes? And just what has been stolen? If you'll come along wi' me, we'll take a nice little stroll down to the station and you shall turn out your pockets and explain what you were doing running down the street at this time in the morning. I should say you were disturbing the peace, which can earn you a night in the cells.'

Mo watched with awe as Cyril tried to jerk himself free, whereupon the policeman put his whistle to his lips and blew a resounding blast. Cyril screamed a curse, freed himself and set off at a run, with the policeman in hot pursuit.

When they had gone the young man who had grabbed Mo released her, and Jimmy emerged from the shadows, grinning. Mo opened her mouth to demand an explanation but Jimmy shook his head. 'No talking until we're back in Miss Trent's room,' he said in a low voice. 'We don't want to disturb the peace.' He smiled at his sister. 'I think we're safe from Cyril for a while at least.'

Mo took two steps towards Jimmy and collapsed into his arms. She fought to stop herself crying but two fat tears rolled down her cheeks. 'Oh, Jimmy, you're safe,' she murmured into his corduroy jacket. 'But who's this feller, and who's Miss Trent? And why can't we go back to Major Williams's house?'

Jimmy opened his mouth to speak but was hushed by a tall slim woman in a neatly belted mackintosh, who must have been hiding in the porch. She smiled in a very friendly way at Mo, but sank her voice to a whisper. 'It's far too late to go to the Williamses' now. Mr Bloggs here will let them know you're safe in the morning. Now, no more talking until we're indoors.'

Mo nodded dumbly; she did not understand what was happening, but the man in uniform and this tall and beautiful lady seemed to be on their side, and that was all that mattered. Adrenalin had kept her going, fear and excitement lending her strength, but now she was beginning to realise how very tired she was, and how she longed for her bed, either the one which awaited her at Major Williams's or the cosy dormouse-nest beneath Mr Theaker's second-hand clothes stall. Being Mo she would naturally have died rather than admit her total weariness, but she was grateful enough for the arm which Jimmy put round her shoulders as they walked. She would have liked to whisper 'Is it much further?' but pride kept her silent and soon she was glad she had not complained, for really it was only a short way to Orange Street, where the beautiful lady lived. The young man seemed to live there too, for he put his own key in the lock, opened the door and ushered everyone inside. Mo noticed that he did this very quietly, and looked all round as though to satisfy himself that no enemy lurked in the long shadows before he closed the door again.

Once they were all in her room, the tall lady – Miss Trent – lit the gas fire and went across to a cupboard, producing from its depths a large tin of Heinz vegetable soup. She poured the soup into a pan, lit the Primus stove and returned to the cupboard to bring out four bowls and a loaf of bread. 'I think we all need something warm after our adventure,' she said cheerfully. 'And now, Jimmy, I think you should explain to your sister exactly what happened to you, and then Maureen can tell us how she came to be out in the middle of the night when she was supposed to be in bed and asleep in Major Williams's house.'

Chapter 6

When the various stories had all been told, Mo, as well as Jimmy, knew they had found two new good friends.

'Lucky for us that I blundered into Miss Trent's back yard, and she realised that I was in desperate need of help, and not simply searching for someone to buy my holly,' Jimmy told his sister impressively. 'Heaven knows what Cyril would have done if he'd caught me.'

'And lucky for all of us that Mr Bloggs is a Salvationist and knew both the major's name and his address,' Miss Trent put in. 'Of course we went there first, Mo, in case you were sound asleep and not worried at all, but you had already left. The Williamses were very concerned, of course, but Jimmy assured them he had a pretty good idea of where we were likely to find you, and Mr Bloggs promised to go back tomorrow and tell them how we got on. Oh yes, luck has been on our side tonight, but we mustn't assume that we're safe, or that luck will always be with the righteous – by which I mean you Trewins, of course.' She glanced at the two children, and then at the railway worker. 'You note I say *we* and not *you*, because I'm sure

Mr Bloggs will agree that we're on your side, and will do everything we can to help you.'

'Of course,' Frank said, but he sounded uneasy. 'Only I shan't be much use to anyone after the holiday because I'll be back on the engine, learning the road from Liverpool to Manchester.'

Mo had been sitting on the edge of Miss Trent's bed, eyes half closed and on the verge of sleep, but at Frank's words her eyes shot open and she stared across at him. 'Road? But I always thought trains ran on rails!' She eyed the young man seated opposite doubtfully. 'Ain't that right? That puffer-trains run on rails?'

Frank grinned. 'I'm what you might call apprenticed to the railways,' he explained. 'One day I'll be an engine driver, if I pass all my exams and learn the roads – which is just another word for rails, really – but until then I'm only a fireman. Do you understand, queen?'

'Ye-es,' Mo said slowly. 'So you won't be able to look after us except when your engine brings you back to Liverpool.' She twisted round towards the older woman. 'What about you, Miss Trent?'

'I shall have to look for a job, even though teachers who have been dismissed after only one term aren't exactly sought after,' Miss Trent admitted. 'In fact I'm not at all sure yet what is best to do. You see, apart from luck we have other advantages on our side, one of which is that the Huxtables have never seen either me or Mr Bloggs. That may be useful, but I don't see that we can do anything until the

Christmas holidays are over. I have to move out of this house on New Year's Eve, so we shall need to think about our moves after that extremely carefully.'

Jimmy turned appealing eyes upon Miss Trent. 'This here room of yours has been a real refuge in a time of trouble; if we can just stay here until Cyril's ship sails . . .'

'Of course you can,' Miss Trent said at once. She hesitated. 'Look, it's very late. Why don't we all go to bed – you can share with me, Mo, and perhaps Jimmy can sleep on the sofa in your room, Frank? – and tomorrow we'll start to make plans: not least for ensuring that we all have a jolly good Christmas!'

By six o'clock on Boxing Day the oddly assorted group had enjoyed what they all agreed had been a splendid Christmas. Jimmy gave Mo the toy dog with its torn ear, and she gave him the stick of nougat that Miss Trent, on her behalf, had managed to buy. Despite the lure of bright lights, cheap prices and a delicate covering of snow, neither Mo nor Jimmy had dared to leave Miss Trent's cosy room, but on Christmas Eve the three of them had cut Jimmy's holly into saleable bundles, which Frank had taken to Great Homer Street as soon as his shift had ended. He had sold the lot, and had returned triumphant to the house in Orange Street bearing all the essentials for a delicious Christmas dinner.

Jimmy had wondered aloud how Miss Trent

would manage to cook everything on the Primus stove, but it soon appeared that Frank knew more than railway engines. With the help of Miss Trent's nail file he managed to get into their landlady's beloved kitchen, and on Christmas Day itself they feasted on chicken, sprouts, roast potatoes and gravy, followed by Christmas pudding and custard. Miss Trent had bought a box of Christmas crackers for a paltry sum at the very end of trading on Christmas Eve, and these had been pulled with much hilarity. Soon everyone was wearing a colourful paper hat, reading each other's mottoes and jokes with many a groan, and feeling that the party mood was made all the sweeter by the fact that they were on forbidden ground. Afterwards they pushed the big table out into the corridor and played games, though despite the fact that the streets were almost deserted Mo insisted upon drawing the curtains, fearful of watching eyes.

When the twenty-seventh dawned, Jimmy realised how sensible Miss Trent had been to insist on a break to enjoy themselves and revel in the spirit of Christmas. When they had restored the kitchen to its normal state and were sitting round the table eating cold chicken, potatoes baked in their jackets and slices of the ham which Mr Theaker had contributed, via Major Williams, to the holiday fare, they were all relaxed and each was eager to air his or her ideas. Miss Trent had made a large trifle, and as the spoon was scraped around the last smears of fruit and sponge cake she stood up and rapped on the table. 'Right; I'm afraid that for us Christmas is over, and serious life must begin again. I know we've all been thinking frantically how best to solve the Trewins' problem, and I mean to lead off with my own theories, if nobody minds.'

Everyone thought this was sensible, so Miss Trent began. 'Mo and Jimmy are in a very unfortunate position,' she pointed out. 'In normal circumstances I should advise them to go to the nearest police station and demand protection; but from what? For one thing, their father let them stay in the Huxtables' charge; he even agreed to the Huxtables moving into number four and letting their own house, and everyone in the Court knows he sends Mrs Huxtable his allotment at the end of every month. She has never allowed the children to write to their father, nor given them any letters that might have come for them. Unfortunately, neither Jimmy nor Mo ever went to the authorities to complain of their treatment. Mrs Huxtable no doubt saw to that. And now we have a situation which has made every-thing even more difficult. Mo says she saw Cyril open a parcel addressed to you both—'

'I did see him,' Mo cut in. 'It had our Christmas presents in it, and then he took them upstairs. And he had a glittery necklace too,' she added. 'Don't you believe me, Miss Trent?'

Miss Trent laughed and ruffled Mo's curls. 'I'm just telling it as you would have to tell it to the scuffers,' she explained. 'You see, darling, there were no witnesses apart from yourself who could be called upon to give what is known as "corroborative evidence". It would be your word against Cyril's, and the police might well think a six-year-old could be mistaken. And why would they think there was anything special about a parcel of toys? As for the necklace, it could just be glass, and a present for his mum. They might even think you'd been asleep and dreamed the whole thing.'

'But what about the threats?' Jimmy said after a longish pause. 'That isn't a perishin' dream, I can tell you. Oh, Miss Trent, are you sayin' we've got to let Cyril beat the pair of us to a pulp before the scuffers will listen to our story?'

Miss Trent leaned across the table and patted his cheek. 'What I'm trying to say, dear Jimmy, is that without an independent witness we have no proof that Cyril ever had the necklace, and only you and Mo have heard him threaten you with violence for taking it – or whatever it is he thinks you took. I think it would be difficult to persuade the police to help you when there is no evidence that any crime has been committed.' She looked around the table; Jimmy and Mo looked frustrated and on the brink of tears, whilst Frank looked very thoughtful indeed. He was frowning heavily, but the frown cleared suddenly and he spoke.

'I think our best bet is to wait until Cyril's ship sails. Then we will ask Jimmy to appear openly in the Court and do anything he can think of to get Mrs Huxtable in a temper. Then he must run away, not too fast, so that Mrs Huxtable waddles after him and the rest of us can get into the house, lock all the doors and have a really good search for the necklace. What do you think of that idea?'

They all agreed that this might well work, for who could say that it was not the fall down the stairs which had caused Cyril to forget completely that it was he himself who had hidden the jewels, if jewels they were?

Much enamoured of their plan, Jimmy rose early on the morning Cyril was due to sail and went down to the kitchen, where Frank was already making breakfast. Outside, the brief spell of mild weather had been replaced by a bitter wind, and when they had cleared away the dishes Jimmy wrapped the thick scarf which Mr Theaker had given him as a Christmas present around his mouth and nose, meaning to walk up to Lime Street station and see Frank off to work.

They had only walked a few yards when Jimmy spied Nutty walking purposefully ahead of them, a box beneath his arm. There were few people about, so Jimmy told Frank it was an old friend and the two of them hurried to catch the other boy up. When they reached him, however, they got a nasty shock. 'Wharron earth are you doin' here, Jimmy?' Nutty asked, glancing around him. 'Haven't you heard? Cyril Huxtable's ship sailed without him. He's been effin' and blindin' ever since, sayin' it's all your fault, though how he could possibly blame you no one can imagine. But if I were you I'd steer clear of the Court until he calms down.' He stared inquisitively into Jimmy's face. 'What's his problem, anyhow? What can a kid like you do to a feller what's twice your size and has three times your strength? Or is it summat you knows? My mam cleans the Cuckoo's Nest and hears all the gossip. She says as the captain of the *Sugar Trader* don't trust Huxtable because of summat what happened on their last voyage; don't know what, but I spec he prigged some cash and the cap'n found out.'

'Sounds possible,' Jimmy said thoughtfully. 'He won't get another berth, though, if he's been caught thieving, will he?'

Nutty shrugged. 'Dunno; it's probably just gossip anyway. His shipmates hate Cyril and would like to see him taken down a peg.'

'But you're sure he hasn't sailed?' Jimmy said, voicing the thought uppermost in his mind. 'So what does we do now? Don't tell anyone, Nutty, but the fact is Cyril hates us because he thinks we took summat of his. Oh, oh, oh, whatever ought I to do?'

Nutty grinned. 'Glad it's your problem and not mine,' he said cheerfully. 'That Huxtable will kill someone one of these days; just make sure it ain't you, old pal.' And with that and a cheery wave he left them.

'Well, that's our plan done for,' Frank said, causing Jimmy to jump, for he had completely forgotten the other man. 'If you ask me you'll be best away from Liverpool, for the time being at any rate. If you stay here you'll be waiting the whole while for a hand on your shoulder or a blow on the back of the head. And poor little Mo is nervous enough already. Is there anything keeping you in Liverpool? That horrible old woman half starves you; she takes your father's money and never passes on a groat, and Cyril, now that he might not get another berth, will be constantly on at you. You can't pretend you and your sister can live under a cloud like that. I tell you, Jimmy, clear out while you've still got your health. You talk it over with Miss Trent, and I'll see you when I come back from work tonight.'

Jimmy went straight back to Orange Street and was just in time to prevent Miss Trent and Mo from leaving the house, though as soon as they heard his story Miss Trent announced that they would go nowhere that day. 'Your Nutty is a good friend, and so is Frank Bloggs,' she said. 'They could be very helpful; if we make up our minds to leave Liverpool we shall need someone in the city to stay in touch and let us know what is happening. There's nothing else to keep you here, is there?'

For a fleeting moment Jimmy thought of his father, who would not know where they were, and knew that the same thought had flickered across Mo's mind, but he told himself firmly that his dad didn't deserve any consideration. However grief-stricken he might have been after Grace's death, he had behaved extremely badly in never checking that Mrs Huxtable was the right person to look after his children. And as for Cyril, Jimmy thought, agreeing that there was nothing to keep either him or his sister in Liverpool, their father probably had no idea that he even existed. He looked across at Mo. She was cuddling her teddy and did not seem to be taking much notice of what the others were about, but she must have felt Jimmy's gaze upon her, because she looked up and answered Miss Trent's question just as Jimmy would have liked to do. 'We used to think our dad would come and rescue us,' she said in a small voice. 'But it's ages since we've seen him. Jimmy don't think he's bothered about us much, so if it's all right with you, Miss Trent, we'll give Liverpool and Solomon Court the go-by. Only where will we go instead?'

Jimmy laughed. 'That's a good question.' He turned to the tall young woman. 'Well, Miss Trent? What do you think?'

'What about your mother's family?' Miss Trent asked. 'You said she was Welsh . . . surely there must have been some coming and going between Liverpool and Wales? Why, they call Liverpool the capital of North Wales! Didn't aunts and uncles or even grandparents visit you from time to time?'

Jimmy shook his head. 'Mam said her family wanted her to marry a neighbouring farmer. In fact, she meant to do so until she met our dad. They made a runaway match of it and cut themselves off from their relatives completely. The only thing we know is her maiden name – she was Grace Griffiths – and that she grew up on a farm somewhere in Wales, only I can't remember where: Rith something,

I think.' He looked enquiringly at Miss Trent. 'What about you, miss? Will you go back to your folks? You said you came here from Yorkshire, didn't you?'

There was a long silence before Miss Trent spoke. 'I can see I shall have to come clean,' she said resignedly. 'I've always kept my past life a secret; as far as possible, that is. I reckoned it wouldn't help my chances in life to admit that I was – am – a foundling.' She turned and smiled at Mo, who was staring at her in obvious puzzlement. 'That means that one morning a housewife opened her front door and found a box on the top step. The box had a baby in it and that baby was me. The housewife thought that I must have been left on her doorstep by mistake, since there was an orphanage only a couple of doors further up the road. I don't know anything about her at all except that she carried me in my little cardboard box along to the Sister Eulalia Home for Girls and handed me over. There was a note pinned to my blanket in true storybook fashion, but I didn't know about that until much later, when I went to teacher training college. You see, when a child leaves an orphanage she's given everything she possessed when she entered the establishment. Some orphans, of course, know all about their past and have relatives who visit them quite regularly, but foundlings are different, so all I was given was a little nightgown, a blanket and a note in a foreign language, which I couldn't understand. At college I was in a dormitory with five other girls, and when I tipped my belongings on to my bed on the first night the girl standing next to me pounced on the note. "Are you Welsh, cariad?" she asked me. "This is yours, isn't it?"

'So naturally I said it was and asked her to translate it for me. I suppose I had hoped for a clue to my identity, but all it said was "Please take care of my baby. I will come for her as soon as I can. Bethan".' She smiled at the two children. 'So if you go into Wales to search for your mum's relatives, and since I have no work at the moment, I might do a lot worse than accompany you, and try to find my own roots.'

'I say, that's real romantic,' Jimmy said, his tone awed. 'So foundling means orphan! Gosh, Miss Trent, then in a way we've all got a connection with Wales. I know Mam could speak Welsh, although she never taught it to us, of course – Dad only spoke English – but it's a clue, isn't it? Or does everyone in Wales speak it?'

Miss Trent shrugged. 'I've no idea. But since we have no other clues, and you intend to leave Liverpool anyhow, we might as well run to Wales as anywhere else. Since your dad was probably already in the merchant navy and based in Liverpool when he met your mum, her family's farm might not be all that far away.'

When Frank returned from work Jimmy put him in possession of all that he had missed, and then the four of them settled once more around the kitchen table and began to plan.

'We'll be travelling by train, so we don't want to burden ourselves with unnecessary luggage,' Miss Trent said. 'Oh, and by the way, please call me Auntie Glenys, because I think that if anyone asks I should say you're my nephew and niece, and we're trying to get in touch with our Griffiths relatives because, although it's probably just talk, they do say there's a war coming.'

'Huh!' Jimmy said. 'Wharrabout peace for our time an' old Chamberlain telling everyone there wouldn't be no fightin'? If you ask me we've enough to worry about on our own account, without someone startin' a war—'

Glenys cut in. 'We're supposed to be deciding where and when we take off for pastures new. Anyone got any suggestions?'

'Pastures new,' Mo said longingly. She grabbed Jimmy's arm. 'Don't that sound nice, our Jimmy? It's like that song they sings in church sometimes: "Sheep may safely graze". Sheep and lambs graze on pastures, ain't that so? Will there be sheep where we're goin'?'

'Maureen Trewin, if you don't stop chattering you can jolly well go to bed and leave us grown-ups to discuss what's best to do,' Jimmy said severely. 'Just button your lip, understand?'

Maureen, far from being cast down, grinned cheekily at her brother. 'Shan't say another word,' she promised. She got up from the table and went over to the curtained window, making herself a little spy-hole so that she could look out at the passers-by, for it was another mild night and though the pavement was by no means crowded there were a few people still about. 'I say, Frank, when you came home . . . Oh, oh, oh . . .' She dropped the thick curtain back into place and turned a white and frightened face towards the rest of the company. 'Jimmy, it's him! Perishin' Cyril Huxtable! He's comin' along the pavement headin' straight for this house!'

'Then gerraway from the perishin' window,' Jimmy hissed. But Frank took his dark greatcoat and peaked cap off the hook and put a finger to his lips.

'It's probably just a coincidence, someone what looks like Cyril,' he whispered. He jerked a thumb at Mo. 'But the littl'un won't sleep until she knows for sure that Huxtable ain't found you. Shan't be long.'

He disappeared from the room, shrugging into his coat as he went, and they heard him unlocking the front door and issuing forth into the moonlight. Jimmy moved over to the window and bent his head, listening. Presently he beckoned to Glenys, who joined him at once. 'D'you think Frank might not be as nice as he seems?' he murmured. 'If so, we're dead ducks.'

Glenys shook her head. 'I'm a fair judge of character and I'd say Frank is very much on our side and just what he seems – an honest man,' she whispered. 'But Liverpool is full of hefty seamen with black beards. I don't think we need worry, but it's best to make sure.'

And presently Frank re-joined them, ruffling Mo's pale curls as he re-entered the room and divesting himself of his outdoor clothing. 'False alarm,' he said cheerfully. 'So back to business.'

Mo took Frank's hand and rubbed it worshipfully against her cheek. 'Thanks, Frank,' she said, beaming up at him. 'Sorry I false alarmed, but until we're away from Liverpool I reckon I'll still be scared of anyone who looks even the tiniest bit like Cyril!'

'Right you are, chuck,' Glenys said, standing up. 'And if we plan to leave within the next few days, we all need our beauty sleep. So I'll come and tuck you up and shan't be long following you.'

When she returned to the kitchen, however, she glanced enquiringly at Frank, who smiled ruefully. 'There's no sense in worrying Mo, but it was him all right,' he said. 'He stopped me, said he'd mislaid the number of the house his young cousins were staying in, but knew it was somewhere along this road and could I tell him if I'd seen any youngsters about. He described Jimmy and Mo to a T. I told him there were no children living here as far as I knew, but he said he'd keep looking because he's sure they're here somewhere. So the sooner you leave the better.'

Glenys packed up some food, checked that the fire was almost out and tiptoed into her bedroom. She began to lay out Mo's clothes, whereupon the child woke and sat up, eyes wide and black in the candle-light. 'It wasn't true, what Frank said about the feller I thought were Cyril, was it?' she asked. 'He didn't want to scare me but I were right, weren't I? It were Cyril?' A hand flew to her heart. 'Is he still out there? Is he like a cat waiting at a mouse-hole, ready to pounce the moment one of us goes out the door?'

Glenys shook her head. 'Of course not,' she said reassuringly. 'Though you, were right about Cyril. Frank didn't want to worry you, but we've decided we must leave now, whilst it's still dark. He's given me a telephone number where I ought to be able to reach him between shifts, so we can keep in touch. I've laid out your clothes, dear, so just you get dressed and go down to the kitchen. We'll go out the back way across the yard and into the jigger. I've already made some sandwiches, so we shan't starve. Frank will see us off on the milk train before going to work.'

Mo, who was struggling into her clothes, nodded. 'I'm glad we're off,' she admitted. 'Only suppose Cyril's still lurking about somewhere and sees us leave?'

Glenys picked up her carpetbag and shook her head. 'Not even Cyril can be in two places at once, and his pals – if he's got any – have more sense than to hang around the streets all night. Now stop imagining horrid things, pull the covers straight on the bed, and we'll be off.'

Chapter 7

An hour later the three of them were on the train and waving to Frank. It was still dark, and Mo was discomposed when, as the train drew out, a man in seaman's clothing waved to them. Jimmy assured his sister that the man had merely been waving at someone further up the carriage, but it had made Mo uneasy and she did not begin to relax until they had picked up speed. The train was practically empty and Mo enjoyed herself hugely, as indeed did Jimmy, for neither of them had ever travelled by rail before. Jimmy remembered his mother telling him a story in which she had imitated the sound of the train wheels clattering along the lines and crossing the points. 'Ticketyboosh, ticketyboosh, ticketyboosh' their mother had told them the engines said, and scarcely had the train pulled out of the station before both children, noses pressed to the window, were imitating the sound. They marvelled at fields, woods and copses, dimly seen in the dawn light, watched cows being driven to the milking sheds, and saw early risers going off to work. The train was not a fast one and it stopped at every station, but nothing spoiled their enjoyment of this, their first train ride. Indeed everything pleased them, even the fact that the rolling stock was old and it was a no-corridor train. 'It means we can't go along to the privy, or to a refreshment car if there is one,' Glenys said rather regretfully, but Jimmy assured her that this made him feel safer than ever.

'Even if Cyril had seen us get aboard the train, and followed, he'd be stuck in his own compartment until the train stops,' he said gleefully. 'I say, Miss – I mean Auntie Glenys, ain't this just prime? I'd like to travel by train for days and days.'

It was late afternoon by the time they reached the border town from which Glenys thought their search should start, and by then she was heartily sick of cardboard cups of railway tea and the continual stopping of the little train. She checked the compartment to make sure they had left nothing behind and smiled her thanks at a fat red-faced farmer who was helping Mo to descend from the carriage. They had travelled for the last fifteen minutes or so of their ride with the farmer and his wife, and as Glenys adjusted the straps of the small haversack on Mo's shoulders the farmer remarked that it was a strange time of year to start a walking holiday.

'It's not exactly a holiday,' Glenys began, but the farmer and his wife were already moving away, and Glenys suddenly felt very alone and almost crushed beneath the weight of responsibility for the two children. She led them across the platform and on to a paved road, where several other passengers from their train were already heading away from the station.

'No point in asking directions into town; we'll just follow everyone else,' she said, falsely cheerful. 'We'll have to find somewhere to spend the night, and then tomorrow we can start asking questions. I'm sure the local people will know everybody who lives in the area, and I don't imagine Griffiths is a common name.'

Mo said nothing, and even in the dusk which was beginning to fall Glenys could see that the child looked tired and worried. And why not, Glenys asked herself as they crossed the road over the railway line. They seemed a long way from home, and suddenly she began to wonder whether this whole expedition was not just a huge waste of time. After all, there had been a family rift; Grace and her new husband had gone their own way and lost touch with her parents completely, it seemed. Even if they managed to find the Griffiths – and it was a big if – then they might be told that it was the duty of the children's father, not their mother's family, to take care of them. Of course they could explain that the children were in fear of Cyril Huxtable and tell the whole frightening story, but that did not mean they would be believed. In fact, weighed down with both responsibility and her haversack, she began to wish she had never agreed to try to help Mo and Jimmy.

What was more, she acknowledged now, the reason she had thrown herself into the children's search was that ever since discovering that she herself was Welsh she had longed to find her own family. But without any sort of clue as to her mother's identity, apart from a first name which for all Glenys knew could be shared by half the young women in Wales, how could she possibly hope to trace the poor girl who, twenty-six years previously, had been forced to abandon her baby on someone else's doorstep? Yet she had heard of others, abandoned at birth, who had managed to trace their parents; why should she not be equally fortunate? Indeed, in her heart she had hoped that when they discovered the children's relatives, the Griffiths might, in gratitude, agree to try to help in her own search. So I'm not just doing this for the sake of Jimmy and Mo, if I'm honest, but for my own sake too.

Nevertheless, Glenys told herself, as a gentle rain began to fall, I've been a complete fool. I have little money and I've saddled myself with two children who have no money at all. Perhaps I should have encouraged them to go to the police after all, but oh no, I couldn't just do that. I had to say I'd look after them, see that Cyril Huxtable didn't touch them. Whatever was I thinking of? He's a big hefty man with three times my strength, and I dare say if he got really nasty he'd be prepared to attack all three of us. And what do I do to protect them? I bring them to a foreign country and intend to set them down amongst people who may prove to speak scarcely a word of English. We should have started our search in Liverpool – there are heaps of

Welsh people there. Why didn't I think of that? But I'm Miss Awfully Clever Glenys Trent, who never takes advice or asks for suggestions, but goes her own way. And now I'm stranded in a town of which I know nothing with two frightened children who turn white at the mere mention of the name Huxtable. And what I aim to do with them in a strange town as it grows darker and darker and the street lamps wink on, I have no idea whatsoever.

It was at this moment that Glenys spotted something ahead of them, and realised it was the swinging sign of an inn. She gave Mo's small hand a squeeze and spoke in her most schoolmistressy voice. 'There now, aren't we in luck? A nice little inn, not too big and expensive, which I do hope can give us a couple of rooms for the night. Once we've settled in, I'll order us a meal and we can start asking questions. Wouldn't it be marvellous if we found your family on the very first day of our quest?'

By this time they had reached the inn, which was called the Glas Fryn. As they neared the door it opened and the smell of hot food and beer came wafting towards them. The man who came out started to close the door behind him, then noticed them, grinned, and held it open. He said something in Welsh and then called out to someone behind him. Before Glenys could open her mouth Jimmy said, 'We're lookin' for somewhere to spend the night. Does this place have rooms to let?' The man ushered them inside and then called out once more to the man behind the bar, and Glenys realised that this was the first time in her life she had been on licensed premises, unlike Jimmy who, she knew, was in the habit of earning a few pence by scrubbing down pub floors or washing up large quantities of dirty glasses.

Telling herself that what she had imagined as a den of vice was clearly no such thing, she chided herself. You have got to start living in the real world, Miss Holier-than-Thou Trent.

The man behind the bar raised his eyebrows at her and smiled pleasantly. 'Can I help you?' he asked. He looked at Glenys's coat, furred with a mixture of rain and snowflakes. 'Come off the train, did you?' He jerked his thumb at the man still hovering by the door. 'Dick there seems to think you're after finding if the Glas Fryn lets rooms. Well it do, but not at this time of year – no call for it, see, 'cos folk don't walk the hills in the winter. But you might try Mrs Hughes, three or four doors on. She's a keen one on earnin' a few extra bob, though I can't promise . . .' He stopped speaking, dismayed. Miss Holier-than-Thou Trent had burst into tears.

Afterwards, she wondered whether it was the best thing or the worst that she could have done. The man behind the bar shouted: 'Cath, Cath, come you through here. There's folk wanting lodgings,' and whilst Glenys was blowing her nose and wiping the tear tracks from her cheeks a round and motherly woman appeared from the back premises. She wore a large white apron over a black wool dress and was drying her hands on a striped tea towel. She smiled across at Glenys.

'How can I help you, dear?' she asked, and her fat and comfortable voice held a trace of the Liverpool accent with which Miss Trent had grown familiar during her one term in the city. 'Wanting a room, was you? Well, as I expect Mr Jones told you, we don't do rooms at this time of year, but Mrs Hughes, four doors down the road, might be willing.' She cocked her head on one side and shrewd little eyes scanned the bedraggled trio. 'And if you're the new schoolteacher, come to instruct the kids whilst Miss Jones is ill with the measles, I know for a fact she's expecting you.' She tutted. 'Miss Jones's mam should have seen that she took the measles when she were a kid, then we shouldn't be in such a pickle now.'

Glenys was shaking her head when Jimmy spoke up. 'That's right; my auntie is a schoolteacher,' he said firmly. 'Can you show us which is Mrs Hughes's house, please? I don't suppose she's expecting my little sister and me, but – but . . .'

'But we's had the measles and our mam died a while back, so Auntie Glenys said we could come with her so long as we promised to behave,' Mo put in.

The fat woman chuckled richly. 'You'd best be good if you're goin' to live with Mrs Hughes, else she'll turn you out,' she said. She came out from behind the counter, crossed the bar and held the door open, then pointed. 'See the house with the blue curtains and a light showin' through? That's

Mrs Hughes's place. Knock good and loud and then wait, because she lives in the back.' She turned to go back into the pub, but Glenys put a hand on her arm to detain her.

'Oh, excuse me, but what do we do if Mrs Hughes won't take us in? She won't be expecting a couple of children . . .'

'I wouldn't worry about that, my dear,' the fat woman said. 'If there's money in it Mrs Hughes will be first in line.'

She turned away and this time Glenys did not attempt to stop her, but picked up her carpetbag, seized Mo's small hand, waited for a moment whilst Jimmy picked up his own bag and then set off at a fast walk towards the blue curtains.

They reached the house and Jimmy knocked loudly on the door, and then the three of them waited in the drizzling rain. Mo, who had been unusually silent, suddenly piped up. 'I'm cold and wet and I want to go home to where there's street lights,' she said miserably. 'Why couldn't we stay in that nice cheerful pub? I liked it in there; it was warm and cosy and it smelled of food, and I's hungry.'

Glenys was about to remind her of the no children on licensed premises rule when they heard shuffling footsteps approaching the front door, and it was pulled open by a tiny woman who Glenys thought could have been any age between forty and seventy. Glenys opened her mouth to explain, but before she managed to get a word out Mrs Hughes said, 'A message I had to say you wasn't comin', 'cos you've got the measles yourself,' she said crossly. 'Or are you the replacement for the replacement?' She gave a little snort which might have been amusement or disapproval. 'But you'd best come in, else you'll catch your death and I can't and won't nurse sick persons, whether it's measles or pneumonia.' She did not wait for a reply, but turned away, opening the door on her right, and gesturing her unexpected guests to enter the small and stuffy parlour thus revealed.

Glad to be indoors, but somewhat nonplussed by their reception, Glenys herded the children into the parlour, then went and shut the front door. In the murky grey of the evening it had been difficult to get even an impression of Mrs Hughes, but the parlour was lamplit, though icy cold, and at last she was able to take stock of the landlady. She was very small, perhaps only a few inches over four foot tall, and though Glenys had thought her fat she now realised that scarves, shawls and cardigans had been piled on haphazardly, one on top of the other, until she was as round as a ball. She gestured Glenys to sit down and took a chair herself, whilst Mo perched on a pouffe and Jimmy leaned against the empty sofa.

Glenys looked at the older woman more closely. She had a large hooked nose, shrewd little eyes behind blue-tinted spectacles, and a thin-lipped mouth which made Glenys think uneasily of rat-traps. She was not a prepossessing figure, but Glenys told herself firmly that it was wrong to judge by appearances, and began to make the speech she had rehearsed as they walked towards the blue curtains. 'I'm so sorry that I was unable to contact you earlier in the day . . .'

Mrs Hughes cut her short. 'You'll be wanting two rooms, right? I've a little slip of a room for the boy, just a bed and a washstand, and a double which you can share with the girl. I does a good breakfast and can provide an evening meal for an extra couple of bob a head. But cold it is in here; follow me.'

She led them down a dark corridor and into a brightly lit kitchen, sat them down at the table and began to make a pot of tea, producing some home-made biscuits and offering Mo a glass of warm milk. The largest black cat Mo had ever seen was sitting on the hearth rug, apparently staring at a picture which hung on the wall. Mo gave a frightened squeak. 'Them's witches!' she said. 'They's wearin' witches' hats!' Then she pointed at the cat. 'And he's a witch's cat . . . oh, Auntie Glenys, I don't want to stay here.'

Mrs Hughes gave a creaky little laugh. 'We don't wear those hats no more, cariad, even on Sundays; that's a real old picture that is. I'll tell you the story behind it one day. And me cat's not a witch's cat, either. He's Solomon Grundy, 'cos he were born on a Monday. Only if you's scared of cats . . .'

Mo promptly flung herself on her knees beside the cat and Mrs Hughes started forward in alarm, but then relaxed as the big animal began to purr for all the world like a tractor. 'He likes you,' she said as the child began to stroke the huge domed head. She turned back to Glenys. 'Now, to business.'

By the time Glenys had seen Jimmy into his 'little slip of a room', helped Mo to undress and put on her cotton nightie, and asked Mrs Hughes what time she would like them to come down to the kitchen for their breakfast, she had begun to think they had fallen on their feet.

Next morning they sat down to porridge and boiled eggs, as well as tea and toast, and the saga of the supply teacher who was supposed to have come to take the place of Miss Teleri Jones was explained, and Glenys's own position made clear. Both Miss Jones and the supply teacher had succumbed to the measles, leaving the school with no teacher at all. 'But a school with only one teacher?' Glenys had exclaimed in astonishment as the other woman explained the situation. 'I didn't know such things existed; good Lord, this is the twentieth century, not the nineteenth! But as it happens I'm a teacher, and I'm looking for supply work. And, of course, I'm on the spot. I noticed there was a public call box quite near the station. If you could furnish me with the telephone number of the Education Department, perhaps we could come to some arrangement.'

'There is no need to go to the public box; I am on the telephone. It is necessary for bookings in high summer,' Mrs Hughes said haughtily. 'You are welcome to ring the Education Department; there's a box for the money beside the phone, and the exchange will tell you what you owe.'

Later, when Glenys had called the Education Department, been given the necessary details and accepted the job, she went down the road to the station and telephoned the number Frank had given her. It rang out for a long time, but no one picked up at the other end, and Glenys pressed button B to get her money back. Disappointed, she stepped out on to the pavement. Never mind, she told herself, I'll try again sometime. I'd really like to let Frank know we're all right and starting afresh.

When term started, Glenys prepared for her first day at the school by eating a hearty breakfast and adjuring Mo to hurry as they had a good walk in front of them. Jimmy had refused point-blank to go with them to what he called 'the babies' school', and Glenys had laughed and agreed that a few extra days' holiday would do him no harm. 'So you're staying here today?' she said now, helping herself to a round of toast and buttering it. 'Perhaps you can meet a few of the locals – ask them whether there are many farms in the area,' she added mean-ingly, while across the table Mrs Hughes raised her eyebrows.

'A good thing it is for us – and no doubt for you too – that you was on a walking holiday in our area just in time to step into Miss Teleri Jones's shoes until she gets over the measles,' she observed. She gave a grim little chuckle. 'You didn't arrange it? No, no, Miss Jones is a very upright woman, a pillar of the chapel, but it does seem strange, don't you think?'

'I believe I did tell you we were not on a walking holiday,' Glenys said rather stiffly. 'I teach at a private school; they have much longer holidays, so we decided to try to contact relatives who we believe live somewhere in this area . . . the name's Griffiths. Do you know a family by that name?'

Mrs Hughes chuckled. 'I know a lot of families by that name, all living within five miles of the town,' she assured Glenys. 'Have you anything other than a surname to go by? A trade perhaps, or a nickname?'

Glenys hesitated. 'The children's mother was called Grace,' she admitted at last.

Mrs Hughes shook her head. 'It generally goes with the fellers, not the girls,' she said. 'Do you know how many Dai Hugheses there are just on this one street?' She began to tick them off on her fingers. 'Dai the coal, Dai the cane – his father was the schoolmaster – Dai the bread, and the one they call Dai Tacsi . . .'

'Stop, stop!' Glenys cried, half laughing and half dismayed. 'I can see this is going to take much longer than I had imagined. Tell me, are we going to find Griffiths all over Wales with only nicknames to distinguish one from t'other? Only I'd not realised . . .'

Mrs Hughes nodded portentously. 'Yes, a hard task you have set yourself,' she said. She stared curiously up into Glenys's face, her eyes suddenly

sharp behind the blue lenses. 'You say they're
your nephew and niece; an odd thing it seems
that none of you seem to know very much about
your family . . .'

Glenys stood up quickly and reached for her
shoulder bag. 'Well, now we are doing what we
may to change that,' she said sharply. 'Eat up, Mo;
I want to get settled into my classroom before the
majority of my pupils arrive.'

Bristling with affront, Mrs Hughes began to clear
the table, and before Glenys could leave the room
the landlady spoke again. 'One rule I forgot to
mention, Miss Trent. My guests are welcome to use
the facilities of this house, but not between nine
o'clock in the morning and six o'clock in the
evening. In between those hours they must amuse
themselves.'

Glenys had a hand on the doorknob, but now
she spun round. 'Oh, but Mrs Hughes, you said
nothing of this.' She glanced towards the window,
at the distant prospect of rain-shrouded hills.
'Jimmy's very quiet and helpful; he'll give you a
hand in any way he can, and in this weather—'

'Rules is rules,' Mrs Hughes interrupted. 'Different
it would be if you was with the children yourself,
but I know lads and I know my house. Take him
with you to the infant school, for without the Welsh
he'd be no use to Mr Feather, who runs the school
for the older children.'

'Oh, but—' Glenys began, but Jimmy interrupted
her.

'It's awright, Auntie Glenys,' he said firmly. 'I'll occupy meself one way or another. I seen a nice roomy woodshed agin the privy in Mrs Hughes's back yard, and today's market day, so I've heard. I love a market I do, and sometimes a likely lad can earn hisself a few pennies, helpin' to herd sheep or drive a pig out of a pen and into the sale ring. Don't you worry about me, I'll be fine.'

For a moment Mrs Hughes looked dumbfounded, but then her expression changed to one of annoyance. It was clear to Glenys that the landlady was deliberately making life difficult for them, probably because she resented Glenys's refusal to pander to her curiosity, and the younger woman tried not to show the dismay she felt. Market day probably only came round once a week; what would Jimmy do on the other four?

But Mo, who was still eating, slid off her chair and went over to the coats hanging beside the back door, jerking her own and Glenys's off the hooks and taking them over to the table. 'Jimmy will be all right,' she said reassuringly through a mouthful of toast and marmalade. 'I see'd a barn up the road when I looked out of our window this morning – if it rains he can shelter in there. And there's shops to look at, 'specially if he's earned a few pennies helpin' at the market. Oh, aye, Jimmy'll be just fine.'

The man leaned on the long counter. 'I came here believing you might help me, and all you've done is ask a lot of damn fool questions,' he said in an aggrieved voice. 'I'm telling you, someone's kidnapped two children, and I bloody well know who did it.'

The large police constable behind the counter pulled a form towards him and picked up a pencil. 'Who?' he enquired stolidly.

'Huxtable,' the man said impatiently, and began to spell it.

'Address?'

'Solomon Court, off the Scottie,' the man said viciously. He snorted and smote the counter with a large fist. 'What the devil does the address matter? They aren't there now, because, as I've been trying to tell you, they've been bloody well kidnapped.'

The police constable leaned back and folded his arms, which seemed to infuriate the man on the other side of the counter still further. But Constable Jones was not the man to frighten easily. 'Proof?' he asked, and seeing the man's eyes flame added stolidly: 'We've only got your word for it, sir. So before we discuss whoever kidnapped these children, if anyone did, I'd like to have a few details . . .'

Across the counter the man's dark eyes bulged, but then he turned away. 'Thanks for nothing,' he said bitterly. 'I thought I'd get help, but all I've had is obstruction, so I'll continue with my own search. There's a reward in it for anyone who finds them before I do, but you needn't bother to apply.'

The constable got ponderously to his feet, but before he could even come out from behind the counter the man was opening the door and letting in the wind and the rain. The constable blinked as the wind picked up the papers lying on the counter and swirled them into the air. 'Just you come back here, sir . . . I want a word with you,' he began, even as the door slammed. Hastily he crossed the room and opened the door, peering out, but the man had disappeared.

Chapter 8

It had stopped snowing. Ever since Glenys had taken on the job of supply teacher it had snowed on and off, but Mrs Hughes's rules, it seemed, were indifferent to the weather. Once the clock in the kitchen over the mantel announced that it was nine o'clock a grim-faced Mrs Hughes ejected Jimmy without so much as glancing at feathery flakes that might be falling from a dark grey sky. After the first day Miss Trent had insisted upon making him a packed lunch from bread, cheese and apples bought in the small town, and with this he had to be content. Jimmy could tell from the hard look in their landlady's eyes that guests were not welcome to make packed lunches, but when she had grumbled that she did not want people working in her kitchen when she was preparing breakfast, Glenys just shot her a glance in which amusement and displeasure were nicely mingled. 'Rules is rules, Mrs Hughes,' Glenys had said, imitating their landlady's tone. 'Young Jimmy here leaves the house when we do and comes back when we do as well. I must remind you that, had your rules been less inflexible, we would have paid for evening meals here. However, since school finishes at three thirty and we are not welcome in your house until after six o'clock, we have had no alternative but to eat in Cath Jones's kitchen.'

Mrs Hughes had said nothing, merely screwing up her mouth until her lips had all but disappeared. 'I might relax the six o'clock rule . . .' she began, but Glenys, sensing that for once she had the advantage of the old woman, forestalled her.

'It's all right, Mrs Hughes, we're managing very well,' she had said. 'Mo and I, of course, simply remain in our warm classroom until we can go to the Glas Fryn, and Jimmy has found a friend whose parents are delighted to welcome him after school hours, when I must admit I should not like to think of him wandering the streets.'

Mrs Hughes sniffed. 'I take it you're referring to that idle woman Mrs Dai Bread,' she said disdainfully. 'She'd take anyone in she would. I'd not like a lad of mine . . .'

But here Glenys had held up a warning finger. 'No gossip *if* you please, Mrs Hughes,' she said briskly. 'I saw Miss Teleri Jones this morning and she hopes to be back in school in a week, so we shan't impose on your – your hospitality for much longer.'

But now the snow had stopped and Jimmy was sitting on the top of his friend's pigsty wall waiting for Wynne to appear. The baker's son was no lover of school and already Jimmy knew that he was being blamed for Wynne's erratic attendance, but as the weather worsened more and more children who normally came in to the town from villages several miles distant failed to arrive, and Wynne assured him that once the ice on the pond was thick enough to bear there would be more absentees yet. Jimmy reflected now, as a spiteful little breeze blew down the neck of his corduroy jacket, that his first opinion of Mrs Hughes had not only been the right one but was also shared by at least half the towns-folk. Their landlady was known to be what Jimmy would have called clutch-fisted and Wynne described succinctly as mean as hell, but however much she might grumble about the extra work involved in accommodating two children as well as the supply teacher, everyone knew there was little fear of her giving them notice. It would have meant losing their rent money, and this she was obviously not prepared to do.

Sitting on the pigsty wall, Jimmy swung his legs backwards and forwards and thought about the weekend ahead. A party of boys and girls from Wynne's school meant to go sledging, taking a packed lunch and indulging in all the ploys which the snowy weather allowed. Wynne had told him that parents usually provided the young snow-ballers with flasks of hot tea and hefty cheese sand-wiches, and Mrs Dai Bread had offered to supply Jimmy's food as well as her son's.

'An' after school on Friday you and me will go off and make slides,' Wynne had said. 'You won't have a sledge, bein' as how you're stayin' with the old witch, but she might let you borrow an old tin tray or somethin'.'

Jimmy had shaken his head regretfully. 'She wouldn't lend me a cold in the head,' he had said dismissively. 'She guards that perishin' house as though it were Buckingham Palace. But the next time she goes out shopping I'll sneak back in – not into the house, since she's the only woman in this town what locks her doors, but into the outbuildins. I'll surely find somethin' amongst the old clutter.'

But now, sitting on the pigsty wall, Jimmy knew ruefully that he would have to disappoint his friend. He had rootled, poked and pried, both in the woodshed and in what she termed the *twll gogoniant*, where she threw anything not wanted at the moment, but she thought might come in handy in the future. But neither search, though thorough, had led to the finding of even the tiniest tray, so it looked as though Jimmy would have to content himself with snowball fights and similar pleasures.

He was still sitting on the wall and swinging his legs when he remembered the old biscuit tin in Mrs Hughes's kitchen. It was square and much battered but the lid, he thought, might be used if he squeezed up small. He wondered how he could acquire the tin, then put it out of his mind as his friend came slogging up the lane towards him. As they set off towards the hills where they would practise both the art of sledging and the making of slides, he admitted to Wynne that he had not managed to find a tray but had hopes of a tin lid for the next day. His friend shrugged.

'It doesn't matter; we'll take it in turns on mine,'

he said generously. He chuckled. 'I bet your sister will breathe fire when she finds we've gone sledging without her.'

Jimmy shook his head. 'She won't,' he assured Wynne. 'She's not like that. For one thing, she's never sat on a sledge in her life, 'cos when our mam was alive she said such things were dangerous for girls, and then the woman we lived with never let us do anything except work in the house and do her messages. That's shopping,' he added hastily, seeing bewilderment on his friend's face. 'I don't know why it is, but everyone in Liverpool – or all the kids at any rate – calls the shoppin' "the messages".' He grinned widely. 'So you Welsh rabbits ain't the only ones to have two languages,' he concluded.

Wynne laughed. 'I reckon all kids is the same: we have one language for grown-ups and another what we use between ourselves. See ahead? That's the hill we're makin' for. It ain't as high as Moel Famau, and Snowdon makes it look like a molehill, but it's the highest one around here, or at least the highest that you can sledge down. You get a grand view from up there, too; you can see for miles.'

'I wouldn't say I were much of a one for views,' Jimmy panted as they reached the summit. 'Do it have a name, this hill? Gosh, don't the town look little when you see it from here?'

'I s'pose it just looks so little to you because you're used to a great old city,' Wynne said. 'My sister had a toy farm a couple of years back. It had little pigs, little cows and even a little farmhouse.

She loved it for ages, and even now she plays with it a couple of times a week. Does your sister . . . what's up? Why are you grabbin' my arm?'

Silently, Jimmy pointed down the hill towards the town. Glenys had bought him an old pair of rubber boots just like Wynne's, and now he was pointing at their tracks, which led plainly from the town below. 'See that man follerin' our boot marks?' he said in a hollow voice. 'He's too far away for me to see his face. Is he – is he anyone you know?'

Wynne shrugged. 'I dunno. Does it matter?' he said indifferently. 'I don't know every bleedin' feller what climbs in the hills. I expect he's a farm worker takin' a short cut home for his tea.'

Jimmy looked desperately around him, but all he could see was snow, smooth and even, with only their footprints breaking the monotony. And the man was getting nearer; a big man, red-faced from the climb, but even as Jimmy moved closer to Wynne he realised that the man was a stranger; not a Huxtable but an unthreatening farm worker, as Wynne had guessed. The man grinned at them. 'Afternoon, both,' he said cheerfully. 'Make the most of the weather, because there's a thaw forecast for tomorrow.'

'Thanks for the warnin', Bob,' Wynne said cheerfully. 'We'll get some tobogganing in whilst the snow lasts, though.'

The man continued on his way and Jimmy felt quite light-headed with relief, but the small incident had reminded him that they were not here just to enjoy themselves. Glenys's job finished today and he supposed that, since he had visited every Griffiths in the area without finding one who had heard of his mother, it was pointless for them to remain. He realised Wynne was staring at him. 'What was up with you when you first saw Bob?' his friend asked curiously. 'I can tell you, you looked as though you'd seen a ghost. Did he remind you of someone? Someone who scares you? Now I come to think of it, for all I know you could be a thief or a murderer, fleeing from the cops as they say in the cinema. I'm sure you looked scared enough.'

It was Jimmy's turn to shrug and feign indifference. 'You don't know much about me because there isn't much to know,' he said. 'But if you're interested, from a distance Bob looked a bit like a neighbour of ours back home in Liverpool. He's a seaman, and Mo and I steer clear of him when we can, so it was a nasty shock to see someone who looks like him coming up the slope of the hill.'

'But why should he be here, in the middle of nowhere?' Wynne persisted reasonably. 'I don't get it, laddo. You said he's a seaman, but we're miles and miles from the sea. So why did you look so scared?'

Taken off his guard, Jimmy spoke without reserve. 'Can you keep a secret?'

Wynne nodded, 'Course I can; that's why me nickname's Oyster.' He laughed. 'Go on then, what's this secret?'

'The feller I mentioned has got a grudge against

me and Mo,' Jimmy admitted. 'It seems he took something he didn't oughter have had, and hid it away, not knowin' at the time that Mo was watchin' him. It wouldn't have mattered except that he took himself off to bed – he were drunk as usual – and when he woke up he couldn't find it. So of course he thinks either me or Mo took it, only we didn't, honest to God we didn't.'

'Cor!' Wynne said, round-eyed. 'It's like one of them stories in the *Boy's Own Paper*! But what can he do to you, this chap? You've only got to go to the police and tell them the whole story and they'll see you safe.'

Jimmy laughed bitterly. 'One, we don't think they'd believe us – you must admit it's a pretty unlikely story – two, if he catches us he'd nigh on kill us before we could get to the scuffers – that's the police – and three, we'd need an armed guard for the rest of our lives, or at least until Cyril accepts that we didn't do nothin'. Why, he near on broke Mo's little arm once when I'd done somethin' to annoy him, so you see we can't take chances. Catch one catch 'em all, you might say.'

'Cor!' Wynne said again. He frowned. 'But you've only told me half the story. How about the other half? What did young Mo see this neighbour hidin'?'

Jimmy grinned as his friend's eyes positively bulged. 'Gold sovereigns? Jewels an' that?'

His smile fading, Jimmy sighed. 'It were a necklace, all sparkly and glittery Mo said, though Auntie Glenys thought it were probably just glass.'

Wynne looked disappointed, but then he perked up. 'That's another thing. Where does Miss Trent fit in? You said it were chance that you arrived here just when they needed a teacher, 'cos you were really lookin' for your family – is she helpin' you do that?'

Jimmy thought for a moment. 'You swear not to tell anyone?'

'Cross me heart,' Wynne said promptly. 'We can seal it in blood if you want.'

Declining this generous offer, Jimmy went on to describe how Miss Trent hoped to find the girl who had abandoned her on a doorstep twenty-six years before, and Wynne's eyes almost popped out of his head.

'Well, if I hadn't heard it from your own lips I'd have thought someone were tellin' tall stories,' he admitted. 'So are you goin' to stay with the old witch? Only you've spoken to all the Griffiths I can think of round here and you've not come across anyone who admits to havin' a relative who married an Englishman.' He grinned at his friend with more than a trace of mischief. 'Not that anyone from this area would admit to an English relative if they could help it,' he concluded.

Jimmy grinned too. Because Miss Trent was teaching all day and Mo stayed with her, it had fallen mostly to him to ask questions. Folk were polite, but now that Wynne had mentioned it, he realised that everyone had been quick to deny any knowledge of a Grace Griffiths who had been unwise enough to marry an Englishman and lose touch with her roots. So now he looked rather helplessly at his friend. 'Are you tellin' me that people have told me untruths?' he asked incredulously. 'Oh lor', don't say all that trampin' from farmhouse to farmhouse has been for nothin'!'

Wynne shook his head. 'It's all right, I were havin' you on,' he assured Jimmy. 'The Welsh are proud of their family connections, and they'd certainly never lie to you. But remember, it's more than twelve years since your mother went off to Liverpool to marry without her family's approval. I dare say it was the talk of the town at the time, but people forget. Now, want to have first go on the sledge?'

When Miss Trent opened the door to Jimmy well after ten o'clock that evening, she tutted over his soaking raiment and sat him in front of a far better fire than Mrs Hughes would have allowed had she been awake. But the landlady always went early to bed, complaining that she had to be up betimes in the mornings; Mo, on the other hand, who could never now be persuaded to go to bed until she knew her brother was home safe, raised heavy eyes when he came in and asked him rather sleepily whether he had had fun.

'Yes, I had a grand time. But when we first got up there I had quite a scare – well, an adventure you could call it. I was looking back at our footprints, and . . .'

He began to tell the story of his fear that Cyril had

caught up with them and his subsequent relief when he identified the stranger as a farm worker, but halfway through he noticed his little sister's apprehension and hastily brought his narrative to a close. 'Tell you what, Mo, if the frost holds I'll take you with me when we go sledgin' next,' he said. 'But you'd best go to bed now; you look wore out.'

Glenys shook her head. 'Wait a bit, Mo my love,' she said quickly. 'What Jimmy has just told us is, in a way, what I've been wanting to talk to you about. Jimmy, what would you have done if the man following you really had been Cyril, or one of his cronies?'

Jimmy frowned. 'But it wasn't. I thought I made that plain enough.'

Glenys sighed. 'Don't you understand? *Listen*, Jimmy! What would you have done if the man following you *had* been Cyril Huxtable?'

Jimmy began to say that it was just his foolishness which had made him assume the man was after him, but Mo slid off Glenys's knee and went and gave her brother a poke. 'You're stupid you are,' she said scornfully. 'Auntie Glenys is asking what you would have done if the man following you hadn't been a farm hand. Would you have burrowed into the snow, like an ostrich?' She giggled. 'Hiding all of you except your bum? Or would you have run further into the hills, or headed here? I suppose you could have done that, only then you might be leading Cyril straight to me and Glenys. Go on, answer the question!'

'Gosh, Mo, you've a head on your shoulders,' Jimmy said admiringly. 'I was so scared that I suppose I'd have run further into the hills, looking for a hiding place.'

'Oh yeah? What about your footprints?' Mo said derisively. 'What you should have said is: *I'd have panicked*. Now if it had been me, I'd have persuaded Wynne to go down and tell a lot of lies whilst I sneaked off.'

Jimmy began to tell Mo, rather unkindly, that she was just as foolish as he was himself, but before his little sister could summon up a retort Glenys interrupted.

'All right, all right, given the weather conditions it's a very difficult question to answer. So let's put it another way. How would you let us know the danger we were in? Pretend you've come down from the hills without being seen, but then you discover he's hanging around the railway station. What would you do then?'

There was a short silence, and then Jimmy spoke sullenly. 'I don't know, and I'm tired of this silly game. I suppose whichever one of us found out that Cyril had caught up with us would make their way back here. Then the three of us could sort out the problem.'

He was looking at Glenys's face as he spoke and saw that she was smiling. 'Good lad; you've gone straight to the heart of the matter. There are three of us in this tangle and I really do think it's important that we stick together. You know my job here ended today, so I've told Mrs Hughes we shall be off on

Monday, and when we leave, which we shall do as unobtrusively as possible, we must carry on being Auntie Glenys, and her nephew and niece. Remember, if Cyril really is still looking for you, it will be for two ragged little children – sorry, Jimmy – who would scarcely stay in a nice house as paying guests.' She pointed at Mo. 'I know you don't like plaiting your hair, or rather you don't like *me* plaiting your hair, and you complain that the headscarf tickles your chin. But it's things like that which will put him off the scent. Now, what are we going to do next? The railway runs from here right to the coast, so I thought we might go on to Bangor, since it's possible I might get work there.' She smiled at them. 'How does that appeal to my fellow adventurers?'

Jimmy said it sounded like a good idea, for he had seen how his little sister's face had brightened at the mere mention of the seaside. 'You'll enjoy that, won't you, Mo?' he said encouragingly. 'If Bangor is a fair-sized town, we could both go to school, so I'd make friends of my own age. Come to that, if there's a harbour I could probably get work on one of the fishing boats – I'd like that. In fact I wouldn't mind if we *never* went back to Liverpool.'

Glenys laughed. 'Well, I don't know about that. The Huxtable problem can't last for ever,' she temporised. 'I think we'll have to return to Liverpool one of these days; we can't spend our whole lives running away.'

'I can,' Mo said dreamily. 'But we wouldn't be running away, we'd be making . . . what was it

Frank said . . . oh, yes, making a new life for ourselves, ain't that so, Glenys?'

'You may be right,' Glenys said. 'But something has just occurred to me. No one knows how to get in touch with us. I haven't been able to reach Frank on the number he gave us, and I'm a little cautious about writing in case the letter falls into the wrong hands, so what do you think we should do? We really need to know what's happening at the Court. Suppose we found someone really reliable to look after the pair of you while I returned to Liverpool to find out what's going on . . . is that possible?'

'No, you can't go,' Mo said, clinging tightly to Glenys's hand. 'You said yourself we should stick together: auntie, nephew and niece.'

'True,' Glenys said, smiling down at the little girl. 'I just wish I could get in touch with Frank.'

Mo brightened. 'Never mind. If we go to the seaside I'll be able to make sand pies and paddle in the little waves. I just can't wait!'

'Oh, go to bed, baby,' Jimmy said, laughing. 'You think of this whole thing as a holiday adventure, whereas Auntie Glenys and I know it's deadly serious. But surely we must have outwitted Cyril the moment we stepped aboard that train. How could he possibly know where we are? Unless he's much cleverer than I think, we ought to be safe enough. Off with you, Mo!'

His sister opened the door into the corridor, squeaked as the cold air rushed into the warm room, and then turned a suddenly pale face towards her brother. With infinite care she closed the kitchen door again, then tiptoed to where Glenys and Jimmy stood staring at her. 'What's up?' Jimmy said, then lowered his voice as Mo made a frantic signal. 'What's the matter, silly? You look as if you've seen a ghost.'

'Not a ghost. It's Mrs Hughes,' Mo hissed. 'I thought you said she was in bed?'

'I thought she was,' Glenys admitted. 'Are you sure you saw her, darling, and it wasn't just a shadow? The stairs creak and I didn't hear anything. Oh, damn, damn, damn! Did I mention where we were going? But why should she care? She can't possibly be in league with the Huxtables, so unless they come knocking and asking for us we've nothing to fear. And anyway, the kitchen door's pretty sturdy; I doubt if she could have heard much through it.'

'Of course she couldn't,' Jimmy said, with an eye on Mo's pale face. 'Don't worry, chuck, she can't do us any harm.' He looked significantly across at Glenys and dropped his voice. 'Imagination,' he murmured, tapping the side of his forehead with one finger. 'Now let's go to bed. Today has gone on quite long enough.'

Chapter 9

Grumbling, Mo bade everyone goodnight in a subdued voice and left the room whilst Jimmy and Glenys tidied round, for, as Glenys said, if they were to leave within a day or so they might as well leave a good impression behind them. She was banking down the fire and brushing out the ash when the kitchen door opened and Mo shot back into the room, then closed the door carefully behind her. Then she turned a pale, frightened face towards the others. 'When I were passing the witch's bedroom door I looked at it and it were closing,' she said in a scared whisper. 'She'd been listenin', Auntie Glenys, I'm sure as sure. Oh, what'll we do?'

Across his sister's head Jimmy winked at the teacher. 'Too much talking,' he murmured. 'She gets like this when she's over-excited.' He turned to his sister. 'Come on, queen, just think; the old witch shuffles along panting and grumbling. If she'd come downstairs we'd have heard her – and if she'd heard us she'd have come in and told us off; she loves doing that. Now you go off to bed and don't worry any more. If the old woman hadn't shut her door properly she might have felt a bit of a draught and got out of bed to close it. Now no more fretting; promise me?'

'Course I does,' Mo said sounding relieved. 'I never thought how she wheezes and mutters when she walks. G'night, Jimmy; Auntie Glenys will tuck me up when she comes to bed.'

Some time later, Mo woke from a strange dream. She had been on the platform of the little station surrounded by her friends and anticipating a trip to the seaside, for in the dream it was high summer and the children were off on a school trip to Prestatyn. She was full of excitement, and was about to climb into a carriage already occupied by some of the other girls when a voice called her name urgently. 'Mo, Mo! Someone's on the telephone asking for you!'

The voice had come from knee level, and when she looked down there was Solomon Grundy, Mrs Hughes's big black cat. Mo promptly squatted and reached out a hand to smooth his velvet fur. 'I never knew you could talk, Solly,' she said wonderingly. 'But if it's the telephone at Banc-y-Celyn I can't possibly answer it. If I try, the train will leave without me, and Jimmy and Auntie Glenys are already aboard. So you see . . .'

The big cat blinked its big green eyes and put a demanding paw on Mo's knee. 'The train will wait; you can take the call from the public box on the station,' the cat said. 'It's important.'

Mo awoke. The dream had been so real that she had already slid her feet out of the bed when common sense stopped her. How foolish she was to think that a dream was anything but a dream. She was just cuddling down once more, however, when she heard the shuffling footsteps of their landlady heading for the stairs. Mo nudged Glenys, on the other side of the big double bed. The teacher rolled over, clearly still more than half asleep. 'Whazza time?' she enquired in a sleep-drugged voice. 'Has the alarm gone off? Oh, I feel as if I've only just got into bed.'

Mo glanced at the clock. 'It's nearly five o' clock . . .' she began, then stopped. Glenys had heaved the covers up over her shoulders and was clearly fast asleep once more.

Mo sighed. Probably Witchy was just going to use the privy, and yet . . . and yet . . . the cat had said the phone call was urgent; suppose the old woman was up to something? It was Mo's duty to find out what.

She slipped out of bed and padded across the lino to where the long cardigan lay on top of the chest of drawers. She pulled it on, wishing she had some slippers, for her feet were growing colder with every moment. She was tempted to get back into bed, but curiosity now forbade her abandoning the adventure. She stood on the landing looking down the flight of stairs, and heard the click of the latch as their landlady entered the parlour. She did not attempt to shut the door behind her, but shuffled across the room, sank into a chair and unhooked the telephone from its perch on the wall. She gave a number as soon as the operator answered, but since she gave it in Welsh Mo was no wiser. In fact, she was beginning to turn away when Mrs Hughes spoke into the receiver. And she spoke in English!

Mo crept down the rest of the stairs and slid into cover behind the coat rack which stood close to the parlour door. What on earth was Mrs Hughes doing telephoning someone in the middle of the night? But she was very soon to find out, as an irascible voice at the other end said loudly, in the way of the slighty deaf, 'What? What's that you say? Who's phonin' me at this bleedin' unearthly hour? Is that you, Lizzie? If so, what the devil do you mean ringin' at this time in the morning?'

'I'll tell you why I'm ringing,' Mrs Hughes said. 'Remember you told me your mate what's married to a policeman said there were a hue and cry out after a couple of kids what had gone missin', believed kidnapped, an' a reward offered for infor-mation what leads to them bein' found? Well, sis, I do believe I've been harbourin' them kids for the past two weeks, not knowin' they weren't legit.'

The other speaker said something Mo couldn't quite catch and then Mrs Hughes broke in. 'Yes, I know – there were no mention of a teacher. It never occurred to me they weren't what they claimed to be until this evenin', when the boy came back late from sledgin' with his mates. They thought I was safely tucked up in bed so they took over my kitchen.' Here Mo distinctly heard her grind her teeth. 'Never asked, of course, but they had what you might call a bit of a conference. I were about to go in and ask what they thought they was doin' when I heard the name Huxtable, which was who your mate said was wanting to find them. So I stayed me hand and heard the teacher say somethin' about goin' back to Liverpool one day because they couldn't spend their whole lives running away.'

There was an exclamation so loud that Mo heard it distinctly, and also the sentence which followed. 'You keep your hands on them kids and we'll claim the reward, half each,' the woman said. She must have then asked how long the trio would remain in Banc-y-Celyn, for Mrs Hughes replied: 'Till Monday, that Miss Trent said, so we're all right for a bit, but we'll have to talk again because I'm in me nightgown and fair freezin'. But I'll ring you again after nine o'clock, when they'll be out of the house. Do you know who's givin' the reward? The scuffers?'

This time Mo was so keen to hear the answer that she actually pushed the parlour door a little wider and heard the reply distinctly. 'I'm not sure. It could be the Huxtables, I reckon, whoever they are. But I'll speak to my mate and find out a bit more.'

By the time Mrs Hughes put the phone down Mo was halfway up the stairs, and she shot into her bedroom to find Glenys sitting up and staring at the alarm clock. She began to ask where Mo had been but Mo jumped into bed and clapped a hand over the teacher's mouth.

'Hush,' she whispered urgently. 'I'll tell you what

145

I've been doin' in a minute, when Witchy has gone back to bed.'

Mo told the story rather well, she thought, though she left out any allusion to the black cat. It had, after all, only been a dream. And she was glad she had said nothing about Solly when Glenys accepted her story without question and began to look for her clothes. 'As soon as you're dressed you nip up to Jimmy's room and wake him,' she hissed. 'We've got to get away from here. Tell Jimmy to dress like lightning and pack his stuff into his bag. Are you sure she's gone back to bed, love? Only I don't fancy walking into her . . .' she glanced at the alarm clock, 'at five in the morning and explaining that we're doing a moonlight.'

Mo nodded. 'I heard her bedroom door shut,' she said, and disappeared to wake her brother.

Presently all three of them foregathered in the kitchen, Jimmy still rubbing the sleep from his eyes. 'What I don't understand . . .' he began, but was interrupted.

'Explanations can come later; you've got the bare facts and that will have to be enough for now,' Glenys said. 'We'll catch the first train that leaves the station.'

They let themselves out into the windy darkness. Glenys had left the outstanding rent on the kitchen table with a note to Mrs Hughes explaining untruthfully that they were going back to Liverpool since she had heard that a job awaited her. Then they made their way to the station, only feeling safe once they were on board a moving train, heading deeper into Wales. Glenys had made each of them a packet of sandwiches and had left an extra few shillings so that Mrs Hughes could not accuse them of stealing her food as well as cheating her of the reward. 'Not that she'd ever have got a penny out of the Huxtables,' Jimmy remarked, sinking back in his seat, as outside the window the countryside grew lighter. 'What'll we do, Auntie Glenys, if we don't find our mam's relatives? As you said, we can't run for ever.'

'We'll disappear into the countryside like a raindrop into a puddle,' Miss Glenys said gaily. 'Goodness, it's getting quite light, and it must be pretty mild because the fields are showing more green than white. Furthermore, I've had a thought. As soon as we stop at a station big enough to have a public call box we'll have another go at reaching Frank.' She chuckled. 'Mrs Hughes and her horrible sister aren't the only ones to make use of the telephone system. I won't try a tiny station, because everyone knows that operators in country districts listen in. But where the branch line goes off, I think we might try there. At least we can tell Frank which town we're heading for and he can tell us about this reward. It should make interesting listening.'

The train was a slow one, stopping at every tiny station. Sometimes passengers came aboard, sometimes goods such as boxes of groceries or livestock were loaded into the guard's van, but whenever there was a telephone box there was also a queue. Even when the train was moving, it seemed to crawl along; work on the line, a porter at the last station had told them. 'This 'un will be a couple of hours late, if you ask me.'

'A couple of hours!' Glenys had said. She had reached out and patted Mo's cheek. 'Never mind, love. You've been so good and patient that when we've got some spare money you shall buy yourself a little treat.'

Mo had smiled, stretched and yawned, and later she had stood up and gone out into the corridor, returning to say she was sure she could walk faster than the train was travelling. 'When we get to the next station, I'm going to run up and down the platform so's I'm really tired, then perhaps I can sleep until we reach where we're going,' she had announced.

But now the train had stopped again and there seemed to be some sort of altercation between the station staff and the passengers, for there were voices raised in protest, and a general outcry when they were told that this train would not take them all the way to its advertised destination.

Mo, nose pressed to the window, turned to Glenys. 'Even if I got down and tried to push my way through, it wouldn't be possible to run backwards and forwards along the platform,' she said. 'Oh, but there's someone selling drinks – cups of tea and that – from a sort of trolley thing further down the platform. Would you like a drink, Auntie

Glenys? If you give me some money I'm sure there would be time for me to join the queue and buy us a cup of tea. This train won't be going off in a hurry, by what the guard said.'

Glenys agreed that this was a good idea, but when Mo had jumped down on to the platform she called her back. 'Wait a minute, love. Is that a telephone box I can see just round the corner of the station buildings? If so, I do believe I might try to get in touch with Frank.' She hesitated, looking up and down the crowded platform. 'Tell you what, I'll go to the call box and you go to the drinks trolley, and if either of us see the porter waving his green flag we'll warn the other one and get back on the train. Jimmy, put our bags on our seats and don't let anyone move them.'

Glenys headed for the phone box, glancing at the station clock as she did so and noting that this was a time when it had never occurred to her to ring Frank; she had always been at the school. For once there was no queue at the box, so she went inside, laid out her pennies in a long line and lifted the receiver. She gave the number to the operator and to her considerable astonishment and delight it was Frank himself who lifted the receiver at the other end.

'Oh, thank God it's you, Frank,' Glenys said gratefully. 'We've been living in a small Welsh village, searching for Griffiths, but we're on the move again. I can't explain why . . . no time. Can

149

you tell me what's happening at Solomon Court?'

There was a noisy crackling and then Frank's voice, distorted and faint, spoke in her ear. 'Glenys? Where are you?'

'We're in transit,' Glenys said. She hesitated. 'Look, I'll ring you at the same time tomorrow and give you our new address. But what's happening your end?'

The line buzzed and crackled again. She thought Frank said, 'Don't stop there . . . farther . . . not safe for you and the kids to . . .' *crackle, crackle, crackle.*

Desperately, Glenys raised her voice to a shout. 'We're heading for Bangor, but we've decided to stop at Deniol on the way . . .' The line buzzed and Frank's tiny voice seemed to get even tinier.

'Terrible line . . . might catch up with you . . .' The line crackled again.

'Catch up where? In Deniol? Do you mean you will catch us up, or the Huxtables?' Glenys said desperately. 'This perishing line . . .'

But at this point the operator's voice cut in. 'Place six more pennies in the box, caller,' she said, and her voice too, was distorted. Glenys grabbed her pennies and began to feed them desperately into the slot provided, but just as she finished the line went dead.

Cursing softly beneath her breath, Glenys tried to reach the operator to ask to be reconnected, but it was useless. She thought that whatever the trouble was further up the line it must have affected the telephone, and pressed button B to get her money back, without success. Crossly, she thrust open the door of the box, and as she went across the platform an elderly porter caught her arm. 'Excuse me, miss, been tryin' to telephone, have you? That there box should have a sign on sayin' *Out of order*.' He wagged his grey head. 'Button B isn't workin', either, but if you come along to the office we'll refund your money, because it's our fault, see?'

'I'd be most grateful,' Glenys began. 'I lost a shilling in pennies and I need it urgently to contact my friend. Is there another box in the village that's in working order? If the train stops here long enough . . .'

But once more the porter was shaking his head. 'There's a box all right, but the train's as full as it can hold, and will be drawing out at any moment. It's the one the workers from the quarry up the hill there . . .' he gestured vaguely to the tree-covered hills nearby, 'catch to get home, only today of course it's late and tempers are a bit frayed. So unless you want to miss it . . .' He plunged a hand into his uniform pocket and handed Glenys two sixpences, saying as he did so: 'Sorry it's not pennies, miss, but no doubt someone will change this for you.'

Glenys took the sixpences, thanked him, and waved to Jimmy and Mo, who were leaning out of the window and making signs that she should hurry, though the train was still stationary.

As soon as she was aboard the two children bombarded her with questions, but Glenys could only shake her head. 'It was a terrible line, and in the end we got cut off,' she told them. 'I think Frank said we should get as far away as we can; it sounded as though he was afraid the Huxtables might catch up with us otherwise. However, if we carry on at this rate we might not get much further than Deniol anyway, so I think we'll just wait and see how we feel when we get there. I asked him what was happening his end, but I don't think he could hear me. Still, at least we're in touch again. I mean to ring him at the same time tomorrow, and we must just hope for the best.' She took Mo's hand and began to push her way through the quarry workers, but Jimmy jerked at her arm.

'It's no use going back to our compartment, Auntie Glenys,' he said. 'They wouldn't let us save the seats because we're only a couple of kids, and of course they've been working the early shift and want to sit down. So we brought our luggage into the corridor, and when they get off we'll be able to find seats once more. One of the men told me it's normally only a twenty-minute ride to his station, but it might be longer today because of the work on the line.'

Glenys sighed, but when the train stopped at the next small station and a couple of the men got out, she and Jimmy were able to grab their seats. She offered Mo her knee, but Mo had seen another attraction. A boy had come on to the platform, staggering beneath the weight of a wooden crate. This was a quieter station than the last one and he went along to the guard's van shouting for someone to give him a hand. Mo jumped down and ran along the platform, seizing one end of the crate and peering through the slats at the occupant, a puppy. It was black and white and fluffy, and Mo recognised it as a border collie, for she had recently watched fully grown dogs of that breed herding sheep. The boy pushed the crate into the guard's van and left with a brief word of thanks. Mo climbed into the van and knelt beside the little dog to read the label.

'You're going to travel with the guard, little fellow,' she cooed, ferreting in her pocket for the remains of a cheese sandwich which she had decided to save for later. 'Are you hungry? You can have my sandwich, little man, and I'll just run along the train and tell my brother and Miss Trent that I shall go the rest of the way with you. I'd love a dog of my own, so perhaps, when I'm given some money for being good, I could buy a puppy.' The puppy, which had wolfed the cheese sandwich, wagged its plumy tail and cocked its head to one side. The guard, who had been watching indulgently, pointed out the puppy's empty water bowl, and an equally empty bottle, inside the crate. 'I'll fill it,' Mo said eagerly, extracting the bottle through the slats of the crate. 'And I'll tell my auntie that I'm going to travel in the guard's van from now on to keep my new friend company. Is that all right?'

The guard grinned. He was a short, thick-set man with one yellowing tooth and twinkling little eyes. 'You make sure your auntie agrees before you come back, cariad,' he said. 'You'd best hurry; we're well behind schedule already and likely to be too late for folk wanting to catch a connection.'

But Mo was already out of hearing, tearing along the platform intent upon reaching the carriage in which she knew Jimmy and Glenys awaited her. Jimmy beckoned her from the window, and she ran over to him. 'There's a puppy in the guard's van what needs water and a friend,' she gabbled. 'I's fetchin' him a drink, then I'll stay in the guard's van till we leave the train. Only you'll have to fetch me out of the guard's van, or I shan't know when to get off.'

'Right you are,' Jimmy said, and went back into the compartment to tell Glenys as Mo hurried off to fill the puppy's bottle at the outside tap. It was only half full when the train gave a warning whistle. Mo cursed softly beneath her breath, turned off the tap, rammed the cork back into the bottle and straightened up. Fortunately the guard's van was always at the tail of the train and she was sure the friendly guard would make certain that she got in. She started to trot towards it as the train began to creep slowly out of the station, and then her heart went cold, for a tall, heavily built man was walking along the platform peering in at every window as it passed him. Mo realised with a stab of fear that he would be bound to see her if she carried on. For the first time, she looked around her. She had been so intent on the puppy that she had scarcely noticed that the station was in thickly wooded country, ideal for hiding in. She contemplated dashing across the platform full tilt and leaping aboard the guard's van before the man could react, then dismissed the idea, for the simple reason that the guard had just slid the long door closed. Mo stared, almost unable to believe her eyes, but then remembered that she had promised to get her aunt's permission before journeying with the puppy. She had done so – well, Jimmy's anyway – but the guard was not to know that. He was simply doing his duty, and Jimmy, of course, would assume she was safely in the van.

Even as Mo wondered what best to do, the man turned away from the train and came striding towards her. She caught a glimpse of heavy eyebrows drawn together in a frown and a duffel coat with the collar turned up to hide most of his face, and then he spotted her. 'Hey, you!' he shouted. 'Come here. I want a word with you!'

For one terrifying moment Mo stood statue still, staring at the man approaching. Then she threw the bottle at him with all her strength, hearing it break into a thousand pieces as it bounced off his chest and hit the platform, and then she was running, dodging in and out of the trees, slipping and sliding, panting with effort, until she could no longer hear him crashing through the wood behind her. She found a space where the undergrowth had filled in a gap where trees had fallen and wriggled into the thickest part of it. For a long time she simply lay there, peering out between the tough stems of dead bracken, brambles and nettles. It was only then, in the silence, that she put her hands over her face and began to cry.

Glenys had told Jimmy about the man who had looked into the compartment – Jimmy had been in the lavatory at the time – but she had attached no significance to it, since the man had scarcely glanced at her before scowling and moving on. 'He didn't get on the train, but anyway I'm pretty sure he was nothing to do with us,' she had assured Jimmy. 'He had thick black eyebrows and a bushy black beard. He looked like a seaman, or so I'd judge from his clothing, but I imagine he was searching for a pal he'd expected to meet at this time, and hadn't heard about the two-hour delay.'

The train stopped at their destination, and Jimmy leapt up to lift down their bags before grinning at Glenys. 'What's the betting Mo will want to stay with the puppy until she can hand it over to its new owner?'

'Well she can't,' Glenys said decisively. 'If we find your relatives and they agree to her keeping a pet that's one thing, but she really must learn to do as she's told, so you make it pretty plain that she has to come along straight away.' As she spoke she was collecting crumpled sandwich wrappings and empty cardboard cups, and casting an eye around the compartment to see that all was as it should be. Then she and Jimmy went into the corridor and along to the nearest door to step down on to the platform. 'Give me the bags, and you go and winkle Mo out of the guard's van. I'll wait by the ticket office. Tell her she's got to come now, no matter how much she pleads to accompany the puppy; I've got her ticket, and they won't let her out of the station without it.'

Jimmy sighed, and held out a hand. 'You go ahead, Auntie Glenys,' he said. 'Give me my ticket and Mo's, and you can be fixing up a lodging whilst I prise her away from the puppy.'

Glenys shook her head. 'If I turn up without any children I may be welcomed by a landlady who only takes adults and would be unpleasantly surprised when you two arrived,' she explained. 'I'll wait for you.'

'Right,' Jimmy said. 'I'll go and check the guard's van. Meet you at the ticket office in five minutes.'

But five minutes later Jimmy could only shake his head, an anxious frown marring his usually cheerful face. 'She didn't travel in the guard's van. The guard didn't worry – he just assumed you hadn't agreed to it,' he explained. 'He did say that Mo could have re-joined the train at any number of places, only she would have had to have got a lift to do so, and you know very well she wouldn't have done that. Where can she be?'

Seeing their worried faces, a porter came over to ask if they needed any help. Quickly, Glenys told him what had happened and the porter sighed. 'Kids! They're more trouble than they're worth, I'm tellin' you. How old was this 'un? Ten? Twelve?'

157

'She's six,' Jimmy said, his voice wobbling. 'Only six.' He turned to Glenys. 'What'll we do, Auntie Glenys? Can she have been kidnapped? Oh why on earth didn't she get into the guard's van, or even just get aboard the train and walk up the corridor until she found us? What possible reason could she have for hiding away like a thief in the night?'

Glenys chewed her lip, but the porter spoke up.

'She might have been in the toilet block, or the waitin' room, and not realised the train were leavin' till it were too late.'

Glenys shook her head. 'She's only six, but she's a sensible child,' she said. 'She'd have gone to the station master's house, or asked the way to the nearest bus stop. She wouldn't have just disappeared. Is there a public telephone near here? Can you give me the number of the last two or three stations? She has no money on her, you see.'

The porter grinned. 'We can do better'n that,' he said proudly. 'The station master here, Mr Alf Grimes, can send a message to every station on the line.' He turned to Jimmy. 'Is she your sister? Well. don't you worry, young feller, we'll have her back wi' you before you know it.'

An hour later Glenys had used some of her precious savings on a local bus which trundled them back through beautiful countryside to the place which they now thought of as the puppy station. To Glenys, and to Jimmy too, it looked just like all the other stations they had passed, with one difference. 'There's glass scattered all over the platform there,' the keen-eyed Jimmy remarked. 'Someone's tried to clear it up, but there are fragments in between the paving slabs. I wonder . . .'

'It can't have anything to do with Mo,' Glenys was beginning, when Jimmy pounced on something which had rolled a short way away.

'She was filling a bottle so the puppy could have a drink, and here's the cork,' he said triumphantly. 'If she was surprised whilst filling it, it could have got dropped. But even that shouldn't have stopped her getting on the train, unless she thought she saw . . .'

Mo lay in her little hideout until her heart stopped hammering and she was certain there were no signs of pursuit. Even then, however, she hesitated to leave the safety of the woods. She was sure the man who had shouted at her must have been Cyril, but in her mind the figure grew and grew until he was twice the size of Cyril and three times as dangerous. She had barely caught a glimpse of his face, but now it was clear in her mind: thick, angry eyebrows, dark pockmarked skin, mean little eyes and huge ham-like hands. If he had removed his hat, she felt sure it would have revealed a red spotted handkerchief and a black eyepatch; all the markings of a pirate, in fact. I ought to go back to the station, Mo told herself. Jimmy and Auntie Glenys will be worried when they realise I'm not in the guard's van. But why haven't they checked yet? She began to feel aggrieved. Cyril chased me into the woods and no one came to rescue me, even though I'm only little. Jimmy should have come to help me, and so should Glenys. It's very wicked to leave someone to look after herself whilst you go off in a warm and comfortable train. Forgotten were the hours spent sitting, bored and cold, in the cheerless compartment as the train chugged deeper into the hills, and as dusk fell Mo got angrier and angrier. It wasn't right. Auntie Glenys had said they must stick together, and what had she and Jimmy done? They had gone off, abandoned her, left her to be very nearly caught by their dreaded enemy. How she would reproach them when she saw them again; if she *did* ever see them again, that was.

But now, though the sound of pursuit had long since stopped, she fancied she could hear voices, and presently saw the gleam of artificial light as someone with a lantern made his or her way along the edge of the wood. Mo gave a squeak; she would know that voice anywhere! Oh, how she would give it to Jimmy when they met! She stood up and ran towards the light.

Despite her intentions, thoughts of revenge crumbled away the moment she emerged from the trees and flung herself into her brother's arms. She had meant to blame him, to tell him and Auntie Glenys just what she thought of them, but instead common sense reasserted itself.

'I'm sorry, I'm sorry,' she wailed. 'I was frightened.'

'You little idiot,' Jimmy said fondly, lifting her

up to give her a big hug. 'You said you were going to travel in the guard's van, but you didn't get on the train at all! Whatever happened to make you run into the woods instead of getting back on to the train? We thought . . . we thought someone had kidnapped you!' The station porter had accompanied them on their search, and Jimmy was reluctant to mention Cyril's name in front of a stranger who might demand all sorts of explanations. The warning glance he received from Glenys told him she felt the same, so when he saw the porter's eyebrows shoot up he changed it to a joke. 'To tell you the truth, queen, I thought you'd probably let the puppy out of the crate by accident and were searching the woods for it.'

Mo was indignant. 'As if I would,' she said. 'But there were a man, Jimmy – he shouted "come here" at me, sounding rare angry, and I thought he'd tell the station people that I were thievin' their water, so I ran into the trees. He followed me for a bit, but then he give up and I thought I'd come back to the station and see if I could catch the next train.'

'Well, why didn't you, then?' the porter said, in a grumbling voice. 'That would ha' been the sensible thing to do.' He was swinging the lighted lantern as he spoke, and Mo gave him a brilliant smile.

'I couldn't find my way out of the wood,' she said simply. 'I walked around for ages, and then I sat down on a log and had a bit of a weep, and then I heard Jimmy's voice and ran towards it, and the rest you know.'

'But who was the feller what chased you into the wood?' the porter grumbled.

'We've no idea, have we, you two?' Glenys said quickly. 'But I do believe that you should report him as dangerous.' She lowered her voice. 'What might have happened had he caught up with my niece, before she hid in the trees? I shudder to think!'

The porter nodded, and lowered his voice in his turn. 'You are very right, miss. Happily, we found the child before harm could come to her, but the feller must be reported. Do you think she will be able to describe him?'

Jimmy started to say that he could describe the man perfectly well himself, which caused the porter's eyebrows to shoot up his forehead once more. 'That is, it must have been the man Auntie Glenys saw through the window of the train,' Jimmy gabbled. 'He almost pressed his nose against the glass, didn't you say, Auntie Glenys? He had these thick eyebrows . . .' He gave the same description of the man that Glenys had given him, though Mo stuck out her lower lip.

'I saw him first, and I was the one he chased so I should be the one to tell the scuffers, not you,' she said mulishly. 'He had this big scar on his cheek and a black patch over one eye . . .'

Everyone laughed. 'And a parrot on his shoulder shouting *Pieces of eight, pieces of eight*,' Jimmy said. 'Oh, Mo, I think you ought to leave descriptions for someone who wasn't frightened out of their life at the time.'

'I wasn't frightened,' Mo said belligerently. 'I'm brave as a lion I am! Why, I only cried a little bit.'

Jimmy gave her a playful shake. 'Course you did,' he said comfortably. 'And now let's get back down to the station, otherwise we'll arrive in town too late to buy fish and chips for our supper.'

Mo was about to argue when she caught Jimmy's eye and subsided, realising that he had described Cyril Huxtable as exactly as was possible.

'I'll go and give Ifan tacsi a ring,' the porter said. He winked at Glenys, who was delving in her elderly leather handbag for her purse. 'Don't worry, miss. It ain't that far by road to Deniol, so it shouldn't break the bank.' He pulled a gunmetal watch out of his waistcoat pocket and consulted it. 'He'll be here in no time; he'll have just finished his tea,' he said, and disappeared into the office. True to his word, the taxi drew up a few minutes later with a scream of brakes and a fat little man with ginger hair jumped out to help his passengers aboard. The porter watched as Glenys joined the children on the back seat. 'All aboard. And rest assured, if that feller turns up again, he'll get a pretty hot reception!'

Half an hour later they had arrived in the market town of Ruthin, Glenys having simply asked the driver to take them to the nearest lodging-house he could recommend.

'You'll find Mrs Buttermilk is just grand with kiddies, and knows every soul for miles around,' their taxi driver had assured them, stopping his cab directly at the foot of eight steep steps leading to the front door of a tall thin house which leaned perilously towards the one on the opposite side of the street. A sign in the window read *Vacancies*. Glenys had looked at the quaint old house, the gleaming window panes and the net curtains looped back to show a cosy firelit interior, and had voiced her fears aloud. 'Forgive me, but it looks expensive,' she said. 'As I told you, we're looking for relatives who used to live in these parts, and it may be some while before we contact them, so we need something quite cheap. This house is so delightful that I imagine Mrs Buttermilk can charge what she likes.'

The taxi driver slewed in his seat to grin, revealing large yellowing teeth. 'Aye, you'd be right in what you might call the normal way,' he agreed, his grin widening. 'But this house is halfway up Ffordd Hilbre, so whatever you want, the town square at the top or the recreation ground at the bottom, climb you must, and then there's them eight steep steps. So Mrs Buttermilk's lodgings are often vacant, and that means she has to keep her prices down.' He named a sum which had Glenys smiling with relief and struggling out of the cab, but before she had done more than get one foot on the roadway the taxi driver gestured her back to her seat. 'I'm used to them steps; if you're willing, I'll book a double and a single room and help you up with your luggage.'

So some time later, Glenys, Jimmy and Mo found

themselves sitting in the cosy parlour which was set aside for guests and enjoying a cup of tea and a Welsh cake, liberally buttered, whilst in the big stone-flagged kitchen Mrs Buttermilk was preparing a meal for which she would charge them a very reasonable sum. Jimmy looked around at the comfortable chairs, the little bookcase upon which many of his favourite titles were displayed, and the log fire roaring up the chimney, and spoke through a mouthful of Welsh cake. 'We've fallen on our feet this time, don't you think, Auntie Glenys? I doesn't care if we never find a Griffiths so long as we can stay at Ty Bryn. I've got a grand bedroom overlooking the street; it's only small, but it's cosy, like my little room in the Court before . . . oh, well, no point in lookin' back.'

'And no point, alas, in believing that we can stay here for long, unless I can find work,' Glenys said ruefully. 'When I went down to the basement kitchen to pay Mrs Buttermilk – I've booked us in for two nights' supper, bed and breakfast – I asked if there was any chance of a teaching job around here, and, to be blunt, there isn't. Then I mentioned Griffiths, and oh, Jimmy, there are hundreds of them.' She peered out of the window and up into the sky. 'Mrs Buttermilk says it always snows here, so there's no point our searching for a dry and cosy barn because there's no such thing. However, she did think that one of the outlying farms might give us beds in what they call bunkhouses, which the holidaymakers hire when the weather's warmer.

And, she says, someone on those farms might have work for a strong young woman.' She giggled. 'She meant me, of course. So immediately after breakfast tomorrow I think we should start visiting.'

Mo, who had curled up on a chair with eyes shut and toes pointed at the fire, suddenly opened her eyes. 'Cyril will be real cross when they haul him off to the police station,' she said with satisfaction. 'Serves him right for frightenin' little girls. Serves him right for pokin' his long nose into other people's railway carriages . . .'

Glenys and Jimmy exchanged indulgent looks. It was clear to them both that the cosy armchair, the roaring fire and the welcome Mrs Buttermilk had given them were rapidly sending Mo into the land of nod. 'Serves him right, serves him right . . .' she said dreamily, as Glenys lifted her up and carried her to the bedroom – and the big double bed – which they were to share. She was still murmuring 'serves him right' as Glenys helped her out of her travelling clothes and into a white cotton nightie. The last thing Glenys heard, before she closed the door and went downstairs for supper, was Mo's small, smug voice: 'Serves him *jolly* well right.'

After hearing Mo's description of her horrible experience Jimmy did not expect to fall asleep without a struggle, for losing Mo and then hearing how she had been pursued by a man whose description certainly fitted that of Cyril Huxtable had upset

Jimmy deeply. Tossing and turning in his small but comfortable bed he told himself that now they were beyond the reach of both parents it was even more his duty to look after Mo and see she came to no harm. And what had he done? He had let her get off the train and trot around looking after some puppy or other. Of course it was not his fault that Cyril had come on to the platform to search the train and had got between Mo and the guard's van, but he told himself he should have checked that she was aboard and not merely taken it for granted. When he thought of all the things which might have happened to a little girl of six, apparently abandoned by her companions, his blood ran cold. It was not just Cyril who might have harmed her. He had read stories in the newspaper . . . but he refused to allow himself to think of them now. What *had* happened was bad enough without letting his imagination run wild, and anyway they had been lucky. Mo had returned to them unscathed, and now all they had to do was find their mother's family and ask to be taken in. Once the Griffiths were convinced that they were speaking the truth about the Huxtables, the scuffers could be called in to find whatever it was Cyril believed he and Mo had taken, and all would be well.

Jimmy sighed deeply, tucked his hand beneath his pillow, and, at long last, fell asleep.

Chapter 10

When Glenys awoke a wintry sun was shining, and for some reason she felt optimistic, sure that in this pleasant little town they would run the Trewins' family to earth. She rolled over in bed and found that her companion had abandoned her; plainly the sunshine had given Mo her confidence back. The smell of bacon which came floating through the half-open door made Glenys's nostrils twitch.

She swung her legs out of bed, washed rather shrinkingly in the cold water contained in the ewer, and went downstairs. She hesitated in the hallway, trying to remember which door led to the kitchen and which to the parlour, but then she heard muffled voices from the door on her right and feeling rather foolish, for she had promised to be up betimes, she tapped lightly on the door and went in.

The first sight which met her eyes was Jimmy and Mo seated at the table with bowls of what looked like porridge or cereal before them. Also at the table were a couple, probably in their mid-twenties, who turned as the door opened and smiled at the teacher, chorusing 'Good morning' as she came fully into the room. Mrs Buttermilk was at the stove, manoeuvring a mighty frying pan as she dished out crisp bacon and golden-yolked eggs on to half a dozen plates.

'I'm sorry I'm late,' Glenys began, but the land-lady shook her head.

'You're just in nice time you are, my dear,' she assured her guest. 'There's porridge to start, unless you'd rather have cereal, a good hot cup of tea to go with it and piles of toast with butter and marma-lade to fill the chinks. As my hubby always says, "An empty sack won't stand up", so just you tuck in, my dear, and don't worry about time.' She began to hand around plates of bacon, egg and sausage, saying as she did so: 'But I must introduce you to my other guests. Them's Mr and Mrs Horner, what's just here for a couple of days' hillwalking.' She turned to the young couple and gave them a roguish look. 'Last time they come they was Miss Clark and Mr Horner. I tease them that they only got wed to save the price of two single rooms.'

Glenys smiled at the young couple, who were both blushing furiously. 'Nice to meet you,' she said. 'I'm Glenys Trent, the children's aunt. We've come here to try to contact the children's relatives on their mother's side. Their name is Griffiths, but it turns out that Wales is full of Griffiths, so we've had no luck so far.'

Having handed round all the plates Mrs Buttermilk took her place at the head of the table and picked up her knife and fork, nodding to the others to follow suit. 'I'm a Griffiths myself,' she said conversationally. 'The reason they call me Mrs

Buttermilk is to avoid confusion, 'cos there's at least half a dozen Griffiths families livin' in the town, and more on the outskirts of course.' She raised a plump hand and began to tell off her neighbours on her fingers. 'One, there's Mrs Icecream because she makes her own in the summer; two, there's Mr and Mrs River because their land runs down to the river; three . . .'

But here Jimmy interrupted. 'Do you think you could write them down for us please, Mrs Buttermilk?' he asked eagerly. 'It would be a great help in our search.'

Mrs Buttermilk nodded. 'I'll write a list,' she promised. 'But if your good aunt is taking care of you . . .'

Glenys broke in. 'I'm only what you might call an honorary aunt,' she said glibly. 'The children's mother and myself were best friends, and when I heard that their father had gone back to sea after her death and not been next or nigh them since, I thought their maternal relations should be told. I knew, of course, that Grace had lost contact with her parents when she married an Englishman, so when I lost my job it seemed the sensible thing to do was to bring the children to Wales to find them, in the hope that they might offer them a home. So any help you can give us would be appreciated more than I can say.'

Mrs Buttermilk appeared to accept this explanation without demur, and after all, Glenys comforted herself, it was the truth, more or less. The young couple, tucking into the delicious and generous breakfast provided by their landlady, murmured that they too would help if they could. 'Grace is an unusual name for a Welsh woman,' Mr Horner said. 'Tell you what: we've noticed in the past that all these villages have a very efficient bush telegraph system. If you start enquiring about a Grace Griffiths at one end of the county it'll be common knowledge among folk from the other end by the time you go to bed that night.'

Mrs Buttermilk nodded wisely and addressed herself to Jimmy. 'If your relatives is local, we'll find 'em in no time,' she promised. 'Just you leave it to us, lad.'

But Glenys had had another thought. Suppose Cyril Huxtable too did just what Mr Horner had suggested? He must be lodging somewhere, and even if he was sleeping rough he would have to eat, which would mean visiting towns and villages. Suppose he made use of the same bush telegraph? She looked wildly at Jimmy and saw that he was looking wildly at her; clearly the same thought had entered the head of her young charge. She was thinking desperately of ways to counter this latest snag when Jimmy's face cleared, and he spoke.

'The thing is, Mam's relatives don't know she's dead; it's bound to be a blow to them, even though they quarrelled, so we'd rather tell them ourselves. Then we can judge whether they really want us or whether they would just be doing their duty, which might be uncomfortable for Mo and me. So if you could put the word around without mentioning us, we'd be very grateful.'

'Mebbe you're in the right of it,' Mrs Buttermilk said slowly. 'Yes, I'm sure you are. But don't you worry: family is important to the Welsh, so don't think you won't be welcome. And Ruthin folk are a friendly lot, so we'll do everything we can to help.'

Jimmy had been busy loading his fork with a generous mouthful of bacon and sausage, but at these words he looked up sharply. '*What* folk?'

'Ruthin folk,' Mrs Buttermilk repeated, puzzled. 'Folk who live here in Ruthin.'

'But is this town called Ruthin, then? We saw the sign and it looked like—'

Light dawned on the landlady's face. 'Oh, I see – that's a mistake a lot of English people make. You see, in Welsh the "u" is pronounced like an English "i", so R-u-t-h-i-n is pronounced Rithin.'

Jimmy said no more, but the glance he shot at Glenys was so full of excitement that it was all she could do to wait until they had finished their meal and helped the landlady to wash up before demanding 'Well, Jimmy? What did Mrs Buttermilk say to make you look as though you'd lost a penny and found a pound?'

'Oh, Auntie Glenys, don't you remember? Back in Liverpool, when we were discussing where we should go, I said that all we knew about our mam was that she lived on a farm near a place called Rith something. It was Ruthin, I'm sure it was – as

173

soon as Mrs Buttermilk mentioned it I remembered as clear as clear. It must mean we really are close to where Mam grew up . . . in a farmhouse with roses round the door!'

Glenys smiled. 'You won't see roses in January no matter how hard you look, I'm afraid, but it does sound as though we ought at least to find someone who can tell us whether your Griffiths relations are still in the neighbourhood. So why don't you and Mo make your beds and then wrap up in your warmest clothes whilst I nip down and ask Mrs Buttermilk if I can put together a packed lunch for us, and then we'll make a start.'

By the time they had visited half a dozen farms Glenys could see that Mo was beginning to despair of ever succeeding in their quest. The trouble was the farms tended to be some way apart, and sometimes when they knocked at the back door it was answered by a young girl who could tell them very little, save the name of her employer. Even when this was Griffiths – and they found two such quite early in their search – neither of them knew anything of Grace. It was a bitterly cold day, and when they sat down in the lee of a tumbled-down elm to eat their packed lunch, Mo had reached the whining stage, wanting nothing more than to turn for home, and even Jimmy remarked morosely that he suspected that when he took off his boots his feet would come with them.

It seemed to Glenys that some of the farms were

in a state of dilapidation which must make them almost unworkable, but Jimmy, who had spent much of the last fortnight visiting farms in the vicinity of their first stopping place, said that farmers didn't care about appearances; sometimes the dirtier the farmyard the more comfortably situated was the family who owned it.

But winter days are short and the sky had a threatening look; Glenys suspected that there would be snow before many hours had passed, so she gave in to the children's pleas that they should only visit two more farms and then turn for home. The time she had earmarked for ringing Frank was approaching, too, and she did not want to miss it.

The first farm they visited was called Ridgeways, and turned out to be owned by an Evans family. It was a prosperous-looking place, reached down a narrow lane with high banks on either side which must, when spring came, be starred with primroses and violets. And no doubt in June with wild strawberries, Jimmy said longingly, and added that if his mother's family owned a farm like this they should certainly be willing to take on a couple of kids who would cost them almost nothing.

Mrs Evans herself answered the door, and said at once that there was another farm a couple of miles off. 'But I believe a bad state it is in,' she warned them. 'The Depression has hit farming families cruel hard; cheap imports, see? If they'd had a big family of lads, same as us, they could have weathered the Depression, but as it is the old folk couldn't cope. I believe they're living just in the back of the house, and my good man says if it weren't for their vegetable garden they'd have likely starved.'

'Did the family have a daughter what ran away with an English seaman a dozen or more years ago?' Jimmy asked eagerly.

Mrs Evans shook her head. 'We wouldn't be knowin' about anythin' what happened more'n five years ago, when we bought old Mr Davies out and moved up from our small farm in the Vale of Clwyd to this 'un. I can't tell you anything about the Weathers' family.'

'Weathers? We're looking for folk named Griffiths,' Jimmy told her in a disappointed tone. 'My mam was a Griffiths before she got married.'

Mrs Evans was a plump and jolly woman, dark-haired and dark-eyed. She had been smiling, but now her face grew thoughtful. 'Weather isn't their proper name, just what we call them. You know how it is in Wales when you've got four or five families all with the same surname. It's quite possible their real name is Griffiths.'

Jimmy and Glenys both nodded their comprehension, but Mo looked curious. 'Why do you call them the Weathers?'

Mrs Evans laughed. 'Because their farm has a weathercock on the roof of the big old barn. And they call me Mrs Redhead because my husband has red hair. But I'd best not keep you, as you have a fair walk ahead of you. Be sure to give the Weathers the good word from myself and my family.'

'We will; and thank you,' Mo said blithely. She seized Glenys's hand. 'I do hope it's our mam's relatives,' she said as they returned to the lane. 'Oh, Auntie Glenys, I've got a feelin' in me bones that soon as soon, me and Jimmy's goin' to have a grandma and grandpa, and a proper home of our own; I can't wait!'

Glenys smiled at the little girl, but she too was growing tired, and suddenly she realised her own position. At present she was the nearest thing to a relative the two children had, and they treated her with affection and respect. But if this old couple really were her charges' grandparents then they were bound to look upon her in a different light. Glenys, who had always known she was a foundling, realised that once the children were settled in this beautiful countryside they would have no further need of her. Oh, they had kind hearts and a great many good intentions, but things would change, and she was not at all sure that, for her, it would be for the better. But though she hesitated for a moment she chided herself for so doing. It would be shabby indeed to grudge the children success, so she pinned a bright smile on her face, took Mo's hand, and set off at a smart pace along the high-banked lane. 'I think you're right, Mo,' she said. 'Best foot forward, troops.'

They followed the twistings and turnings of several small lanes, and would have missed the farm altogether but for the weathercock twirling on top of the big old barn as the wind caught it.

Glenys saw that both Jimmy and Mo were looking tired, but as she pushed open the rickety gate which led into the neglected front garden Mo tugged at her hand. 'Look!' she whispered. 'Oh, Auntie Glenys, look!'

Glenys's eyes followed the little girl's pointing finger, but her brain could make little sense of Mo's excitement. The front of the house was clad in shining ivy, whilst the ground at their feet was scattered with the scarlet and gold leaves of a Virginia creeper. But when she stepped forward to examine the door more closely, she saw what the child had been pointing at: a tiny white rose, paper thin on its bare twig. Not the rose of high summer, indeed, but none the less a rose for all that.

Chapter 11

Glenys reached up to an old brass knocker, a bull's head, green with neglect, and rapped sharply. Then she turned to Mo. 'You're a very observant little girl. I'm sure you really are right, and this is your mother's old home. But why are we standing here waiting for someone to open the door? Mrs Evans told us that the old couple had moved to the back of the house. Come on.'

The three of them left the door and turned into an overgrown pathway which led to the farmyard itself. There they paused, looking around them. What they could see was shabby but not neglected; Glenys glanced towards the farmhouse and noted that the red-and-white chequered curtains that hung at the windows of what she guessed to be the kitchen were faded but clean. Then a dog, a black and white border collie who had been lying on the cobbles, jumped to its feet and gave a warning growl, wagging its plumy tail.

Jimmy laughed. 'His tail says "come in", and his mouth says "stay out",' he remarked. 'Shall I knock on the back door, Auntie Glenys? I'm sure I just saw movement through that window.' Without waiting for an answer, and ignoring the dog's low growl, he stepped up to the door and beat a tattoo upon the blistered paintwork with his knuckles.

They barely had to wait thirty seconds before the door swung open to reveal a large black-bearded man with a scar etched across his forehead. He was grinning. Glenys's heart jumped into her mouth. 'Sorry, wrong house,' she gabbled, and turned to run, but Mo was ahead of her, streaking across the cobbles. But Jimmy, to Glenys's astonishment, gave a shriek and leapt forward.

'Dad! Oh, Dad!' he cried, clasping the man around the waist and burying his head in his broad chest. 'Oh, Dad, where have you been?' He twisted in the man's grasp. 'Mo, you little idiot, don't you recognise your own father when you see him?'

The man let go of Jimmy and held out a hand. Mo had stopped and was staring back at the house, eyes round with fear. 'That's not our daddy,' she said doubtfully. 'Our daddy didn't have a beard; nor he didn't have a horrid cut on his forehead. Oh, Jimmy, it looks awful like Cyril Huxtable to me; and awful like the man who chased me at the puppy station.'

The man sat down on the step and smiled at Mo. 'Don't tell me my bright little button *still* doesn't recognise me,' he said. 'It was understandable on the railway platform, but now that you've had a good look at me . . .'

Mo gave a strangled sob and threw herself into his arms, pushing Jimmy aside. 'So you recognise

me at last,' her father exclaimed, in a voice somewhere between elation and tears. 'I'm so sorry I
frightened you at the station, but I've been hunting
for you for what seems like weeks, and then, when
I saw you at last, I wasn't sure it really was you.
You've grown, queen, and it's over a year since I
saw you last. Now we'd best go indoors, because
explaining what's been happening to us all is going
to take some time. And I can introduce you to your
grandparents.'

Glenys looked at them. Sam Trewin had risen to
his feet with Mo still in his arms, and Jimmy was
leaning against his shoulder. They looked so happy,
such a complete family group, that envy flooded
her, and she spoke more sharply than she intended.
'How do you come to be here at all, Mr Trewin?
For all your children knew you might have been
dead.'

Sam Trewin looked her up and down, and it was
not a friendly look. 'Who are you?' he asked. 'When
I first arrived home I learned that the children had
disappeared. Are you a Huxtable? Because the
neighbours told me the Huxtables must have had
something to do with it.' His gaze swept her again,
his inspection insultingly thorough. 'I suppose you
posed as a friend when you took them away from
Solomon Court.'

Jimmy wrenched himself free from his father's
grasp, and Mo turned in his arms and seized a
handful of his strong black beard. 'You shan't say
nasty things about Auntie Glenys,' they shouted,

almost in chorus, Jimmy adding, 'If she hadn't taken us away from Liverpool we'd likely have been dead by now, because Cyril Huxtable got it into his head we'd stolen something of his, and he nearly broke Mo's arm once just because he thought I'd eaten a bit of his pie.'

'Oh, Jimmy, thank you, but it really doesn't matter,' Glenys began, turning to retrace her steps along the path, but she was stopped by Jimmy's hand grabbing her arm.

'Don't go, Auntie Glenys; our dad doesn't know the truth and we need you to tell it,' he said urgently. 'And if he sends you away he can send us away as well, because we know you're our friend, and have done nothing to hurt us in any way.' He turned to look defiantly up into his father's bearded face. 'And if you think she's like the Huxtables, what have starved and beaten us and never give us so much as a penny of the money you sent, then Mo and me don't want to have anything to do with you. So there!'

Sam Trewin heaved a sigh. 'All right, Miss whatever your name is, you'd best come into the kitchen. My in-laws won't mind hearing the story again, and we need to hear your version of events. Come along.'

Glenys opened her mouth to say that she would do no such thing, but Mo seized one hand and Jimmy the other. 'He don't mean to be nasty, Auntie Glenys,' Jimmy said urgently. 'And you'd like to meet our mam's parents, wouldn't you? You must want to know the truth as badly as we do, and besides, where would you go? Back to Mrs Buttermilk's?'

Glenys felt a sob rising up in her throat and choked it back. Jimmy had put his finger on the nub of the matter. She had talked about finding her relatives, but knew it was just a dream. She was alone, as she had always been, and unless she found a job within the next month to six weeks she would be in a parlous state indeed, with no money, no home, and no prospects. Unhappily, she followed the Trewin family into the kitchen. It was a large room, shabby but clean, and lamplit, for it was growing dusk outside. There was a black-leaded range in which a good fire burned, a square wooden table, a number of ladder-back chairs, and a low stone sink with two wooden draining boards. Glenys thought it felt homely and pleasant.

As they entered the kitchen, two elderly people seated on either side of the fire got shakily to their feet. They both smiled at the children, then turned to Sam. 'So you were right, Sam; you thought they'd come here,' the woman said. She turned back to Jimmy and Mo. 'I'm your granny – your nain, as we say in Wales – and I welcome you to Weathercock Farm. This is my husband, your taid, and we'd be happy for you to live with us for as long as you should wish. Indeed, since you will inherit the farm one day, the sooner you move in here and get to know our ways the better. We've plenty of bedrooms.' She smiled sadly and put out a caressing hand to ruffle Mo's hair. 'I can't believe you are actually here, because until a few days ago we didn't even know we had grandchildren. We knew Grace had died because your father sent us a telegram, but he didn't mention you and he forgot to include your address, although we couldn't have come to the funeral anyway, because Taid was in hospital with pneumonia, and far too ill to be moved.' Nain wiped a tear from her eye as she remembered that terrible time.

'I think it might be quite nice to live here,' Mo said cautiously, 'but what about our dad? And what about Auntie Glenys? We wants her to live with us, doesn't we, Jimmy?'

Glenys was about to reply that she did not wish to be a burden when old Mr Griffiths spoke, his voice heavily accented and his breathing wheezy. 'Jumping ahead of yourselves you are,' he commented. He turned to Glenys. 'No disrespect, miss, but we've yet to hear how you come to be travelling with our grandchildren. Sam here told us Jimmy and Maureen had left Liverpool with a woman he'd never heard of. So before we make any more plans for the future I think we must hear your story. Sit yourselves down – you too, Sam – and we'll start as we mean to go on, please. Whoever is speaking must be allowed to do so without interruptions. Questions can come at the end.'

His wife laughed but patted the couch, indicating that the children should sit beside her. 'I think we should start with the children, and Miss Glenys can pick up the story at the time she entered it in real life,' she said. 'Off you go, Jimmy and Mo!'

'That's a poem,' Mo said approvingly. Glenys had sat down beside her and smiled at the remark.

'Very true. So far as I can make out, the story really begins with Mo herself. As it was told to me she was cleaning sprouts so that Mrs Huxtable might sell them to folk for their Christmas dinner . . .'

She looked enquiringly at Mo, who nodded vigorously. 'And I saw Cyril Huxtable opening a parcel . . .'

Glenys sighed. 'Start at the very beginning,' she said. 'One morning a few days before Christmas, when you were doing the sprouts . . .'

The story unfolded far more coherently than one would have expected. Everyone was amused by the tying together of Cyril's bootlaces, but annoyed that the Huxtables could think Mo would steal anything from anyone, 'let alone a piece of what I dare say was probably costume jewellery', Sam had surmised. And having heard how the other man had abused his trust and ill treated his children, Sam said he would have cheered had Cyril broken his neck. Glenys's side of the story followed, and she made no secret of the fact that she thought Sam a cruel and uncaring father to leave his children in the care of people whose bad reputation should have been known to him. Having heard Glenys's explanation, one would have thought that Sam would have looked upon her with a kindlier eye, but this did not seem to be the case. He resented her criticism of the time he had allowed to elapse before coming back to Liverpool, and she resented it when he said, frankly, that had she not run away with them he would have been reunited with his children weeks earlier. She pointed out sharply that she was not psychic, could not possibly have known that he would return. 'I thought you a most unnatural parent,' she told him coldly. 'And who could blame me? You did not seem to care what happened to Jimmy and Mo, whereas I, being on the spot, could understand their desperation to get away from Liverpool and the Huxtables.' Sam began to justify himself, but his father-in-law shook his head chidingly.

'Miss Glenys has told us the story as it appeared to her,' he said. 'Don't forget what we said.'

His son-in-law had reared up, his face reddening, but at his father-in-law's words he sat back in his chair and grinned resignedly. 'And here was me thinking I'd got my temper under control at last,' he said ruefully. 'It's got me into enough trouble in the past, one way or another. If it hadn't been for my temper Grace and I could have got married from here, helped you run the farm and lived happily ever after, but I couldn't bear to be told when I did things wrong. I was a young hothead in those days, and I admit now that I behaved very badly.' He smiled sadly at his children, sitting demurely on the couch beside his mother-in-law. 'I won't bore you by telling you about the big row which resulted in my persuading Grace that I could never be a farmer, and that I would only marry her if she would come back to Liverpool with me and agree to my going back to sea. That's an old, old story, and one I'm deeply ashamed of.'

He was silent for a few minutes, a frown creasing his brow. Then he looked up and let his gaze roam around the assembled company. 'I'm going to tell things, not as I learned them myself, but as I think they really happened,' he said.

Jimmy began to say something, but subsided as Mo kicked him sharply in the shins. 'Shurrup,' she hissed. 'You heard what Tai . . . Taid said – let our Dad tell wi'out interruptions.'

'Thanks, Mo,' Sam said. 'I'll start at the very beginning, which was the day after we docked and I was walking along the quay, on my way back from the post office where I'd just sent off your Christmas parcel. I wasn't taking much notice of my surroundings, and then someone – or some-thing – hit me hard on the back of the head. I fell forward, and found myself face down in the oily water of the dock and only half conscious. Of course I tried to swim to the surface, but just as I reached it something struck me a stunning blow on the forehead – you can see the scar – and I lost consciousness completely.'

'Oh, poor Dad,' Mo whispered. 'You might have been killed!'

'I very nearly was,' Sam said ruefully. 'But a passer-by must have fished me out, and I'm afraid I can't tell you much of what happened after that, because someone had stripped me of my clothing and everything I possessed so that when they took me to the hospital no one had any idea that I was a seaman off one of the ships. The *Mary Anne* had been due to sail on the evening tide, and no doubt she did so, with Captain Able believing I had jumped ship as seamen sometimes do. I was unconscious for ten days, but at the end of that time I came round to find myself in a hospital bed, with absolutely no idea how I got there, or even who I was. Fortunately for me, because I didn't speak the language, one of the doctors was an American and he and I got quite friendly. He told me about his family back in the States, but of course I couldn't reciprocate because I could remember nothing of my life before I opened my eyes to find myself in hospital. The doctor, however, was sure that I would recover my memory, and one day, when I was taking a walk around the town, I saw a boy of about your age, Jimmy, pushing a little girl on a swing. The sight of those two children disturbed me, though I could not have said why. They were in a playground with two or three swings, a slide and a sort of roundabout, and whilst I was watching them the little girl jumped off the swing and came hurtling through the air, and I caught her, and the moment I held her in my arms my memory came flooding back. I remembered everything: my darling Grace dying, taking a berth aboard the *Mary Anne*, and leaving you children in the care of the Huxtables. I stood the little girl down very carefully and she ran back to the swing, and after that I just sat down on the dusty earth and tried to make sense of what had happened. My American doctor friend had told me not to try too hard but simply to open my mind to thoughts of the past, and over the next few days that was what I did. The memories came at their own pace and would not be hurried, but when I remembered that Grace had died I knew I must come back home as soon as possible. My arrangement with the Huxtables had included my sending money home to cover the rent and other expenses, and of course I had not done so for some time.'

Jimmy beamed at his father. 'So you never knew Mrs Huxtable ill-treated us,' he said.

Sam shook his head. 'And I promise you, Jimmy, that had I known, nothing would have prevented me from sorting her out.'

'I knew it!' Jimmy said exultantly. 'I knew you wouldn't let us down. Well, we both knew, didn't we, Mo?'

Mo stared at her brother, a pink flush gradually creeping across her face. 'We didn't know!' she said indignantly. 'We thought he'd forgot all about us.'

Sam groaned. 'I've been a rotten dad to you, both of you,' he said remorsefully. 'But I'll make it up to you somehow. Now let me finish my story.' He smiled across at his in-laws. 'I know you've heard all this before, but I dare say you won't mind listening to it again,' he said. 'Or if you need to be doing other things you could leave me to tell it for the second time.' The Griffiths, however, exchanged an affectionate glance and shook their heads.

'It's a complicated tale,' Taid said. 'Confusing, like. No harm in hearing a repetition, hey, Mother?'

His wife nodded. 'Fire ahead, Sam,' she said.

Sam Trewin took a deep breath, thought for a moment, and then began. 'Once I had regained my memory and knew that my darling Grace was dead and my children were coping alone, I got a berth on the next ship heading for Liverpool.' He smiled at Jimmy and Mo. 'When we docked I signed off, for I meant to get work ashore and look after you myself. I went straight to Solomon Court, and you can imagine my horror when I went to number four and the door was opened by a slovenly woman with greasy hair whom I scarcely recognised; she seemed much fatter and more unkempt than I remembered. Perhaps I should have taken warning, but all I cared about was that this woman had looked after you – fed and clothed you – for over a year, when I had abandoned you. So, foolish though it seems now, I was truly grateful, and believed everything she told me. I asked where you were, and it was then that she told me you'd been kidnapped. I did not stop to ask myself why anyone should want to steal a couple of penniless kids, but headed straight for the police station, and if I hadn't walked slap bang into Nutty I'd have reported you missing there and then.

'But Nutty enlightened me. He said that Mrs Huxtable was a wicked old woman and her son was worse. He told me Cyril had near on broken Mo's arm once, and had been ranting and raving at Christmas about getting his hands on you both, but then his ship had sailed without him and now no one knew where he was. I didn't know what to think, still less what to do, except to carry out my original intention and report you missing, only I said it was definitely Cyril Huxtable who had taken you. But then I had a stroke of luck. I met an old pal who had a second-hand clothes stall and he told me that Cyril thought Mo had stolen something of his and that he was after your blood. Good old Harry knows a liar from an honest man and he didn't believe a word of it. He took you kids to the Salvation Hall and handed you over to a Major Williams, and within a couple of days you had disappeared.' He glared at Glenys. 'Don't you understand? If you'd not paid for the kids' tickets and taken them off into Wales I would have sorted the whole thing out, but before I could do anything *you*, Miss Schoolteacher, had whisked them away.'

Jimmy could stay silent no longer. 'But when we told our story I explained that Cyril caught me cutting holly, and Auntie Glenys saved us both by letting us stay in her house,' he said indignantly. 'Me and Mo *told* you that Cyril knew we'd taken shelter somewhere on Orange Street, and after Frank had spoken to him, and found he was determined to stick around until he found us, we knew we had to get away, not just from Orange Street but from Liverpool itself.'

191

Sam nodded, though reluctantly. 'But it was not sensible just to take off with only a vague idea of where you were going. You were lucky that it was me who caught up with you and not Cyril Huxtable, because I imagine he's disappeared because he too is looking for you.' He turned to Glenys. 'I dare say you did it for the best, but it was more of a hindrance than a help. Sheer interference I'd call it.'

Glenys sniffed. 'If we're going to get personal I can't help thinking you a very neglectful parent,' she snapped. 'Oh, I know you were nearly drowned and lost your memory, but what about that first year? There was nothing wrong with you then. You could have come home any time and made sure that your children were in good hands. So if we're casting blame, Mr Trewin, I think you should take your share.'

Sam felt his cheeks grow hot. The fact that there was some truth in what she said did not make it easier to accept, so he went into the attack. 'Good God, woman, why did you take no notice when you *finally* rang Frank and he told you the children's father had turned up? I know he did, because Major Williams introduced us before I left Liverpool and we've spoken regularly ever since. And if you'd taken the trouble to ring him a bit more often yourself I could have met you days ago and brought my children to safety much earlier. In case you've forgotten, we still don't know where Cyril is.'

Glenys stared. 'I don't know what you mean,' she said. 'Frank said nothing about their father!'

'He told me he did,' Sam said doggedly. He felt strongly that it should have been he who had brought his children to Weathercock Farm, not a jumped up schoolteacher who thought she knew it all.

But Jimmy was grinning. 'I know what happened, and when you remember what a bad line it was, it's easy to understand,' he said. He turned to Glenys. 'You thought Frank said we should go farther, right down to the coast, but I bet that wasn't what he said at all. He must have said he'd seen our father.'

Sam made a rude disbelieving noise, but his mother-in-law tutted and gave him a reproving look. 'Of course, that's the obvious answer,' she said. 'I think you should apologise to this young lady, Sam, because if it hadn't been for her that Huxtable person might well have got hold of your children, though what he intended to do if he caught them heaven only knows. Now come along, do the decent thing. There's no shame in admitting you're wrong and apologising for it.'

Sam began to say that the whole episode would have been cleared up weeks ago had the young teacher not interfered, but at this point Mr Griffiths leaned forward. 'I've not said much, young Sam, because I know you've been under a fair amount of strain,' he said. 'But remember, it was your temper and your refusal to apologise which led to us losing our only child.'

Sam took a deep breath and released it in a low

whistle, and the hot colour which had invaded his face gradually faded. He turned to Glenys. 'I'm sorry, I jumped the gun,' he said gruffly. 'You did your best by my children; did what I should have done, had I been in my right mind. The reason I didn't return sooner isn't easy to explain, particularly to anyone who didn't know Grace.' He turned to Mo. 'Sweetheart, you're the living image of your mother, so much so that when she died I found it hard to look at you. I'm sorry, my darling; I never meant to tell you that, but it was the true reason why I sent every penny of my wages home, and never came myself.'

Mo raised a hand to her wet eyes and rubbed them dry, then gave an enormous sniff, and clambered on to her father's knee. 'Nutty's mam said that I were too like Mam for comfort,' she said in a muffled voice. 'Does that mean you'll go away again, our dad? Because it ain't my fault, the way I look.'

Mrs Griffiths stood up. 'Of course your daddy won't go away again,' she said briskly, and Sam saw that her eyes were shiny with unshed tears. 'Why, there's enough work on Weathercock Farm to keep all of us occupied, and if this war they're talking about really happens, then the country will need every mouthful of food we can grow, because they won't be bringing in supplies from abroad.'

'When the war comes, which it most certainly will, those of us in the merchant fleet will be called up by the Royal Navy,' Sam observed. 'And that means, my poor little button, that I shall have to go to sea again. But I shall make sure Liverpool is my home port, and in my absence you will be well looked after by Nain and Taid.' He looked encouragingly from Mo's smiling face to Jimmy's serious one. 'What do you think of that, you two?'

'Can Auntie Glenys stay with us?' Mo asked at once. 'She's my bestest friend, so she is.'

Sam laughed, but once more he felt resentment rising up in his chest. If that woman hadn't interfered it would be he who was his daughter's 'bestest friend'. But he could scarcely say so, and certainly not in front of his in-laws. Instead he glanced towards the schoolteacher and saw her shaking her head.

'Darling Mo, I'd love to stay here with you and help on the farm; it would be fun as well as my duty. But I'm afraid I'm just the right age to be called up and posted to somewhere like the Outer Hebrides!'

Sam breathed an inward sigh of relief. He knew he was being mean and selfish, but he found himself hoping that Glenys would indeed join up and be posted far away. However, he realised it would not do to let such feelings show. 'Why not join the Wrens, then we could both go to sea,' he said jokingly.

And he was disproportionately upset when Mo said at once: 'Oh, that would never do, Daddy. If she can't stay here with us we wants her where we can visit her, doesn't we, Jimmy?'

Sam looked at his son, who had been quieter than usual, and read in his eyes more than he wanted to see. Mo was only a baby and accepted things at their face value, but Jimmy was older and looked deeper than his sister. He had read Sam's mind, and Sam realised that Jimmy would soon begin to see that the older man was jealous of his children's affection for the schoolteacher. Hastily, he tried to put things right. 'Well, Miss Trent, you're very welcome to stay with my parents-in-law, I'm sure,' he said quickly. 'But you told us yourself that when you left Liverpool with my children you were not being entirely altruistic. You were looking for your own family, and I imagine you will want to continue to pursue your search. Naturally, any help we can give . . .'

He was watching Miss Trent's face as he spoke, and saw the colour in her cheeks gradually fade until her face was perfectly white and her big blue eyes, when she turned them on him, seemed to burn. 'It's quite all right, Mr Trewin,' she said quietly. 'I won't intrude on your family now you have all managed to find one another. I shall continue my own search and need no help from anyone, and now I'd better go back to Mrs Buttermilk's house and explain that the children are staying here. I shan't set out on the next stage of my journey until tomorrow, but I think it best that we say our goodbyes now.' She had been sitting in a comfortable armchair, but got up and went over to give Mo and Jimmy a kiss. 'Cheerio, kids,' she said, and Sam realised that she had recognised his antagonism and was doing her best not to let the children see her hurt.

Feeling ashamed, he suggested that she might stay for the evening meal before returning to the town. 'I'll see you safely home afterwards,' he said, 'and then I'll bring the kids into town tomorrow to see you on your way.'

Mr Griffiths began to speak, to say that Glenys must not refuse their hospitality, but his wife hushed him. 'I'm going to prepare a meal for us all and Miss Glenys will no doubt be happy to give me a hand,' she said firmly. 'It will be bacon from the pig we killed last autumn, and our own good eggs. Children, Sam and your taid will show you round the farm whilst Miss Glenys and I prepare the meal.' She smiled kindly at Jimmy and Mo. 'Give us thirty minutes and the food will be on the table.'

Chapter 12

Mrs Griffiths shut the door firmly and turned to her guest. 'You mustn't mind my son-in-law; he obviously adores those children and is deeply ashamed that it was a total stranger – yourself – who helped them when they were in need. He hasn't been here long, but he's been a tower of strength in that time. Even though he was worried sick that harm might come to Jimmy and Maureen he did everything he could to make our life easier. What's more, he promised he would stay here and work to bring Weathercock Farm back to the condition it was in when he took our Grace away. He's no farmer, but he put his mind to learning our ways and how he could be most useful, and if he left tomorrow we would miss him sorely. Years ago he was impetuous and hot-tempered, but he's learning to control himself. Unfortunately, he may find it harder to overcome his tendency to jealousy. He has been both rude and ungrateful to you but believe me, give him a few hours to think over his behaviour and he'll be apologising and begging for forgiveness.' She went to the pantry and came back with some rashers of bacon. 'I'll deal with this whilst you lay the table; you'll find cutlery in the dresser drawer and crockery on the dresser itself.' She walked over to the window and peered out into the farmyard. 'It'll be a full moon tonight,' she remarked conversationally. 'At this time of year that usually means a hard frost. Now tell me, Miss Trent, just how do you intend to trace your family? Trent isn't a Welsh name, so there must be another reason that makes you think you might find them in Wales.'

For a moment Glenys was tempted to tell this friendly, easy-going woman just how fragile that reason would seem to be, but pride forbade such a move. Since she left the orphanage she had never told a soul, not even the children, how very alone she felt, and how pathetic would be any attempt to find the woman who had given birth to her. All the matron of the orphanage had been able to tell her was that she had been left on the housewife's doorstep in a cardboard box which had once contained apples. And what did it matter anyway, Glenys thought. But Mrs Griffiths was looking at her with raised brows. 'How do you intend to trace your family?' she repeated.

Glenys shrugged. 'I don't. I meant nothing to them, which is why I have such a strong fellow feeling for your grandchildren,' she said rather stiffly. 'But I have no wish to come between your son-in-law and his children, and because of his attitude I'm afraid that might happen if I was here long. So tomorrow I shall get on the train for Rhyl and hope that either there, or further along the coast at Llandudno, I may find employment of a sort which will suit me. Of course, if I'm only a matter of twenty or thirty miles from Weathercock Farm I should very much like to visit from time to time . . .' she gave her hostess a sudden, rather twisted smile, 'when your son-in-law is not around, that is.' She smiled again. 'I can see you are about to protest, but let there be honesty between us. You say he has a jealous nature; well, I have a certain amount of pride, and don't mean to put the children in the position of having to choose between us. Naturally they would choose him, but even so they may still retain affection for me, so it's best that we part. Don't tell them, please, but when they come down to Mrs Buttermilk's house tomorrow I shall be long gone.'

Her hostess, jiggling a pan now full of bacon rashers, began to say that this was not a good idea, that the children would grieve and their father would feel guilty, but Glenys shook her head. 'They may feel that for a little while – not Mr Trewin, but the children – but I'm certain it won't last,' she said positively. 'Remember, I've been a teacher now for several years and I know the way children's minds work. I have been their friend, but I'm also a reminder of times they would rather forget. So truly it's best that I disappear from their lives and let them throw themselves into being young farmers, which I am certain will suit them down to the ground.'

'But you said you would visit . . .' the older woman began, and then stopped as the kitchen door opened to reveal Mr Griffiths and the three Trewins.

'Come along in and sit yourselves down,' Nain said at once. 'Wash your hands, you children, and I'll start cooking, because Miss Trent wants to get back to Mrs Buttermilk's place before midnight!'

Glenys began to protest, to say that Mrs Buttermilk would no doubt give her a meal, but the older woman, though she smiled, shook her head. 'I don't want it said that a guest came to my house and left without good hot food inside them.' She twitched the curtain aside and looked out, then let it drop with an exclamation. 'It's snowing! Ah well, that settles it. Dad and Sam will get the trap out, harness the pony and drive you back to town. Now sit down, everyone.' She turned to her husband. 'I don't suppose this young lady will drink our homebrew as you and Sam do; I dare say she'd prefer a nice hot cup of tea.'

Glenys realised that to protest, to try to insist that she should leave at once, would be churlish, so she sat down at the table and was grateful when Mo took the chair on her right and Jimmy that on her left. Smiling rather stiffly, she helped herself to bread and butter.

When they had all taken their places, however, and were beginning to eat the food their hostess set before them, Glenys was glad she had stayed. The bacon was delicious, the tea hot and sweet, just as she liked it, and under the influence of the meal conversation gradually ceased to be stilted, and became easier. Sam Trewin told the story of his very first voyage as a lad of sixteen, when he had jumped into his hammock and it had promptly ejected him, to the amusement of his shipmates; and rather to her own surprise Glenys capped his story with a reminiscence of her own first day as a teacher. It was the start of the new school year and she had been teaching the infants when one of them suddenly got up from her little chair and announced she was going home because she did not like school after all. Glenys had no idea what to do. She tried to reason with the tot, but when she took a step towards her the child hurled her pencil case in her general direction and set off, at an incredibly fast pace, for home.

Mo, who had been listening round-eyed, popped a piece of bacon into her mouth and spoke rather thickly through it. 'Oh, Auntie Glenys, whatever did you do? And what a naughty little girl to throw her pencil case.'

Glenys smiled. 'She wasn't really a naughty little girl; in fact she was the daughter of the school's headmaster, but she was very spoilt. She thought she could do just as she liked, but she soon learned her mistake. When I ran out of the classroom after her all my pupils followed, and Mr Mathias saw the children streaming past his classroom windows so he came out to see what was going on. He gave a great bellow, ordering the children back to their class-room at the top of his voice, and I was just wondering whether I should tell him that it was his daughter who had started the riot when he said, "Hands up who was responsible for this behaviour?" and to my surprise his daughter, little Margaret Mathias, put her hand up at once. "It was me," she said. "I don't like school. But I did like you and my mammy said and came here, so may I go home now, please? I've been to school." Mr Mathias grinned at me and then turned back to his daughter. "School isn't just for a day," he said gently. "And in your heart, little Margaret, you know it. You've seen your sister Mary going off to school each morning in term time, and that's what you will be doing until you are a really big girl. Now go back to your classroom and don't let me hear any more nonsense about running away."'

Everyone sitting round the table laughed, though Mo said rather wistfully that she had seldom been allowed to go to school. 'The Huxtables kept Jimmy and me at home and never explained to the teacher that we weren't sagging off,' she said. 'And then there was the boots rule . . .'

Nain raised her eyebrows. 'The boots rule? What was that?' she enquired.

It was Jimmy who answered. 'No boots, no school,' he said succinctly. 'And if the teacher thought you were sagging off, or you was caught by the attendance officer during school hours, you could get the cane.'

Mo broke in. 'I asked old Ma Huxtable to tell the teacher it were her that kept Jimmy off when she sold his boots, but she just laughed. Oh, how we hated that woman, ain't that so, our Jimmy?'

Sam Trewin groaned aloud. 'If I'd only known
. . .' he began bitterly, but Glenys broke in.

'You couldn't have known, and I reckon we all
appreciate what you'd have done if you'd had the
slightest idea of how your children were being
treated,' she said. 'It was a pity that no one at the
school looked into why they were so seldom there,
but teachers are busy people and in many ways
their hands are tied.'

Sam stared at her. 'But you were their teacher;
you could have found out what was happening,'
he said through gritted teeth. 'You chose rather to
sit back and let them get on with things until they
came to your door that night . . .'

Jimmy suddenly jumped to his feet and banged
both fists down on the table. 'Are you deaf, our
dad?' he shouted. 'We've told you and told you
that Auntie Glenys saved our bacon, and though
she's a schoolteacher – or was, rather – she didn't
teach at our school but at a posh high school for
girls, and anyway we didn't meet each other until
the Christmas holidays! You'd better say sorry for
the rude things you've been saying, or Mo and me
will never speak to you again!'

There was a startled silence, but when this was
broken it was not by Sam but by Glenys. 'It's all
right, Jimmy,' she said quietly. 'Your father was not
to know how I was situated since I didn't choose
to tell him. And now, since we've all finished this
excellent supper, I really must be going.' She turned
to the Griffiths. 'Thank you so much for your

kindness and hospitality; I shall never forget you or Weathercock Farm.' She turned back to Jimmy. 'It's very kind of you to come charging to my rescue like a knight on a white horse, but it really isn't necessary. After all, your father has only got to put up with me whilst I make my farewells, and then he can forget all about me.'

Mo promptly burst into tears. 'Don't leave us, don't leave us,' she wailed. 'I know Daddy says he'll stay with us on the farm but he left us before and he'll leave us again, I know he will.' She sniffed, and added in a watery tone: 'Daddies have to go away to earn money so's they can look after their children; that's how awful things like the Huxtables come to happen. Oh, Auntie Glenys, why don't you and our daddy get married? Then you could stay with us and it wouldn't matter when Daddy went off for a job.' She sniffed again, then knuckled her eyes, leaving her face smeared with dirt. Glenys, very embarrassed, began to mumble something, but Mo grabbed her arm and rubbed her face against the older woman's shoulder. 'Please, please don't leave us! Our Jimmy and me loves you, so we do.'

Glenys looked across the table and saw the look of black jealousy on Sam's face. She sighed inwardly; what an idiot the man was! It must be obvious to everyone except him that the child was in danger of being overwhelmed by the happenings of the last few days, and was fighting to keep familiar things and people about her. But it would not last. Once she, Glenys, had gone they would miss her for a while and sometimes talk about her when they were discussing their adventures, but knowing children as she did she was confident they would soon put her to the backs of their minds. Their new school would provide them with friends and the farm itself would employ all their spare energy. Furthermore, their father would have time for them, something which he had not had before, so that the relationship between them would flourish and grow. But she realised that to put this into words was impossible, and even if it had not been, it would have caused unnecessary distress. Jimmy and Mo would insist that she was essential to their happiness, Sam would glower and keep trying to put her down, and Nain and Taid, whilst rejoicing in their grandchildren, would be embarrassed and humiliated by their son-in-law's attitude.

To ease the tension she offered to wash up, and when that was done and all the crockery and cutlery put away she touched her hostess's arm and flicked a glance towards Mo, curled up in an old basket chair, eyelids drooping. 'She's had a long day,' she murmured. 'Is there a bed made up? I appreciate that you didn't know you were going to have guests, but if we could settle her down with a pillow and some blankets in your own room so that she wouldn't wake and find herself apparently abandoned she should have her sleep out. Tomorrow things won't seem quite so daunting, and she'll accept that I'm no longer around. Can that be arranged?'

Her hostess nodded. 'Of course it can, but I think it would be best if she shared the attic room with Jimmy for the time being. She's been through more than a little'un should have to cope with these last few weeks, and she'll want to know her brother's close by. Will you wake her?'

Glenys shook her head. 'I'll carry her up; she's not heavy . . .' she was beginning, and was actually taking the child in her arms when Sam crossed the room in a couple of strides and scooped his daughter up.

'She's too heavy for you to cart all the way upstairs,' he said gruffly. He marched off, and Jimmy ran over to have a private word with Glenys.

'I do understand you want to leave now,' he said earnestly. 'But Mo and me want you to promise you'll send us your new address just as soon as you've got one. I'm sorry our dad wasn't very nice to you and I can't explain why because I don't understand it myself. Will you promise, Auntie Glenys?'

Glenys hesitated. 'It would be better if we went our separate ways, Jimmy,' she said. 'You are starting a new and exciting life, the sort of life you deserve, and so is Mo, of course. You'll be going to a new school, meeting new people, even learning a new language, and now that you've found your own family you can forget all about Cyril and his horrible old mother. They'll never learn where you are, and even if they did your grandparents would see that you were kept safe.'

'Oh, them,' Jimmy said disdainfully. 'I'm not

worrying about them! I'm pretty strong, you know, Auntie Glenys, so if they were to turn up here tomorrow I'd punch the pair of them on the nose, tie their wrists with strong rope and send for the local scuffers to throw them into prison. I could do it, honest to God I could, especially if we have lots more good meals like the one we had tonight.'

Glenys laughed. 'I'm sure you could; or you could tie their bootlaces together and push them down the stairs,' she said. 'But if it will make you happy, dear Jimmy, I'll send you my address, and that's a promise. Only it may not be for a while because I really do need to find a job of some sort just to keep myself.'

Jimmy smiled. 'I know, everyone needs money,' he said. 'But suppose you have difficulty finding work, Auntie Glenys? What will you do?'

'If I can't find work in somewhere like Rhyl or Llandudno then I suppose I shall have to go back to Liverpool,' Glenys said reluctantly. 'There's always something a qualified teacher can do . . .'

'But if you go back to Liverpool you might walk slap bang into Cyril or his mam,' Jimmy said, sounding agitated. 'He's a brute and a bully; if he thought you could tell him where we were he'd not hesitate, and it would be you lying in hospital instead of our dad.'

But Glenys was easily able to refute this suggestion. 'Neither of the Huxtables has ever laid eyes on me,' she reminded him. 'And nor I on them for that matter, so you needn't worry, Jimmy. For one thing I can't see myself returning to Liverpool, and in the unlikely event of them finding out I'd been with you and turning up on my doorstep I would go straight to the police.'

At this point Sam re-entered the kitchen, and actually smiled at Glenys. 'She didn't even wake when I popped her into bed,' he said softly. 'She looked so pretty and sweet cuddling her cheek into the pillow that I would have given her a kiss, only I didn't want to rouse her.' His expression changed. 'Are you ready for the off, Miss Trent?' he asked briskly. 'Because if I'm to get the trap out and catch the pony . . .'

Glenys spoke up at once. 'You are not going to get the trap out, thank you very much,' she said firmly. 'I walked here with the children and I shall walk back without them, but I won't bother you or Mr Griffiths. I shall enjoy the walk, especially now that the snow has stopped and the moon is at the full. It will be a positive pleasure to see the countryside by moonlight.'

To do him justice, Sam looked horrified. 'You can't possibly walk all that way alone,' he said. 'And don't suggest that Jimmy should accompany you, because the poor kid is asleep on his feet.'

Glenys bit back a sharp retort. 'I know he's tired and I wouldn't dream of taking him all that way,' she said. 'I'm not a nervous person, Mr Trewin, so I have no qualms about a moonlight walk. In fact I shall enjoy it.' As she spoke she crossed the kitchen and took her coat off the hook by the door whilst

Sam, thoroughly discomposed, for it was clear she had no desire for his company, was protesting that he would willingly help Taid to fetch out the trap and catch the pony. 'Because it's snowing hard, Miss Trent,' he protested.

Glenys interrupted. 'I understand your concern, but did you not hear what I said? There's a full moon, no clouds and a clear frosty sky. The clear frosty sky means that the snow has stopped, and the full moon means that it's as light as day outside, so I can enjoy my walk without fear of tripping over an unseen branch or falling face down in a puddle.'

Sam actually laughed. 'Well done; you are more of a country woman than I knew,' he said approvingly. 'But though I may be only a seaman, I trust I am still a gentleman, and a gentleman does not let a young woman go off on a long walk alone. Suppose the Evanses' old bull should take fright at seeing a stranger walking along the lane and decide to challenge you? Suppose a badger comes out of his sett and scares the life out of you? Suppose clouds race across the moon and the snow starts again? My dear Miss Trent, a thousand and one things could make your walk more perilous than pleasurable. Don't deny me the satisfaction of seeing my children's saviour safely back to her lodgings.'

It was said lightly, but Glenys knew an olive branch when she saw one, and she realised she would have to accept his offered companionship, though it went against the grain to do so after he had been so rude. Across the lamplit kitchen the old couple were listening intently, and she knew they were hoping she would not deny Sam the chance to make amends. Accordingly, she smiled at them and then began to push her arms into her coat and do up the buttons. 'Thank you, Mr Trewin. I had not thought of any such obstacles to a simple country walk, and I shall be glad of your company.'

Sam shrugged himself into his duffel coat, pushed his feet into his boots and held open the door for her to pass into the yard. Then he turned to his in-laws. 'The snow may have stopped but there are a couple of inches on the ground still, so it's as well I'm accompanying our friend here,' he said. 'When snow lies on ice like that, one wrong step can mean a broken ankle, so you may be sure I shall be careful.'

'That's a good fellow,' his mother-in-law said approvingly. 'We've got enough on our hands without having to nurse an invalid. If I were you I'd link arms; that way you can hold one another up.'

'That way we can pull one another down,' Glenys said humorously, making no attempt to take the arm Sam was offering. 'Goodbye, Mr and Mrs Griffiths, and thank you so much. I promised Jimmy I'll keep in touch but I doubt I'll be able to visit. However, it's been a pleasure knowing you. Now, Mr Trewin, off we go!'

They crossed the yard cautiously, Glenys uneasily aware how extremely slippery snow on ice is, and Sam swung the big dilapidated gate open. He ushered her through, then took her hand in a firm grip, saying as he did so: 'Better safe than sorry, Miss Trent. This is treacherous weather and I imagine quite treacherous country when the snow hides the pitfalls one could easily avoid in fine weather. Now, why don't you tell me a bit about yourself.'

Glenys raised her eyebrows and looked up at the dark face above her own. He wasn't exactly handsome, but despite the way he had treated her she thought him an attractive man. He might look grim, but when he smiled his whole face changed, and not only could she see a likeness to Jimmy, but there was a gentleness in the way he smiled down at her which gave the lie to his previous behaviour. Mrs Weather had been right; it was shame over the way he had neglected his children which had made him behave so unpleasantly towards her. 'There's nothing much to tell,' she admitted. 'Why don't you tell me about your life? It has to be more exciting than mine because you've travelled. You've seen New York, Mexico – even the place where you were attacked – Malvonia, wasn't it? As well as Ireland, Portsmouth, Norway . . . oh, a heap of different places, all of which I should love to visit one day.'

'Yes, I've seen a great deal of the world, more even than I've told my children about,' Sam admitted. 'But if you want the truth, Miss Trent, a seaman sees very little of the countries he visits, as a general rule. You see, one pulls into a harbour, the dockers swarm aboard to unload your cargo, you may have a meal in a quayside restaurant or a few drinks in a pub, and then you're off again. But you have led a very different life. In short, Miss Trent, you are an enigma and one which intrigues me. Are you hiding some dark secret? But there is an honesty and openness in your face which makes me think not.'

Surprise tricked Glenys into answering more frankly than she intended. 'I'm a foundling, so I have no knowledge of my relations,' she said. 'When I was found on someone's doorstep and taken to the orphanage there was a note in Welsh pinned to my shawl and when I went to college a friend translated it for me, and then and there I decided that one day I would travel to Wales and see the country for myself.'

Sam's eyebrows shot up. 'I'd never have guessed it; you seem far too intelligent for the product of an orphanage,' he said, thereby putting Glenys's back up, for she resented any criticism of the home which had taken her in.

However, she spoke calmly. 'Well, the orphanage saw me through college and supported me until I got my first job. Then, when I met Jimmy and Mo and we talked over what would be best to do, I told them that I, too, wanted to trace my Welsh relatives so that the children should not feel that I was only coming here for their sake.'

'That was very good of you,' he said. 'You must know that unless you have a name, the chances of your tracing anyone who by now must be in her mid-forties at least are pretty slight. Obviously nobody tried to claim you, so for all you know she might have moved far from Wales, or even out of Great Britain altogether. So where will you go when you leave this area, Miss Trent?'

Glenys shrugged. 'I don't mind where I go so long as I can find a teaching post which will pay me enough to keep body and soul together,' she admitted. She looked up at him again, this time with a twinkling smile. 'So don't be afraid that I shall hang around here or make any claims on Mr and Mrs Weather or on you. If I can't find work in Rhyl, or perhaps Llandudno, I suppose I shall have to try Liverpool or London. I'm very independent, you see.'

Sam squeezed her hand. 'I'm certainly not *afraid* that you'll stay in the area – the children would be delighted – but suppose I could find you a job? Or perhaps it would be better to say that I would like you to consider living at Weathercock Farm until you find something more to your taste. 'I don't like to think of you trudging round the countryside searching for work, when you've saved my children's lives . . . no, don't deny it. But for you they might have fallen into the wrong hands and believe me, I'm grateful.' He squeezed her hand again. 'You did what I should have done and because I'm ashamed of my behaviour I've been very rude to you. But all that's over, so can we call friends?'

Glenys was only too glad to agree and was surprised when Sam pulled her to a halt in order to shake her hand. 'Pax!' he said. 'And now I shall tell you how I knew you were on your way to Weathercock Farm? It's a pretty complicated story so listen hard.'

Glenys giggled. 'It can't be as complicated as ours,' she assured him. 'There was scarcely anyone in Liverpool who didn't either help or hinder us. Carry on, then!'

'Well, when Harry Theaker told me he'd left the children at the Salvation Hall, I went straight there and spoke to Major Williams, who seems to have been especially kind to Mo. He told me that the children had made friends with another Salvationist, Frank Bloggs, and took me to meet him that very evening. Frank, of course, knew all about you setting off for Wales with the children, and said you were going to let him know how you were getting on, so I stayed in Liverpool for a couple more days to see if there would be any news. But you didn't ring, so I decided to swallow my pride and come down to see whether I couldn't make my peace with Grace's parents and wait for you here.'

'And of course, being the lovely couple they are, they welcomed you with open arms,' Glenys said, smiling.

'Well, not quite that, but I think they are starting to forgive me,' Sam said. 'And then you rang Frank, so he contacted me and told me you were going to Deniol, but he'd looked at the timetable and was pretty sure I'd be able to meet you at Llanerch – the puppy station! – but of course we didn't know about the two-hour delay. I'd almost given up when

I saw Mo . . . and the rest you know. I returned to Weathercock Farm to wait, because I was certain, now, that you would turn up there.'

Glenys had begun to say that he had been proved right when he gave an exclamation. 'How far would you say we've walked? Only it's been some while since I saw the moon, and those dark racing clouds look pretty sinister. Surely we should have reached the outskirts of Ruthin by now?'

Glenys looked round her, but before she could reply the wind snatched the words from her lips and it began to snow in earnest. In two minutes what had been a calm night was calm no longer. A vicious wind whipped the surface of the snow and before either of them could remark upon it, they found themselves in the heart of a blizzard. Snow was coming at them horizontally and within moments they both looked like snowmen, and the intense cold made Glenys accept without question the arm Sam slung around her waist. 'Hang on to me,' he shouted, for the noise of the storm was so great that even the strongest voice had to be raised. 'Did you recognise where we were before the blizzard struck?'

Glenys shook her head and ice trickled down the back of her mackintosh collar, causing her to shrink even closer to Sam. 'How could I possibly know where we are when I don't know the country at all?' she shouted. 'Oh, Sam, this is horrible. Is that a house on our left, or just a thicket?'

Sam swung her round until they both faced the

direction she had indicated. 'It's just a thicket,' he said, speaking directly into her ear. 'The fact is, Miss Trent, that I haven't been here long enough to be sure of my way even in good weather. But if we keep walking along this track we're bound to come to a labourer's cottage or somewhere similar where we can seek shelter.'

'But which way shall we go? Can't we go back to Weathercock Farm? If we're walking towards Ruthin surely we should have come across some sort of dwellings by now.'

Sam sighed. 'I think you're right. I wonder how long it is since we set out? We seem to have been walking for hours. I think we might try turning right here.' They fought the blizzard to make the turn, which at least meant that the wind was coming at the back of them, but after ten minutes Sam pulled her to a halt. 'We've gone wrong somewhere,' he shouted. 'Let's go in the opposite direction and see how we get on.'

Glenys gave an exclamation. 'I think I see a cottage a couple of hundred yards ahead on our left,' she said. 'Whoever lives in it is bound to offer us shelter on a night like this.'

Halfway to the cottage she began to wonder if they would ever arrive, for the wind was in their faces now and despite trying hard to be brave she couldn't help a little moan escaping her lips. Sam stopped immediately. 'Are you all right, queen?' he asked anxiously. 'If you can't go on I'll carry you over the last few yards.'

Glenys wiped the snow off her face and glared up at him, though she knew he could not see her, what with the dark and the snow. 'You will do nothing of the sort!' she shouted. 'Don't make me an excuse to linger; best foot forward, Seaman Trewin!'

She heard him give a muffled snort of laughter and then they were in the shelter of the cottage and making their way around to the porch, which they could just make out through the whirling flakes. There was no light coming from any of the windows, but Sam beat a tattoo on the wooden front door and did not seem particularly surprised when it gave under his onslaught. With a grunt of satisfaction he pushed it wide and bundled his companion into the darkness inside. Then he produced a small torch from his pocket and swung it round to illuminate their haven. 'It's abandoned; there are a good few cottages like this now that farming has almost ceased to pay dividends,' he said. 'It's lucky for us it still has a roof and four walls to protect us from the weather.' He pushed open a door on his right, then backed out hastily. 'Sheep dung,' he said succinctly. 'Give that other door a push, would you? I reckon it'll be the kitchen – or was, rather.'

He was right, for as soon as they entered the room with its low sink and earth floor Glenys saw that this had indeed been the cottage kitchen, and by the look of things was now being used for general storage. There were piles of old newspapers and sacks as well a mound of dusty hay, and though outside the storm raged on more fiercely than ever she realised that she felt almost comfortable. She went over to the low sink, suddenly aware that she was very thirsty, but there was no tap or pump so she turned away with a disappointed sigh and looked towards Sam, who was spreading newspapers on the floor and covering them with piles of hay. The glassless window was small and at knee height, but when she commented that this seemed strange Sam shook his head. 'Not strange, convenient,' he said firmly. 'We don't want a view; we want to keep the weather out. There're cardboard boxes stacked up over there which will fill the gap quite nicely, and this . . .' he indicated the result of his labours, 'will make a very good bed for two, because if you ask me this weather is going to last for the rest of the night and I've no intention of venturing out into it whilst we can stay in this convenient shelter. I've put newspapers down for a mattress because tramps always tell you newspapers make excellent bedding. Take off that soaking wet coat, that thing you've got on your head and your boots, and we'll snuggle up in the hay like a couple of little dormice and won't poke so much as our noses outside until we can see where we are.'

Staying out of the blizzard seemed sensible enough, but Glenys was quite determined not to share a bed with him even if it was made out of newspapers and hay. She took off her short boots and then hung her coat and sopping headscarf over the window, which made Sam Trewin give a crack of laughter and tell her she would make Robinson Crusoe proud. 'Thanks, but I'll be quite happy curling up on what's left of the hay,' she said, turning towards him. Then she gasped. 'Oh! Are you – are you *very* wet? Only my dress isn't too bad at all, and I certainly don't intend to take it off.'

'My trousers are soaking,' Sam said equably. 'And very likely your dress is in the same state. Look, you silly girl, no one is likely to walk in on us, and tomorrow we'll have a long walk ahead of us, because I'm pretty sure we took more than one wrong turning and have ended up a long way from Ruthin or Weathercock Farm. We both need a good sleep, so stop being ridiculous! Do you imagine that I'm going to ravish you?' He was laughing, but the look he gave her was friendly and not mocking. 'I promise you I'll stick to my own side of the bed, trousers or no trousers. Will that satisfy you?' As he spoke he was hanging his own clothing across the window. Then he snapped the torch off, plunging them into almost complete darkness, and the next thing Glenys knew she was being lifted up and dumped unceremoniously in the makeshift bed, with Sam's broad chest against her back and his warm arms about her.

She began to protest, to say that people would talk, but Sam Trewin just chuckled. 'Shut up and go to sleep. I promise I'll take the greatest care of you and not do anything to frighten or upset you,' he said, and now his voice was serious. 'Goodnight,

Glenys. Remember, you saved my children, so I could never harm a hair on your head.'

Glenys gave one last despairing wriggle and managed to put several inches between her back and Sam Trewin's chest, but the cold draught which whistled into the gap was so unpleasant that she hastily returned to her former position. Sam chuckled. 'Good girl. We have to share our warmth or we'll end up frozen solid,' he said. 'It's not as if there's a soul for miles around who could offer us any better shelter. Just relax; morning will come soon enough.'

'Yes, I suppose you're right,' Glenys said dreamily. 'Goodnight, Sam . . . oh!' Her neat, schoolmistressy bun of hair had come loose as soon as she removed her headscarf, and now she felt Sam's hand smoothing it away from the back of her neck.

'Why oh?' he asked.

'Because – because you called me Glenys and I called you Sam, and I was determined to stick to Mr Trewin,' Glenys said after a pause. 'Oh, Sam, I'm *so* sleepy!'

And Glenys Trent, schoolmistress, was fast asleep.

Glenys awoke. It was still dark and for a moment she wondered where she was. Then she remembered vaguely that yesterday she and someone else – she could not remember who – had been fighting their way through a blizzard. She had been so cold! But then she and her companion must have reached both shelter and safety, and now she felt warm as

222

toast and happier than she had felt for many a long day.

It was tempting to put the blizzard out of her mind and let herself sleep once more; after all, it could not be very late, for there was no sign of stirring from the house around her. But which house was it? Was it the house with eight steps owned by the woman with the funny name, or was it the farm that she and the children had found at the very end of a long and tiring search?

Glenys sighed. She was too tired to struggle out of bed just to find out which house she was in. She was sliding down a pleasant hill into sleep once more when somebody, somebody close to her, gave a tremendous yawn. At the same moment she realised she was not alone in what she had believed, only seconds earlier, to be a large and comfortable bed. She frowned in an effort to remember just where she was. She knew Mo was quite capable of climbing into bed with her, had done so several times, but the yawn had not sounded as though it came from a little girl. Suddenly she realised that the arms which were holding her did not belong to a little girl either. Shock, like a bucket of cold water, washed over her and she struggled upright as memory flooded back. She had been trying to get back to Mrs Buttermilk's tall house in Ruthin, and Sam Trewin had insisted on escorting her. Now she remembered. Within perhaps thirty minutes of leaving Weathercock Farm the blizzard had caught them unawares, and they had lost their way. Unable to see the weathercock on the old barn which had guided Glenys and the children straight to the farm on the previous day, they had tried one direction and then another and had finally sought shelter in an abandoned cottage.

Glenys tried to pull herself out of the bed, which meant freeing herself from the confining arms which held her. What on earth had possessed her? She remembered telling Sam that she would sleep on what little hay was left after his bed-making activities; what had changed her mind? She was a well brought up young woman and should have known better than to share any bed, whatever the circumstances, with a man. So now she twisted in Sam's embrace, wrenched herself out of his arms and woke him by the simple expedient of punching him in the chest and then tugging at his thick mop of curling black hair, hissing as she did so: 'Wake up, Sam Trewin. How dare you make me sleep in the same bed as you, even if it is made out of hay and newspapers?'

'And sacks, and a couple of cardboard boxes,' Sam said dreamily. 'But it's better to be warm together than cold apart.'

Glenys sniffed and scrambled to her feet, shivering as the cold air struck her and horrified to find that she was only wearing her white cotton petticoat. 'Did you . . .' she began indignantly, but then she remembered removing her soaked dress and, with chattering teeth, hanging it beside her equally soaking coat. Trembling with the cold, she crossed to the window and took it down. It was not dry but it was no longer sodden, only damp, and she began to struggle into it, turning to where Sam, without any of the embarrassment she felt, was stepping into his stout denim trousers and pulling on his thick navy blue jersey over his blue shirt and what she blushingly supposed to be his underwear.

'Everyone will know we spent the night together,' she said, her voice shaking a little. 'I don't suppose you'd like to invent some story which will save my reputation?'

Sam laughed. 'We'll pile up the newspapers in a corner and spread the hay out all over the floor and say we staggered in here at the height of the blizzard, lay down on the hay and slept until it grew light. Will that satisfy you?' He smiled at her and she read understanding and a little amusement in his face. 'My dear Glenys, you really mustn't be so prudish. Of course it would have been a good deal nicer had we discovered two beautiful beds with blankets and pillows and a pair of pyjamas for myself and a night-dress for you, but things like that only happen in fairy stories.' He looked her up and down with a critical eye. 'No one would dream that you'd not spent the night in your dress, nor I in my denims and jersey, so stop worrying that your reputation is ruined, because it's nonsense.' He walked over to the window, no longer hidden by their clothing, and bent down to peer out. He stared around him for a moment then straightened up once more. 'I can't recognise anything, I'm afraid; snow changes a landscape completely. But presently I'll climb the nearest hill and no doubt see some landmark I recognise.' He turned to smile at his companion. 'I'm sure you've read *The Wind In The Willows* by Kenneth Grahame. Do you remember the bit where Mole goes off by himself into the Wild Wood? He curls up inside a hollow tree because he's afraid of the Faces, and in the night it snows . . .'

'. . . and it completely changes the look of everything,' Glenys finished for him.

Somehow the simple fact that they both knew the children's classic made it easier to laugh with him when he said, longingly: 'And after that they found Badger's front door and sat down to an excellent supper in his kitchen, and next morning there was oatmeal porridge and buttered toast for breakfast. What a pity we aren't Mole and Rat, for I fear we'll have to do without any breakfast at all today.'

As they talked Glenys had been following his suggestion that they should dismantle the bed so that the cottage would look as it had done on the previous day, though judging from the look of the place no one had been here for many weeks. Now she dusted her hands and stood back. 'My mouth waters even at the thought of a cold drink,' she admitted. 'Aren't you thirsty, Sam? My mouth is so dry it's like a desert. In fact as soon as I've got my boots back on I shall go outside and eat some snow.'

Sam, shrugging himself into his duffel coat, nodded agreement. 'There'd have been a well within a few yards of the back door,' he observed. He caught her arm and pulled her over to the window. 'See that mound? That, I'm sure, will be all that's left of the well, and the mound next to it will be the shed where the good man who once lived in this cottage kept his tools.'

'I see,' Glenys said. She looked shyly up at the man beside her. 'Or perhaps it was the privy.'

Sam looked down at her, a grin hovering. 'I doubt that there ever was one; such niceties do not always extend to a solitary cottage,' he said. 'I'm afraid you'll have to do as the cottagers once did; see the other mound, the much shorter one? I reckon that's the muck heap. If you go round the far side of it you'll be out of sight – not that I'd dream of peeping, mind you.'

Glenys glared. 'I should hope not,' she said tartly. 'And as soon as I've – I've taken advantage of the facilities I think I should come with you to the hill. Then, if there are still no landmarks, we can simply keep walking until we see something that we do recognise.'

Sam agreed with this infinitely sensible plan, and as soon as Glenys was ready they set off, closing the cottage door behind them. 'Because if anyone else is benighted and lost in a blizzard I wouldn't like to think we had ruined the only shelter for miles,' he said. Turning to take one last look at the cottage, Glenys realised for the first time that others had come this way in the night, for she saw a great many slotted footprints where sheep had taken advantage of whatever shelter the broken-down walls of the cottage afforded, and some human footprints, too.

'It's a good thing we were still sleeping when the shepherd came for his flock,' Glenys remarked as they pushed their way through the thick snow towards where they hoped the road would be. 'What an adventure we shall have to tell Jimmy and Mo when we see them! Only I expect they will say that we should have made ourselves some sort of shelter in that thicket,' she added, pointing.

'Yes, and that we should have snared a rabbit or fished a trout out of the nearest stream,' Sam agreed. He grinned down at her. 'I shall put all the blame on you and say that you were too finicky to start building a cabin of willow wands. Not that there are any willows around. Oh, look.' They had reached the top of a small hillock, and saw below them a forest of closely packed trees which stretched for some considerable distance.

'We've reached the Wild Wood, and beyond the Wild Wood is the wide world,' Glenys said, and just as she said it the clouds parted and the sun gleamed gold on the snow-laden branches, turning the scene into a thing of beauty.

'Isn't that something?' Sam said softly. 'And of course that must be the forest you can see from the back bedroom window in Weathercock Farm. It used to be Grace's room, but she moved out whenever I was staying with the family because, bless her, she was always generous and thought her room a good deal nicer than the little one in the attic into which I would have had to squeeze my six foot two.'

'That's the room Jimmy will be having once Nain has got things sorted out,' Glenys said. 'She sounded as though she really wanted the children to live on the farm. I do like your mother-in-law, Sam.'

Sam nodded. They had been standing side by side staring out across the glittering scene, but now he put an arm round her waist and turned her towards a tiny point of golden light which the sun had just illumined. 'See that? It's the weathercock on the big barn. We're lucky that it's a clear day, because it must be all of five miles away, but now we know which way to walk we'll be there in no time.'

'It's all very well for you, with your great long legs; it will take me a good deal longer than "no time" to walk five miles,' Glenys said apologetically. 'However, when I think of last night's delicious smell of frying bacon I do believe I might actually run to keep up with your long strides. And there'll be a kettle jumping on the hob, and a jug of creamy milk from the dairy . . .'

'Shut up,' Sam said laughingly. 'I'm sure we needn't waste time eating snow, because I believe it doesn't quench your thirst, so we'll put all our energy into walking, if you please. You'll find it easier going if we link arms.' He looked down at her, the smile lurking once more. 'Having spent the night together, linking arms seems pretty tame.'

They set off, Glenys remarking that she hoped

he would keep the way they had spent the night to himself, but presently she had other things to think about, for the snow was more than a foot deep and hid all sorts of obstacles for the unwary. One moment her boot sank into soft snow and the next she was banging her toes on a hidden rock. But they kept their eyes fixed on the weathercock, and sooner than she would have believed possible they saw the sunken lane which they knew led directly to the farm.

'It's just occurred to me to wonder whether there were search parties out looking for us last night,' Sam said suddenly. 'Mrs Buttermilk will have expected you and the children to arrive on her doorstep and my in-laws must have assumed that I would leave you at your lodgings and then return to the farm. Goodness, I hope to God they didn't alert the police, or the neighbours, otherwise we shall be unpopular.'

'And there will be talk,' Glenys said resignedly. 'Oh dear, and talk is what I most want to avoid. Not that it will really matter, come to think, because I'll be on my way as soon as the snow clears.'

Sam was beginning to answer when she checked him, a hand on his arm. 'Listen!' she commanded. 'It's the children!' And sure enough, rounding the next bend and tearing towards them, well muffled up in coats and scarves, came Jimmy and Mo.

'Where have you been?' Mo shrieked as she panted up to them. 'I went into your room, Dad, as soon as I woked up this morning and you weren't there. But I didn't cry, and I went back up to our room and shook Jimmy and he said you'd have stayed with Mrs Buttermilk, else you'd have got lost, 'cos there were a great blizzard, you know, and Nain said you don't know the country well enough to walk around when it's under snow. She said only a idiot would have come home in them conditions.'

'Very true, my bright little button,' her father said, winking at Glenys. 'But we're starving hungry, 'cos we got lost in the Wild Wood on our way back, so we've had no breakfast. You know the book Miss Glenys has been reading to you?'

'Yes, I remember it,' Mo said. 'It snows in the Wild Wood . . .'

Jimmy, who had stopped to examine a deserted bird's nest in a thicket, came galloping up and interrupted his sister. 'I 'spect Mrs Buttermilk gave you both breakfast,' he said, 'but our Nain says you'll be hungry all over again after your long walk, so she told us to run ahead of you and she'll start cooking at once.'

'Well, you won't arrive at the farm much before we do, because your nain was right, and we're hungry as hunters,' Sam said. 'We've also got pretty wet, and as soon as we reach the farm we shall want to borrow a couple of dressing gowns and dry our clothes out before the kitchen fire, so you two run ahead and tell Nain we're not far behind you.'

When Sam and Glenys, closely following the two children, burst into the kitchen at Weathercock

Farm, they received a grand welcome. 'We realised you must have taken shelter during that blizzard, for how on earth you managed to reach Mrs Buttermilk's we could not imagine,' Nain said. 'As soon as it was light Taid fought his way to the Evans farm to telephone her from there, only the lines were down so he got no response. We were just talking over what best to do when the children came panting in to say you were on their heels.' She turned to Glenys. 'I take it Mrs Buttermilk gave Sam a bed for the night?'

Glenys began to speak, but Sam overruled her. 'We got hopelessly lost, to tell you the truth,' he said frankly, 'so we took shelter in a cottage. I couldn't tell you where it was save that it was sheep country. I hope Mrs Buttermilk wasn't worried; with any luck she will assume that Glenys and the children found their relatives and stayed with them, but when the telephone wires are restored I'll ring her from the Evanses' to set her mind at rest. I'll ring Frank, too, and let him know their story has had a happy ending!'

'There we are then; everything settled,' Nain said placidly. She looked at her dressing gown-clad guests. 'Sit yourselves down; you must be starving indeed. And Taid and I have a suggestion to make.' She turned to Glenys. 'I know you're a school-teacher and I know you want a proper job, but whilst this dreadful weather lasts you have little option but to remain with us and I can tell you we need all the help we can get.' She smiled at her husband, already seated at the table and about to address a large plate of bacon and eggs. 'Considering our age we think we've managed quite well. We've always kept pigs, half a dozen milch cows and a pedigree Hereford bull at stud. What we have chiefly lacked is workers to milk, to feed, to doctor when necessary and do a thousand and one others things. If we'd had more ready cash we could have employed a labourer or two, but as it was we dared not spend the money because we needed it for foodstuffs for the animals, as well as ourselves. So you see, if you are prepared to work alongside Taid and me you'll be more than paying for your keep.' She slid a plate of bacon, eggs and fried bread down in front of Glenys and another in front of Sam. 'Is that fair?'

'It's more than fair, it's extremely generous,' Glenys said, picking up her knife and fork. 'But you must remember I'm a totally unskilled worker so far as farming is concerned. You might find that I was more of a nuisance than a help.'

Nain shook her head. 'That's not important. Taid and I can manage the milking, but carting fodder into the fields, carrying the swill across to the pigsties, searching out the hens if they get lost in the snow and don't return to the henhouse are all jobs which you and the children should be able to tackle. Winters are always hard, so we keep a stock of food in, but money being so tight means that it's largely what you might call staples: flour, lard, sugar and so on – enough to keep Taid and me

233

until the weather breaks. But this year we shall be providing for four extra, so there will be trips into Ruthin to be made, too many for an old couple like Taid and myself to tackle even after the snow melts. So if you and Sam were willing to stay on, why, you'd be doubly welcome. Will you consider it, my dear?'

The children had joined them at the table and were eating slices of homemade bread spread with homemade jam, and now Jimmy smiled at Glenys. 'You ain't the only one who'll be learning, Auntie Glenys,' he told her. 'We ain't going to be super-cargo, we're going to be real good helpers, ain't we, little sister?'

Mo turned towards Glenys, and spoke through a mouthful of bread and jam. 'That's right, Auntie Glenys, we's going to be workers same as you and our dad,' she said. 'Supercargo is what they call someone who pays to travel on a working ship; ain't that right, our dad?'

'That's right, button,' Sam said, spearing a piece of bacon and winking at Jimmy. 'But we'll start working our passage the moment I finish this grand breakfast, by beginning to clear the yard.'

Chapter 13

Although Glenys had assured her host and hostess that she would be quite happy to remain on the farm as a worker until the weather cleared, she was secretly worried that Sam's first antagonism would rear its ugly head once more now that they were constantly with the children. Jimmy clung to his father, wanting to show him that all had been forgiven and forgotten, but Mo, Glenys thought, was still a little wary of a man she could scarcely remember. She tended to attach herself to Glenys, and though Glenys did her best to encourage the child to get to know her father it was uphill work. Mo chatted away to Nain and Taid and to Glenys herself, but she was still shy with Sam. At first, Glenys had thought that Sam might think she was deliberately encouraging Mo to work with her rather than with him, but Sam showed no signs of the jealousy which had upset her when she had first met him. And then one day, when she and Mo were in the kitchen baking scones whilst the men carried bales of hay out to the cows in the high pasture, she discovered at least one reason for Mo's attitude to her father. Until now Glenys had avoided the subject, but that morning, after they had been snowed in for the best part of two weeks, Taid had sniffed the air and said there was a thaw coming. 'Shan't be shut in much longer,' he said cheerfully. He turned to Mo. 'You and Jimmy will be able to start school by the end of the week. See if I'm not right.'

Mo's obvious pleasure at the prospect of spending large parts of each day away from the farm prompted Glenys to try to find out why the child seemed so ill at ease in her father's company. When they had finished cutting out a tray of scones and slid them into the oven to bake, Glenys asked the question on her mind. 'Mo, my love, has your dad said anything to upset you?'

Mo had been making a little figure out of the remains of the scone mixture, but now she looked up and shook her head, then dropped her eyes to her work once more. 'Don't know what you mean,' she said. 'This here scone boy what I'm making is for Jimmy. If there's enough pastry over I'll make one for Taid; I'll make one for Daddy too if you like, so long as he doesn't try to kiss me.' She shuddered expressively. 'I don't like beardy kisses; they scratch.'

Glenys laughed. 'I've always thought your father's beard looks very soft, but soft or bristly you can't be frightened of a beard. I mean, it's like saying you're frightened of a finger, or a toe.' She laughed and Mo laughed with her but, Glenys thought, a trifle uneasily.

'I'm not frightened of anything,' Mo said defiantly.

'It's just that horrible Cyril has a beard and – and sometimes when my daddy's worried or cross he looks a bit like Cyril.'

'Oh, I *see*,' Glenys said, vastly relieved. So that was why Mo avoided her father's company! But she would have to talk seriously to the child, because although he had said nothing on the subject she knew Sam was both hurt and puzzled by his daughter's attitude. Glenys remembered that in the early days of their acquaintance she herself had tended to treat him with kid gloves: he was so big, so dark and, she supposed, so frightening to a small child, though she herself now knew him for what he was: a gentle giant. Indeed, she realised that when the snow cleared and the time came for her to leave it would be Sam that she missed the most. He had been everything that was good and kind to her, showing her how to carry out every task she undertook in a way which saved her strength. She had stood by and watched him learning to milk the cows and he had been delighted when she proved to be a better milker than he was, congratulating her and saying, with a twinkle, that she would make some lucky farmer an excellent wife.

So now, in the warm kitchen, Glenys considered how best to tackle Mo's lingering fear of her father. It was no use saying that Sam was nothing like the hateful Cyril Huxtable, because irrational fears can rarely be talked away. Instead, Glenys probed a little deeper. 'But Mo darling, Cyril Huxtable is far away and you're very unlikely to meet him again. It's very hurtful to your daddy when you turn your face away when he gives you a goodnight kiss, or . . .' her eyes settled on the manikins the child was making, 'or when you make everyone else a scone boy and don't make one for Daddy. What's the reason, sweetheart? It can't just be because Daddy and Cyril both have beards.'

Mo heaved a deep sigh and began to put her family of little men on to the baking tray which Glenys had greased for her. 'The night you and Daddy were lost in the snowstorm I had a terrible dream,' she said reluctantly. 'I dreamed that Daddy had strangled you and he carried you back and threw you down on the kitchen floor. He said you had kidnapped his children and he hated you, only then you weren't dead and you sat up and your face was all purple and horrible and when you started to scream I looked at Daddy and he was laughing. I could see big black teeth in his black beard, and he said he would eat you up, and then I realised it wasn't my daddy at all but horrible Cyril. And then I woked up and started to wail, so Jimmy woke too and I got in his bed and he cuddled me until I fell asleep.'

'Oh, you poor baby; what an absolutely horrid dream,' Glenys said, very distressed. 'Did you tell Jimmy about it? Sometimes it's better not to try to keep frightening things to yourself. But I promise you, your daddy wouldn't hurt anyone, least of all you or Jimmy. He's a very kind and gentle man, and he loves you very much.'

238

Mo looked doubtful. 'He was horrid to you when you first met,' she pointed out, and then added with the shrewdness of one a good deal older than six, 'He's nice to everyone now, but I can't help remembering that awful dream.'

Glenys began to clean down the table so that she and Mo might lay it ready for the next meal. She was thinking hard. If Mo told Sam about the dream he would do his best to reassure her, but being only human he might be upset by the fact that she had seen him as a bad person, the enemy rather than the hero. She could not leave things as they stood at present, she must do her utmost to put things right, but how? She knew that Sam's original jealousy of her had disappeared and they were now good friends, and she did not want to spoil the relationship by mishandling such a sensitive subject. She was still pondering over what best to do when there was a knock on the back door and it was flung open to reveal a scruffy man in working clothes. He gave her a broad grin. 'All right if I come in, missus?' he asked. ''Tis mortal cold out here and Master said I were to tell you to put the kettle on.'

There was no need for Glenys to assure the stranger that he might come in out of the cold, for he was already inside, slamming the door and making his way determinedly towards the kitchen table, a hand already reaching for the scones.

'Hang on a minute; don't touch the baking until you've washed your hands,' Glenys said quickly.

'I'll pump you some water and then you can tell me who you are. I can see you're a farm worker . . .' Inside her head she was thinking *and I can smell you're one, too.*

Mo looked up from her task of laying out the cutlery. 'He's Pete the Sheep,' she informed Glenys. 'He's a shepherd and he works for the Evanses 'cos they've got a whole load of sheep, but Taid employs him for the odd couple of days when he needs an extra pair of hands.' She turned from Glenys to the stranger. 'What do you want?' she said baldly. 'I thought Taid said you needn't come to us until the snow was completely cleared away and spring was coming through.'

The little man gave her a malevolent look. He was small and almost square with eyes like dull pebbles set in folds of flesh and a loose-lipped mouth. He was filthy dirty and looked as though he had not seen water or soap for several weeks, and when Glenys drew another tray of scones from the oven he snatched one without so much as a by your leave and crammed it into his mouth. Then he sat himself down at the table and grinned at her, revealing that he only had one tooth.

'Any more of them little scones in the oven?' he asked hopefully. 'I could do with another one to go with a cup of tea I see you're a-makin'. And I'll be bound you've butter in the larder; I does like butter on a scone.'

Glenys sighed, but already she had learned that country folk seldom refused food to anyone, so she took one of the scones off the cooling tray, split it and spread it with the butter she had placed ready on the dresser behind her. The little man crammed the buttered scone into his mouth. 'Master'll be comin' along in a few minutes with your young man, missy,' he said thickly. 'Them scones is prime. I could do with another.'

Glenys shook her head. 'I think you've had quite enough,' she said firmly. 'And now, if you want to see Mr Griffiths . . .'

The man clapped a filthy hand to his mouth and spoke through his fingers. 'If I weren't forgettin'! The missus – Mrs Evans – said she were in the grocer's a couple of days ago when Mrs Weather come in. She telled the missus she were after dried fruit to make farmhouse loaves to sell at the market when the weather clears. Only the chap had run out, but this mornin' when the missus got a lift into town with the milk lorry, Mr Jones at the shop give her a big ol' bag of dried fruit for Mrs Weather.' He plunged a hand into the great flappy waterproof he wore, and produced a large blue bag with the word *Sultanas* printed across it. 'There you are, missy,' he said triumphantly. 'Payment for your scones, if you like, only Mrs Evans said you can pay her next time you're passin'.'

'Thanks very much,' Glenys said, trying to take the bag of sultanas without coming into direct contact with her visitor's filthy paw. 'Tell Mrs Evans . . .' But the man was hastily slurping a large mug of sweetened tea, and cut across her.

'I'll tell her,' he said hastily. 'But I hear the master and your young feller a-comin' across the yard, so I'd best be off.' He had not bothered to remove his boots or overcoat when he came into the kitchen, and now went straight to the back door and opened it, letting in a cold draught of air and a few flakes of whirling snow, and leaving behind him not just the dirt from his boots but a good deal of dung as well. 'Thanks for the grub, missus,' he shouted over his shoulder. 'I'll tell your man that the kettle's steamin' on the hob, and the scones is out of the oven and ready for eatin'.'

'Thanks, but . . .' Glenys was beginning when the little man suddenly turned in his tracks and came back into the kitchen, still leaving the door wide.

'I'll take a couple to see me on me way,' he said, and before Glenys had done more than open her mouth he had snatched two scones from the pile on the wire cooling tray and was charging across the kitchen and into the yard, apparently oblivious of the fact that he had failed to close the door.

Glenys and Mo exchanged startled looks. 'That's Pete the Sheep,' Mo repeated unnecessarily. 'He lives down in one of Taid's farm cottages. I don't like him.' She crossed the room and slammed the door, wincing as the cold air rushed in.

'I don't like him either,' Glenys agreed. 'He ate two scones and put another two in his beastly pocket, so now we shall be short when Jimmy and the others come in.'

'No we shan't. What about the little scone boys

242

I made?' Mo said indignantly. 'Where's Nain? I expect Dad and Taid have brought the cows in, so she's probably milking.'

Glenys looked at the clock above the mantelpiece. 'She'll have finished by now. Want to put your coat on, poppet, and give her a hand whilst I get on with the cooking?'

Mo did not need asking twice. She dived across the kitchen and grabbed her coat from its peg, but as she began to put it on a thought clearly occurred to her. 'I'm going to give the biggest scone boy to my daddy,' she said, just as the back door opened to admit the three male members of the household.

Sam and his father-in-law kicked off their wellington boots and came into the kitchen in their stockinged feet. Taid said, in a tone of deep displeasure, that someone had been trekking mud in, and Mo was just starting to explain that it was Pete the Sheep when Jimmy entered the room and slung his coat at its peg on the wall. He, too, kicked off his boots, then looked around the kitchen with approval, taking a deep breath of the warm food-scented air. 'It's brass monkey weather out there, even though Taid says the thaw is coming,' he said. He pointed accusingly at the dirt and dung on the floor. 'Who did that? And where's Nain?'

'She'll be along in a minute,' Sam said. 'She told me she meant to begin weaning Violet's calf, and that takes time.' He turned to his daughter. 'I'd better go and give her a hand; you can come with me if you like.'

243

'Oh yes, I'll come,' Mo said, beaming up at him. She had already put her coat on and now Sam did up the buttons for her. He was smiling delightedly and Glenys, realising that Mo had taken her words to heart, felt a great weight lift from her shoulders.

'Tell Nain to hurry if she wants to have a scone hot from the oven,' she said. 'I don't suppose my scones are anything like as good as hers, but they're the best I can do.'

As soon as they were out in the farmyard, Mo seized her father's hand. 'Taid says when the thaw comes Jimmy and me'll be able to go to school,' she said. 'But it doesn't feel as though the snow is going to me. It's still mortal cold, ain't it?'

'It'll be warmer in the cow byre,' Sam said. 'When you get half a dozen cows all in a small space they create warmth, you know.'

'Yes, and their breath smells lovely even though they haven't been on grass for ages and have had to make do with hay,' Mo observed as they entered the byre. Her grandmother was at the far end and had presumably just finished feeding the calf, for the big-eyed, long-legged little creature was prancing around the small enclosure, eager to get back to the security of his mother's side.

'Hey, Nain, have you finished? I've come to help you, and so's Daddy,' Mo shouted.

Nain turned at the sound of her granddaughter's voice and reached for the gate to the small pen, but before she could come out the calf knocked her aside

244

as it darted ahead of her through the gate. The old woman gave a startled squeak and Sam ran forward to prevent the calf from escaping, but it dodged round him and made for the open doorway.

'Give your grandmother a hand up, Mo,' Sam commanded. 'I'll go after the calf; it could break all four legs if it tries to run across the icy yard. I reckon it knows Violet is in the big barn and wants to join her.'

Mo ran to her grandmother, who was lying motionless amongst the straw. 'Are you all right, Nain?' Mo asked anxiously. 'It were all my fault, shouting out like that and taking your mind off what you were doing. Nain? Are you all right?' She threw herself down beside her grandmother.

Nain groaned but tried to give Mo a reassuring smile. 'I'm all right, but we've got to catch the calf before it damages itself,' she said in a thread of a voice. 'And it wasn't your fault, cariad, but my own. I should have remembered that the calf would want to go to its mother.' She sat up, but Mo could see that it cost her an effort to do so. 'Go and help your father to catch that calf.'

Before Mo could obey she heard a triumphant shout, and smiled reassuringly down at her grandmother. 'Did you hear that, Nain?' she asked. 'That shout, I mean? It were Dad and he said "Gotcher", so that's all right. Let me help you up. Auntie Glenys has made a batch of scones and I helped her, so she said to hurry in and have one whilst they're still hot.' She seized her grandmother's hands and tried to pull her to her feet, but Nain gave a shriek of pain and shook her head.

'No, cariad, I think it will take more than your little strength to get me on my feet,' she said. 'Perhaps you'd better go to your father and get him to come and lend me his strong arm once the calf is safely shut in the big barn with his mother.'

'Oh, but I don't want to leave you, Nain,' Mo said distressfully. 'Dad's bound to come over to the byre as soon as he's penned the calf, to make sure you're all right.' She stared anxiously into her grandmother's face. 'You're awful pale, Nain. Where does it hurt?'

'It's my bloody leg,' her grandmother said, then smiled feebly as Mo's mouth dropped open. 'I'm sorry, cariad. Your taid and I hardly ever swear, but there's times when a bad word just pops out, and this is one of them. Fetch Sam, because I don't want Taid coming out here and trying to move me.'

But even as she spoke Sam's large figure appeared in the doorway. They saw him look round then turn to leave, clearly unable to see them crouching in the straw. Nain tried to call him back, but it was Mo's shrill voice which brought her father running. 'Dad, Nain's fell down and can't get up,' she shouted. 'I tried to help but she were too heavy and she wouldn't let me fetch Taid 'cos she said only your strong arm would do. Did you get the calf?'

Sam crossed the intervening space and entered the catching pen, looking down at his mother-in-law with deep concern. To Mo's surprise he did not immediately try to pull the old woman to her feet but squatted beside her and put an arm about her shoulders. 'If I fetch Taid . . .' he began, but was immediately frowned down.

'Taid's too old to be lifting heavy weights and I'm not exactly a frail flower. If Mo will run for Glenys, and Taid's walking stick, then the two of you can get me to my feet.'

But getting Nain to her feet only proved that she was more seriously hurt than any of them had realised. Sam took one look at her leg and commanded that a chair be brought. 'But don't let Taid bring it out; Jimmy can do that,' he told Mo. 'It's mortal slippy in the farmyard and we don't want Taid laid up with a broken ankle as well as Nain.'

Mo shot off, big with news, but she remembered Nain's insistence that she wasn't to worry Taid, and merely said that Jimmy and she were to carry the kitchen chair to the byre. Before Taid had finished wondering aloud what had happened to the milking stool, they and their burden were halfway across the yard. Presently Sam and Glenys carried the chair with Nain perched on it into the kitchen and stood it down as close to the fire as they could get, and one glance at Nain's strained white face was enough to put Taid on the alert. To his anxious enquiries Sam replied briefly that he thought his mother-in-law's leg might have suffered a fracture. 'I'll go along to the Evanses' and borrow their phone and we'll have Nain in hospital before you can say knife,' he said cheerfully. 'They won't

247

want to keep her there long, probably just for a couple of nights, but if I'm right they'll want to plaster that leg. Do you hurt anywhere else, Nain?'

'Yes, I hurt all over and want nothing more than my bed,' Nain said crossly. 'What a thing to happen, and just when we've been getting on so well! And if I know hospitals they'll want me under their eye for days, and the doctor will try to insist that I keep to my bed when I do get home. Oh, damn, damn, damn, why couldn't it have happened to somebody else? Why was I such a fool? I should have guessed that the calf would rush forward as soon as the gate was open.' She turned to her husband. 'I'm that sorry, Gethin. I'm pretty sure I shan't be able to help on the farm for a few days at least.'

Taid smiled grimly and then, to Mo's astonishment, bent over and kissed his wife's weathered cheek. 'Don't you worry, lass,' he said bracingly. 'Why do you think I've let these young people make themselves at home in our house, eh? It's 'cos I knew in me bones we were going to need them.'

Nain gave a watery little laugh. 'You always were a bit of a joker, Gethin Griffiths,' she said. 'You know very well that our visitors would have been welcome under any circumstances.' She glanced around the kitchen. 'I could just do with a hot cup of tea and one of those scones, and whilst someone's providing me with that little snack you, Jimmy, can brush up all the mud and dung I see on the kitchen floor.' She tutted. 'There you are, I only have to turn my back and rules about taking dirty boots off go by the board. Why are you putting on your duffel, Sam? No need to go ringing for an ambulance. If someone can help me up the stairs to my bed I'll be fit as a flea by morning. I don't want you breaking *your* leg trying to telephone, because now I'm in the warm with folk round me I'll be just fine.'

Taid began to protest, but Sam cut across him. 'We don't know what you've done to your leg, Nain, and you've a fine big bruise on your forehead as well, so don't you go trying to stop me from either fetching a doctor or getting you to hospital,' he said firmly.

'The Evanses are newcomers but they seem kindly, and I know Mr Evans has got one of them baby Austin cars,' Taid put in. 'If an ambulance can't get out to us, Myfanwy, I reckon he'd give you and me a lift to the hospital.'

As they talked Jimmy was struggling into his coat and winding a large, rather ragged scarf around his neck. 'I'm going with you, Dad,' he announced. 'It's a fair walk to the Evanses' farm, and Nain's accident should have taught us a lesson: it's dangerous to go out alone when the weather's so bad.'

'I'll go too,' Mo piped up, but then she hesitated. 'Only Nain didn't fall through slipping on the ice, she fell because of me and the calf.'

Jimmy chuckled, but insisted upon donning his boots and following his father as Sam opened the back door and began to cross the farmyard. Mo rushed to the door to close it for him, shouting that

249

they must be careful and to take Flush the sheepdog with them. 'If you breaks your legs you can send Flush back with a message,' she shouted. 'Do you want a pencil and a piece of paper to write SOS on?'

Her father laughed and shouted back that it was not necessary, and then he and Jimmy disappeared into the lane, carefully shutting the five-bar gate behind them.

Chapter 14

Glenys awoke to find bright sunshine pouring in through her bedroom window and sounds of movement drifting up from the farmyard below. For a moment she was puzzled; why did she feel so happy, as though something really nice awaited her? And then she remembered. It was the second of September and the weather remained brilliantly sunny. Rain would have been most unwelcome, for it was the day Nain was going to leave the house for the first time since her accident. Her injuries had proved to be more extensive than they had first thought, and she had been hospitalised for three months and then under what she called 'house arrest' for months more, meaning that Glenys's presence was indispensable, and much appreciated. But by now Nain was doing a good deal of the cooking and some of the housework, and was eagerly looking forward to collecting the eggs and scattering corn for the impatient hens, perhaps tipping the pigswill into the troughs and certainly picking bunches of flowers from her beloved garden. She had promised the doctor that she would be sensible and not 'overdo herself', as she put it, and in return the doctor had agreed that her house arrest could end on this particular date, for it was Nain's seventieth birthday and the family were going to give her a surprise party to celebrate both her anniversary and her return to normality.

The doctor, however, a grey-haired, bustling little man from Swansea, had grown serious, warning Glenys that though national events might not be uppermost in their minds at the moment, when the great day arrived they might find themselves with more to consider than a birthday party.

'It can't have escaped your notice, even in the midst of the harvest, that Mr Chamberlain has been trying to negotiate a peace deal with those damnable Huns,' he had said. 'He's going to talk to the nation on Sunday morning, at around eleven. I'm sure everyone hopes for peace, and for the brownshirts or whatever they're calling themselves this time round to back down and stay out of Poland, but I remember the last lot and I doubt it. And Mrs Weather's party is supposed to be on Saturday, isn't it? What will you do? Call off the celebrations?'

Glenys had shaken her head. 'We'll celebrate Nain's birthday on the second of September what-ever that Hitler decides to do,' she assured him. 'Weathercock Farm is a long way from Nazi Germany, thank the Lord, but if it is to be war then we'll face it when it comes and not anticipate trouble before we have to.' She gave a small shudder. 'We went to the flicks last winter and the sight of those evil men bombing Spain . . . oh, well, best not to think of it.'

The party was going to be held in the harvest

field, for Nain had made no secret of the fact that she was growing more and more eager to leave the house, and the doctor, a sensible man, had told Glenys privately that he knew the value of a really nice surprise when a patient had been confined for as long as Mrs Weather.

'I don't want anyone to think that I don't appreciate the way you've all rallied round and taken on twice the usual amount of work,' Nain had assured them. 'But now that I can walk with only a bit of a limp, surely I can actually be of some use? I'd like to watch the harvesters at work and share the harvest tea, and the stories and laughs as well. If you, Glenys my dear, and you, dear Sam, will take an arm each I'm sure you could get me there safe and sound, and it would be such a treat.'

She had sounded so wistful that Glenys almost burst into tears, and it was at that moment that the idea of having the party in the harvest field instead of in the farmhouse was born.

'All the neighbours will be working on your twelve-acre, so it will be as much of a surprise for them as for Nain,' she had told Taid as they milked the cows. 'We'll bring the sandwiches, sausage rolls and other savouries down first, and then we'll get Jimmy to blow a blast on his harmonica and you and Sam can process down the lane and into the field with the candles already lit on the cake and we'll all sing Happy Birthday. Do you think Nain would like that?'

Taid thought it was a grand idea and very soon

the children began to talk secrets, planning what they would give Nain for her birthday, arguing and plotting, until Sam told them that they would give the game away simply by their behaviour. 'You carved a little wooden bird when the big beech fell in the gales,' he reminded Jimmy. 'Carve another and give it to Nain; she'll appreciate it more than the most expensive trifle you could buy in a shop because you made it yourself.' He smiled at Mo. 'And why don't you embroider a Peter Pan collar for Nain to sew on her blue dress? Could you manage that? Just lazy daisies and love knots? Nain would be tickled pink that you'd tried, because she knows embroidery bores you to tears.'

Both children agreed to the plan, and very soon decided to go to bed early at weekends so that they might toil over their birthday presents in peace, and if Nain had an inkling of what such strange behaviour might mean, or wondered about the whispered conferences which ceased abruptly whenever she entered a room, she never said so much as a word.

Now, Glenys slid her legs out of bed and crossed the broad expanse of linoleum to where her washstand with its flowery ewer and basin awaited her. Once, she and Mo had shared this room, but that was because it meant Glenys was handy when the little girl had a nightmare. Now Mo's bad dreams were a thing of the past, and she slept happily in her own pretty room on the opposite side of the landing, though if she woke first Glenys was apt to come round to find the little girl's weight on her protesting stomach, whereupon she tried to bury her head in her pillow and assure Mo, with pretended annoyance, that she was still fast asleep.

Because the harvest could not possibly be postponed just because of a birthday party, Glenys washed and dressed as fast as she could and then went down to the parlour, where Nain had been sleeping whilst she found the stairs rather too much. Rather to her surprise, Nain still appeared to be slumbering, but as she turned in the doorway to sneak out again Nain turned her head and grinned at her.

'Pass me my teeth, cariad,' she whispered. 'A feeling I have that I'll be receiving visitors before too long, and I want to look seventeen again and not seventy.'

'Happy birthday, dear Nain. You certainly don't look seventy,' Glenys said. 'I won't deny that you looked pretty grim when you were carted off to hospital with all your broken bones, but since then you've shed years.'

'Aye; done me good the rest has,' Nain acknowledged. 'You've been grand, so you have, and if you have time I'd not say no to a nice hot cup of tea and a bit of a hand to get dressed, but not if you're too busy. I know what it's like at harvest time.'

'I'm never too busy to spend time with you,' Glenys said with perfect truth, for she and the older woman had grown very attached to one another. She handed Nain the little blue box which contained her teeth and turned to the door, but was called back.

'A nuisance it has been, having me downstairs

and the rest of you up,' she said firmly. 'Tonight I intend to go back to my own room with Taid. If you can just put out my clothes each night then Taid will help me dress in the morning. Not that I need much help now.'

Glenys agreed happily, knowing that it would do Nain good to regain her independence, and went to the kitchen to make the cup of tea with which Nain always started the day.

By the time she had carried it through to the parlour there were sounds of stirring upstairs, and when she returned to the kitchen, having left Nain cradling her cup in her hands, the back door opened and Sam and Taid came in. Glenys, measuring oatmeal into the big black saucepan, turned to smile at them. 'Pour yourselves a cuppa,' she said cheerfully. 'I've already drunk mine, and Nain is probably draining her teacup even as I speak.' She turned to Taid. 'Morning, Taid. I've set out Nain's best clothes on the chair by her bed. If you take your tea through to her you can give her a hand to dress whilst I make the porridge and Sam does the toast. Knowing the kids they'll be down as soon as they smell cooking. They've been longing for today, and can't wait to hand over their presents.'

Presently the children bounced into the kitchen, shouted a greeting and went straight to the dresser, in the top drawer of which they had hidden their gifts. They grabbed the little parcels and disappeared into the parlour whence presently came the sound of Nain's appreciation and praise. Sam and

Glenys exchanged smiles. The celebratory day was getting off to a good start.

By the time Glenys had got the children into their beds that night she was exhausted, but very happy. It had been a splendid day, she thought, sitting down at the kitchen table between Sam and Nain and pouring herself a cup of tea, a positively wonderful day. The corn was harvested and in stooks, waiting to be stacked, the guests had been royally fed, and the weather, despite some early fears, had been perfect. The sun had shone from a cloudless sky and not one disagreement had arisen to spoil the atmosphere, though it was a well known fact that some of the guests had not been on speaking terms for years.

'Well, my love? I dare say you're wore out, but you've given my old girl a day to remember, that's for sure!' Taid beamed at Glenys, and then reached over and patted Sam's shoulder. 'And I can't leave you out, Sam, because I know well that you and Glenys planned the whole day . . . and what a day it's been!'

The four adults were sitting round the kitchen table, the men with mugs of Taid's home brew, the women with cups of tea. Nain was wearing her new Peter Pan collar, which she kept touching as though to make sure it was real, and Taid, seeing the movement, got to his feet, bent creakingly over, and kissed his wife's cheek. 'Well, old lady?' he said fondly. 'I think it's about time you were in bed after such a day.'

Nain protested, but when Sam said that since Glenys had done the washing up he and Taid would dry and put away, she agreed that she was indeed weary. 'But it's a happy weariness,' she assured them, getting to her feet. She turned to Glenys. 'If you've finished the washing up, cariad, will you come upstairs with me and help me to get out of this very fine, Sunday-go-to-meeting dress? Then you can come down again and make sure that the men have cleared away properly.'

Sam and Taid protested that of course they would clear away properly, and Glenys and the older woman headed for the stairs. Pushing open the old couple's bedroom door, Glenys realised that she had never been in this room before. Taid had dealt with the bed-making and general tidying whilst his wife could not do so.

She looked around her appreciatively. There was a rose-patterned carpet on the floor, and the curtains at the window, she saw when she went across to draw them, were also covered in roses. There were two bedside cabinets and a washstand – more roses – two easy chairs, and a walnut wardrobe and dressing table. Nain had followed her into the room, and now smiled around possessively as Glenys said: 'What a pretty room! Knowing how fond you are of roses in the garden I suppose I should have guessed that you'd have them in your room as well.'

Nain nodded and sank into one of the easy chairs – basketwork, with roses on the cushion – with a little sigh. 'It's good to be back,' she said, as though she had been away for years. 'This was my parents' room when I was a girl and I had the room you have now, which was Grace's room, as I expect you've been told. Of course the furnishings are different, but the view is the same.' She was regarding Glenys and obviously expected a reply.

'Yes, Sam mentioned it once,' Glenys said, feeling a little awkward. 'You don't mind? My being in Grace's room, I mean.'

Nain smiled fondly at her. 'Mind? My dear, you've been like a daughter to me, and if you had ever known Grace you would know that she was not only pretty but generous and sweet-natured as well.' She got to her feet and crossed the room to her dressing table, picking up a photograph in a silver frame and handing it to Glenys. 'I don't suppose you've ever seen a photograph of our girl. She was only sixteen when this was taken, and I dare say life changed her a little, but not very much.'

Glenys took the photograph and stared down into the lovely oval face. 'She's not just pretty, she's beautiful,' Glenys said softly. 'And . . . yes, there is a striking likeness to Mo. No wonder Sam found it so painful.'

'I must tell you, my dear, that you and Grace would have loved one another like sisters, because in some ways you're very alike,' Nain said softly. 'You've been so good to my grandchildren, to say nothing of how good you have been with Taid and me, and then there's Sam; you get on so well together and he's not always an easy man, as you know. But you've tamed the dragon. Oh, I know you've had your disagreements, but there has been no hint of bitterness, and believe me, Taid and I are grateful for that. You love the farm, don't you?'

'I do,' Glenys acknowledged, then added gently: 'But you mustn't think I'm trying to take Grace's place.'

'My daughter was a wonderful girl,' Nain said. 'But she wasn't strong, and farm work . . .'

She might have said more, but at that moment Taid called up the stairs. 'Would you like a mug of hot milk by your bed, Myfanwy?'

'Yes please, Gethin,' his wife called back. 'One teaspoon of sugar, remember.'

'I'll get it and bring it up to you on my way to my own bed,' Glenys said tactfully. She could just imagine how much milk would be left in the mug if Taid attempted to carry it upstairs. 'Good night, dear Nain. Do you realise how rarely I've heard you and Taid using each other's proper names? Myfanwy; how pretty that sounds!'

Nain chuckled. 'Go on with you,' she said affectionately. 'Goodnight, cariad.'

The next day dawned as fair as the previous one. Nain always prepared and served a cooked breakfast on Sundays, not just porridge but bacon and eggs with plenty of crisp toast and marmalade to follow, but today, Taid announced, when they were all gathered round the kitchen table, would be anything but a normal Sunday in other ways.

'Mr Chamberlain is going to tell us how Hitler has responded to our ultimatum that his troops get out of Poland or put themselves on a war footing with Great Britain,' he reminded them. 'I know we've all refused to let the thought of war affect our lives but this announcement is too important to miss, so I've told Pete the Sheep and the families who rent the other two cottages that they can come and listen with us.'

Nain had been helping the children to lay the table, but at these words she stopped short and sighed. 'Oh, I do pray it will be peace,' she said. 'Women were not expected to fight in the last war, but I knew girls who nursed sick soldiers in France and had some dreadful tales to tell. We don't want that again.'

Taid nodded. 'You're right, old lady,' he said. 'War's a wicked thing, but it's up to the strong to protect the weak, and Poland is a little country. The Nazis have already gobbled up Austria and Czechoslovakia and it's time someone stood up to them, like we did in the last lot.' He swung round and pointed a finger at Jimmy, who was staring at him, pink-cheeked and starry-eyed. 'You think it'd be a lark, a bit of fun,' he said. 'Well, you're wrong, but each generation has to make its own mistakes. And now you run down to the cottages and tell them if they want to hear Mr Chamberlain's speech they'd best be here by a quarter to eleven.'

Jimmy beamed, but then his face fell. 'Do I have to go before breakfast?' he asked. 'Oh, Taid, can't it wait till after?'

Everyone laughed, and Taid looked up at the big clock over the mantelpiece. 'After will be fine,' he said.

Glenys, who had stopped filling their plates to listen, started to dish up once more. She disliked Pete the Sheep, who was now a permanent part-time employee of Weathercock Farm. Nasty, dirty, creepy little man, she thought to herself as she slid eggs on to the warmed plates. The minute he gets into this kitchen he starts hinting that he's had no breakfast and can smell bacon, or anything else he happens to fancy. I still think Taid might have employed someone else, but he says he couldn't do that, not with Pete living in one of the farm cottages. If only someone could persuade him to wash from time to time . . .

Sam, making toast in front of the open range, turned and grinned at her. 'You don't like Pete, do you?' he said, reading her mind with uncanny accuracy. 'There's nothing wrong with him; he's just an appetite on legs. Is that why you don't like him? Because he comes up here when we're eating and makes everyone feel uncomfortable?'

Glenys turned and smiled at him. 'How petty you must think me! No, it's not just his never-ending appetite and his freely expressed opinions.'

Sam returned her smile. 'It's the dirt, I suppose,' he said. 'He's got a tin bath in his cottage and the use of the well, so he has every opportunity to clean himself up. I dare say it would do him good to dip his head into a bucket of water occasionally but

262

he's a darned good sheep man. And if we're going to expand our flock we shall need his expertise.'

'Right; then I'll put up with him,' Glenys said. 'And now sit down and have your breakfast before—'

There was a crashing thump from outside the back door and it burst open to reveal the subject of their conversation, who came straight across the room and settled himself in the nearest chair. 'Mornin' all,' he said cheerfully, seeming not to notice the startled looks trained on him. 'I 'member yesterday – cor, that were a grand party, missus – the master said old Chambermaid was goin' to make a speech today about this 'ere war, an' we was all invited up here to listen. The O'Connells is comin', but I don't know about the Davieses, 'cos I couldn't ask 'em – they don't let me into their garding, let alone the cottage.' He caught Sam's look and hastened into further speech. 'It ain't nothin' to do wi' me; never a cross word have I uttered to that stuck-up bitch . . . well, well, less said the better, but I don't know what I've ever done to them.'

The last words were uttered in a self-pitying whine, and Glenys would have sworn that he was slurring his speech; surely he could not be drunk at this time of the morning? And suddenly his proximity was too much for Glenys's self-control. Before she could prevent them, words popped out of her mouth. 'I expect it's the smell,' she said sharply, 'or the muck, of course. Try washing, Pete, and the chances are you'll be invited to Buckingham Palace, and perhaps you'll be welcome at the

Davieses' too. And the broadcast takes place at eleven, not eight o'clock.'

To her surprise a slow brick-red blush crept up from the man's filthy, collarless shirt to invade his face. He thumped his fist on the table and half rose to his feet. 'That weren't called for, missus,' he said coldly. 'It's all very well for you, you've got yourself a tidy billet up here and think you've got no need to be polite to old Pete the Sheep.' He pointed a trembling finger at Glenys. 'I may be dirty . . .'

'You damned well are,' Sam interposed, having obviously decided to take Glenys's part. 'And now if you've had your say, Pete, you'd best toddle off home and come back at eleven to hear Mr Chamberlain . . . *Chamberlain*, Pete . . . talk to the nation.'

Pete swung round to face Sam. 'You're no bloody angel,' he said in a hissing whisper. 'If I were to tell what I know . . .'

But at this point Taid interrupted. 'You've been drinking, Pete, and at this hour of the morning too,' he said quietly. 'I saw you leaving the party last night with a bag full of food which my wife had given you; I hadn't realised you'd taken that big flagon of cider as well till I saw it was missing. Now just you apologise for the things you've said.'

Pete sank back in his chair once again and the tide of colour receded from his face. He lowered his head, clearly not wanting to meet his employer's eyes. There was a short silence before he spoke. 'I'm sorry for what I said,' he muttered. Then he looked up and the glance he shot at Glenys was openly malevolent before he dropped his eyes again, veiling them with their puffy lids. 'Sorry, missus,' he mumbled. 'I didn't mean no offence, but I've got no woman to cook or make a meal for me . . .'

His voice faded into the whine once more and Glenys saw her opportunity. The moment he lifted his eyes again she gave him her biggest and brightest smile. 'I was rude and said things I shouldn't. I'm sorry, Pete; I should have remembered that a man living alone has no one to cook for him.' And then, unable to resist, she added: 'But living alone doesn't mean you don't have to wash.'

Pete's mouth opened and shut a couple of times and once more the look that he cast at her was unmistakably hostile. But then he must have remembered that Taid was listening to every word, for he gave a little bob of his head. 'You're right, of course, missus.' He cast a wistful look at the food on the table. 'I'd best be on me way then, but I'll be back in time to hear that speech.'

Nain had been an amused listener, but now she too stood up, wagging a hand at Pete to indicate that he should sit down once more. 'I won't have it said that anyone who came to Weathercock Farm went away hungry,' she said briskly. 'After all, a man who's drunk deep of our cider can't be blamed for having no hold on his tongue.' She turned to Glenys. 'Give him a couple of rashers between two slices of bread and he can eat it on his way to the well. But you've learned some home truths today, Pete, and unwelcome though they might have been, you must take them to heart. So I give you fair warning, because that's my way, that on the days you're working for us you'll get a bacon butty to eat in the yard and nothing more, until you stop smelling of sheep dung.'

Glenys expected a repetition of Pete's outrage at the accusation of being smelly, but instead he took the big bacon sandwich she was holding out with a mumbled thank you, scraped back his chair and stood up, addressing himself to Nain. 'Thanks, missus,' he said almost humbly. 'I'll mind your words, and mind my tongue, too.' Then he grinned round the assembled company, displaying his one yellow tooth. 'Mornin' to you all, ladies and gents.'

Everyone chorused 'Good morning', and said nothing else until the door had closed behind their visitor. Only then did Sam let out his breath in a long sigh. 'Phew!' he said. 'That was a nasty one!' He turned to Glenys. 'Can you believe that nobody has ever criticised him before? It seems impossible. But he certainly behaved as though he were astonished that anyone should think him dirty.'

Glenys had been standing throughout the encounter, but now she sank into her chair, pulling her plate of bacon and eggs towards her. 'I know I only spoke the truth – he really is filthy, and he smells like a midden – but it was wrong of me to say it in front of the whole family,' she said remorsefully. 'I expect that's why the Davieses won't have anything to do with him, but even so . . .'

'Even so he had it coming to him,' Taid remarked.

'Now let's forget Pete and get breakfast over and our chores done so we can come in and listen to the wireless with a clear conscience. Kids, you're on egg collecting today, and mind you bring back a good basketful; Sam and I did the milking and now I shall have to load the churns on to the trailer and take it down to the main road because the milk lorry waits for no man. Glenys will want to get the housework done and a cold lunch prepared for later. Sam'll check the flock and Nain can put her feet up.' He held out a hand to Glenys. 'Pete didn't upset you?' he asked in a low tone. 'I knew he'd taken a flagon of cider but I never thought he'd drink most of it in one go, and at this time in the morning too.'

Sam walked over to where Glenys had begun to wash up the breakfast things and put a hand against her neck, beneath the tumble of fair curls. 'Don't let it worry you,' he said gently. 'It isn't often that Pete has a flagon of cider all to himself, and it clearly went to his head. By tomorrow he'll have forgotten every word you uttered, and besides he's in considerable awe of Taid. After all, Taid could sack him at any time and kick him out of his cottage; he won't forget that.'

Glenys twisted round to look up into his face. 'But I'm not his employer; he can be as rude to me as he likes and I'll still have to feed him,' she observed. She smothered a laugh. 'But at least he won't be coming into the house again. I don't mind feeding him if I can do it at a distance.'

Presently the men and the children left to carry

out their chores and Glenys began to clean lettuce, spring onions and radishes. Nain, sitting at the kitchen table slicing cucumber, looked keenly into Glenys's troubled face.

'I don't doubt you spoke without thinking, but who can blame you?' she asked reasonably. 'Pete's got a nasty tongue on him and a bad reputation amongst the village girls; that's what you dislike, isn't it?' She had pulled the kettle over the fire earlier and now she got to her feet and made two cups of tea, pushing one across to the younger woman and raising her eyebrows. 'That's right, isn't it?' she repeated. 'You don't like the way Pete leers, and some of the remarks he makes are not suitable for Jimmy's ears, let alone Mo's.'

'I know,' Glenys said. 'But don't worry, Nain. I can put up with him provided he doesn't come indoors.'

Promptly at eleven o'clock Nain turned the wireless on, and the tenants joined the family in the kitchen. Pete came with them, for the first time since Glenys had met him wearing clothing which could not have stood up by itself. His face was pink instead of mud-coloured and his nails were not black-rimmed. He sidled in last, casting Glenys a look of mingled triumph and hatred, and she guessed that the cleaning up process had been as unwelcome as it was thorough. She would never have known what had happened when Pete went back to his cottage, had not Jimmy, having delivered

Taid's message to the tenants, seen Pete draw a bucket of water from the well. The little man had then knocked on the O'Connells' door, and after he had had a brief chat with Liam O'Connell both men had disappeared into Pete's cottage. Jimmy had not been able to resist creeping round the back and thus had heard every word of the story which Pete had told his neighbour, though he toned down the language slightly when he repeated it to Glenys.

'That bitch won't have me in the kitchen unless I'm clean,' Pete had grumbled. 'It ain't her kitchen, conceited slut, but she's got the old folk under her thumb so I've axed you here to help me fill my tin bath.'

'Clean out the cobwebs, you mean,' Liam O'Connell had said jocularly, in a not unfriendly tone. 'All right, I'm game. The missus and kids are out looking for blackberries, so we shan't be disturbed.'

There was a short pause and then, as Jimmy told Glenys later, the truth came out. 'I'm not that keen on soap and water, so you'll have to throw me into the tub,' Pete had said. 'But suppose you put a bucket of hot in with the cold, I dare say I wouldn't fight you quite so hard.'

Gleefully Jimmy had listened as what sounded like a pitched battle took place inside the cottage, and presently a transformed Pete had come stumbling out of the back door. He had not seen Jimmy crouching behind the water butt.

'He was mother naked and pink all over and cursing like a docker,' Jimmy said happily. 'He went into the old privy and came out lugging a tattered old bag. It must have had his clean clothes in it because when he and Liam staggered out of the cottage carrying the bath between them and emptied the filthy water on to that patch of weeds he calls a garden he was wearing clean trousers, and Liam was laughing fit to bust, and Pete told Liam if he told a soul he'd kill him. But he was laughing too, and he told Liam he could have the rest of the cider he'd nicked from the farm as a thank you. So I waited till they went back into their cottages and hightailed it back here.'

The kitchen was big, but by eleven o'clock it was full, for the tenants had brought their families, knowing that, whichever way it went, this would be a historic occasion. When the announcer introduced Mr Chamberlain complete silence descended, even the children ceasing their chatter, guessing from the way the adults behaved that they should not say a word as the thin, sad voice began.

I am speaking to you from the cabinet room at 10 Downing Street. This morning the British Ambassador in Berlin handed the German government a final note stating that unless we heard from them by eleven o'clock that they were prepared at once to withdraw their troops from Poland, a state of war would exist between us. I have to tell you now that no such undertaking has been received, and that consequently this country is at war with Germany.

Chapter 15

When the tenants had departed, taking Pete the Sheep with them, Nain rose to her feet. 'Well, now we know what we're in for,' she said briskly. 'We've brought the Huns to their knees before and no doubt we'll do it again, but we are ill prepared. Last time we were told not to hoard, but this time I think we should buy in anything which will keep. I dare say the shops will be out of tinned goods in a couple of days; we must make sure at least some of them are here.'

Taid spoke up. 'Farmers have been treated pretty badly by the government in the past, but they'll need us now,' he said with some satisfaction. 'They'll have to stop bringing in cheap imports from foreign countries when ships have to face U-boats and torpedoes. Workers on the land will be needed more than ever before, though they'll most be pretty old, I reckon, because young fit men will be needed in the armed forces.'

Nain was frowning. 'I wonder if they'll ask us to take any evacuees,' she said. 'I've been reading a lot about it in the papers – goodness knows I've been stuck in the house long enough to have written them myself – and it seems the government intends to get as many children as possible out of the cities, especially the ports, because they think there'll be heavy bombing raids, as there were in Spain. So they want the kids safely in the country. I suppose if they ask us we'll have to say yes, but now they've revived the Land Army there's no doubt that a couple of Land Girls would be a lot more useful!'

Smiling at this eminently practical observation, Glenys glanced at the clock above the mantelpiece. Its hands pointed at noon. Sam and Taid, still chatting, went outside to resume their chores, while Jimmy and Mo lingered in the kitchen. 'What's for dinner, Auntie Glenys?' Jimmy asked. 'I know it's usually cold on a Sunday, because we go to church for the morning service, but today's different, isn't it?' He looked hopefully from her to Nain. 'You made some pasties yesterday, didn't you? I'm rare fond of a pasty.'

Glenys laughed, but shook her head. 'It's the usual Sunday lunch: luncheon meat, bread and butter and a salad which Nain made earlier. And don't tell me that's no meal for a hard-working man, because I've heard it all before.'

Jimmy sniggered. 'Oh well, it was worth a try,' he said. He held out a hand to his sister. 'Come on, Mo; we haven't finished collecting the eggs. I know we've cleared the boxes in the poultry house, but there's always one of the hens who lays astray; how about coming with me and trying to find her nest?' He looked up at the clock and then at the table, bare save for a salt and pepper shaker, and heaved a sigh. 'Or you can help the women to get our dinner if you'd rather,' he added. Mo shook her head and he started to push her in front of him out of the kitchen, but then he stopped short and turned her round to face him. 'Why are you crying?' he asked suspiciously. 'I didn't hurt you when I gave you a shove, did I?'

Once more Mo shook her head. 'No, you didn't hurt me, but I's sad,' she said in a small, choked voice. 'When Nain and Taid were talking in the kitchen I remembered the Court and all the kids what was our friends . . . oh, Jimmy, I don't want them to be killed by bombs or U-boats and torpedoes! Some of 'em were real good to us when we lived there; if a bomb fell on Nelly or Nutty I'd be real upset. But you think it's all a lark, don't you, Jimmy? Well, it might be a lark for us because we're in the country already, but it will be real serious for kids what live in the Courts.'

Glenys put the handful of cutlery she had been holding down on the table and went straight to Mo. She picked her up and cuddled her, then sat herself down on a chair with Mo on her lap. 'Mo darling, didn't you hear what Nain said? The children are going to be evacuated.'

Mo reared up. 'Does that mean they'll come along and prick you with a needle, and shout at you if you yell, because it's for your own good?' she said fearfully. 'I've had evacuation and I don't want no more.'

Jimmy snorted. 'Evacuation isn't the same thing as inoculation, you idiot,' he said loftily. 'It just means you're sent into the country to be safe. You want your pals to be safe, don't you? And when they're in the country they're called evacuees, because they've been evacuated from their homes, see?'

Mo nodded. 'I understand now,' she said. 'Might they come here, our Jimmy? Oh, and suppose they do come here and then write home and tell their mams and dads they're with us. And then suppose the neighbours tell the Huxtables where we've gone?' She rubbed her eyes vigorously. 'Oh dear, oh dear, oh dear, I just knew something nasty would happen when I woke up this morning and realised the party was over. And I didn't go with Jimmy to the cottages so I missed seeing Pete in his skin like a poor dead rabbit . . . oh, aren't I the most unluckiest girl in the world?'

Glenys laughed, gave the child a brief hug and stood her down on the kitchen floor. 'You're a very kind and thoughtful girl,' she said. 'Now, I really don't need any help with a cold meal, so you run along with Jimmy and see how many eggs you can find. Dinner will be in half an hour, and though the pasties are for tonight Nain made an apple pie earlier for dessert.'

Jimmy seized the basket standing by the back door and the two of them went out, wrangling amicably over where the hen who laid astray was most likely to be, and Glenys settled down to lay the table and make some dressing with oil, cream and vinegar to pour over the salad.

Promptly at twelve thirty she went to the door to call the family in, and was quite surprised to realise that the sun was beaming down from a blue sky and the birds were singing lustily. Somehow Mr Chamberlain's speech had ruined the lovely day, for her at any rate, and she could not help contrasting the way she felt now with the way she had felt yesterday. Yesterday had been perfect, the happiest day of her life so far, but today worries predominated, foremost among them the fear that Sam would feel bound to return to the sea. It was a dangerous place in peacetime, but in war it was much worse. Still, no point in fretting ahead of time, so with everyone seated she served out the food and tried to keep her anxiety to herself.

However, it was only natural that the war formed the main topic of conversation. Nain was quite frank. 'Food will be rationed, and it will be the poor who suffer,' she said. 'The rich have a way of getting round regulations, which is why I said we should get hold of as many tinned goods as we could.' She turned to Glenys. 'You wait and see, my girl; we farmers and tenants will have no choice but to take in evacuees, which is only right and proper, but the folk at the hall and at the bigger houses round about will be making their plans this very minute. They'll get relatives down from London and Cardiff and other big cities and when the billeting officer comes round they'll show him that they've not a square inch of space left un-occupied. As for food, they'll pay double price and get produce to which they're not entitled.' She chuckled grimly. 'Oh aye, that's how they behaved in the last lot and they'll do the same again, believe me.'

'Then tomorrow the kids and I will go into town and buy up as many tinned goods as we can afford,' Glenys said. She grinned ruefully at the older woman. 'If the townsfolk have left us any, that is! Would anyone like more salad? Sam?'

Sam shook his head and pushed back his chair. 'No thanks; I don't fancy rabbit food today for some reason,' he said. 'Jimmy, can you and Mo manage the clearing away and washing up, if Glenys and I leave you to it? I'd like to take her for a walk; there are things we need to talk about. Is that all right with you, Nain?'

'Of course it is. I'll help the children with the clearing up, and then Taid and I will go up to our room and have a rest on the bed,' Nain said. 'It's been a thoroughly disturbing day and the sooner it's over the better.' She sighed. 'Two wars in one lifetime is two wars too many. And don't you waste your time together talking about this war, because if you mean to go back to sea . . .'

Glenys looked at Sam with dismay. 'Oh, Sam, no! It isn't as though you aren't needed here, because you are. And there are the children to consider, remember. They've already suffered the loss of their mother. Don't leave them without a father as well.'

'Who said anything about leaving them without a mother?' Sam said as they left the kitchen, closing the back door behind them. 'Glenys, my dear, I'm a good deal older than you but we get on extremely well and the children, it seems to me, think of you as something very much closer than an aunt. I know that when we first met I treated you like an interloper, an enemy almost, but since then I've grown to appreciate your many good qualities . . . oh, hell, I'm doing this all wrong, aren't I? But we've only known each other for seven months and I wouldn't normally have spoken so soon . . .'

By this time they were in the lane and heading towards open country. Sam struck his forehead with the back of his hand and cast an apologetic glance at her. 'I'm doing this awfully badly, aren't I? But I know people will talk, and if I do as I know I must and go back to sea, you will have to face it alone . . .'

'Talk about what?' Glenys asked indignantly. 'Oh – they think I should go back to teaching and leave the job of helping on the farm to one of them. Is that it? Some people are so nasty . . .'

'Well no, it isn't exactly that,' Sam said, looking hunted. 'It's more they think I'm the Weathers' son-in-law and therefore will probably inherit the farm . . .' He stopped speaking and stared helplessly at his companion. 'Don't you see what that means? Oh, Glenys, I didn't want to have to spell it out, but it's clear that I must. They think you're setting your cap at me, and that when I go to sea you'll . . . you'll work at making yourself indispensable to Nain and Taid and the children, so that when I come back . . .' He hesitated, and then, seeing her expression, said quickly, 'Don't look so angry, girl. It's always the same in small communities; people positively enjoy thinking the worst, and—'

'Are they daring to say that I've chased all the way across Wales to pin you down and force you to marry me . . . is that what they're saying?' Glenys said, unable to keep the fury out of her voice. 'How dare they think such a thing, how dare they! I've never even thought of marriage, with you or anyone else – oh, I'll make them eat their words!'

Sam tried to put his arms round her but she pushed him away. 'Don't!' she said sharply. 'Do Nain and Taid know about these rumours?'

'No-oo,' Sam said miserably. 'But Nain has hinted that I should regularise the situation by asking you to marry me. Oh, Glenys, I had meant to wait until we had known each other a little longer, but now that war is a certainty . . .' Once more he tried to put his arm around her, but again she pushed him away.

'So you were only asking me to marry you because your mother-in-law thinks it's a good idea!' she said furiously, feeling the hot blood rush into her cheeks and invade her face. 'And won't I be useful? A mother for your children, a nurse for your parents-in-law as they grow older and a worker for your farm, and all free! Well, you can forget it, Sam Trewin. I shall catch the train to Bangor tomorrow and put my name down for a teaching job, or for any job for which I'm qualified, in fact. And failing that I suppose you think I'll come back here with my tail between my legs and beg to be allowed to take up your very obliging offer after all. Well, you're out there! Because I wouldn't marry you if you were the last man on earth.'

She flung away from him, but Sam, too, had a temper when roused. He grabbed her by the shoulders, swung her round and kissed her long and passionately. When he pushed her away he was breathless, and she could see by the sparkle in his eyes that he was as annoyed as she.

'I should put you across my knee and give you a good spanking,' he said, his breath coming short. 'Just think over my proposal, and the next time I ask you it had better be "yes please Mr Trewin" or I'll never ask you again.'

Glenys scrubbed at her mouth with the back of her hand, a childish gesture, but one she felt fitted the occasion. 'Don't bother to ask me again, because the answer will still be the same,' she blazed. 'And don't you dare follow me, Sam Trewin, because I need to be alone. Tell Nain and Taid that I'll be in for supper,' and on these words she turned away and ran up the rocky lane, only casting one look across her shoulder to make sure he was not following.

* * *

Glenys walked and walked, and when the lane petered out into a rocky outcrop she simply abandoned it and went across the moors. It took her a good half hour to calm down, and even then the memory of his hard hands gripping her shoulders and his hard mouth clamped on to hers kept reminding her of her grievances. If he had only said he loved her, just once, she could have forgiven all the rest. Well, he had not said it because it wasn't true. All he wanted was a free mother for the kids, a free housekeeper, and a free nurse for when the grandparents were older. But what about the kiss? *That* had not felt like something he would have given to a proxy mother, housekeeper or nurse. It made her wonder whether he really did love her a little, but if so why in God's name could he not have said so? And then there were her feelings for him. True, she had never contemplated marriage, but for several months now she had not been able to imagine being without him. She knew him to be strong-willed and quick-tempered, but he rarely showed either of these traits now that they had – or she had thought they had – a pleasant and friendly working relationship. Marriage had never entered her head, however, and she would have sworn it had not entered his head either. She thought about this as she strode across the moor, scarcely noticing where she was going. If only he had not more or less told her that he was offering marriage in order to save her from gossip and innuendo! Come to that, if only she had not lost her temper, screamed at him like a fishwife and marched away. If only, in fact, she had behaved with dignity and decorum. But she had not, and she supposed, shamefacedly, that she would have to eat humble pie, tell him that, though she had no intention of marrying him, she was honestly ashamed of her behaviour and hoped that he would forgive her so that they might resume their friendship, which meant a good deal to her.

By the time the sun was setting in a glory of tiny pink clouds, Glenys realised that she was exhausted. She stopped by a little stream and splashed water in her face, but knew she was most definitely not looking her best. She would simply have to recover herself a little before facing Sam once more. But where should she go? She could scarcely expect to re-enter Weathercock Farm without running the gauntlet of critical stares as well as questions. She could just imagine Mo: 'Where's you been, Auntie Glenys? Did you fall down in a bog? Why, you've muck up to the knees, nearly as dirty as Pete the Sheep. And is that hay in your hair?'

Glenys glanced down at herself, and despite her weariness she had to bite back a laugh. She was dirty, scratched and bruised, and her hair, she guessed, must look like a bird's nest. She had torn the skirt of her pink gingham dress, and one of her sandals lacked a buckle. Once more, the desire to laugh nearly overcame her. She could not possibly face the family quite yet; she would definitely try to tidy herself up a bit before she went indoors. She needed somewhere private, but definitely not the farmhouse itself. Fortunately, she seemed to have walked in a large circle, because when she looked around her she realised she was less than a mile from the farm. As she made her way towards it she considered its various outbuildings, and finally decided on the tack room. Besides saddles and bridles, the horse brasses which the enormous Clydesdales had worn to shows in the past, and various brushes and combs, it contained a mirror, so that whoever was showing the horses might check their own appearance as well as their charges'.

In the yard, Glenys filled a bucket at the outside tap, and stole into the shed, closing the door softly behind her. She removed as much dirt from her person as she could, then found a brush and set to work on her pale hair until all the tangles had disappeared. When she had finished she looked searchingly at her reflection in the mirror. Not too bad, she congratulated herself. Now I'll stroll casually in at the back door and tell them I wanted to be by myself for a bit . . .

But before she could carry out this admirable plan, someone in the stable next door spoke her name. Immediately, she was on the alert. Was that Sam's voice? No, and neither was it Taid's or Jimmy's. A moment's listening told her the answer: it was the hated Pete the Sheep, and he was talking to a sharp-faced, spiteful woman who went by the name of Phoebe Smith. She was almost as dirty as Pete himself, with thin, greasy black hair which hung to her shoulders and a whining, unpleasantly nasal voice. She lived in an ancient caravan in the woods and was much disliked and distrusted by all the locals, who swore that Phoebe Smith would thieve anything not nailed down and would lie like a flatfish if it was to her advantage to do so. But Glenys knew the other woman was frequently seen around with Pete, and began to listen without feeling that she was eavesdropping; the tack room was Weathercock property, after all.

'Ah, Pheeb, but you ain't heard the worst yet, not by a long chalk . . .'

Yes, that was Pete's voice, sly and breathy. And Phoebe was with him, no doubt couched down in the hay of an empty stall and probably – ugh, ugh – as near naked as time and circumstance allowed. She heard her name again. 'That stuck-up bitch Miss High and Mighty Glenys ain't no better'n a poor man's tart, for all that she gives herself airs. One night last winter, when the snow were down and thick, deep as me knees or deeper, I had cause to visit a sick ewe what I'd bedded down in that old cottage, the one with four walls barely a-standin'. Well, when I were seein' to the ewe I heard noises comin' from the next room, the one with a smashed winder. So I nips out an' I sees someone's hung clothin' over the empty winder, so I make meself a spy-hole, and what d'you think I sees? Why, I sees Miss common-as-muck Glenys, nekkid as the day she were born, a-squealin' an' a-tellin' the feller on top of her to do it agin, so acourse he did. And the feller was that Sam Trewin, whose wife ain't been more'n a year or two dead, a-humpin' an' a-wheezin' while she shouted at him to go faster, an' she sank her teeth in his neck and clawed at him and yelled till 'twas a miracle they didn't scare my old ewe to death.'

Phoebe gave a snicker of amusement. 'I wouldn't ha' believed it, an' her so prim and proper,' she said. 'Now what say you an' me takes ourselves down to your cottage an' a proper bed?'

There was a short pause, presumably whilst Pete considered the question, but then he grunted what was obviously agreement. 'I got the rest of the food what the old woman gimme last night,' he said thoughtfully. 'We could have us a little party, and then . . .' He chuckled, and even without being able to see him Glenys could easily imagine the lascivious look on his face.

The woman agreed that this would suit her fine, and with a great rustling of straw and some hoarse laughter the two trespassers left the stall in which they had been disporting themselves and headed, Glenys assumed, for Pete's cottage. After their footsteps had faded away, there was an interval of silence and Glenys suddenly realised that while she had been listening she had somehow managed to get right across the tack room, as though physically distancing herself as far from the disgusting couple as she could get. She was crouching by the door, and could not understand how she had got there. Horror, and the lies which had tripped so readily off Pete's spiteful tongue, must have propelled her. She had always disliked Pete the Sheep, had known that she had roused his enmity, and now she realised that the previous winter, all unknowingly, she had played into his hands.

Glenys cursed beneath her breath. She had feared that taking shelter in the abandoned cottage might lead to unpleasant rumours, but what choice had they had? And now she remembered the boot prints they had seen in the fresh snow when daylight came and they left their refuge. She got slowly to her feet. Was this why Sam had asked her to marry him? Was this the kind of 'talk' he had wanted to spare her? She wondered whether he could have heard this particular rumour, but then she remembered that Pete had always been in awe of Taid, and guessed that the shepherd had held his tongue, if only because he must have known that if it came to Taid's ears Taid would undoubtedly sack him and throw him out of the farm cottage.

Outside, it was growing dark, and if she did not go in soon someone might come and search for her and that someone might be Sam. The thought galvanised her into action. She dusted down the skirt of her pink gingham dress, tucked her fair curls behind her ears, cast one glance around the tack room to make sure there was no sign of her recent presence, and set off across the farmyard.

As she had guessed, the family was at supper. One of Nain's pasties sat forlornly on a crumb-spattered plate in the centre of the table, alongside two large platters of sandwiches. Everyone but Sam looked up and smiled as she entered the room; Sam kept his eyes studiously lowered to his plate. Jimmy and Mo said accusingly, in chorus: 'You're late!' but though Taid murmured a greeting, his wife looked at her long and hard.

'Are you all right, my dear? I saw that dreadful Phoebe Smith cross the yard a while back. She's a nasty piece of work, always out to do mischief. I wondered if you'd fallen foul of her.'

Glenys assured her, airily, that she would never take any notice of anything Phoebe said since the woman lied as she breathed, but inside she was thinking *trust Nain to pick up on one's emotions! None of the others have noticed that I'm not feeling quite myself.*

Jimmy, chewing busily, jerked a thumb at the empty chair beside his own. 'We've saved you a pasty, and the sandwiches on the blue plate is cheese and pickle, and the ones on the plate with the pattern of green leaves is egg and lettuce,' he said thickly. 'There's tea, cider or homemade lemonade . . .' His face clouded. 'It ain't fair, Auntie Glenys. Nain won't let me have cider but you can have it, even though you're a woman.'

Glenys smiled at him and hesitated, not knowing whether to take the offered seat, but Sam made up her mind for her. He pushed his own chair back with a loud squeal and got to his feet. 'I'm going out to put the milk into the churns,' he said gruffly. 'If you've finished, Jimmy, you can come and give me a hand.'

Jimmy stared at him, eyes rounding with astonishment. 'I *haven't* finished,' he said. 'There's some of Nain's bara brith for afters, and I love bara brith.'

Mo, sitting opposite him, leaned forward and took a piece of the richly fruited bread. 'I loves it, too,' she confided. 'Why don't you take two pieces, our Jimmy, and then Daddy and you can eat it outside?' She turned to Glenys. 'Jimmy and I never did find the nest of the hen who lays away, Auntie Glenys, so if you eat your pasty up quick we can go out too and take our bara brith with us.'

Glenys smiled, though it was an effort to do so. 'I'm afraid it's too dark to go out nest-hunting now, poppet. And I've got a shocking headache, so the only thing I want to do is go up to my bed and sleep. Is that all right, Nain? I know from experience that the pain in my head needs darkness and quiet even more than it needs tea and sandwiches.'

'Of course you must go. You could take a couple of sandwiches and a piece of fruit loaf up with you,' Nain suggested, but Glenys shook her head, and was surprised when Taid got to his feet and came round the table to where she sat.

'I mebbe don't notice as much as Nain, but I can see today's upset you,' he said kindly. 'It don't do to take all the troubles in the world on your own shoulders, cariad. Things will work out, see if they don't.'

Glenys was grateful for his solicitude and would have said so, but fortunately Jimmy had ignored Mo's helpful suggestion and was tucking into his bara brith at the table, and now he piped up, 'I 'spect most of the troubles are still on Mr Chamberlain's shoulders,' he said, and Glenys realised that she had completely forgotten what day this was. Even the fact that Britain was now at war with Germany had shrunk into insignificance beside the emotions of the afternoon.

Jimmy, Mo and Taid were all looking at her sympathetically, obviously thinking that the coming war was on her mind; only Nain shot her a twinkling glance before helping herself to another sandwich.

'You'll get over it,' she said cheerfully, and Glenys could not decide whether she was referring to anxiety about the war or to the quarrel with Sam. But she did not intend to give herself away and merely smiled her gratitude at the offer of refreshment whilst still shaking her head.

'No, thanks, Nain; I can always come down later and make myself a snack if the headache eases off,' she said. 'But in case it doesn't, I'll say goodnight now.'

Once in the security of her own room, Glenys lay down on the bed and let peace encompass her. She had invented the headache but now, lying quietly in the dark, she could feel the stirrings of pain in her temples and knew she was probably in for a restless night. She tried to make herself relax, to put the events of the day out of her mind, but she soon realised she would have to face up to making a decision. As she saw it she had three options: to stay where she was and let people believe what they wished to believe, for she had no doubt that there were those who suspected what Sam had spelled out, and would pass on the gossip as fact; to marry Sam despite knowing that he did not love her; or – oh, God, and this was the course she knew it would be wise to take – to leave the farm, with no promise of a forwarding address. It might look like running away, it might even *be* running away, but at least it would scotch the rumour that she had set her cap at Sam and had come all the way across Wales to Weathercock Farm in order to feather her nest. How she was supposed to have known that the Weathers had anything she wanted she could not imagine, but the more she thought the more she favoured the option of leaving the farm.

There were several good reasons for this. Nain might have prompted Sam to offer marriage, but what was marriage without love? It would be a millstone around both their necks, and much though she loved the children and admired Nain and Taid, she could not stomach being thought the sort of person who would scheme and plan simply to get a ring on her finger. Furthermore, although most young and fit men would go into the forces now war had been declared, surely the government would leave one reliable person in charge of every farm. On Weathercock Farm that person would be Sam, unless he were married and his wife still on the spot, in which case she would be expected to take over in his absence. And Sam must stay, for the children's sake even more than for Nain and Taid's.

Glenys's head thumped, adding to her misery. She lay on top of her bedclothes, wrestling with a problem which had now shrunk to one stark choice: to go or to stay. It broke her heart to think of the children's unhappiness if she left; they had gone through so much, had sailed such rough seas, and now they believed they had come into a safe harbour. Glenys was not conceited, but she knew the children loved her, and was determined that they should never have cause to think she did not love them too. She would leave a letter for Nain and Taid, explaining that she had gone in order that Sam might stay, and she would write to them regularly, but would never put an address on her correspondence. And anyway, she told herself, she had been a teacher for long enough, to know that children's memories are not long. She could imagine Mo, in a year's time, saying innocently; 'Miss Trent? Who's that? Oh, I know, it's the new lady at the post office . . .'

Glenys's mind dwelt rather sadly on this image for a moment or two, but presently she forced herself to return to her next move. She had decided that going away from the farm was the right thing to do. Thinking back over her past as she lay in the warm dark, she realised, perhaps for the first time, that she was woefully inexperienced. Sam had been kind to her, but he had never given any hint that he loved her, and she had no idea how one encouraged – or for that matter discouraged – a young man to show his feelings. Come to that, she did not even know how to show her own. She had been reared in an orphanage for girls, had gone to a school for girls, had even gone to a training college for girls, and then she had taught in a girls' academy. Her months at Weathercock Farm, in fact, had been her very first experience of how pleasant a friendship with a young man could be. She had enjoyed Sam's company immensely, but then Sam was not a young man; he was at least a dozen years older than herself, and a widower to boot. He had fathered two children and clearly, compared to herself, had a good deal of worldly knowledge. If I had agreed to marry him, Glenys told herself, it would have been an unequal match. I could help Taid run the farm, and I could look after the children, and help Nain run the house, of course. But the other side of marriage . . . she felt her cheeks glow at the thought . . . is a closed book to me, and one I don't particularly want to open. If we were in love with one another it would be wonderful, but as it is it is just frightening, so I think the only choice I can honestly make is to leave.

Having made up her mind Glenys slid off the bed and went over to the window. She pulled the curtains back and looked out. The dark sky above was lit by a thousand twinkling stars, but when she looked to the east she realised that dawn could not be far distant. If she were to get away before anyone was up she must write her letter to Nain and pack her few belongings at once, then steal down the stairs and make for the railway station, though if she were to be pursued that would be the obvious place to look. And if Sam does come after me it will be proof that he truly does love me, even if he doesn't know it, she told herself wistfully as she got down her trusty haversack from where it had been sitting on the top of her wardrobe, ignored now for many months. Yes, if he finds me, if he begs me to come back, I shall see it as a sign that I've made the wrong decision and will return with him to Weathercock Farm.

Chapter 16

Twenty minutes later, with the straps of her haver-sack fastened and her shoes in one hand, Glenys was tiptoeing down the stairs. As she passed Sam's door she was unable to prevent herself from glancing wistfully at it; she even slowed her down-ward flight for a moment, secretly hoping that the door would open and Sam would emerge to ask her what she was doing up at such an unearthly hour. But the door remained closed. That's proof that he has no particular fondness for me, she told herself, starting off down the stairs once more. If he had he would have sensed my presence and got up to discover what I was doing creeping about the house at five o'clock in the morning. Deliberately, she came down hard on the sixth stair from the bottom, which always squawked when trodden on, and was almost outraged when no bedroom door creaked a response. Not even Nain, who had particularly sharp hearing, came out to see who was up so early. But as she gained the kitchen Glenys reminded herself of the events of the last week: Mr Chamberlain's speech, coming on top of Nain's party and the days of excited preparation that had preceded it, must have been the final straw. No wonder they were all sleeping soundly!

Automatically, she glanced up at the clock; heavens, in another hour it would be full daylight. She must buck her ideas up, for to be caught actually on the premises would be so embarrassing, and would call for so many explanations, that she would be forced to abandon her scheme. Then, halfway to the door, she saw the sandwiches. Glenys, who had had no supper, in fact had eaten nothing since a salad at lunchtime the day before, felt the saliva rush to her mouth. She approached the table, and saw that the sandwiches were not on a plate but on top of a small sheet of greaseproof paper, and beside them was an apple and a slice of farmhouse fruitcake. It looked almost as though Nain had prepared a picnic for her, knowing that she was going away. For a moment, Glenys felt as though someone had slapped her in the face; this was rejection, complete rejection! But then she thought of what she knew of Nain and realised that, if the food indeed held a message it was that Nain wanted her to know she was loved.

She wrapped the sandwiches and the fruitcake carefully in the greaseproof paper, put the food into her haversack and cast one valedictory glance around the kitchen; she had known more happiness here than she had believed existed. Then she propped her letter to Nain against the tin of Saxa salt and headed for the back door. It wasn't even locked; had Nain realised that the key screeched in the lock like a lost soul? Had she deliberately eased her way? But it was no use conjecturing; Glenys shut the door as stealthily as she could, crossed the farmyard, and went through the little side gate into the lane. She did not know the time of the first train to anywhere, but remembered that the milk lorry had to get the churns down to the station to connect with it. She turned briskly towards the road. Already a sense of adventure gripped her. She told herself she could go anywhere, do anything. Now there was a war to take into consideration, she was pretty sure that someone with her experience of farming would be eagerly accepted as a worker. She had read an article – she supposed it was an advertisement really – raving about the wonderful work of the Land Army, which was manned, she believed, entirely by women. There were pictures on station platforms and in other public places of unbelievably glamorous girls clad in neat-fitting and elegant costumes, harvesting grain in sunny cornfields, picking apples or plums from leafy branches or crouching over full baskets of strawberries so beautifully painted that they looked real. Yes, I'd make a really useful Land Girl, Glenys told herself.

As the thought entered her mind she turned into the main road and was walking confidently along the verge when she heard a heavy vehicle approaching from the rear. Immediately her heart gave an excited little bump; it would be the old jalopy which Sam and Taid had agreed would ease their lives considerably. Or it might be the tractor, even though Sam said it needed twice the fuel . . .

It was neither. The disappointment Glenys felt when she looked over her shoulder and saw an army lorry behind her was almost overwhelming, but then common sense reasserted itself. She was still a long way from the railway station; if she could flag the driver down . . .

The lorry drew up alongside her, the window was cranked down, and a young voice said cheerfully: 'Wanna lift, mate?'

'Yes, please – I'm on my way to the station,' she began, but was swiftly interrupted.

'Well, wharra daft thing to do. Trains cost money; that is they do if you ain't in the forces. You gorra train pass?'

'No, but I've got money for my fare,' Glenys said defensively. 'Where are you going?'

The young soldier revved his engine impatiently. 'All the way there and back agin,' he said. 'I deliver all acrost the country, wharrever they're short of and wherever they're short of it: Liverpool, Chester, Wrexham . . . Where's you want to go? Only gerra move on, else I'll be late for my first delivery.' He revved the engine again, and almost as though impelled by the roar Glenys hopped up the step and into the passenger seat.

'Thanks very much,' she said breathlessly as the young man pushed the gear lever into first and the huge lorry hiccuped, lurched and began to move forward. 'Did you say your first stop was Liverpool?'

The young man shrugged and swung the wheel, blinking his lights at another vehicle as the two passed. 'Depends,' he said airily. 'I can take you to Liverpool; there's plenty of work down at the docks for us drivers. Of course, now war's been declared we'll be on the go from morning till night, and from night till morning, come to that. What's your trade, mate? Goin' to work in one of them factories? I believe you can make uniforms, or parts for aeroplanes, or even guns and that in the factories on Love Lane.' He chuckled. 'Odd name for factories doin' war work, wouldn't you say? But they pays real well, and of course if you're a docker you can't go wrong.' He glanced sideways at her and grinned ruefully. 'But they don't employ women on the docks, worse luck. So if you're lookin' for work, well they say the services always put a square peg into a round hole, so you'd best pick the factory you'd like rather than let the authorities choose for you. I tell you one thing: don't you go suggestin' that you'll work in munitions 'cos the stuff them girls handle turns their skin yellow as bloody daffodils. I gorra cousin – Queenie, her name is – what works in munitions, an' she's been an' gone and got allergic to some oil or other what they use.' He turned to grin at his passenger. 'Looks as though she's got the measles, 'cept she had 'em when she were five. Now the perishin' government have said she can make parachutes, which is another thing they've got women a-doin'. Fancy yourself with a needle and thread?'

'No, not at all,' Glenys said firmly. 'I hate sewing

and I'm rotten at it. I've been working on a farm this past year, so I thought the Land Army would probably suit me best. And I'm volunteering, not being conscripted, which should make a difference, shouldn't it?'

'The Land Army? Have you seen their uniform? Them awful baggy breeches are enough to put anyone off, as well as them great clumpin' shoes. I seen 'em at dances, a-treadin' on their partners' feet wi' their great hooves. Now Liverpool's a port, so there are plenty of them little Wrens in their black silk stockin's . . . but what's wrong with the army, eh? You've not mentioned the army and it's the one service I can really tell you about . . . the ATS, I *should* say.'

'Oh yeah?' Glenys said sarcastically. 'Got a girl-friend in the ATS, have you? If so, I can understand your enthusiasm . . .'

The young man drew the lorry up behind another of the same ilk. 'Girlfriend? Don't you have eyes in your bleedin' head?' he said scornfully. 'I'm *in* the perishin' ATS.' He snatched his cap off his head, revealing that he – or rather she – had a neat bun of light brown hair on the top of her head, and turned to face her passenger. 'Well I never bloody did! You thought I were a perishin' feller, and me with a figure what's the envy of the rest of my section!' She laughed uproariously, jerking the lorry into first gear once more and beginning to creep forward. 'Well, to be took for a perishin' feller!' she repeated.

Glenys clapped her hands to her hot cheeks. 'I'm most awfully sorry, but the fact is it's still dark and it never occurred to me that a woman could drive a huge lorry like this one. I know there were women in the last war but I thought they were mainly Land Girls and nurses . . . but I'm very, very grateful and I'd like it if you'd tell me how you came to get the job of a driver.'

Her companion snorted. 'Forget the Land Girls, and you can't join as a nurse unless you really are one, if you see what I mean. What's wrong with the ATS?'

'Nothing, nothing at all,' Glenys said hastily. She felt she had put her foot in it and was remorseful, especially since the driver had been good enough to give her a lift. 'Tell me all about it; the ATS I mean,' she added. 'I hadn't really considered which service, and I only thought of the Land Army because of my previous experience. Do you think the ATS could find a niche for me? Before I moved into Wales I was a fully qualified teacher in a girls' private school, with a certificate and everything,' she added rather self-consciously. 'I don't suppose it would be very helpful, though . . .'

Her companion whistled. 'I should think they'd jump at you!' she said frankly, as the slow-moving line of vehicles drew to a halt once more. 'Tell you what, I'll drop you outside the TA office in Liverpool . . . no, no, I've got a better idea. You said you have money for your fare; there are cheap lodging houses near the docks and one of 'em – the fellers call the landlady Mrs Churchill, 'cos she's rare fond of old Winnie – lets us gals have a room cheap. It's not a long way from the recruiting office, so you could stay there whilst you make up your mind.'

Once more the traffic edged forward and, to Gleny's dismay, as the lorry began to pick up speed the driver turned to her and thrust out a hand. 'How do you do? I'm Dorothy Ward, Dotty to me friends.'

'I'm Glenys Trent,' Glenys said as their hands met. 'I say, do keep your eyes on the road. The lorry ahead is going to stop, I feel it in my bones.'

Her companion chuckled. 'You'd better apply to be a driver – Driver Mechanic is what they call my section. I'm not saying the pay is particularly good, you can earn more in other trades, but the training is first class, and though there's a lot of sitting around you'll get exercise right enough. Still, you'll get a load of information from the recruiting office.'

Glenys sighed, bidding farewell in her mind to the possibility of breeches and a green jersey, WAAF blues, a Wren's black silk stockings and a nurse's cap and apron. She owed this young person more perhaps than mere thanks. Aloud, she said: 'I *shall* apply for the ATS, Dotty. Will they issue me a uniform at once?'

Dotty gave a crow of amusement. 'Because of old Chamberlain – the gals call him "Potty"; I expect you can guess why – recruiting offices are goin' to be overwhelmed. You'll be lucky to get an armband at first, though once they realise you've gorra proper qualification I dare say they'll find up a uniform from somewhere.'

The traffic began to move, this time more rapidly, and presently the two girls shared Glenys's sandwiches and tea from Dotty's flask. After that, as the stars paled and the sky brightened, Dotty told Glenys all about the ATS as seen through a driver's eyes. 'But could you drive already?' Glenys asked uneasily.

'No, the ATS taught me. I take it you can't drive?' Dotty said.

'I've driven a tractor many times and Sam lets me drive his old jalopy into town, but I don't know whether I'd dare to say I could actually drive,' Glenys admitted.

'Who's Sam?'

'Sam? Oh, he's just the son-in-law of my old employer; no one of any particular importance,' Glenys said airily, and realised as she said it that she was speaking no more than the truth. Regardless of Sam's feelings for her, if she had felt anything stronger than sisterly affection for him she would surely have left him a note, and it had not once occurred to her to do so. But as the light grew stronger, Dotty's chatter seemed to fade and Glenys realised that she was visualising the scene in the kitchen when the family assembled for breakfast. She sighed. She hated inflicting pain, but she told herself that she had done the right thing by leaving. So she sat up straighter and watched the passing countryside and would not let herself think of the people she had left behind.

In the farmhouse kitchen, Nain was already stirring the porridge and Taid was sitting in front of the stove, toasting slices of the bread which his wife had made the day before. He had seen the letter addressed to Nain leaning against the drum of salt but had said nothing, realising that his wife would probably read it when she had finished cooking breakfast, and presently Sam and the children clattered down the stairs. Jimmy and Mo began to do the tasks which they performed every morning, fetching jars of marmalade and Marmite from the pantry, checking that their books were in their school satchels, feeding the cats – there were three of them – with saucers of milk and finally sitting themselves down at the table as Nain served out porridge into five of the six dishes they had laid out. Mo stared at the empty dish. 'Has Glenys already had hers?' she asked plaintively. 'I got up early 'cos it's the first day of school after the holidays, only I know the corn harvest isn't finished and I thought I'd ask Glenys if we could have a day off to help.'

'Glenys isn't here,' Nain said rather guardedly, glancing at Sam, but there was no sign on his face of either distress or annoyance. So they did quarrel, Nain thought. 'But she's left me a letter, which I've not yet read. However, the time has come to do so. Eat up your porridge, children; whether it's school or the harvest, you'll still want to face the day with your stomachs lined.' As she spoke, she picked up the envelope, slit it open and pulled out the page it contained. She read it quickly to herself and then aloud:

'Dearest Nain and Taid,

'You've been so good to me, so kind and generous, but I've thought it over carefully and listened to people talking, and this helped me to come to a decision. Whilst I am at the farm the government will think that Sam does not have to be here, which means he will go back to sea, leaving Weathercock in my far from capable hands. Of course we all know that it will be you and Taid who make the decisions and take the responsibility, but that's not how the War Office sees things. If I leave, then Sam will almost certainly be allowed to stay, and for the children's sake I have decided that I must be the one who goes . . .'

At this point, Mo flung back her head and howled like a dog, tears streaming down her normally rosy cheeks. 'I don't want my daddy, I want Glenys!' she wailed. 'He went away and left us before, and he'll do it again.' She turned a tear-blubbered face towards her father. 'Where's she gone? She must be goin' by train . . .' She leaned across and grabbed her brother's arm, causing him to spill porridge all down his clean school shirt. 'Jimmy, we've got to go after her. If we beg and plead ever so hard, maybe she'll come back.'

Sam pushed back his chair. 'I'll go to the station and see what I can do,' he said resignedly. 'Just let me finish my porridge and I'll take a couple of rounds of toast with me. If the porter can tell me where the train she boarded was bound, then I suppose I could follow her . . .' He jerked a thumb at Mo. 'And don't give me any more cheek, madam, or you'll get a good hiding.'

'She won't come back for you, not if you were nasty to her,' Mo said sullenly. She turned to her brother. 'Make Daddy go *now*. Oh, I'd rather go meself!'

Nain stepped in at this point. 'You've not heard the whole letter,' she said reprovingly. 'Glenys says she has found a clue to her mother's whereabouts so she will no longer be alone in the world. Then she says: *I wish you nothing but good and shall never forget your kindness to me. I'll write regularly, and when this wretched war is over I'll come back to see you.*'

Sam, by this time, had scraped his porridge bowl clean and left the table, and was heading for the back door. 'I shan't be long,' he called over his shoulder. 'Daft girl. The Min of Ag will know that Taid is quite capable of running the farm, just as Nain is equally capable of running the house, so neither I nor Glenys is necessary. I'm going to re-muster whether she comes back or not.'

Jimmy abandoned his own half-eaten breakfast and followed his father out of the kitchen. 'I knew you'd go, Dad, and so you should, 'cos it's your duty,' he said importantly. 'I'm thirteen, nearly old enough to do a man's work. So don't you worry, but go off on your ship and come home when you're on leave. Taid and me can cope.'

Nain sent Mo off to make the beds whilst she and Taid had their own breakfast, but Mo, halfway to the stairs, turned abruptly. 'Nain, shall I make Glenys's bed? Do you think Daddy will catch up with her and bring her back?'

'No, I don't think he will; even if he catches up with her she isn't going to want to come back,' Nain said gently. 'I think we have to accept that we may not see her for some time. So you must be a brave little girl and help in the war effort, as Jimmy will.'

Mo turned to peer down into the kitchen. 'But shall I make her bed?' she enquired patiently. 'You didn't answer that part of me question.'

Nain sighed. Oh, dear; how literal children were. But an honest question deserved an honest answer. 'No, dear,' she said decidedly. 'Leave that room until last. We'll fold up the bedding – apart from the sheets, which I will launder – and put it into the chest at the end of the bed to await her return.'

She waited until the child was out of sight, waited in fact until she heard Mo open her own bedroom door and slam it casually behind her, then turned to Taid. He was smiling. 'You knew she'd gone before you even opened the envelope,' he said, his tone neither accusatory nor surprised. 'Has she been plan-ning this for days? Did you know?'

Nain shook her head. 'Not exactly; all that nonsense about Sam being allowed to remain if she left was probably only put into her head by the Prime Minister yesterday, and as for having found a clue to her mother's identity, how, pray, could she have done that? No, it's nothing so simple; I think she's on a quest, though not to find her mother. What Glenys is searching for, and hoping to find, is herself. Poor child. Just think of our Grace and compare her childhood – and young womanhood too for that matter – with Glenys's. Brought up in an orphanage, never knowing the love of a parent or the attention of relatives, and then pushed out into college because she was so clever. She was always expected to take her own decisions and make her own way. Even friendships must have come hard for her, because I expect that when she was in the orphanage she was cleverer than the other girls, and folk don't like feeling inferior. And even though she would have been surrounded by a great many clever young women when she went on to college, she would have found it difficult to integrate; they would have had relatives, school friends, even boyfriends. Glenys knew herself to be alone, knew herself to be different, so she seized on the children's desire to find their mother's relatives and pretended that she, too, was looking for the woman who had abandoned her. It was probably the first time she ever felt needed. So it's not surprising that when Sam's attitude towards her softened, she believed herself to be in love with him . . .'

'Perhaps she was,' Taid said thoughtfully. 'The mind of a young woman is a closed book to me, but I imagine she must have felt herself rejected when they quarrelled yesterday, which you tell me they did, though I saw no sign of it. She's had so much rejection that more would have been hard to bear.' He frowned. 'But if you suspected that she was going to run away, why did you not try to stop her? I know she isn't a young girl – she's twenty-six isn't she – but she's young in experience.' He looked reproachfully at his wife. 'You should have stopped her, Myfanwy.'

Nain, however, shook her head. 'No, I thought it was the most sensible thing she could have done. She needs to mix with men and women of her own age. You see, Gethin, here on the farm she only meets folk like ourselves. The services need bright, clever girls and Glenys is very bright and very clever. She will begin to see that she is appreciated and admired, no longer in the background but a valued member of whichever discipline she chooses. Her self-confidence, which is nil at the moment, will grow and flower. Leaving us will be the best thing she's ever done.'

Taid reached across the table for the butter and began to spread it on his toast. 'You're a wise old woman, Myfanwy Griffiths,' he said. 'I always knew you had the brains and I had the brawn. Unfortunately, brawn lessens with age, but wisdom increases.'

Nain laughed and tapped him affectionately on the cheek. 'Nonsense; it was just women's intuition,' she assured her husband. 'And now let's get

307

on with our chores; Sam will be wondering what's happened to you, leaving him with all the milking to do when he gets back from his unsuccessful search.'

Taid got stiffly to his feet. 'So you don't think Sam will find her?' he asked, and was not surprised when Nain shook her head.

'No, I don't, and a good thing too. Sam's had months to make her love him if he had wanted her to do so; as I said, she's gone in search of herself, and woe betide anyone, even Sam, who gets in her path.'

Chapter 17

March 1941

Glenys swung her heavy lorry into the parking space, cut the engine, switched off the lights and sat for a moment, arms crossed on the wheel, staring dully ahead. The trouble with driving, she reminded herself, was that it left you a great deal of time for thinking, and in her case, hard though she tried to prevent them, her thoughts tended to go straight back to Weathercock Farm.

It was all very well to tell herself that she was living a different life, owed allegiance to the ATS and to her work: she still could not banish the ache which crept into her mind the moment she let down her guard. She told herself that she had chosen to leave the family who had been good to her, that she had done the sensible thing, and when she was actively engaged she could control the impulse to send them her address, beg them to write, perhaps arrange a visit.

The worst times came in the wee small hours, when misery and despair engulfed her, and would not be denied. She would lie in her bed in the hut, willing the hours to pass, even wishing that the alarm would sound, that raiders would cross the coast, so that she would have something other than regrets to think about.

Other girls, she knew, were also probably lying awake in the dark, fighting their own particular demons: a boyfriend who had not returned from a raid on Germany; a relative seriously ill, perhaps needing her; or even something as trivial as a kit inspection next day when she had laddered her last pair of lisle stockings and would be in for a wigging from the section leader.

And I have no right to torture myself by imagining Sam's ship being torpedoed, Sam sinking into the black waters, reaching for a spar, too proud to call for help . . . by now he probably has some natty little Wren to worry over him. But the children . . .

She was sure they would be mixing with evacuated kids from a dozen different backgrounds; she had no fear for Mo, who made friends easily, but she was worried about Jimmy. Suppose he did something foolish? She knew the merchant navy recruited young boys, and ever since arriving at the farm Jimmy had flourished, gaining not only height but also muscular development. He could easily pass for fifteen, and immediately the picture in her mind of Sam struggling in a dark sea was replaced by one of Jimmy, in that same dark sea, frightened and alone, trying to swim to safety when there was no safety to be had.

For the thousandth time, Glenys choked back tears. What nonsense this was! For all she knew,

Sam and Jimmy were still both working on the farm and probably enjoying every minute. If they thought about her at all, it would probably only be when one of her letters arrived, and she could not deny that the weekly epistles to Weathercock Farm were a thing of the past. In fact, she was lucky if she managed to find time to scrawl a couple of pages every other month.

The trouble was, of course, that because she did not want them to know where she was or what she was doing, her correspondence lacked a certain sparkle. She never once admitted that she was a driver, but when she mentioned a journey let it appear that she was travelling as a passenger. She had not even told them to which service she belonged, because if Sam knew and did *not* come looking for her, then she would really feel that her cup of unhappiness overflowed. At least this way she saved herself from the ultimate humiliation of not even getting a reply, however brief, from Sam, or Nain, or even Taid. After all, it had been eighteen months since she saw them last; why should they think twice about her?

A sharp rap on the window interrupted her reverie and Glenys wrenched her mind back to the present. It was Driver Bennett, who had parked her own lorry in the space alongside, and the two girls smiled at one another as Glenys opened her door and dropped to the ground. They both walked round their vehicles, checking that all was well, then set off towards their hut. 'Better clean up before we go to the cookhouse or Sarge will have our guts for garters,' Jane Bennett remarked. 'I'm oil to the eyebrows; good thing we wear overalls, because service dress isn't designed for dirty work.'

Glenys nodded. 'When I joined – which seems a lifetime ago – they couldn't find me a uniform of any description. If you remember, the sergeant issuing clothing was quite rude; he called me a giraffe.'

Jane laughed. 'And we did our basic training in service dress because some high-up thought we were all destined to be clerks, cooks or waitresses . . .'

Glenys blew out her cheeks, crossed her eyes and made a fanning motion with one hand. 'Can you imagine what our lives would have been like if we hadn't kept insisting that we could drive! Even now I meet members of the public who simply assume that men drive lorries and women make sandwiches . . .'

'I know; doesn't it make you cross?' Jane agreed. 'And there are still people who refer to us as "officers' groundsheets". It's bloody unfair, but comments like that just have to be dismissed as ignorant. I gave a Waaf a lift a few weeks ago, and she told me the men on her station referred to her as the station bicycle because she's been out with more than one fellow.'

Glenys pulled a face. 'Some men are always quick to judge women, though they seem to think that they can carry on regardless,' she said. 'They never seem to take into account that it takes two to have an affair.'

'True,' Jane said, as they began to wash off the grime of the day. 'But it's just jealousy and ignorance . . . is my cap straight? My hair needs a wash, but a comb through will have to suffice for now. I'm starving, so do hurry.'

'Got your irons?' Glenys queried as they reached the cookhouse. 'I asked Katie what they were making for supper and she said stew, which could mean anything.'

Jane plunged a hand into her gas mask case and produced knife, fork and spoon, and flourished them triumphantly under her friend's nose. 'It's the first thing I check when I get up each morning,' she observed. 'No irons, no supper. Though if it's the sort of stew which is mainly turnips, I think I'll go to the Naafi instead.'

As they entered the long building and joined the queue waiting at the counter, someone dug Glenys in the back. She turned and saw Dotty Ward, grinning from ear to ear. 'You two are late; Sarge has been searching for both of you. Where have you been?'

'Oh, on a secret mission up north,' Glenys said airily. 'But where did you spring from, Dotty? I've not seen you since last week!'

Dotty tutted as the queue shuffled forward. 'Wouldn't you like to know!' She picked up a tin plate and held it out in the prescribed manner. Behind the counter, the staff were sloshing mashed potato, overcooked cabbage and watery stew on to the outstretched plates, regardless of the fact that a carelessly aimed ladle might deliver half its contents either on to the floor or across someone's jealously guarded uniform. 'It's probably a posting; you know how the brass hats like to disrupt our lives, and you've been here for months.'

Glenys extended her own plate, frowning thoughtfully. It was true that the girls were frequently moved around, though this did not often apply to drivers, who might be sent to any part of the country at any time. Sometimes they stayed away for several nights, only returning to Liverpool when they had a load for the docks. But it was possible the powers that be had decided she was too happy with her lot; they might even have thought she knew her trade too well and needed to do something different.

The stew that was presently sloshed on to her plate seemed to contain at least some meat, and her portion had carrot and onion as well as a surfeit of turnip, so she thanked the girl in the big wrap-around apron and hair tidy, and followed Jane to one of the square wooden tables against the wall.

Glenys and Jane had joined at the same time and done their basic training together, becoming fast friends in the process. At first the other Ats had made rude remarks about the long and the short of it, because Glenys stood five foot seven in her stockinged feet and Jane barely managed to make five foot, but the ribbing soon stopped when it became clear that neither girl was going to rise to the bait.

They thought themselves very fortunate that they were both posted to the same depot when their basic training had been completed. They had gone straight to Newcastle upon Tyne, and since neither of them had ever been so far north before they enjoyed exploring their new territory, especially when their journeys took them over the border into Scotland and into wild and deserted countryside where they sometimes thought that the very language was foreign. But that had been almost a year ago and now, if Dotty's guess was right, they might well find themselves posted to different parts of the country; which, Glenys thought, might call for some pretty nifty footwork. She remembered an old sergeant once telling her that if you were prepared to put yourself out you could control the service instead of it controlling you, and indeed, had she not borne his words in mind, she might not have attained the rank of driver quite so quickly.

'Hey, dreamy, come down to earth and tell me what sort of a day you've had,' Jane said. 'I heard Dotty say that Sarge had been chasing round looking for the pair of us.' She put down her knife and fork in order to smite her forehead dramatically. 'Oh, woe, don't say it's a posting.'

Glenys laughed. 'Why does everyone's mind immediately fly to a posting?' she enquired. 'I believe you know what it's about . . . c'mon, spit it out, and I don't mean the stew!'

'If you do mean the stew I've half a mind to obey your command,' Jane said, pulling a face. 'I don't know anything.' She glanced at her companion's plate. 'It's not *fair*. Who's Cooky's favourite, then? You've got a lump of meat *and* some carrots! Then it's true what they say about tall people having an advantage over shorter ones. I shall complain to the next promotion board I attend.'

'Oh, shut up,' Glenys said, applying herself to her plate. 'Tell you what, Janie, this stew isn't half bad! And there's treacle duff for afters, my favourite.' She looked hopefully at her friend. 'You keep telling everyone you're trying to slim, so why not let me have your portion of duff?'

Jane began to speak but was cut short. 'Private Trent, I've been a-searchin' for you, and Bennett here, this hour an' more.' The sergeant's voice was plaintive. 'Come to my room as soon as you've finished guzzlin', and no delayin' tactics, if you please!'

'Yes, sarge,' Glenys said obediently, 'as soon as we've finished our treacle duff.' She looked at Sergeant Reeves's large, brick-red face and bristling grey eyebrows, half expecting a reproof for even mentioning it, but instead he nodded.

'Oh, awright, finish the pud.' He looked with disfavour at their battle dress blouse and trousers, which was the uniform drivers usually wore except on special occasions. 'Better change them trousers for skirts, though, if you want to make a good impression . . . but enough said. Get a move on or

316

the officer will put me on a charge for keepin' him waitin'. And furthermore, he'll think I've shot my mouth off which I were told particular not to do.' He put a finger the size of a pork sausage across his lips. 'Very hush-hush; walls have ears,' he muttered.

Glenys was about to remind him that they had both signed the Official Secrets Act when he turned and fought his way past the queue of incoming service men and women. Once he was well out of earshot, she raised her brows at her friend. 'If there's one thing which makes me curiouser and curiouser, as Lewis Carroll would say, it's a sergeant with a secret,' she observed. 'And now let me concentrate on finishing this stew.'

Jane got to her feet. 'I'll go and fetch the duffs for you, and then I'm going to change. Meet me in the hut in twenty minutes.'

Glenys thought of saying she would skip the pudding and go with her friend, but changed her mind when Jane plonked two helpings of duff before her and whisked away her empty tin plate. Treacle duff was Glenys's favourite of all the cookhouse's rather uninspired puddings, so she seized her spoon and began to wield it with all possible speed. The sergeant was a kindly man, who got on well with all his drivers; it would not be fair to keep him waiting. She scraped the second plate clean, and hurried to the hut where Jane awaited her. At lightning speed, she changed into her skirt, rubbed a duster across her neat brown boots, gave her hair in its curly bob a couple of taps with her hairbrush and then raised her eyebrows at her friend. 'Ready?' she said. 'Do you know, I've been giving the matter some thought and I believe it might be a very good thing if we changed our trade. I enjoyed driving at first, but it's become pretty humdrum, wouldn't you say?'

Jane didn't reply until both girls had checked their appearance in the long mirror by the door and left the hut. 'Become pretty humdrum?' she repeated. 'The trouble is, ninety per cent of our work is simply ferrying various things from the docks to other ATS sections. In the early days it was more of a challenge, because we went much further afield.'

Glenys nodded. 'And now we know everything, the top brass is going to consult us,' she said sarcastically. She pushed open the door to the administration block. 'Well, we'll know soon enough.'

She tapped briefly on the door marked *Sergeant Reeves* and poked her head round it. The sergeant was sitting behind a large desk, with a pile of papers in front of him. He looked up, grinned and got to his feet. 'Better late than never,' he rumbled. 'Go down the corridor until you come to Lecture Room Three and go in and sit down.' He glanced at the clock on his desk. 'The officer will be along in five minutes, so just sit quiet and wait.'

He ushered them out of the room and Glenys nudged her friend. 'Did you see those papers?' she hissed. 'Remember those tests? They didn't tell us why we had to take them or what it was all about, but my intelligence paper was on top of the pile – I spilt some ink on it, and I recognised the blot.'

But at that moment they reached Lecture Room No. 3 and went inside. The room was almost full, and a couple of the girls already seated murmured a greeting. One of them, a pretty redhead named Maisie who had done the physical fitness test in the same group as Glenys and Jane, asked them if they knew what was going on, but before they could answer the door behind her opened and an officer strode in, removing his cap as he did so to reveal short, curly blond hair which was exactly the same colour as his tiny toothbrush moustache. Glenys jumped to her feet and saluted, as did everyone else, and then obeyed the sergeant's instruction to sit down once more. She knew the officer's name was Captain Dorrington, and thought she had heard someone say he was with the Intelligence Branch, but he was often to be seen coming and going to the Officers' Mess so she supposed he must be seconded to their regiment.

The captain had acknowledged the forest of hands with a salute of his own so stiff and correct that she wanted to giggle, and now began to leaf through the pile of papers the sergeant had given him. Glenys seized the opportunity to hiss to Jane that you couldn't help admiring his blond good looks, and then he began to speak.

'Two or three weeks ago, a hundred young women between the ages of nineteen and thirty-five sat an intelligence test and then were put through an extremely rigorous programme to test their physical fitness. Some of those who passed the intelligence test failed the physical, but to our pleasure just over fifty of you – the young women in this room now – passed both intelligence and physical tests with flying colours. Congratulations.' He smiled slightly, and for the first time Glenys realised that, despite his rank, he was probably no more than twenty-four or five. 'Now, you must all realise that as the war progresses, the need for men on the front line increases. Many of you in the ATS are already doing men's work: women have taken on the driving of heavy lorries, and almost a hundred per cent of our clerks, military police, PT instructors and telephonists are now women. And still the need for men on the front line becomes ever more urgent. So our thoughts have turned to the ack-ack batteries. The top brass consider that if we could find women strong enough and intelligent enough to work the searchlights there would be a great saving of manpower. You were the pick of those asked to sit the tests, and are the first to be offered the opportunity to go on a six-week training course on searchlights. Any questions?'

A hand in the front row shot up. 'Please, sir, what if we can't start them great heavy generators? I've got a brother in the site just up the road from our house and he says it's real hard; I doubt I'd be able to do it myself.'

Captain Dorrington smiled thinly. 'We've thought of that,' he said. 'A man will be given the task of starting the generators, and once they're up and running we think you'll be able to cope.'

The girl, who had stood up to deliver her question, sank back into her seat and Glenys, highly daring, raised her own hand. 'I'd like to give it a go, sir,' she said, sounding far more confident than she felt. 'But suppose we get through our training and go to a searchlight battery and find we can't manage it; what then? Can we return to our previous jobs?'

The captain exchanged a look with the sergeant which Glenys interpreted as being of the 'poor little woman' variety. 'We don't doubt your ability to do the job. The reason why we hesitated at first to bring the ATS into searchlights was to do with location: ack-ack batteries are a long way from HQ and other amenities. You could be expected to get your own meals, and to manage such things as washing your own uniforms, et cetera. But obviously it won't suit everyone, and since we would prefer volunteers to pressed men it is important that you think carefully before agreeing to take on this most arduous task.' His keen gaze travelled slowly from face to face, and when he spoke again his voice was far more relaxed and friendly. 'Well, young ladies? You will be issued with extra clothing: when women were first brought into the army it was assumed that they would not have to face inclement weather conditions. And of course, though in time women will take the positions of command in the searchlight batteries, at first the more senior positions will be filled by men.' Once more his keen gaze swept the audience sitting before him, and once again that slow and very attractive smile softened his features. 'It is very gratifying to see that it would be quicker to take the names of those not interested in being re-mustered than to record those willing to undertake what I have to tell you could be a dangerous trade. Anyone not wishing to re-muster to the ack-ack battery section, please raise your hand.'

A subdued chuckle ran along the ranks a moment later as the captain said drily: 'Sergeant! Have you made a note of the names of those not wishing to re-muster?'

Everyone laughed as the sergeant, grinning sheepishly, said that he had done so, but Glenys had thought of another question and raised her hand again, catching the captain's eye and speaking quickly, before he could give the command to dismiss. 'Please, Captain Dorrington, since we may be seconded to remote places and will obviously have to rely upon one another far more than we do now, will it be possible for friends and colleagues to stay together?'

She half expected a freezing set-down, but instead he nodded slowly. 'Yes, I'm sure that can be arranged. Any more questions?'

There were none, and upon being dismissed the girls congregated in small groups outside their huts. 'I just hope, when we finish our training, we can get a few days' leave,' a tall, athletic girl said hopefully. 'My home's in Devon, and I've not been able to get to see my parents once since I joined.' She turned to Glenys. 'What do you think? I heard you talking in the Mess the other day and you've not been home either, have you?'

Glenys hesitated, not wanting to have to explain that she had no desire to return to the farm, but Jane, the only person there who knew she was a foundling, cut in quickly. 'Well, unless they post us to the Outer Hebrides, we ought to be able to visit our families more often. I dare say it's true that the army is much meaner with our time than the air force or the Navy, but most of us have been in at least a year and that's a long time to go without seeing family and friends.'

The pretty red-headed Maisie hugged herself. 'My folk live in Penzance. We're a family with a tradition of going into the Navy, so Mum and Dad are used to my brothers being at sea for long periods, but I must say they grumbled when the army didn't let me go home. What good is a forty-eight when you're trying to get from Newcastle to Penzance? Oh, well, I suppose it's all part of being at war. And Lucy there . . .' she indicated a serious, dark-haired girl who had just turned from another conversation, having heard her name, 'Lucy was brought up by an aunt she doesn't like, so they're both positively grateful to the army for keeping them apart.' She raised her voice. 'Isn't that so, Lucy?'

The dark-haired girl smiled and nodded. 'Yes, Aunt is glad of any excuse which keeps me at one end of the country and her at the other,' she said. 'But what do you think about all this, girls? I did wonder whether the army was thinking of girls on the ack-ack batteries when we took those intelligence and physical tests. I mean, look at the Waafs! I've watched the girls on the balloon site and they cope without the help of any men, and cope very well, too. But look, from what the captain said it sounds as though there's a chance that if we go to the basic training in groups, we might actually re-muster in a group as well. Let's put all our names together – the girls from this hut, I mean – and see if we can at least begin our new careers together. The army can only say no, after all.'

Jane and Glenys – and the rest of their battery – enjoyed the training and felt at the end of it that they were now capable of handling anything the service might throw at them. They learned how to spot an enemy plane from the others criss-crossing the sky above them, to manoeuvre the long arm which controlled the elevation and movements of their searchlight, to receive and relay information using a head and chest radio set, and to operate the generator. When the postings came through Jane and Glenys hugged one another, for they had both been posted to the same battery, but when Glenys took a closer look she hissed in her breath. No. 94 battery, on the outskirts of Liverpool, was to be their new home.

They had received their posting in the normal

way, via the bulletin board in the Mess, and one glance was enough to show them that the whole of their training group had been posted on the same day. There was a general feeling of satisfaction. Virtually everyone in their section had been posted to the surroundings of a city south of Newcastle, so it would be quite simple to travel together. 'It'll seem odd going by train and not driving ourselves,' Jane confided, when she and Glenys went to their hut to start packing. 'Personally, I was expecting to go to London, but of course the Huns' main objective now is to hit the ports so hard that shipping can no longer be relied upon.' She sighed, and Glenys remembered that before the war Jane's boyfriend Paul had sailed from Liverpool. She had quite envied Jane the affections of the tall, friendly officer, who was first lieutenant on one of the flower class corvettes. But only a matter of days earlier Jane had received a letter from him telling her that his corvette had been torpedoed. He was safe, having been picked up by a cruiser, but he thought it only fair to tell her that he had, whilst in hospital ashore, met Someone Else, a nurse named Marilyn, and they meant to marry before he put to sea again. The news had knocked Jane sideways. She told Glenys she had never dreamed that Paul might fall in love with another; all her fears had been that he might be killed in action, and now she had to face a new enemy: jealousy. She and Paul had known one another since childhood, and even to think of going out with anyone else would have seemed, to her, like infidelity. Both sets of parents were saving up so that as soon as their son and daughter got leave together they could host a grand betrothal party . . . perhaps even a wedding. Now, Jane told her friend miserably, she would have to break the news to them, for she was pretty sure that Paul would duck out of admitting what he had done for as long as possible.

'I always knew he was beautiful but weak,' she had confessed. 'But I told myself he would change, grow more responsible. Well, perhaps he has – after all, being torpedoed, and wounded in action, whilst your erstwhile companions drowned, is enough to make anyone, after thanking God for their deliverance, take life a bit more seriously.'

Glenys had sympathised in every way with her friend's distress, but could not help pointing out that Jane had had a lucky escape. 'And now you'll be able to accept invitations to go to the NAAFI dances and so on,' she had said. 'In fact, as soon as we settle into our new batteries and have a night off, we'll go to the local dance hall – there are lots in Liverpool – and see whether we can find ourselves a dashing officer or possibly even a handsome Spitfire pilot apiece.'

But that had been before they had actually reached their new home, and when they did so, and had settled into the hut previously shared by fourteen men, they realised that airy talk of going to dances was airy indeed. Buses ran from the camp to the battery, and no doubt as they settled in they would find others equally determined to find some way of entertaining themselves, but they were a long way from the city centre and at first they were too busy with their new work to even think about trying to get there.

Glenys was sitting at a table in the cookhouse, writing a letter to Mo, when Jane walloped her in the back and peered over her shoulder. 'What on earth are you finding to write home about?' she asked. 'You never get any letters back – oh, and I can tell you why not. It's because you don't put your address at the top of the page. What a halfwit you are!'

Taken off guard, Glenys stared at her for a moment and then, most unexpectedly, burst into tears.

Jane stared wide-eyed, and took a cautious glance around the room before sitting down at the table opposite her friend. 'Hush!' she said quietly. 'Don't make a scene; everyone's staring at us.' She glanced out of the window; the sun was shining and a gentle breeze moved the branches of a tree nearby. 'Let's go for a walk and you can tell me all about it.'

And as soon as they were alone the whole story came tumbling out, all about Sam and the children, Nain and Taid, and Weathercock Farm. Jane was fascinated and told Glenys, frankly, to stop being such an idiot. 'How can you be so foolish?' she said. 'Of course you must give them your address. Oh,

Glenys, think of that poor little girl, longing to tell you how she's getting on. It's downright cruel.'

Glenys shook her head. 'I can't,' she wailed. 'You don't understand; if I give them my address they'll think it's because I want Sam to come after me, and I don't.'

Jane narrowed her eyes. 'Was this Sam Trewin your feller?' she asked. 'Why do you care if he comes after you, if he's no more than a friend? Come on, spit it out.'

Fortunately for Glenys, at that moment Jane spotted the truck which was waiting to pick up anyone who wanted to go into the city, and grabbed her arm. 'Look, the liberty truck. If we run we can catch it. That's why I was coming to find you. I know you wanted to see *Mr Smith Goes to Washington*, so why not come with me? But first stop messing about and put your address at the top of that letter. Honestly, Glenys, you're so sensible in other ways and so silly in others.' As she spoke the driver of the liberty truck revved the engine, and though the girls ran they did not make it in time to get aboard.

'Damn, damn and damn again,' Jane said wrathfully, slowing to a halt as the truck careered out of the gates. 'And I really did want to see that film.'

Someone dug Jane in the ribs and she turned to glower at Jack Keithley, their corporal. 'Don't,' she said crossly. 'We've missed the perishin' bus because Private Trent is a twerp, and there isn't a service bus into the city which would get us there in time to see our film.'

'Ho yes there is, in a manner of speaking,' the corporal said placidly. 'I've got a pal with a share in an old bullnose Morris; he came by to pick me up because we want to see *Stagecoach* at the Forum. Fancy a lift, young ladies?'

Jane, always at ease with the men on the battery, immediately accepted the invitation for them both. 'Only who's your friend?' she asked rather suspiciously. 'Not that ferrety little fellow with the ginger hair and the squint?'

The corporal laughed, but shook his head. 'No, it's not Sandy. He's a married man; his wife's a Waaf, didn't you know? And just to have everything plain and above board, neither I nor Lance Corporal Rigby is married. So you can come with us without strings, as they say. All right?'

Just then the bullnose Morris drew up outside the gates and the driver got out, and both girls recognised the darkly handsome young man who had recently joined their battery. There had been much speculation amongst the searchlight crew, and the girls realised that if they accepted the corporal's kind invitation they would be the envy of the section.

Glenys opened her mouth to ask Jane what she thought, but Jane was already speaking. 'It's very good of you and we do appreciate it,' she said gratefully. She grinned cheekily at both men. 'I notice you haven't queried our marital status. But as it happens we're as single as you like; a couple of innocents abroad, that's us.'

'Well, I am relieved,' Corporal Keithley said sarcastically, helping the girls into the back seat of the Morris. 'No one wants to sit in the front? Off we go then, young Rigby, and let's hope the films are as good as they're cracked up to be.'

Chapter 18

Glenys awoke when the sun, slanting through the window of the Nissen hut, fell across her face. For a moment she just lay where she was, curled up in her bunk, but then she glanced at her alarm clock, whose face read five fifteen. She smiled to herself. Reveille would not be sounded for another forty-five minutes, so she might as well go back to sleep. After all, the only thing she had to look forward to was brekker in the cookhouse – porridge or cereal, burnt toast and a smear of – yuck – marrow jam.

Glenys pulled the blankets up, but after five minutes she pushed them down again. After brekker came drill on the parade ground, and since the sun was shining and spring had well and truly sprung she might as well get up and have a quick wash, then have a wander round until it was time to go to the cookhouse. Or she could take advantage of her early rising and bag a shower, but what chance was there that the water would, for once, be hot?

Hot water! That reminded her that there was something other than drill to anticipate with pleasure. Today was her section's turn to march right across the city to the bath house, where they would wallow in hot soapy water, dry themselves off on the somewhat inadequate issue towels, and then march back to camp, where she and Jane would decide what to do with the rest of the day. Tonight was Glenys's last night on duty before she was due for what the officers called 'a spot of leave', a week for which she had not yet made plans.

She lay quiet for a few minutes, then leaned over and dug Jane in the back. 'Wake up, it's a lovely day,' she hissed. 'If we get up now we can be first at the cookhouse, then we can check our uniforms and so on and perhaps find a way of disguising our towels and soap and that for bath parade.'

Jane groaned and sat up, rubbing her eyes. The previous night had been a busy one for the girls on searchlights and Jane had been on the predictor, which meant she had had to track the target visually and pass the information on to the gunners. The other members of the section had not been idle, of course. Glenys was a spotter because she had done well on the aircraft recognition course; she had a good memory and found it easier than most of their team to pick out the identifying features of the planes making for the docks. She used this gift to good effect; already their team had accounted for several hits. Her worst fear, however, was that she might make a mistake and cause a friendly aircraft to be shot down . . .

'What's up?' Jane's sleepy voice cut across her musings. 'Oh, hooray, bath parade! And I haven't forgotten I said you can have a bit of the

332

rose-scented soap that French flyer gave me at the last NAAFI dance if you can hack it off the bar.' She chuckled. 'Is that why you're awake early?'

'I'm awake early because you were snoring,' Glenys said, pushing her blankets right down and getting out of bed. 'And having woken, I'm going out to enjoy the sunshine. Come with me, there's a dear.'

She half expected an indignant refusal but Jane, though she groaned, agreed, and after a very quick – and cold – wash in the half-empty ablutions hut they presently joined the queue for porridge and toast in the cookhouse and dipped their mugs into the enormous bucket of tea at the end of the line. 'After the parade I thought we could catch a bus into the centre, get our shopping over early, and then see a flick, if there's anything decent on,' Glenys suggested as they settled themselves at a table for two. 'Only don't you go and fall asleep like you did in *The Hunchback of Notre Dame* because it's dead embarrassing.'

Jane giggled. 'All right, all right, I'll do my best to stay awake, only I've never really got used to working seven or eight nights on the run,' she said. 'What's showing?'

Knowing her friend's weakness for cowboy films, Glenys pretended deep thought. 'Dunno, but there's bound to be a Western on somewhere. I like a comedy myself, but I'll go along with whatever you choose.'

When they got back to their hut they found a

scene of frantic activity, with girls in various stages of undress screaming at each other and swapping items of clothing, button sticks and lanyards whilst others made vague dusting motions at the floor, walls and windows.

'What's up, Daf?' Glenys asked the nearest girl, who was busily polishing her buttons and humming a popular tune as she did so. 'No, don't tell me . . .'

'Some high-up is doing the rounds and we've been picked on for a kit inspection,' Daf explained. 'I told our dear leader that we would be on bath parade just as soon as we'd done our PT, but she said we'd been chosen because our section downed three German aircraft over the course of the last fortnight, and we should be very pleased with ourselves. But they're halving the length of the PT demo, praise be to God.'

Glenys pulled a face. 'I knew it, I just jolly well knew it! Still, if they really halve the PT demo, that's something. Thanks, Daf; you always know what's going on.' She began to strip the sheets from her bed and square up the blankets, but Daf shook her head.

'No, dearie, this is a special inspection for some reason. Beds are to be made up so that the visiting officer or whatever believes we are really cosy,' she said. 'Apparently we aren't getting enough new blood in the ack-ack section, so they're having a recruiting drive and we're part of it.'

'Oh! Thanks, Daf,' Glenys said, beginning to

make up her bed again. 'They've not cancelled the bath parade, I trust?'

'Not so far,' Daf conceded, holding her tunic up and regarding it critically. 'Better get your PT stuff together, though . . . glory, what a day!'

Jane, replacing her biscuits – her name for the sections of her mattress, which she had just piled on top of one another – unfolding her blankets and giving a low moan as she searched for unladdered stockings, said she just wished high-ups would descend on the men instead of them, but Glenys, though she laughed, said it was natural, particularly if the visiting officer was a man. 'Gives them a thrill to order girls about and see their knickers and suspender belts laid out for their approval,' she said. 'And we're better at that sort of thing than the fellers. Oh, drat, is that a step I hear? Stand by your beds, Gunners!'

The kit inspection went well, only one girl having the humiliation of seeing her neatly arranged possessions thrown on the floor because she had not made up her bed, though she had squared her blankets correctly, and the PT session went even better. Glenys thought that the lovely sunshine helped, and when PT was over and the girls were back in their hut getting towels, soap and clean underwear ready for the bath parade, she gave Jane a nudge. 'Whilst we're in the city centre this afternoon we might go to Lyons and have sausage and chips. It would make a change from PS.'

Jane grinned. 'Peculiar stew,' she said. 'The girls

335

– and some of the blokes – nickname everything and everyone. They used to call you "Frozen Fanny", as I recall, but they've not done that for a while.'

'No, and they'd better not,' Glenys said. 'I'd see the bombardier and get them put on a charge. Hey, the girls are forming up into two lines, bath towels at the ready; better get a move on, Gunner Bennett!'

Marching smartly through the streets of Liverpool, Glenys was aware that all her section regarded bath parade with mixed feelings. Their way led them past several enormous factories, and as soon as the factory girls spotted them the jeers would begin to fly. Some of the more hot-tempered girls were wont to reply in kind, though always beneath their breath, but as their bombardier had pointed out the first time they were verbally attacked, the ATS were always immaculate and could afford to ignore the factory girls. Those in munitions were yellow-faced as daffodils, save for their hands which would have done credit to a coal miner, and whilst their overalls might be clean at the beginning of the week, after two or three days of wear they were stained, oily and filthy. Hair was dragged back with bits of string and fingernails were grimy, although the bombardier was at pains to point out that none of this was actually the fault of the girls themselves.

'The thing is, you can damn well take no notice, because you know it's only jealousy,' she had informed them as the girls quickened their pace, eager to escape from the tide of insults. 'Eyes front *if* you please!'

The attitude of the factory girls had been painful at first, but now it was accepted as something to be ignored, and Glenys and Jane exchanged wry looks as Swithin, who had been promoted to lance bombardier only the previous week, gave the order to wheel right and the factories were left behind.

The bath house was a large building, steamy and warm, and Glenys thought the pleasure of having a hot bath more than made up for the insults of the factory girls. There were not enough tubs for everyone to bath at the same time, so Swithin adjured them to remember that others were waiting. 'Five minutes to wash, five minutes to soak and five minutes to get dry,' she reminded them as they took their places at the head of the queue. 'And don't fill the tub over the four inch mark.'

'Don't do this, don't do that . . . what about dressing? Surely you don't expect us to march out of the bath house in the buff?' Glenys said cheekily. 'Just because you've been promoted doesn't mean you can boss your old pals around.'

'Yes it does,' Swithin contradicted. She sniffed. 'Oh, someone's got scented soap. Is it you, Bennett? Can I have a borrow when it's my turn for the tub?'

'So long as you don't leave it in the water to go all soft and squishy,' Jane conceded, and was about to expatiate on this theme when the door against which Glenys had been leaning opened and a damp-haired, pink-cheeked girl emerged, beaming. She started to say 'In you go, Trent', but Glenys had already shot into the cubicle, slammed the door and begun to hurl her clothes on to the wooden rack provided. It was tempting to fill the tub to the brim, but naturally she did not do so. Instead she filled it exactly to the four inch mark, and jumped in. Jane's lovely soap was much appreciated, and by the time Glenys was neatly dressed once more she was at peace with the world.

She left the cubicle door open and went out into the street, where a couple of benches had been erected so that bathers who had to wait for others would have somewhere to sit. Jane, who had finished first, was in a particularly sunny mood. 'It made me think of home,' she murmured dreamily. 'Our house didn't have a bathroom when we moved in – Friday nights Mum filled the tin bath in front of the fire and the family took turns while Mum timed us by the kitchen clock. Of course, before the war we could have had the water right up to the brim, but since we had to carry it in from the pump in the yard and heat it up in the biggest saucepan Mum possessed we never did – fill the bath right up, I mean. But in 1936 Mum and Dad had an extension built on to the kitchen; it's got a tub, a hand basin and a lavvy, and there's even a bench in the garden so in the summertime there's somewhere to sit while your hair dries. But we still take our turn to get clean, just as we do here.'

'Sounds nice,' Glenys said, plonking herself down next to her. 'I hope the others hurry; if there are enough of us perhaps Swithin will let the early birds go on ahead. Then we'll have time to hang our towels out to dry and snatch a bun or some biscuits from the Naafi before we catch a bus to the city.'

Even as she spoke, Swithin appeared. 'There're enough of you out to make a respectable column and you've already had an unscheduled kit inspection, so you might as well form up in twos and get going,' she said. 'Trent, you're in charge; see that they get home safe, there's a good girl. I'll round up the stragglers. See you in the cookhouse.'

An hour later Glenys and Jane had hung out their towels in the beautiful spring sunshine and were heading for the bus which stopped outside the camp and would take them into the centre.

'I'm not at all sure I really want to spend such a perfect day in the cinema,' Glenys said as they climbed aboard the bus. It's not often we see the sun.'

The conductor, overhearing, gave a low whistle. '*Rebecca*'s showing,' he informed them. 'It's a grand fillum so it is. You don't want to miss it.'

'Cheeky sod,' Jane said as he moved away, but she was careful to keep her voice low. 'Tell you what, I can see you don't want sixpenn'orth of dark, so we'll go to the shops and then I'll go to the cinema by myself. I don't mind so long as it's not a romantic weepy; I do so hate it when the lights go up for the interval and my face is all smeary with tears.'

Glenys laughed. 'Right. If you really don't mind I'll go for a walk instead – I've always been intrigued by shipping, and though I did go on the overhead railway once, before it was bombed, you can't get close to the ships the way you can if you walk along the Dock Road. What time shall we meet afterwards? Six o'clock?'

Jane agreed to this, and presently they reached Ranelagh Street and dived into Lewis's. Used, by now, to empty shelves and a scarcity of goods for sale, they still found it thrilling to be in a big store, and by the time they had visited every department and actually come upon a tiny amount of makeup for sale, they felt that they had had a really exciting day out. Glenys bought a lipstick and a pale brown eyebrow pencil which, though it did not go perfectly with her ash blonde hair, was better than a darker shade would have been. Jane, blessed with very dark and gleaming curls, bought rouge and a tiny pot of eye shadow. 'Though when we'll get the opportunity to flash our new makeup, heaven alone knows,' she said rather ruefully. 'What's the point of getting all dolled up for a NAAFI dance? And now, dear Glenys, I must be off or I'll miss the beginning of the film.' She sighed dramatically and cast her eyes heavenwards. 'Imagine missing even a minute of Laurence Olivier or Joan Fontaine. Meet you outside the Corner House at six. Not that you'll be in any hurry to leave the bright lights since you've got a week's leave coming up, you lucky thing you.' She hesitated outside the cinema of her choice and faced her friend. 'Look, I wouldn't dream of interfering, you know that, but I do think you ought to go back to the farm now that you haven't got the excuse of being too far north to make it there and back in your time off.'

Glenys felt the blood creep up her neck and flame in her cheeks. 'I can't go back yet,' she said. 'I left because I got too fond of someone and I knew he wasn't fond of me. Oh, we were friends all right, but nothing more. Now you get off and swoon over Laurence Olivier whilst I go down to the docks for a good look at the shipping.'

Jane did not need telling twice. They were on London Road and already a short queue was forming outside the cinema. She did turn and give Glenys a quick wave, however, and Glenys shouted: 'Lyons Corner House, six o'clock. Shall I order for you if I'm first?'

'Might as well; sausage and chips and a penny bun for pudding,' Jane bawled. 'Be good, and if you can't be good . . .'

'. . . be careful, and if you can't be careful buy a pram,' Glenys finished for her. Then she saluted an imaginary officer, clicked her heels the way the Jerries were supposed to do, and headed for the docks.

As she went she told herself, not for the first time, that she really ought to go back to the farm. Despite Jane's urging she had never given them her address, but she had said that the ATS girls were always being posted to different parts of the country and if she ever got near enough to Weathercock Farm she would definitely come and see them.

But I don't want to send a telegram and frighten you out of your wits, she had explained. *So I'll just turn up when I'm able.*

As she prowled along the pavement, peering sideways at the shipping, she wondered again what she should do. If Sam had not re-joined the Navy and was still at the farm, there was their unresolved quarrel hanging over her head. If, on the other hand, he had re-joined the Navy, then she would not see him but would suffer afresh the agonies of fear which attacked her whenever she thought of him afloat on the treacherous sea. It would be almost worse to know he was in constant peril than to see his contempt because she had run away. If only the pleasant friendship they had shared could have been something warmer. But it was no good wishing; if she'd had any sense at all she would never have left him, but would have worked at their relationship until it was strong enough to bear whatever lay ahead of them.

Glenys sighed, looked up at the towering shape of the nearest ship, lingered for a moment, and then set off at an even faster pace. Life was full of 'if only's. She had missed her chance of happiness through her own foolishness, and now it was too late to repine.

* * *

342

Sam saw the slim blonde in the familiar uniform as he had done a hundred times before and knew it could not be Glenys; it never was. But he followed, knowing that this was his last chance before he was whisked off to join his ship. Sealed orders were the order of the day now, but rumour had it that they were bound for distant waters, probably the Med, to join the fleet there. Embarkation leave such as he had just enjoyed was only granted to men who were about to be stationed abroad. So if it really *was* her this time . . . Sam quickened his pace. As if conscious of his pursuit the girl also seemed to speed up. There was something in her walk, the way she held her head, the swing of her hips . . . and then he threw caution to the winds and began to run, desperation coming to his aid. 'Glenys!' he shouted. 'Wait! Glenys Trent, will you turn round?'

For a moment he thought she had not heard, but just as he reached her she stopped and turned towards him, and it was Glenys.

Sam did not hesitate. He dragged her into his arms and began kissing her frantically. Forehead, nose, cheeks . . . mouth. When he had first grabbed her she had mumbled a protest and tried to pull away, and then suddenly her arms were tightly round his neck and she was responding to his kisses. When he finally released her, he was murmuring, 'I love you, I love you, I love you! Oh, Glenys, I should have said that ages ago. What a fool I was. Say you love me too!'

Glenys heaved a great sigh and for a moment leaned her head against his chest. 'Oh, Sam, of course I love you,' she whispered. 'But we're in uniform; you could get us court-martialled! Can't we go somewhere a little less public so we can talk? You see, I thought you didn't want me; I thought you were only interested in getting a mother for Jimmy and Mo and a housekeeper for the farm. That would have been all right if I hadn't loved you, but I knew I couldn't bear it if you married someone else.' She smiled mistily up into his face, tears forming in her big blue-grey eyes. 'Oh Sam, I'm on my way to meet someone, and she'll be waiting for me. Look, I'll be free tomorrow – I've got a week's leave. Could we meet then?'

Sam shook his head. 'No, my darling. I'm first lieutenant aboard the *Hunter*; we sail on the early tide and won't be back until God knows when. Our orders can only be opened once we're at sea, but I imagine we shan't be back in Blighty for a long time. But I'll write to you at the farm and you can write to me at my given address, and the moment I come back into port we'll get married, because all I want in the world is to be with you.' He pinched her cheek. 'I've been searching for you ever since you ran away, and now when I find you we must part almost immediately. Oh, Glenys, Glenys, how can I bear to let you go?'

How can I bear to leave him, Glenys asked herself as she stood and watched him go aboard the

Hunter. She ached to run after him, to beg him to stay, but she knew he could not. And presently she walked back to the Corner House, feeling as if she were floating a foot above the ground. That Sam loved her she no longer doubted. She loved him too, loved him with all the strength of her once lonely heart. But I'll never be lonely again, because whatever happens Sam and I are together now, and will remain together till death us do part, Glenys told herself. Dear God, if I'd known being in love was like this I'd never have left the farm. Why didn't I *make* him show his feelings; and why didn't I show him mine, for that matter? I knew I loved him, I just didn't know whether he loved me, and of course my silly pride wouldn't let me admit to a love which I was not sure was returned.

And now a week's leave would give her plenty of time to get back to Weathercock Farm, and face the task of explaining why she had left, and how she and Sam had resolved their differences. It'll be my first visit in nearly two years, she thought. I wonder how things have changed? I wonder if Nain and Taid will be happy when I tell them I've met Sam and all our troubles and misunderstandings are over? At least the kids will be thrilled. Oh, what a fool I was! I kept telling myself not to give in, not to go back until I was sure of Sam's affection. But how could I be sure when I made certain we never met? I really have been a fool, and giving in to Sam just now, admitting how much I love him, must be the only sensible thing I've done since

345

I left Weathercock Farm. I love and am loved in return, and that's enough to make anyone think they are on cloud nine. And I'll see Sam just as soon as his ship comes in, and when peace comes we'll never be parted again.

Chapter 19

'Hey, Beaver! Ernie Beaver! Don't you know you're on perishin' watch? Unless you want me to tip you out you'd better get on your feet and get up on deck, else you'll find yourself on a charge. It's just rung four bells for the change, so I'm off and you're on.'

Cyril Huxtable groaned and opened his eyes, then sat slowly upright. Whenever somebody called him by his new name he had to remind himself not to glance around for his one-time shipmate, Ernie Beaver, whose identity he had decided on the spur of the moment to steal because he dared not go ashore in his home port under his own name. In fact, he was wary about going ashore anywhere, or had been. The reason – which still made his blood run cold – was something that had happened on a previous visit to Liverpool. Ever since the incident of the necklace – which had turned up, just as his mother had predicted, when he had finally secured another berth and Mrs Huxtable had stripped his bed of its filthy sheets so that she might take them to the wash house – he had been looking for an opportunity to do a little thieving on his own account. When the air raids had begun in 1940, he had followed the example of his drinking pals whenever he was on shore leave, and when a raid started had helped himself to anything not closely guarded before the all clear sounded. And not immediately, but soon enough, he had remembered just where he could find the most valuable loot of all.

So when his ship had next docked in his home port and a raid had started he had set off to the area where the people with money lived. When he reached the house he was heading for, he simply lumbered up the garden path, ducked under the branches of a flowering tree and, heart thumping, put a cautious hand on the kitchen door handle. He knew an old lady lived here with her niece, a simple soul who frequently left doors and windows unlocked, but he was pretty sure they would have gone into the country to escape the bombs, probably to relatives who would see them safe. In the good old days, as he now thought of them, he had owned a long ladder and had come round Princes Park on his shore leaves cleaning windows for a local contractor called Freddie Cummins. On one occasion he had looked through a bedroom window and seen old Mrs Rathbone sitting in front of her dressing table with a beautifully carved wooden box open before her. He had frozen, statue still, and had seen the sparkle of precious stones and the gleam of gold before she had closed the lid, pushed the box into the dressing table drawer and hobbled out of the room.

Greed had caused his eyes to sparkle, might have led him to throw caution to the winds then and there, but at the very moment his hand stretched out to open the window he had been hailed from below. 'Hux! *Will* you get a move on, you lazy bugger! This may be beer money to you but it's my livelihood! Come on down and go next door.' Freddie Cummins had chuckled. 'I keep these customers 'cos I'm reg'lar and cheap; there's no one as mean as the rich. Go on, shift yourself.'

But that had been years ago; now he knew exactly what he must do, and his reward would be not beer money but a handful of those sparkly stones.

The back door had opened beneath his touch, the click of the latch drowned by the crump of the bombs, and he went like a shadow through the kitchen, across the hall, and up the stairs. He was almost at the top landing when he heard a sound, and glancing towards the half-open bedroom door he had nearly died of fright. An old, old woman stood in the doorway, ghostlike in a white cotton nightie, pointing a trembling finger at him. 'How dare you come into my house!' she said in a frail, shaking voice. 'I'll call the police, I'll have you arrested. I'll . . . I'll . . .'

And on those words she had tipped forward, and though, to be fair, Cyril had tried to catch her, she fell and lay, an immovable bundle, on the landing.

Cyril had left the scene, but not before he had tried to open the dressing table drawer and found it locked. He would have broken it open had he

349

not seen through the window a man in a tin hat and ARP uniform coming up the path. He must have seen the back door swinging open.

It was sheer bad luck that the ARP warden was Cyril's erstwhile boss, Freddie Cummins. Cyril pushed past him, muttering that he had noticed the open door and come in to check that all was well, but Freddie stopped short and reached out to grab his arm. 'Do I know you?' he said uncertainly, but Cyril was already moving again.

He did not know whether he had been recognised in the dark or what had happened to the old lady. He had returned to his ship and resolved not to go ashore again until he had ascertained that the wretched old woman was not dead. But even then he would be in danger if Cummins had recognised him. It was whilst he was still trying to discover whether the scuffers might be on his tail that another thought occurred to him. If only he could become another person . . .

Then had come the attack on his convoy, and when his ship had gone down with most of the crew Cyril had been one of the lucky ones, for he was a strong swimmer and had speedily found himself a spar on which to cling. The sea had been relatively calm; the enemy had gone on their way, knowing that they had scored a kill. Cyril had looked around him and seen, in the dim dawn light, what seemed to be a friendly ship, and had set off towards what he hoped would be rescue.

Then he had seen one of his shipmates, Ernie

Beaver, drifting towards him, his skinny white hands desperately clinging to just such a sturdy plank as Cyril's. He had contemplated leaving the other man to struggle on alone, but even as the thought occurred to him Ernie turned his long, horse-like face towards his approaching shipmate. 'Gi' us a hand, Hux,' he had pleaded. 'I can't swim . . . gi' us a hand.'

Grudgingly, Cyril had begun to swim towards the other man, and it was only when the two spars to which they clung collided gently that the idea had come to him. Here was his chance! He could see Ernie's pay book poking out of his breast pocket. No one was in sight; he and Ernie were alone on the face of the ocean save for the small sloop bearing down on them, and even as Ernie began to thank the man he plainly considered his rescuer Cyril made up his mind. Swiftly, he grabbed Ernie's pay book and thrust it into his own pocket, before bringing his fist down on Ernie's hands and tipping him, without a qualm, into the sea. Ernie Beaver had simply slid down towards the ocean bed far below, and Cyril, looking around him once more, could see no one near enough to have spotted his action. He began to grin, even to laugh, but hastily pulled a grave face as the sloop drew near and cast out a rope ladder and one of the crew leaned over the rail and bade him climb up to the deck as fast as possible. At least Cyril supposed the man said something of the sort, but since he spoke in a language Cyril could not identify his words could only be guessed at. But then another voice had been raised, speaking fractured English. 'What happened to ze ozzer bloke?'

For a moment Cyril, almost at the top of the ladder, felt a pang of icy fear, but he said, as he landed on the deck with a thump: 'Other bloke? What do you mean? There weren't no one else . . .' And then inspiration came to him. 'Oh, you must mean Cyril Huxtable. He were dead when our spars collided and the jolt sent him into Davy Jones's locker, I reckon.'

Lie with conviction and you'll never be found out, he told himself. Believe you are speaking nothing but the truth. This is the moment you get the chance to be a hero, the man who almost saved Cyril Huxtable's life, but sadly arrived just minutes too late.

He did not have long to bask in glory. The rescue sloop handed him over to a merchantman heading first for New York and then for Liverpool, so his celebrity was short-lived. The officers aboard the merchantman merely gave him the berth of a man who had been swept overboard in a storm and kept Cyril's nose to the grindstone.

But now they were approaching Liverpool; he could see the Liver Birds through the morning mist as he stumbled up on deck to take over the watch. This would be his first arrival at his former home port in his new identity, and he just hoped that no one would hail him by his real name. But he had shaved off his beard, and to the best of his recollection no one on this side of the Atlantic had ever seen him without it, so he should be safe enough.

Once he'd had a drink – several drinks – at a pub he had rarely frequented in his old life, he meant to go straight to his mother and enlist her support.

Mrs Huxtable was no longer living in the Court, which had been badly bombed, but had taken herself off to her sister's and got a job cleaning public lavatories and other amenities for the local council. Cyril had toyed with the idea of simply not telling her he had survived the attack on his convoy, but after much laborious thought he had come to the conclusion that she could be more useful to him if she were in on his secret than if he left her in the dark. It gnawed at his mind like a rat at a cheese that someone might reach the Rathbone jewels first and steal them from him, though he doubted anyone else would know exactly where the treasure was hidden. Not much longer, he told himself. Once he got the dressing table drawer unlocked and took the jewels he was sure it contained, he would be able to kiss the Navy goodbye and take himself off to somewhere a good deal safer than Liverpool in wartime. His mind filled with visions of unlimited riches, he performed his duties as the ship docked, then went ashore and gave an urchin sixpence to deliver a scribbled note to his Auntie Letty's address, asking his mother to meet him at Lyons Corner House that very afternoon.

'Oh, Cyril, it's grand to see you, so it is. They told me your ship went down with all hands, and you was missing presumed killed,' Mrs Huxtable said, sitting down heavily at the small corner table. 'And the money stopped coming . . . What happened? Where's you been?'

'It's a long story,' Cyril said vaguely, not wanting to go into too much detail. 'The main thing is, you mustn't call me Cyril any more.' He went on to explain, with certain omissions, how he had come to take over his erstwhile shipmate's identity, and sat back to await his mother's approval. When she said nothing, but merely looked thoughtful, he burst into angry speech. 'What's the matter, you silly old bag? You know the scuffers have been watchin' me ever since some interferin' busybody told them I'd kidnapped them kids. This way I get them off me back once and for all. So what's wrong with that, eh?'

His mother did not answer at once. 'Is this Ernie a local man?' she asked eventually. 'If so, me laddo, the first person to seek out Ernie Beaver is bound to notice he's changed somethin' remarkable. How will you explain that away, eh?'

'Ma, for one thing he was a single man, with no wife, and no family that he ever mentioned, and for another Liverpool weren't his home port,' Cyril said impatiently. 'He were from Southampton, which means that as long as I'm on me present ship no one's likely to put two and two together.' He glared at his mother. 'Satisfied? Want to hear the rest of me plan?'

'Sorry, Cy . . . I mean Ernie,' she said. 'Go on, spill the beans.'

Mollified, Cyril proceeded to tell his mother about the day when he had been cleaning windows at the Rathbone house and had spotted the rich spoils behind the glass, and went on to describe the night of the raid, when old Mrs Rathbone had collapsed at his feet. 'You've got to find out whether she's dead or alive,' he said. 'No one won't accuse me of murder, acourse, 'cos only you knows I ain't dead, but I need to know if she's still livin' in that house. So you write and tell me – only make sure you address the envelope to Ernie Beaver, aboard HMS *Pinewood* – and next time I come home I'll make sure we's set up for life!'

It was a fine hot day, but as Glenys walked along the sunken lane leading to Weathercock Farm she was torn between delight as each familiar scene unrolled before her and the chilly fear that she would receive a well-deserved telling-off for her long absence, perhaps even be told not to visit again.

Halfway across the farmyard she stopped and stared at the large dog kennel, which had been Flush's home as the farm had once been hers. She expected him to come rushing out, giving either a warning bark or an enthusiastic wag of his plumy tail as he recognised her. But no Flush emerged, and Glenys guessed that meant Taid was working in the fields somewhere. But she knew he would not leave the farmhouse empty without a dog to guard it, so Nain and perhaps both children were probably in the kitchen at this very moment. Glenys had bent to peer into the kennel, but now she straightened up, squared her shoulders and headed for the back door. She would take her medicine like a man – no, like a soldier of the ATS – and the sooner she got it over with the better.

She rattled on the back door, knocked, and pushed it open. 'Is it safe to come in or shall I be shot down in flames? I'm so sorry, so ashamed . . .' There was a stifled cry from the room she was entering and then her arms were full of Mo, and Nain was hobbling across the floor towards her, a beam spreading across her face, and Glenys knew that all was forgiven even before Nain's arms enveloped her.

'Oh, you foolish girl, no visitor could be more welcome,' Nain said, her voice shaking. 'We got your letters and longed to be able to tell you all our news, but of course, you naughty girl, that was impossible without an address. Sit down, do, and tell us why you stayed away so long.' She held Glenys at arm's length, looking her over whilst a slow smile spread across her face. 'My goodness, how your uniform suits you! But I do believe you've lost weight; have you been pining for – for a sight of your old friends? But I'm afraid you've missed Sam. He only left yesterday; he will be so disappointed. He's been searching for you . . .'

'I've seen him; that's why I'm here,' Glenys said quickly. 'I was on my way to meet someone, and I was hurrying because I was late and Sam was trying to catch me up. I think he must have been running because I didn't know anyone was behind me until suddenly someone grabbed me round the waist and it was Sam, bubbling over with excitement. Oh, Nain, I knew at that moment what a fool I'd been . . .'

Mo's voice broke in on Glenys's explanation. 'Was you a fool because you didn't come back to Weathercock Farm, or because you went away? Nain said you'd gone to get experience, wharrever that may mean, and I were afraid you might never come back, though Jimmy was sure you would and he's usually right, isn't he?' She grabbed Glenys's hand and pressed it to her cheek. 'Well, he was right this time, wasn't he? You have come back, and if you promise never never to go away again I'll let go of your hand so's you can drink the tea Nain is pouring and have a buttered scone.'

'And you must let Glenys sit down,' Nain said, pouring tea into two large enamel mugs. 'My goodness, wait until the others see you. Taid always said I was wrong to let you go and I was beginning to fear he was right, but now he'll have to admit I knew what I was doing.'

Glenys had seated herself at the table, and now she raised her eyebrows. 'Let me go? What do you mean?'

Nain chuckled, but continued with the task of splitting and buttering scones on which she had been engaged when Glenys had entered the room. 'I knew you and Sam had quarrelled, and while I won't say I have second sight – though Taid always insists that I do – I suddenly knew that you would run away from us, because nothing in your life had prepared you to understand the emotions of a man like Sam, who has had the dreadful experience of losing a loved one. He was trying to be both mother and father to his children, yet I could see, even if you could not, that he was . . . well, more than fond of you, my dear.' Her glance slid to Mo and a smile crinkled her eyes as she addressed her grand-daughter. 'I saw you nick that scone, you little monkey! And now we must let Glenys tell us what's been happening to her.' She turned back to Glenys. 'I can see you have all the self-confidence you lacked when you left us, and that is thanks to the ATS, of course. But I'm more interested in the social side of your life. Do you have a young man? Friends of both sexes?'

Mo gasped. 'Nain, you said a bad word,' she said accusingly. 'You said sex; our teacher says that's a bad word.'

Glenys giggled. 'It's not a bad word, darling, it's just another way of saying boy or girl,' she explained. She looked back at Nain and thought guiltily that the other woman had aged in her absence. She hoped to God it had not been worry over her which had caused the additional wrinkles and the trembling hand. But Nain was still watching her expectantly. 'Well, there have been a couple of fellows,' she admitted. 'But truly, Nain, they really were just good friends. And of course the person who ran away

358

from Sam and the farm is entirely different from the person who works on the ack-ack site, spotting enemy planes so that the gunners can shoot them down, and, in short, is in command both of her duty and of herself.'

Nain looked up quickly, her butter knife extended, and said one word: 'Sam?'

Glenys nodded shyly. 'Yes. He's . . .'

'He's my father,' Mo said conversationally. 'He likes you ever so much. One day when he'd been to the shops in Ruthin asking if anyone had seen you, only nobody had, he *cried*. He pretended the wind had made his eyes water but Jimmy and me knew he'd cried. And after that he said there was no point in searching for you, Auntie Glenys, because he said your letters were postmarked Newcastle upon Tyne, and that's so many miles away, you wouldn't believe.'

'Oh, darling Mo, don't tell me any more,' Glenys said, tears trickling down her own cheeks. 'But I'm back now, and though I shall have to return to my camp at the end of the week I'll try to get back to Weathercock whenever I have a spot of leave.' She turned to the older woman. 'Can you put up with me for just a few nights, Nain? I'll be really good and help in any way you name. And I'll start by helping you to butter those scones . . .'

But on these words the back door burst open and Jimmy and Taid, and a tall dark-haired girl in Land Army overalls, came into the room.

Glenys went straight across to the old man and

359

gave him a hug, then flushed at her own daring. Taid had always been shy with her; now that she thought about it they had never even shaken hands, but now he returned her embrace with delight. 'So you have come back to us. I'm glad,' he said simply. 'But you've missed our Sam.'

The glance Nain shot at him was full of warning. 'It's all right, Gethin; she's seen him,' she said, and turned to the girl who had just entered the room. 'Sally my dear, this is Glenys Trent, who had your job until she went and joined the ATS. Glenys, this is Sally Probert, our much-valued Land Girl. And here's Jimmy. You're lucky to catch him, because he's got a berth aboard one of the ships bringing goods across the Atlantic, and has to return to it at the end of the week.'

The two girls shook hands, but Jimmy was so overcome to find Glenys present that he could do little but grab her hand and tell her in a breaking voice how much he had missed her.

Glenys smiled at him. 'Oh, Jimmy, it's so good to see you! If I'd met you anywhere but here, though, I don't believe I would have recognised you. You're taller than I am now and a good deal heftier! In fact I'm surprised you haven't been called up.'

Jimmy looked gratified. 'I can't join the Royal Navy until I'm a bit older, but for the time being I'm very happy in the merchant fleet,' he admitted. 'At least I'm doing something for the war effort. But oh, Auntie Glenys, it's so good to see you!'

* * *

It was hard, parting from the family and the farm, but Glenys had no intention of getting into trouble through overstaying her leave. Mo and Jimmy insisted on accompanying her to the station, but it was not until Glenys had climbed aboard the train and got herself a corner seat that Jimmy voiced what was probably on his sister's mind as well as his own. 'Glenys, you do know our dad has been desperate unhappy ever since you ran away?' he said, his voice a growl one moment, a squeak the next. 'Have you and he made friends again?'

There was a short pause whilst Glenys felt her face gradually getting hot. She glanced round apprehensively; the train was full of service people saying goodbye to their own friends and families, so with Jimmy's eyes and Mo's fixed upon her she gave an embarrassed little nod. 'Yes, you could say that,' she admitted. 'But your dad was about to go aboard his ship and I couldn't keep Jane waiting, so . . .'

Mo gave a squeak of excitement. 'Next time you come home perhaps Dad will be back from wherever it is he's gone,' she said excitedly. 'Did he give you a cuddle? Jimmy says people who cuddle aren't friends, they're in *looove*; is that true?'

'Sometimes,' Glenys said bluntly, just as the guard blew his whistle and the train began to move.

'Jimmy, Jimmy, gimme a lift!' Mo shrieked. 'I want to give Glenys a goodbye kiss.'

But she was too late. The train steamed out of the station whilst Jimmy was still struggling to lift his sister up – he was not the only one who had put on weight – so Glenys simply waved and waved and shouted that she would be sure to come back to the farm whenever she could. Then she collapsed into her seat and settled down to watch the passing scene as the train steamed on towards Liverpool.

Cyril – now Ernie – climbed into his bunk and lay there unmoving for a moment, waiting for the warmth of the Navy blankets to overcome the terrible cold. As it did so, he reflected sourly that he had made the worst decision of his life when he had taken on another man's identity.

Oh, it had seemed a good idea at the time – it *was* a good idea – it was just that ever since becoming Ernie Beaver he had had the most appalling luck. For instance, no sooner had he returned to sea after the meeting with his mother than HMS *Pinewood* had been sent up to the north of Scotland and then, laden with ammunition, food and God knew what beside, to the Russian port of Murmansk.

And by God, it was cold! If he had had time to pity anyone but himself he would have pitied the pathetic creatures, many of them women, who unloaded the *Pinewood*, who despite the snow, gales and general appalling weather were clad in rags, and so thin and gaunt that many members of the *Pinewood*'s crew saved a part of their own rations to throw down to the skeletal workers on the quayside below.

Not that the dockers got a chance to snatch up the bounty descending from above; the armed guards saw to that. Cyril had seen the guards hitting the women with their rifle butts and then ignoring them, leaving them unconscious on the frozen ground for their companions to take away to God alone knew what horrible igloo or whatever their homes were called.

But much of this passed Cyril by. He had hoped for a posting to some delectable spot in the Mediterranean, but they were to be on the Russian run until the war ended, he supposed viciously; just his luck! Only the other day he had received a letter from his mother telling him that his Auntie Letty had a friend who cleaned a couple of the big houses near Princes Park, and had been willing to nose out what she could about the Rathbones to oblige Letty's sister. The old lady, it seemed, had died in one of the air raids during what was now being spoken of as the Liverpool Blitz, had been found on the landing by her niece without a mark on her, apparently: *the doc said it were a heart attack, brung on by fright, he reckoned.* Naturally Mrs Huxtable had not disclosed the nature of her interest in the affair, but Letty's friend hadn't mentioned any suspicion of foul play, so it looked as though Freddie Cummins hadn't reported Cyril's presence at the scene.

By the time he got to this part of the letter Cyril's anxiety was mounting: what if the house were cleared and sold before he could get back to

Liverpool? But Mrs Huxtable's next words allayed his fears. *The old lady's niece is staying on in the house – old Mrs Rathbone left it to her in her will, they say, and no one can't force her out, not even if she's daft as a brush, which by all accounts she is. Come home soon, son.*

But Cyril couldn't go home, or not yet, at least. Lying in his bunk as the feeling gradually returned to his fingers and toes, he started to plan how he would get his hands on the dressing table, and make himself master of that bulging jewellery box . . .

Chapter 20

August 1946

It was a glorious August day and Glenys, looking around her, felt that she was on top of the world. The war was over and Sam had been demobbed at last; he had served continuously in the Mediterranean since their one brief wartime meeting, so Glenys had not seen him for five years.

She and Jane, however, had been fortunate enough to stay together for a good deal of the conflict, but then the postings had come thick and fast. Glenys had spent time in Northern Ireland, gaining in experience and accuracy as she grew accustomed to uprooting herself, piling into a lorry or on to a train, and taking over some site where searchlights and ack-acks were needed, for she was now a lance bombardier and wore her white lanyard with pride. She had spent her leaves at Weathercock Farm when possible and worried about the volume of hard work demanded of the old people, but despite her fears Nain, Taid and even Mo seemed to take everything in their stride.

But now Sam and Glenys were to be married at long last. Glenys herself had been demobbed only a week earlier, and had hurried back to Weathercock Farm and into Sam's waiting arms.

Nain and Taid had taken it for granted that after the wedding the happy couple would live with them, but Sam, though he thanked them sincerely, said that he had put down a deposit on a farm cottage less than a mile from the Griffiths property. Nain said sadly that she would miss them, but Taid thought it was for the best.

'We'll have Mo to stay for a couple of weeks whilst you settle in, but if you're thinking of going shopping in Liverpool I think you should take her with you. Since VE Day last year I've noticed that she's mentioned her old fear of the Huxtables more than once, and if Solomon Court's been bombed, which is more than likely, it might convince her that they're out of her life for good,' Taid suggested.

Glenys mentioned the idea to Sam a couple of days later as the two of them stood in the cottage, surveying the whitewashed walls and brick floor with an owner's pride, and he agreed at once. 'We'll go on Saturday. It's our first home and we'll enjoy furnishing it and setting out our things.'

Accordingly, they accompanied Mo on a tour of the courts and markets in the area around Scotland Road. She shed a tear when she failed to recognise her old school in the bomb site to which it had been reduced, and was upset to find the corner shop where she used to spend her pennies gone, but she cheered up at the sight of the pile of bricks and rubble which had once been her home. 'You were right, Auntie Glenys. No one could live there any more, so the Huxtables really have gone,' she said. 'I wasn't *really* scared; it was a long time ago and with any luck Cyril might have been killed in the war anyway, but I can stop worrying about them at all now.'

Unfortunately, the shopping expedition itself was not quite so successful, and they returned with only a couple of Utility chairs and a small bedside cabinet. 'The trouble is, everyone's in the same boat,' Glenys said wearily, dropping into a creaking wicker chair in the farmhouse kitchen and accepting the cup of tea Nain offered. 'But we met old Mrs Ransome from Solomon Court – she recognised Mo, which is amazing after all these years – and she told us there's going to be a grand furniture sale just outside Liverpool next weekend. Apparently someone has hired a tumbledown farmhouse with a good deal of land and the usual outbuildings, and he's opening it up as a sort of second-hand emporium. People can take any furniture or clothing or whatnot they want to get rid of and put it up for sale, and everyone who comes in either to buy or to sell will be charged a shilling at the gate. It's a good idea, don't you think?'

The family agreed, Mo saying rather bitterly that it would make a change from cleaning the cottage and adding that Mrs Ransome had said the farm would be open both on Saturday and Sunday, unless it rained.

News of the sale had aroused interest in other

quarters, too. Cyril Huxtable, demobbed and back in Liverpool, had been considerably heartened when he had walked straight into a fellow selling the *Echo*, someone with whom he had been on drinking terms, and the other man had stared for a moment and then looked away. Cyril had known himself unrecognised. The next day, he saw a man in the uniform of a naval rating, a man he had once known well, and the man's eyes had slid over him without a trace of recognition, increasing Cyril's sense that he almost was, in truth, Ernie Beaver.

So it was with a light heart that he set out for Mrs Rathbone's house. He would not try to enter the place in broad daylight, of course, but a little reconnaissance never did any harm, and might stand him in good stead when the time came to make his move. When he reached the house he padded softly round the side and knocked firmly on the back door. It was locked, and when he examined the nearest window he realised that the whole place was positively sealed shut. No one was going to get in without using force.

But just as he was about to leave the property he noticed a note pinned to the front door, and as he conned it a smile spread across his unlovely countenance. The note said that the house was to be offered for sale, but that the furniture would be taken to a nearby farm where a market would be taking place the following weekend, and anyone interested might put in an offer for anything which took their fancy.

Cyril had heard of these sales, and reflected that his luck had clearly changed at last, and for the better. He and his mother could visit the sale, find the dressing table, buy it . . . and then unlock that drawer by fair means or foul and make off with the jewellery, and no one any the wiser. After all, them jewels is naturally mine, since I'm the only feller what knows where they are, he told himself. So all in all, Cyril me laddo, you're on to a winner, and soon Ma and meself will be in clover!

When Saturday dawned the weather seemed set fair, and Sam, Glenys and Mo arrived at the farm in good time. They were able to buy two respectable single beds and a rather ancient brass double, but realised that it would be necessary to come back the following day with a hired van to carry their purchases home. Sam had got chatting to one of the policemen on duty at the market, who had mentioned that his brother-in-law had a small removals business in Ruthin, and they had agreed to get a van from him. Mo wondered aloud why two scuffers had come to the sale, and Sam explained that thieves as well as genuine customers frequented such places.

As the hired van trundled along the country lanes the next day, Mo was describing the contents of their old home to Glenys. 'Our mam had a little rosewood desk which she used when she wrote her letters and paid bills,' she said. 'And there was the most beautiful carpet, pale blue, scattered with pink roses. And a Welsh dresser in the kitchen, and easy

chairs in the parlour, the sort with arms and high
backs, and of course two of the bedrooms were
furnished especially for Jimmy and me; pink for
me and blue for Jimmy. Oh, and I forgot, there was
a cupboard in the kitchen called a maid saver, and
chairs which Mam painted white; they stood round
the big kitchen table, and the china on the Welsh
dresser was real pretty . . .' But at this point Sam
intervened, laughingly accusing Mo of seeing their
old furniture through rose-coloured spectacles, and
in a very few minutes they had arrived at the farm.

Sam and Glenys had decided that today they
would ignore the bedroom furniture and concentrate on the parlour and the kitchen. A great many
of the things on sale for the former needed reup-
holstering, but the stuff for the kitchen could definitely be moved to the farm cottage along with the
beds they had bought the previous day.

'Starting from scratch is an enormous task, when
you think about it,' Sam said as they chose easy
chairs. 'Grace would have been heartbroken to
know that the furniture she once chose so carefully
no longer existed.' He squeezed Glenys's hand.
'You two would have loved one another; you're
very alike in many ways,' he said, unconsciously
echoing Nain. He turned to his daughter, who was
jumping up and down and clearly trying to get his
attention. 'What do you want, darling?' he asked,
laughing. 'There's bound to be a privy somewhere
around, if that's your problem. Just knock at one
of the cottages and ask if you can use theirs.'

His daughter shook her head indignantly. 'No, Dad, it's not that. I've just seen a beautiful dressing table for my room. It's only two quid and it has two little lamps with pink shades and a big mirror. Oh, do come and see. Auntie Glenys will tell you it's a bargain if you ask her!'

'Presently,' Glenys said as Mo bounced up to her. 'I thought we'd take a look at some of the clothes stalls. The dress you're wearing is very pretty, but far too small. And though I'm happy with my ATS slacks and Aertex shirt I wouldn't say no to a cotton frock.'

But Mo, for once, was more concerned with her bedroom furniture. 'I'd love a dressing table all of my own. Can't we look at it first?'

Glenys and Sam agreed, but when they accompanied her to the seller of the bedroom furniture the object of her desire had been sold. 'You must mean the one from the Rathbone house. I just sold it to a big feller with dark hair; he paid one of the lads a bob to help him carry it. You'd best hurry, 'cos I reckon if you offer him a quid more'n he paid me, he'll jump at it. He looks the sort what'd do anything for money.'

Glenys sighed at Mo's entreaties but knew what she was like. If the girl had set her heart on the dressing table, she would not rest until she had searched the entire sales area for its new owner. She cast a glance at Sam, who raised his eyebrows. 'She's always known her own mind,' he said ruefully. 'You know what kids are. I'll start loading the van whilst you and Mo go for a look.'

Glenys nodded. She and Sam had come to an arrangement to hire the driver as well as the van, and he had agreed to transport their belongings to the cottage over the course of the next two days.

Mo and Glenys toured almost the whole sales area without success, but when Sam appeared to say that they were nearly ready to set off with the first load, Mo jutted her lip. 'I've not quite finished lookin' for that dressing table,' she said. 'Can I have another ten minutes?' Sam agreed, and Glenys said it would give her time to have a quick look at the clothes, so Mo went off to search the only part left which was the stables, with their lovely deep mangers and half-doors, similar to those at Weathercock Farm. She went straight there, going carefully from stall to stall, staring up at the names over each manger: Millie, Flossy, Black Prince. Each name board held a variety of rosettes, red, blue, yellow, green and orange, though they were now so dirty that the colours were barely discernible.

Mo noticed a little window giving on to the tack room, and thought she could see movement on the other side. She went nearer and heard voices, then peeped through the glass and made out the dressing table. Even as she began to pluck up her courage to go and ask if she might buy it from the new owner, she saw a large dark-haired man raise an axe above his head and bring it crashing down on the wood.

Mo gasped just as a voice she had once known well came to her ears. 'Cyril! Mind where you're wavin' that perishin' thing. You nearly had me bleedin' ear off,' it said peevishly. 'Why d'you want to destroy it, eh? I quite fancy a pretty piece of furniture, instead of the old rubbish your Auntie Letty thinks so posh.'

Mo stood on tiptoe and peered more closely, then hastily dropped on to all fours. She could not possibly be mistaken; it was the Huxtables! It had been more than seven years since she had seen them last but she would have known them anywhere, particularly the old woman. If only Jimmy were here, he would have known what to do! When they had lived in the Court he had told her to run to him if she was in trouble, but Jimmy was doing his National Service, so she would get her father – and Auntie Glenys, too – to tell the scuffers that they must arrest the wicked Huxtables before they could do any more mischief to her beautiful dressing table. She crawled carefully across the stable floor and did not rise to her feet until she reached the half-door which led out to the yard. Then she ran like the wind, putting as much distance as possible between herself and the Huxtables. When she collided with someone she was already breathless, and for a moment could not answer his: "'ello, 'ello, 'ello? What's up with you, queen?'

'Oh, constable . . . thank goodness! There's a crime being committed not far from here and I want you to arrest someone; two someones in fact. They've got an axe and are breaking up the very dressing table I've set my heart on. Only we'd best fetch my dad in case you don't believe me.' She tugged imperiously at the constable's jacket. 'Please, do hurry, or they'll escape!'

The policeman was beginning to argue as they reached Sam and Glenys, and Sam, conscious that his daughter had a bee in her bonnet about the Huxtables, would have pooh-poohed her fears, but Glenys had never forgotten the wretched state the children had been in when she had first met them, and joined her voice to Mo's. 'I'd be very much obliged, constable, if you'd come with us, especially if Cyril Huxtable has an axe. He's a dangerous man without one, but armed . . . I shudder to think what he might do.'

The policeman looked at Glenys's earnest face and Mo's frightened one, and nodded gravely. 'Lead on, young lady,' he said. 'Maybe you're right and maybe you're wrong, but I do seem to remember the name Huxtable from somewhere, so if it really is him, I'll take him in charge.'

When they got back to the farm, the whole story came tumbling out. Despite his initial objection Sam had agreed to accompany Mo, Glenys and the constable to the stable block and find out if Mo really had seen someone wielding an axe. 'Though why anyone would want to destroy a nice little piece of furniture in this day and age, I can't imagine,' Sam had said. 'It's not as if the weather's cold and the fellow needed kindling for his fire . . . ah, there's the stable. In we go, constable.'

As they entered the tack room, two enquiring faces

turned towards them, and Mo shrank back until she was half hidden by Glenys. The man began to speak, demanding angrily why they were all staring at him and his mother. 'And if you want to know why I'm smashin' this perishin' dressing table, it's to get at my wallet what I'd put safely away in the middle drawer for the journey home, only somehow the drawer got stuck and it's got all my money in it.' He turned to the old woman. 'Ain't that so, Ma?'

'Oh, really?' the constable said, with a world of disbelief in his tone. 'That sounds a pretty thin story, Mr Cyril Huxtable.'

Cyril's eyes fairly bulged. 'Cyril Huxtable?' he said, his voice vibrant with astonishment. 'Who's Cyril Huxtable? I ain't never heard of no one by that name. What makes you think I'm him?'

Sam began to laugh. 'I know this man,' he said. 'And his name's certainly not Cyril Huxtable. He was a rating aboard my ship towards the end of the war. His name's Ernie Beaver, and he and I had several run-ins, Mr Beaver not understanding the difference between yours and mine as regards rum rations and personal property. In fact he's a thoroughly unreliable person whom the Navy will be glad to do without in future.'

But Mo, standing at her father's elbow, gave him a nudge. 'Dad, I don't know Ernie Beaver but I do know Cyril Huxtable, truly I do, and that's who he is, and that fat old woman . . .'

Sam looked from Cyril to his mother, and smote his forehead. 'You're right, Mo; that's the woman who came to the door when I was searching for you and Jimmy.' He turned to the policeman. 'There's something very strange going on here,' he said. 'That woman is definitely Mrs Huxtable, which would seem to indicate . . .'

The fat old woman gave Sam a malevolent look. 'It ain't got nothin' to do wi' me,' she said. She pointed dramatically at Mo. 'As for that kid, she's a real bad 'un, pilferin', lyin', gettin' honest folk into trouble . . . why, she tied my son's bootlaces together so he measured his length down the stairs. Ain't that so, Cyril?'

Cyril was beginning to agree when he saw the trap yawning in front of him and tried desperately to unsay his mother's words, but it was too late. The policeman did not move quickly enough, however, and Cyril was running before the man had so much as produced his handcuffs. Mrs Huxtable wept and wailed and used language seldom heard on the lips of a female, trying to prove that she had known nothing about the false identity which her son had acquired. ''Cos I ain't gettin' done for no murder,' she whined, giving the policeman another reason for taking her straight to the cells.

'Murder bein' a word no scuffer can ignore,' he said solemnly, clicking the handcuffs into place. 'Come along now, and less of that language if you please.'

Mrs Huxtable had promptly begun to protest her innocence, condemning Cyril again without a moment's hesitation. She had seemed quite content to blame her son for everything, and Sam, Glenys and Mo had watched with fascination as she was carried off in a black Maria, cursing freely.

Nain and Taid listened in astonishment to the story of this very odd example of a mother's love, but when it was all told Taid nodded his grizzled head. 'Sometimes we gets a sow which tries to eat her own babbies,' he said. 'We call her a rogue, and some other beast is give her piglets to rear. I reckon your Mrs Huxtable is a rogue, in every sense of the word.'

Cyril Huxtable had been nabbed down at the docks, trying to wheedle his way aboard a cargo boat bound for South America, and was now in custody and about to stand trial for the theft of Ernest Beaver's identity, including the taking of his wages for several years. Mrs Huxtable was also in prison and would stay there for a long time, since not only had she aided and abetted her son in his fraud, but she had abused her position as carer of Sam Trewin's children, stealing money and anything else she could lay her hands on meant for Jimmy and Mo, and interfering with His Majesty's mail. Given her age, it was possible she would spend the rest of her life behind bars.

The riddle of the destruction of the dressing table was a mystery until Mo asked if she might get someone to mend it, and her father had agreed. 'Though why Cyril was chopping it up is beyond me,' he admitted frankly. 'Was there anything of value in the locked drawer, when the carpenter got it open?'

'No, nothing,' his daughter assured him. 'Just a box full of stage jewellery. Dad, did you know Mrs Rathbone was quite a well-known music hall artiste when she was young? The carpenter said his mam had been her dresser at one time, Mrs Rathbone's I mean, only she was called Miss Tilly, Songbird of the North, then. He said that when you're on the stage real jewellery looks insig – insigni . . .'

'Insignificant,' her father supplied. 'Cyril must have believed the jewels to be real. He's quite stupid enough to go stealing something worthless.'

Glenys found it difficult even to pretend sorrow at the old woman's fate, for she remembered the two little waifs, skinny as sticks, who had come to her room on that dark December night. She had thought them delightful children, and had she not intervened they might never have escaped the Huxtables' brutal rule. Glenys sighed, but decided that the Huxtables had got what was coming to them; and anyway, she had more important things to think about.

So now, at the end of September on the actual eve of her wedding, Glenys was trying to be calm and sensible. She had spent the afternoon scrubbing the cottage and rearranging the furniture for the hundredth time. She had made up the bed with lavender-scented sheets from Nain's linen press and she had helped put the finishing touches to the wedding breakfast which would be held, after

378

the church ceremony, at Weathercock Farm. She smiled across the kitchen at her husband-to-be, who was placidly darning socks. Glenys had giggled but Sam had assured her that seamen were past masters at many of the tasks she had once thought to be women's work.

Sam looked up from his task and smiled lovingly at her. 'These past few weeks haven't been as hard for you as they have for me,' he observed. 'It's been like sitting at a table with a wonderful meal spread out before one, unable to take so much as a mouthful. Tomorrow . . .'

Mo had been sitting on the floor stitching away at the rag rug she was making as a wedding present for Glenys. It was almost finished, only needing half an hour's work to complete, but as she dug her needle into the braiding she raised a frowning face to her father's. 'I don't get it,' she said plaintively. 'It isn't as if we mean to eat Auntie Glenys tomorrow, so what do you mean?'

Glenys intervened quickly. 'It's what we call a figure of speech,' she explained. 'We wanted to get married months and months ago, but I didn't want an army wedding and neither did Sam, so I stayed with my section until they decided to demob me . . .'

'Oh, I know all that,' Mo said impatiently. 'But you're going to get married tomorrow so I still don't understand . . .'

Sam put down his darning, bit the end off the wool and grinned at Mo. 'Sorry, poppet, it was a daft thing to say,' he said remorsefully. 'I think the best way of putting it is to say that the past few weeks, with both of us living at Weathercock Farm, have tried our patience somewhat. We were living together without being able to behave as married people. Does that satisfy you?'

Mo thought for a moment and then spoke with her usual devastating directness. 'Do you mean you can't sleep in the same bed together? That's the only thing which will change tomorrow, isn't it? And if I'm right . . .'

Glenys decided it was time to put her oar in. 'You know too much, young lady,' she said severely. 'And if you've nearly finished the braiding on the rug you might nip upstairs and try on your brides-maid dress. It's hanging on the door in our bedroom. And try the satin slippers on as well; they're in the wardrobe by the . . .'

'I know, I know, and I'll be down again in two ticks,' Mo gabbled. 'I wish you could try your dress on too, but Dad might see and that would be bad luck. Oh, how I'm looking forward to tomorrow! Though of course I'll miss you, because Nain and Taid say I'm not to go down to the cottage for two whole weeks. Taid says it's the nearest you'll come to a honeymoon, whatever that may mean . . .'

But the rest of her remarks were lost as she ran up the stairs, still chattering gaily.

Glenys and Sam exchanged a speaking glance and Sam blew out his cheeks in a long whistle. 'Phew! That kid's too knowing by half,' he observed.

'But living on a farm with all the animals around, it would be strange if she didn't know the facts of life.' He sighed and stretched luxuriously. 'Oh, well! Come and sit on my lap so I can give you a cuddle.'

Glenys got to her feet, but before she could take up Sam's invitation the back door opened and Nain and Taid came into the kitchen. Glenys hastily went over to the Aga and pulled the kettle over the flame, promising the newcomers a cup of tea just as soon as the kettle boiled. 'Mo's gone upstairs to try on her bridesmaid dress,' she said rather awkwardly. 'She'll be down in a minute.'

Nain laughed. 'She's only had it on a hundred times since that woman agreed to lend it to her,' she said. 'She's been queening it over the rest of her class for weeks. I keep pointing out that everyone in the school will rush out at eleven o'clock to watch the bride coming out of church – and you, Sam – but she still wants a promise from all her pals that they'll make sure her teacher is there to cheer her on.'

Presently Mo joined them, looking, Sam told her, prettier than any bridesmaid had a right to look. But Nain tutted disapprovingly as she and Glenys laid the table and got out the food which had been set aside for supper. 'You're becoming a conceited little madam,' she said, making shooing movements with both hands. 'Go and take that beautiful dress off before you spill something on it, and don't get too near the fire, because in my opinion that gauzy stuff would go up like a firework if a spark flew up and landed on it.'

Her granddaughter gave a squeak of dismay and fled, lifting up her pink silk skirts and displaying scratched bare legs, down-at-heel ankle socks, and the fact that the pink satin slippers were a trifle too large. 'I'm going, I'm going,' she said as she clattered up the stairs. 'Oh, I can't wait until tomorrow! I just hope that the guests don't eat all the grub while I'm changing, which I'll have to do because we promised Mrs Reynolds that I would only wear the dress for the ceremony itself.'

When her bright head had disappeared and they heard a bedroom door slam shut, Glenys and Nain smiled at one another.

'She's a good girl, despite her funny ways,' Nain said, beginning to slice the loaf. 'It's a pity she can't wear the dress for the wedding breakfast, but she wouldn't enjoy herself if she was worrying all the time about keeping it clean.' She glanced across at Glenys. 'And of course you're in the same position. I'd heard that Pinewood studios rented out wedding dresses that actresses had worn in the films, but I never thought I'd see one. What a good thing your mate told you how to arrange it! It's a pity you have to take it off once you leave the church, but I dare say you won't mind – by then you'll be a married woman at last!'

'At last,' Sam echoed with a quizzical smile. 'I'm staying at the cottage overnight so I don't see my wife-to-be until I reach the church. Glory be, I don't know how I can wait!'

Glenys laughed. 'Remember that you proposed

to me ages ago, when we were both still in uniform,' she reminded him. 'It's a perishing miracle that we're still both sane and in our right minds. Oh, Sam, now that it's getting so near I'm downright nervous.'

'Oh yeah? Well, don't you go leaving me at the altar,' he said sardonically, and began to sing:

> *'There was I, waitin' at the church,*
> *Waitin' at the church, waitin' at the church,*
> *When I found he'd left me in the lurch,*
> *Lor', how it did upset me!'*

Glenys, laughing, joined in the next verse.

> *'All at once he sent me round a note,*
> *Here's the very note, this is what he wrote,*
> *"Can't get away to marry you today,*
> *My wife won't let me!"'*

*

The wedding was a great success, and, as Glenys said, Jimmy's presence set the seal on a wonderful day. He had come home the previous evening and Glenys, Sam and Mo hung on his every word, laughed at all his stories and pressed him to take some pieces of wedding cake and other goodies back to his unit when he left.

Nain and Taid swelled with pride in their tall, handsome grandson, telling him that there was not only a home but a job for him on the farm when he left the army. Jimmy had confided in his father and Glenys that he meant to go to university when he finished his National Service, but he was too fond of his grandparents to admit that he had no desire to work on the land, and simply hoped that when the time came both Nain and Taid would understand.

When they had first begun to plan the wedding, Glenys had been very conscious that she had no relatives of her own to invite, although because she had spent all her leaves since then at Weathercock Farm she no longer felt like a stranger in the Griffiths family. However, she had a great many friends. Indeed, she had issued a wedding invitation to almost the whole of B Section of the ATS, and had been delighted at the response. She had not received one apology, and though they might not be relatives it showed that she was well liked. Confident in her peers' approval, Glenys was sure that Mo was the prettiest bridesmaid anyone could imagine, that Jimmy and his father were the handsomest men present, and that the wedding breakfast itself would be a great success. And it was, for neighbouring farmers, mindful of the rationing that looked set to continue for several years yet, had made sure that their gifts took the form of food. There were hams from those who had recently killed a pig, baskets of eggs, and boxes of fruit and vegetables. In fact, everything needed to make a wedding breakfast something that friends and neighbours would remember for many a long day.

When the meal was over and the barn was being cleared for dancing, Glenys passed amongst her guests, with Nain and Mo at hand to introduce her to anyone she had not already met. One woman, Mrs Amelia Griffiths, whom Glenys had already marked down as a gossip who never lost an opportunity to say something nasty, shook hands as though she were conferring a favour and began to criticise everything around her in a whiny, discontented mutter.

'That dress, Maureen, ain't the sort of thing I'd have let me own daughter wear, if she were still at home, that is. You can see through the skirt; disgustin', I calls it. And as for that white weddin' gown, it's a disgrace to waste kewpongs on finery which won't be wore more than once. And seeing as how Sam's been wed before, I should have thought you'd all have sneaked off into Liverpool and done the deed on the q.t. But there, young people today is all the same: shameless, that's what they are.'

Glenys hid a giggle behind an upraised hand but Mo flushed scarlet and stared hard at the old woman, her eyes flashing with indignation. 'Our dresses are borrowed, not bought,' she said, her voice rising. 'And there's nothing wrong with my father marrying twice because my own mam died, which makes Dad a widower. Anyone can marry a widower; it's just if there had been a divorce . . .'

Nain nudged her granddaughter and pulled her

away from the older woman. 'Mrs Griffiths doesn't mean half what she says,' she whispered. 'She's soured because her daughter ran off with a seaman and was never heard of again. She was one of the blonde Griffiths, so I suspect the sight of you and Glenys upset her, made her think of Bethan.'

'Not her,' Mo said scornfully. 'The only person she thinks about is herself. How *dare* she say Dad was shameless to marry again! She's a spiteful old woman, as bad as Mrs Huxtable. No wonder her daughter ran away, like we did from Cyril and his horrible old mother. I wish we could find Bethan and tell her we don't like her mother either. We could invite her to come and live at Weathercock Farm. What do you think, Aun – I mean Mam?' She turned to appeal to Glenys, but Glenys had moved away and was talking to Taid. Nain, however, smiled and squeezed her hand.

'It all happened a long time ago, cariad,' she said consolingly. 'The trouble was that Amelia was strong chapel and there were rumours . . . but never mind that! As you say Amelia's just a spiteful old woman bent on upsetting folk.' She smiled down into Mo's flushed face. 'Do you know, I believe the orchestra are about to play a barn dance. You wouldn't want to miss that!'

'Dancing!' Mo said longingly. 'Oh, and I'm still wearing my bridesmaid's dress and I promised to take it off before I ate anything! But I was so excited that I only had a few sausage rolls, honest I did, and Dad wouldn't let me taste the champagne – but

I'd best go up to my room and put on the nice frock my new mam bought for me.' She caught Nain's hand. 'Come with me, Nain. I need help to undo this dress, because it unbuttons down the back.'

But halfway back to the farmhouse Glenys caught them up, leading by the hand a weeping small neighbour who had spilt lemonade down her best frock and was saying, between wails, that her mum would scold her something rotten so she would.

'No, she won't,' Glenys said comfortingly. 'I'll tell her it wasn't your fault. You can't help it if a boy carrying dirty glasses cannons into you.' She looked appealingly at her stepdaughter. 'Mo, poppet, I rather want a word with Nain. Would you be a darling and take Marian up to your room and just rinse the lemonade out?'

Mo was willing, so Glenys sent them on their way with a kiss and drew Nain to one side. 'You know what you said about Amelia Griffiths's daughter Bethan – that she'd run away with a seaman and never been seen again? I've just asked Taid when this all happened and he said . . . he said . . .'

Nain smiled at her; an understanding smile. 'That woman is a terror,' she said. 'You don't want to listen to anything she says. As for Bethan, all that is old history. Folk had it that the girl didn't run away with a seaman, only from old Amelia, who never treated her right. Just you forget all about it, my dear. This is *your* day, and you mustn't let someone else's spite spoil it for you.'

Glenys started to speak, then changed her mind.

'It's all right, I was only going to say you were right, as always,' she said when Nain continued to look at her questioningly. 'And don't you dare start washing up; there are others to do that.'

Nain squeezed her hand. 'And here comes Sam to reclaim his wife,' she said gaily. 'And don't *you* dare start washing up, either! As you say, there are others to do that. And no dwelling on what Amelia said,' she added warningly, as Sam came to a halt beside them. 'The past is past: best left to itself.' She smiled at the groom. 'I'm just telling your new wife not to listen to gossip; she'll soon learn it doesn't pay, in the end.'

'That's right,' Sam said. He looked curiously at Glenys. 'What's up? Don't tell me nothing, because I know you!'

Glenys hesitated. She had meant to tell Sam that Amelia Griffiths had a daughter who had run away from home thirty-three years ago, and that said daughter might – just might – be her own mother. But she looked at Sam's kind, generous face and saw in her mind's eye the fat and spiteful face of Mrs Amelia Griffiths. Why should she risk spoiling things by telling Sam a story which was, in all probability, just rumour and gossip? She had thought, once, that finding her mother was important. Now she knew it was not. She had Sam, the children, a heap of good friends . . .

'Well, Miss Innocence? What's on your mind?'

'I'm wondering how long it will be before we can say goodbye to our guests and go to our new home. I love Nain and Taid but I've never had a home of my own . . . Oh, Sam, I simply can't wait!'

Sam kissed her neck and Glenys swivelled in his arms and kissed him back. 'Dearest Sam,' she said lovingly. 'Let's go and join Mo in the barn dance. She's been practising the steps for weeks!'

'Not going to tell me?' Sam said jokingly. 'Never mind. I'll find out when we're alone!'

Glenys smiled and nodded; perhaps she would tell Sam about the mysterious disappearance of fat Amelia's daughter when they were alone, but she knew suddenly that she would do nothing of the sort. The future stretched ahead of her, sunny and enticing; why should she go spoiling it, even for a moment? Yesterday Sam had talked of their new life, and that meant no looking back. A new life was a good thing, a beautiful thing. Glenys gave a contented little murmur, then spoke aloud. 'Come on, let's go to the barn and show them how it's done!' she said against Sam's neck. 'Oh, Sam, we're going to be so happy! And this year we can give the children a real family Christmas!'